W9-BAR-240

The Immigrants

Books by Howard Fast

THE IMMIGRANTS
TIME AND THE RIDDLE
A TOUCH OF INFINITY
THE HESSIAN
THE CROSSING
THE GENERAL ZAPPED AN ANGEL
THE JEWS: STORY OF A PEOPLE
THE HUNTER AND THE TRAP
TORQUEMADA
THE HILL
AGRIPPA'S DAUGHTER
POWER
THE EDGE OF TOMORROW
APRIL MORNING
THE GOLDEN RIVER
THE WINSTON AFFAIR
MOSES, PRINCE OF EGYPT
THE LAST SUPPER
SILAS TIMBERMAN
THE PASSION OF SACCO AND VANZETTI
SPARTACUS
THE PROUD AND THE FREE
DEPARTURE
MY GLORIOUS BROTHERS
CLARKTON
THE AMERICAN
FREEDOM ROAD
CITIZEN TOM PAINE
THE UNVANQUISHED
THE LAST FRONTIER
CONCEIVED IN LIBERTY
PLACE IN THE CITY
THE CHILDREN
STRANGE YESTERDAY
TWO VALLEYS

The Immigrants

HOWARD FAST

HOUGHTON MIFFLIN COMPANY BOSTON

For Bette

THIS BOOK IS PUBLISHED BY
SPECIAL ARRANGEMENT WITH ERIC LASHER.

Library of Congress Cataloging in Publication Data

Fast, Howard Melvin, date
The immigrants.

I. Title.
PZ3.F265Im [PS3511.A784] 813'.5'2 77-9317
ISBN 0-395-25699-2

Printed in the United States of America

s 10 9 8 7 6 5 4 3 2

CONTENTS

The Immigrants

The immigrants were without any deep consciousness of the role they were playing. They did not dream of history or see themselves as a part of history. They partook of a mythology of the place to which they were going, but of the fact of the place they knew little indeed. Misery absorbed them. Nausea absorbed them. The agony of their stomachs absorbed them. In the pitching, shifting, fetid cabin occupied by eight human beings, four of them adult, four of them children, measuring eight feet by eight feet, stinking of a mixture of body odor and vomit, unventilated, they were absorbed by the various degrees of their misery — and this misery appeared to them to go on for an eternity.

On the small, cold, wind- and water-swept deck that was allotted to steerage passengers, there was some relief from the closeness of the cabin, but the North Atlantic in the month of December, in this year of 1888, provided small compensation for the breath of fresh air the deck granted. The deck was wet and icy cold and awash whenever the weather worsened. And the weather was not good during that passage.

Most of the time Anna Lavette spent in her bunk. A dark, good-looking girl in her early twenties, she was in the seventh month of her pregnancy. She had been born and raised in the tiny fishing village of Albenga, in the north of Italy on the Ligurian Sea. Her husband, Joseph, was a distant cousin, not by blood but by the intricate network of Italian family connection. The Lavettes were a family of fishermen, part Italian, part French, part of them in San Remo, part in Marseille. Joseph had grown up in Marseille, a fisherman from the age of ten.

Now, twenty-five years old, he was large, strong, immune to

seasickness, built like a bull, cheerful, and hopeful. His marriage to Anna had been arranged when they were both children, and he saw her for the first time only ten months before, when their marriage took place. He was delighted with his good luck — a wife who was pleasant to look at, round and delicious to embrace, cheerful, and obviously equally pleased with the man chosen as her husband. She welcomed his body as he did hers, and their lovemaking satisfied both of them. If she spoke no French, his own Italian was ample, and she found his French accent attractive. She was also possessed of imagination, and when he told her that his son — he never for a moment considered that it might be a daughter — must be born in America, she agreed.

So they became a part of that vast wash of mankind who were the immigrants, a flow of nations across the Atlantic and into another world. They had been at sea for sixteen days. For the past five days, Anna had lain in her bunk, flushed and feverish, without privacy, without air, her cheerfulness turning into hopelessness, fearing more for her unborn child than for her own life, vomiting out the will to live — with the single gratification that she had married a man who was patient and gentle, who sat beside her for endless hours, wiping her hot brow with a wet cloth, building pictures of what their life would be in the golden land of America.

"No," she said to him once. "No, Joseph, I will die here."

"I will not permit it," he said flatly. "You are my wife. You will honor and obey me and get well."

"I am so miserable."

She did not die, and a day came when the pitching and lurching of the ship ended, and then he picked her up in his arms and carried her up to the deck. She was thin and wasted, but when she saw the sun and the sky and the smooth water of New York Harbor, she knew that she would live and that she wanted to live.

They stood on the deck as the ancient, rusty ship that had been their home and ark for seventeen days wore into Ellis Island — shoulder to shoulder, cheek to jowl. Everyone was on the deck, the old and the young, screaming children, weeping babies, the silent, the terrified, the sick, the hopeful, nationalities and tongues in a flux of sound and tears and laughter. The great lady of hope welcomed them, and this they had been waiting to see. The Eighth Wonder of the World. "Give me your tired, your poor, your huddled masses yearning to breathe free." In five tongues the statistics floated over the babble of sound. She is a hundred and fifty-two feet high and she weighs two hundred and twenty-five tons. Yes, you can stand up there in the torch at the very end of the arm. Across the water, there was the mass of buildings on the battery, but the lady of liberty was something else.

Then on Ellis Island, a ragged rock, jutting out of the harbor, covered with buildings that were stuffed with people, Lady Liberty was laughing at them. They were herded together like cattle, and they whimpered in fear at the mysteries. The smallpox inoculation was a mystery. The hours of waiting were another mystery. There were Turks, and no one spoke Turkish; there were Greeks, and no one spoke Greek. With Italian, it was another matter. An immigration officer spoke Italian fluently, and he asked Joseph how much money he had.

"Seven hundred and twenty French francs."

"Which is French money," said the immigration man, "and what good is French money in America?"

"Mother of God!" whispered Anna.

Warm and friendly, the immigration man took them aside. They were both relieved after their sudden twinge of terror. Here was a friendly face, a friendly soul, and their own tongue.

"You don't mean that our money is worthless?" Joseph pleaded.

"Of course not. But you must have dollars, American money."

"Yes, yes, of course." He explained the matter to Anna. "Women," he said to the immigration inspector. "And she's carrying. She was sick on the passage." "Of course, of course." The inspector's name was Carso. "Paisano," he said warmly, ignoring Joseph's French accent, and Joseph replied, "Paisano." Men understand these things. Carso had a friend whose name was Franco, and Joseph hefted the bundle that contained all their worldly goods, and with an arm around Anna's waist, he followed Carso out of the crowd.

Franco was a small, sharp-eyed, long-nosed man, with a furtive air and a mournful manner. He made it plain that he suffered; he suffered doing favors for softhearted idiots like Carso.

Who needed French francs? Who wanted them? Why did Carso insist upon making his life so difficult? Finally, he weakened and gave Joseph sixty dollars for his seven hundred and twenty francs — about one third of what they would have brought in an honest exchange.

So the Lavettes, Joseph and Anna, the immigrants, came to America.

At the end of five weeks, the sixty dollars was gone. Joseph learned that he had been cheated, and he also learned that there was nothing he could do about it. He learned that the process of being cheated, put upon, robbed, bamboozled was an intricate part of the existence in America of two immigrants who spoke no English and had neither relatives nor friends. The questions in his wife's dark, pain-filled eyes were unspoken, but nonetheless clear. "Look at me with my swollen belly. I'll bring him forth in a coal cellar. That's his inheritance." They had paid seven dollars for a month's rent in advance for half of a coal cellar on Rivington Street. Light came in from two dirty windows, high on the wall. Anna cleaned and cleaned, but there is no way to clean a coal cellar. From dawn until sunset, Joseph offered his body, his intelligence, his great strength. First, at the dockside on the East River, he offered himself as a fisherman. There were no jobs. It was winter, a cold, icy winter, and only the largest boats were going out. For every job on the big boats, there were ten men laid off out of the small boats, and they spoke English. He offered himself in dumb, impotent silence. One day, he found a construction site with an Italian foreman. He threw away his pride and pleaded. "No use, paisano. Come back next week, the week after."

Anna persuaded him, with much argument, to spend two dollars for a heavy jacket. They had to see a doctor, and each time cost them a dollar. At the docks, Joseph met an Italian named Mateo, and Mateo told him that he, Mateo, could find him a job as a deck hand on an excursion boat. No one told Joseph that the excursion boats did not function during the winter. To get the job, to assure it, Mateo would have to have ten dollars in advance. They would meet then at the Battery. At the Battery, Joseph waited five hours in the freezing cold, and then, heartsick, filled with the mortification of the decent man who has been cruelly tricked, he returned to Anna.

The cellar was always cold. At night, they huddled together like two lost children, the great hulk of a man robbed of his manliness, the woman robbed of her joy and cheerfulness and youth, Joseph embracing her swollen body and wiping away her tears. He knew that she must eat well; they came from a land of sunlight and warm winds, where food was life and joy and tradition; but as their few dollars dwindled, they ate only bread and pasta and salt fish, counting out pennies. Soon the pennies would be gone. What then?

Afterward, Joseph would say that they owed their lives and their child's life to Frank Mancini. When he said that, Anna's lips would tighten and her eyes would harden, and Joseph would shrug and say something to the effect of that being the difference between the way a man and a woman looked at things.

Frank Mancini was an elegant gentleman. He wore a black Homburg and a black overcoat with a collar of fine dark mink. He had a scarf of white silk, and his pointed shoes were polished to a glitter. He came into the wretched cellar place where Joseph and Anna lived as if he were entering a palace, took off his hat, bowed to them, informed them that his name was Frank Mancini — in impeccable Italian — and that he had been given their address by Rocco Cantala, who was the foreman at the construction site where Joseph had asked for a job.

To all of this, the Lavettes listened with amazement. This was the first person to set foot in their place, and a person of such elegance and bearing made them speechless. They simply stared.

"I am a labor contractor," he announced.

Still, they stared and waited.

"Forgive me. I have been thirty years in America, and I forget that there are other places and other ways. I forget that the world is not America. I will ask you whether you have ever heard of the Atchison Railroad?"

Joseph was wondering whether it would be proper and polite to suggest that Mr. Mancini remove his coat. It was very cold in the cellar. He wore the jacket that he had purchased, and Anna wore three layers of cotton under her sweater. He decided that in any case it would be presumptuous of him.

"The Atchison Railroad?"

Joseph and Anna shook their heads.

"It is a great railroad, far out to the west. You must understand that America is a vast country — as big as all of Europe. Now this great railroad, which is called the Atchison, has begun the construction of a spur line to connect its main line with the City of San Francisco."

"San Francisco," said Joseph. He had heard the name.

"A beautiful, splendid city that sits like a jewel on the Pacific coast of the United States. Now you understand, of course — "

"Please sit down," Anna said. She had forgotten courtesy; she had forgotten that whatever this place was, it was, nevertheless, their home, and that the wealthy and elegant Mr. Mancini was a guest in their home.

Mr. Mancini examined the three wooden boxes that served as chairs. His expression was dubious, and Joseph looked at Anna disapprovingly. Then Mr. Mancini seated himself gingerly and went on to explain the qualifications for building a railroad, the specific one being men of firm muscle and large build.

"I hire such men," he went on to say, "men who are not afraid to work hard."

"My God," said Joseph, "that's all I want — to work and earn my bread. My wife is with child."

"As I see. May it be born blessed! As I said, the work is hard. I will not deceive a countryman. But the pay is good, twenty cents an hour, two dollars a day, twelve dollars a week — with meals and a place to sleep."

The sudden hope in Joseph's heart died. "You see my wife's condition. I can't leave her."

"But would we want you to? You will find others with wives, with children, too. It's a hard life, but a healthy life. Better than living in a place like this."

"How far is it?" Anna asked uncertainly. "Is it still America, or is it another country?"

"Because my son must not be born in another country," Joseph said firmly.

"Good. Good. I admire that. But I must explain about America. It is a group of states bound together. That is why it is called the United States. You will work in a state called California — a wonderful place, I assure you."

He went on to assure them of all the joys and rewards that flowed from working for the Atchison Railroad. Then he took some papers out of his breast pocket. They were written in English, which Joseph could not read, but Mancini explained that they were only a simple work contract.

A troubled Anna watched Joseph sign the papers. The baby was kicking, moving constantly now. She could no longer remember whether she had calculated the weeks and the months properly.

"Tomorrow then," Mancini said, "at the Lackawanna Ferry on the North River. Seven o'clock in the morning. You know where the ferry is?"

He nodded. That he knew, having prowled the waterfront from 14th Street down to the Battery, looking for work, any work. Now, God be praised, he had work.

That night, Anna pleaded with Joseph not to go, not to take them into another unknown. Her knowledge of geography, place, and distance was vague. She had never been to school, and she could neither read nor write, nor had she any English — for the simple reason that during her time in America she had only the most minimal contact with those who spoke English. Joseph had acquired a vocabulary of a few dozen words, but Anna had been made silent, bereft of voice and will. The passage from Europe had been an eternity of suffering, and she knew that there was no way back ever — no way ever to reach out again and touch family or friends or the things of home, and she clung to the miserable room they lived in as at least something known.

"We will die if we stay here," Joseph said in answer to all her arguments, and she thought, "I will die anyway."

With the first light of dawn, Joseph put together their few possessions, and then they went out into the icy cold to walk across lower New York to the Lackawanna Ferry. When they reached the ferry slip, they joined a group of a dozen men and women and two or three children already gathered there; and by the time Mancini appeared, an hour later, the group had increased to eighteen men, six women, and seven children. Anna's fear increased, and she clung to Joseph. Some of the men were literally in rags, dirty, unshaven, cold, some of them abjectly surrendered to circumstance, spiritless, hopeless, almost all of them immigrants, Swedes, Italians, Poles, their women subdued and troubled, the few children frightened and cowed by the sight of the broad, icy river, and the smoky cloudy unknown beyond it. Mancini was their shepherd. Smiling, confident, wholly in command of the situation, he herded them onto the ferry. Chilled, her fear frozen into silence, Anna watched the gray water slide by and felt cold tears congeal on her cheeks. Not Joseph, not any of the contract laborers spoke; they lined the rail and watched Manhattan drift away into the distance, their faces blank and hopeless.

At the railroad yard, across the river, the contract laborers were fed slices of ham on stale white bread and coffee in tin mugs. Mancini, always smiling and cheerful, assured them that arrangements had been made for their care and feeding on the trip across the country, and then he led them to a part of the yard where a boxcar stood. There he turned them over to a railroad official, who checked them off Mancini's list and herded them into the boxcar. When some of the men began to protest, Mancini assured them that this was no ordinary boxcar. There were toilets at one end of the car, and it was divided into two sections so that the women might have privacy. There were mattresses on which to sleep. Each day they would be given food and fresh water. It would be an interesting and enlightening trip, and they would see a great deal of this beautiful country which they had chosen as their new homeland.

So much for what Frank Mancini told the group of contract laborers in the railroad yard on the west bank of the Hudson River. There was much more that he might have told them that he failed to tell them — that the toilets were filthy and functioned poorly, that the stench would fill the boxcar in short order, that sixteen additional men would join the group in Chicago, that the food would be wretched and in short supply, that they would not have enough drinking water, and that it would be cold beyond belief in the unheated car. He also failed to tell them that the trip across the continent would take seven days.

Seven days in a boxcar, as Anna Lavette discovered, can be an eternity. There was a single primitive latrine built into one end of the car, a traveling outhouse of sorts. There was no heating, no seats, no blankets except what the immigrants had with them, and the food, brought to them at train stops, was a dismal, unchanging diet of cold sausage and stale bread. The population of the car was fragmented by language and origin. The men were quick to anger; frustration became rage. With no other place to vent their fury and despair, men turned on their wives, beat the submissive, inarticulate women, and turned like caged animals on whoever dared to interfere.

For three days, Joseph and Anna huddled together for warmth and watched the life in the boxcar with a growing sense of hopelessness. On the fourth day, Anna's pain began, and at four o'clock in the morning, in the rattling, swaying, cold boxcar, Anna's child was born. A Polish woman and a Hungarian woman served as midwives, and suddenly and miraculously, the strife in the boxcar ceased. Anger turned into compassion, and the tiny bit of squalling life became a sort of covenant and promise to the immigrants. Jackets and coats were given to Anna to warm her and the baby, and in a way, the child became the triumphant possession of the entire population of the car. The husband of the Polish woman who had served as midwife produced a bottle of carefully hoarded plum brandy, and everyone drank to the health of the newborn babe. Their own misery was forgotten, and a babble of tongues and halting translations played the game of finding a name for the child.

Joseph fixed on the name of Daniel. The child was delivered in a lion's den, or its vague equivalent. As for Anna, she was content with the end of the pregnancy and the fact of this lovely, healthy bit of life sucking away at her breast. At least she had milk, and the child would live. And sooner or later, they would find a priest who could baptize him.

Thus Daniel Lavette came into the world in a boxcar rattling across the length of the United States of America. He weighed well over eight pounds, and he sucked manfully and grew fat and round. Years later, doctors would tell Anna Lavette that the manner of the birth and certain complications that must have occurred destroyed her ability to bear additional children. Now she knew only that the pain was over and that a fine, healthy child had been born.

For the first three months of Daniel Lavette's life, he was nursed in railroad camps while his father drove spikes and handled steel rails. Of all this, he was happily unaware. He was equally unaware of the day when his father first saw the hills of San Francisco and decided that this was the place where he would live and be, and his first memories of his father and mother were of the flat on Howard Street that Joseph Lavette had moved into after he found a job on one of the fishing boats that went out of the wharf. The misery of Anna Lavette's illness that came out of a confinement in a filthy boxcar was also prior to his consciousness. He was the only child. There would be no others.

Joseph Lavette had saved forty-two dollars working on the railroad. The experience had turned him into a careful and thrifty man who lived with a nightmarish dread of ever again being penniless, and as the years passed, as he learned to deal with the English language, his life took on a single focus — to become the owner of a fishing boat, to be his own master and never again to be in the position of hopelessness, a leaf blown by the winds of chance.

In 1897, when young Daniel was eight years old, already adept in that strange, complex, and convuluted language called English — still a mystery to his mother — and already going to school and learning all sorts of incredible things about this place, this San Francisco, this California, his father had managed to save six hundred dollars. It had been no easy task. It meant scrimping and saving and going without anything but the barest necessities, and still it was only half of what he needed to buy the boat — not any boat, not one of the lateen-rigged sailing craft that most of the independent Italian fishermen owned, but one of the new power-driven boats; and as far as Joseph was concerned, it was either a power-driven boat or nothing. For this too was the manner and the ideology of the immigrant. The boat was not for him; the boat was for Daniel. Twice already his boss had allowed him to take the boy with him in the off season. His reward was young Daniel's excitement and joy at being out in the bay, and he boasted about it to Anna.

"And why must he be a fisherman?" she asked him. "He's a smart boy. You know how smart he is."

"Meaning that I am a fool."

"No, no. But this is America, and there are other things. Maria Cassala told me that her boy will be an accountant one day. An accountant sits at a desk and wears clean clothes."

"I can't argue with you," Joseph said. "There are things you don't understand — too many things."

Maria Cassala was a kind, openhearted young woman, a Sicilian who was married to a Neapolitan bricklayer named Anthony Cassala. They had been in San Francisco since 1885, or rather

her husband had. Maria had married Anthony in 1892, the year she came to America from Sicily. She had met Anna while shopping, and she had taken the frightened, frail young woman under her wing. To Anna, the Cassalas were a source of inspiration and wonder. They lived in their own house, a frame house on Folsom Street, which Anthony Cassala had built — for the most part with his own hands.

One day Anna confided to Maria Joseph's dream of owning his own powerboat. "He's never content," she said. "Nothing for today — only for tomorrow, and it will never be."

"Why will it never be?"

"Because he needs five hundred dollars. In ten years more, we will not save another five hundred dollars."

"Then," said Maria, "you send him to see my man, Tony. Tony will lend him the money."

"Why?"

"Why? What a foolish question! Because Joseph is a good man."

"But how could we ever pay it back?"

"Joe will have a powerboat, and instead of working for a boss, he'll be the boss. You'll make the money and you'll pay it back. Please, Anna, tell him to go to Tony."

Anthony Cassala, slender, dark-skinned, dark-haired, was indeed that very rare individual, a happy man, happily married, content with his lot, devout and dedicated to his home and his children. He and Maria had two children, Stephan, who was eleven, and Rosa, who was nine. Entirely without schooling, he had taught himself to read and write English, and his son, Stephan, had passed on his grammar-school lessons to his father, teaching Anthony the simple elements of arithmetic.

Early in the year 1903, a small Italian contractor for whom Anthony worked occasionally begged him to lend him a thousand dollars for a period of three months. He promised at the end of that time to pay back the loan with a bonus of two hundred dollars, twelve hundred dollars in all. Cassala knew nothing of the rules or laws or history of interest; he had not the faintest notion that he would be repaid in terms of 80 percent, 20 percent for three months, 80 percent per year, nor was he able at that time to calculate percentages. Neither had he ever heard the word usury. He took his life savings and gave it to his friend; and at the end of three months, the contractor repaid the debt with the two-hundred-dollar bonus. Fortunately, the contractor was also an honest and decent man, and several times more, having to meet a payroll or bills, he turned to Cassala, borrowing and paying, and each time adding a bonus that in yearly percentage figures varied between 50 and 80 percent.

In a community of Italian working people, where wages were low and unemployment and layoffs were frequent, word of Anthony's generosity — for they saw it as such — got around, and he found himself lending small sums here and there and more and more frequently. Because of the very fact of his nature, he was almost always paid back, and within a year after the initial loan, he had become in himself a very small loan company. He asked for no security other than the character of the man who made the loan; he never harassed his debtors; and where it was necessary to extend the loan, he extended it.

It was from his son, Stephan, who went to school and read books, that he learned he was a usurer, and after he had confessed in church and grappled with his own guilts and surveyed his fortunes, he decided to give up moneylending. But the pressures of his countrymen were too great. He fixed his rate of interest, thereby, at 10 percent per annum. His profits were small; he continued to work as a mason, but more and more he found himself pressed into the role of banker for people who had no other place to turn.

In Joseph Lavette's way of thinking, to borrow was to humble oneself. He had endured poverty and hopelessness and despair, but he had never stooped to borrow, and thus he saw it as surrender and humiliation. For weeks he held out against the urging of his wife, but finally his longing for a boat of his own overcame his pride, and he went to Anthony Cassala.

"I have never borrowed before," he protested, "but if I borrow, you have my word as a man of honor — "

He might have gone on and on, but Cassala put him at his ease. "Please, do not lessen my pleasure," Cassala insisted. "I have been waiting for you. The money is yours."

In fact, the money was repaid in a single year, and Joseph Lavette found a friend whom he treasured. But now, the whole sum necessary for the purchase was in his pocket. "No school for Daniel for today," he told his wife. "I go to buy a boat and I will not do so without my son."

"School is more important," Anna said.

"Is the boat for me or for him?"

"He is nine years old. Leave the boy in peace."

"Ah, women," he said in disgust. "The boy goes with me."

That day was one that remained with Dan Lavette all his life. Boat after boat — the wonder and mystery of the new gasoline-powered engines — the lore of boats, the cut of the bow, the curve of the side. A boat, his father explained, is a thing alive. Only when it lies at dockside is it quiet, supine; but when a man fishes, the boat is a part of his living existence. His livelihood and his life too can depend upon the boat. Finally, Joseph Lavette made his decision, and a power-driven fishing boat was theirs.

From that day on, the boy Daniel Lavette lived for Saturdays and for the two summer months when school was out. Each Saturday, before the sun was up in the morning, he was awakened by his father, shaking him gently and whispering, "Up, up, Danny. We fish together."

Then dressing in the cold darkness before dawn, sitting down half asleep to drink hot tea and eat his oatmeal, while Anna protested the barbarism of awakening the child at this hour, then tramping down the steep hill, his hand in his father's; how exciting, how wonderful life could be! Most mornings the bay lay under a feathery cover of mist and fog, before the sun rose and burned the mist away; then the excitement of making the boat ready. Usually, there was a boy to meet them, one of the Italian youngsters whom his father hired — but no more after Daniel turned twelve. Then he did a man's work on the boat, and that was his greatest joy. He adored the enormous, strong, easygoing man who was his father, and he suffered through his school years, hating every one of them, dreaming only of the moment when summer vacation would come and he could spend all his days on the boat with his father.

The good days and the bad; the hot sun or the icy, pouring rain, a glassy bay that was like a fishpond or a raging, churning inferno that took all his father's skill and seamanship to survive. So it went, and the years passed, and the boy who loved the sea became a long-limbed, self-confident young man.

"It's in his blood," Joseph told his wife proudly. "That boy is one damn fine seaman."

Anna, on the other hand, had been undergoing the Americanization of the immigrant; she had other ideas, and she would plead with Joseph, "Why? Why must he be a fisherman?"

"And what is wrong with fishing? Haven't I kept a roof over our heads and food on the table? I'm a fisherman. My father was a fisherman. Why shouldn't my son be a fisherman?"

"Because this is America. It's not Italy. This is San Francisco. Italians are not peasants here; they are lawyers and doctors and storekeepers."

"We never had lawyers in our family. A lawyer is like a bloodsucker. Must my son be a bloodsucker?"

"He could be more than a fisherman. Every day when you go out, I pray to God, bring him back safely, please, please. Is that a life?"

"It's a good life. I don't force him. Ask him. He's sixteen years old. Ask him."

But thinking about it, Joseph wondered. Again and again, during the long summer of 1905, he made mental notes to have a talk with his son. Perhaps Anna was right. But then he would ask himself what meaning there was to any of it if his son left the boat? When the summer ended, Dan announced that he would not return to school. He had a single year remaining to complete high school; but, as he insisted, it was pointless. He had no interest in school. He was a fisherman, as his father had been. Joseph tried to argue with him. Anna wept and pleaded, but already Dan Lavette, not yet turned seventeen, was his own man with his own mind, already an inch taller than his father, strong, a head of black, curly hair, dark eyes, a round face and a firm chin. Self-sufficient, confident, he was not to be treated as a child, and that he made plain.

"I'm a fisherman," he said. "That's my life and that's what I want."

Joseph gave in because he deeply wanted what his son wanted. What is wrong with the life of a fisherman, he asked himself? Compared to the months during which he had swung a hammer, working on the spur line of the Atchison Railroad, it was an almost heavenly existence. He now owned his own boat, which would be his son's boat. San Francisco Bay was a place with a limitless harvest of fish; his flat was clean and not uncomfortable; every night there was food on their table; and in any case, his ancestors had been fishermen for uncounted generations. He had learned to speak the language, and he was no longer a blind and voiceless immigrant, to be cheated and driven aimlessly by chance and necessity. And he was in a city that was a place of beauty, a city of high hills and open vistas where day in and day out the air was washed clean by the cool winds of the Pacific, and where there were thousands of Italians, most of them immigrants like himself.

And there was his friend, Anthony Cassala, and his wife, Maria, who loved Anna. How much more could a man ask of life?

The year was 1906 — almost seventeen years since Joseph Lavette and his wife, Anna, had come to San Francisco.

On Wednesday, the eighteenth of April in 1906, the City of San Francisco was the proud queen of the Pacific Coast of the United States. It had all the attributes and virtues and sins that history requires of a great city, a population of about four hundred and twenty-five thousand, great hotels, splendid mansions of the rich, wretched hovels of the poor, churches, cathedrals, synagogues, colleges, hospitals, libraries, a political machine that competed with Tammany Hall of New York in rapacity and unconcealed mendacity, a city boss named Abe Ruef, a hundred or so wealthy families who displayed their new riches and vulgarity with the same lack of self-consciousness that they displayed toward the piracy of Abe Ruef, and, at the other end of the scale, a criminal element that was already world-famous.

This criminal element ruled and inhabited a district of the city known as the "Tenderloin," or more widely as "The Barbary Coast," a section more or less defined within the limits of Grant Avenue, Clay Street, Broadway, and the waterfront, and appropriately named after the pirate-infested coast of North Africa. Here was a free and dangerous jungle of whores, purse-snatchers, hoodlums, pimps, confidence men, murderers, and thieves of every variety; but since they preyed for the most part on themselves and on seamen off the ships and on citizens who were foolish enough or daring enough to venture into the Tenderloin, the ruling elite of the city tolerated them and their city within a city.

Some five years before this morning of April 18, the teamsters, who were the lifeblood of the city, went on strike. It was a long, violent strike, with no quarter asked and none given, and out of it there came into being a sort of political workers' party, known as the Union Labor Party, and in the election of 1902, the candidate of this party, Eugene E. Schmitz, a leader of the Musicians' Union, was elected Mayor of San Francisco. But as with so many other dreams of organized labor, this one went up in smoke, or as so many put it, down in garbage. Schmitz could only boast that he himself was not a crook; but he was weak and easily corrupted by the crooks who still ran the city, and he gave them full sway and an open field.

Such, very briefly, was the situation of the city on the morning of April 18, 1906. On that morning, a few minutes before 4:00 A.M., Daniel Lavette awakened and looked at the clock next to his bed. His mother and father were still asleep. "Let them sleep," he told himself. It was not the first time he had awakened this early and gone down to the wharf and made the boat ready, so that his father, after a precious extra hour or two of sleep, would come down and find the boat ready to slip its moorings. It gave Dan a good feeling, a sense of his own manhood.

In the kitchen, he made a breakfast of crackers and milk. When his father joined him later, there would be a jug of hot coffee and wine and sandwiches for their noonday meal; now he would not even risk the slight noise of setting water to boil.

Loping down the steep hill to the wharf, he enjoyed as always the sense of being entirely alone in the sleeping city, in the gray broken night that was the dawning, the wonderful feeling of discovery and renewal that always came with watching the first tint of the sunrise.

At the wharf, he leaped onto the boat with the easy agility of youth, stowed away his oilskins, and began to take the nets from the lockers. He glanced up, almost as an act of worship, as the first rays of the rising sun broke through the mist, thinking to himself that if he ever found a girl he was really stuck on, this would be the place and the hour to win her. Then his glance went to the ferry building, where the big clock read thirteen minutes after five o'clock. He took out his own watch to check the time, and then, as he looked at it, the noise began, a great, monstrous rumble of sound, as if the whole world had begun to scream in agony.

At that moment, deep in the bowels of the earth, one great plate of the North American continent, pressing against and building up pressure against another great plate, found the strain unendurable, and the earth slipped. Deep under San Francisco, the earth began to tremble and vibrate. There was the sound of a great, inhuman beast growling and roaring, and then the stable eternal earth shook and trembled like a mass of jelly, and for forty-eight awful seconds this trembling continued. Brick buildings collapsed, furniture danced and skittered, plaster ceilings crumbled and fell, tall, steel-reenforced structures rocked and swayed yet stood firm, but the older buildings of stone and wood crumbled in upon themselves.

Yet when the main shock was over and the thousands of half-dressed or half-naked citizens poured out into the comparative safety of the open streets, they still had no notion of the appalling tragedy that would overtake their city. Strangely enough, the earthquake itself had done fairly modest damage, for 90 percent of the city was constructed in frame houses and they withstand an earthquake best; but in the poorest sections of the city and in the Tenderloin, the oldest structures collapsed; wood and oil-burning stoves had overturned; water mains were broken; and fire began.

So quickly did the fire begin that it appeared to be an integral part of the earthquake. Dan was flung into the cockpit of the boat, and he lay there while the boat rocked and tossed crazily. Again and again, he tried to get to his feet, and again and again the tossing boat flung him back to the deck. When he finally maintained his balance for a moment, the aftershock began and flung him back on the deck. Bruised and battered, he fought to stand up, clawed his way out onto the dock — and now the city was burning. Only minutes had passed, and the city was burning.

For perhaps three or four minutes, Dan stood there, looking up at the ruined city on its wonderful tumbled hills, listening to a new sound, the sound of terror and panic and roaring flames, and then he remembered that he had left his mother and father asleep. He began to run.

Afterward, he had no memory of running up the hill, no memory of anything except the burning building and the crowd of half-naked people standing in the street. When he tried to rush into the building, hands grabbed him and held him. He wept, screamed, pleaded, but still a hand held him, and the old, dry frame tenement building where he had left his parents asleep went up like a torch and folded in on itself.

It was such a fire as no city in America had ever experienced before. For three days it burned, and it consumed four square miles of San Francisco. From the waterfront to Van Ness Avenue to Dolores Street to 20th Street to Howard and to Bryant and then over to the Southern Pacific Depot and then down to the bay again, wiping out the Barbary Coast and the homes of the poor and homes of the rich, too, and the new seven-million-dollar city hall and schools and libraries and churches, five hundred and twenty-one square blocks, over twenty-eight thousand buildings, and almost four hundred human beings dead in the ashes. And for weeks thereafter, smoke rose from the ruins.

Yet in every tragedy, no matter how great, no matter how pervading, there are the lucky and the unlucky. Anthony Cassala was one of the lucky ones. His small frame house, on Folsom Street beyond the edge of the fire-burned area, was almost undisturbed by the earthquake and untouched by the flames. He was a decent human being, reasonably clever yet at the same time rather simple, and he thanked God devoutly for his good fortune. He believed in all sincerity that he had been spared for a reason, and since his only function which might constitute a reason was to lend money, he accepted that function. The catastrophe was too enormous for him to probe any deeper into cause and reason.

Three days after the earthquake, when the first moments of sanity began to return to the ruined city, Anthony Cassala considered himself and his circumstances. He had cash assets of almost eighteen hundred dollars in his home, which was more cash than most of the wealthiest citizens had at that moment. The poor had nothing but the few dollars in their pockets, if indeed they had not been burned out. Those who were burned out had nothing at all — only the robes and trousers and pajamas they were lucky enough to wrap around them.

For the great banks of San Francisco, the great repositories of money and power and wealth, were almost all located within the area that had been burned. Crocker National Bank, Wells Fargo, the California Bank — all of them buried under debris and burned timbers, their vaults sealed shut by the heat, metal safes twisted and melted. These and other giants of high finance conferred with each other, with city and government and army officials, and took measures to keep the burned-out city alive. At Anthony Cassala's house, where already twenty-two human souls were being given refuge and food by his wife, Maria, things functioned on a smaller and more intimate scale. The Italian working people who had fled from their homes half naked, taking nothing with them in their terror as the earth heaved and rolled, wanted for the most essential and immediate necessities, clothing and food and survival for the next hours — and many of them turned to Anthony Cassala.

So on this Saturday morning, three days after the earthquake struck, he sat at his kitchen table with his son, Stephan, beside him. Stephan had a pen and an open ledger. Anthony had a pile of bills and silver dollars in front of him, the dwindling remains of some eighteen hundred dollars in cash which he had hidden in his house when the earthquake struck. He was doling it out five and ten and twenty dollars at a time, while Anthony entered the name of each borrower in the ledger. By half-past eight in the morning, the money was gone. There remained only a list of names in the ledger and the gigantic confusion of a house packed full of homeless people, men, women, and many, many children.

There remained also a notion that had come to Anthony Cassala during all of this — that if these poor working people had left their money with him, somehow it would be available to them now. He said to himself that as soon as things quieted down and the city became a place to live in once more, he would find out something about banks. He felt a desperate need to be alone and to think. He said to his son, "Everyone comes here but Lavette."

"Yes, papa."

"You see Lavette?"

"No, papa," Stephan said.

"Yes, papa, no, papa — " He stood up, looking around the crowded kitchen, women nursing babies, children howling, his wife, Maria, stirring an enormous pot on the stove, three men staring dumbly out of a window.

"Papa," Stephan said. "They are both dead — Anna and Joseph both."

"What!"

"They are caught in the house and burned. I saw it yesterday. The house burned down. There is nothing left."

"You see it, you tell me that! How do you know?" he demanded fiercely. "How to you know they dead?"

"The policeman told me, papa."

"God save me," he said in Italian, and turned to his wife. "Did you hear that, Maria — did you hear what Stephan said?"

She stood at the stove dumbly, tears rolling down her cheeks. One of the men at the window, a plasterer by the name of Cambria, burst into a torrent of words. He had been locked in silence. Now he had a chance to say something. He lived three houses from the Lavettes. He and his wife and his children ran into the street with the first shock. The Lavette house had burst into flames, like an explosion. Lavette, his wife, and his son, Daniel, lived in an apartment on the third floor. They were trapped there, trapped and destroyed.

"All of them? The boy too?"

Where else would the boy be at five o'clock in the morning? Cambria began to explain how he had looked for a priest, but Cassala could listen to no more and he fled from the house into the smoky haze that still covered the city. The firebreak, where they had blasted dozens of houses to stop the flames, was only half a mile from his home, and here he entered into the gates of hell, a whole city reduced to ashes and blackened timbers and piles of rubble. Everywhere, soldiers with fixed bayonets stood guard, and Cassala moved past them apprehensively, for the city was full of stories that the soldiers had killed more people than the earthquake. He was not alone. Hundreds of people were moving slowly on the streets, and families stood in little clusters, looking silently at the blackened ruins that had been their homes.

His friend, Joseph Lavette, had lived on Howard Street, and there Cassala made his way, but as he picked his way among the ruins, he was unable even to determine which was the house, nor did he know exactly what he searched for, charred bodies, confirmation of death, hope of life. And how his memories tortured him! Joseph Lavette had been like a brother to him, Daniel like his own child. After the older Lavette had borrowed five hundred dollars from Cassala to make the down payment on the fishing boat, his gratitude for a loan based on nothing but faith and friendship impelled him to make his boat a Sunday excursion vessel for the two families.

Now, making his way down Market Street toward the waterfront, Cassala recalled all the wonderful Sundays sailing on the bay, putting in at some cove to picnic on good bread and salami and ham and pasta and wine. Was it possible that now it was over and done with and finished, just as everything else in this blackened wasteland was finished? — Yet he went on now, drawn by some faint hope that the boat at least had survived, so that he might look at it and touch something of the old time and the old life.

The wharf was alive, just as the bay was alive. Over the past three days, the fishermen in their fishing boats, among other boats, had taken more than a hundred thousand people, some fleeing the fire, others driven by their own terror, across the bay into the safety of Oakland; and they were still making the passage back and forth, bringing food and medicine and physicians and government officials into the ruined city, bringing back from Oakland boatloads of those who had fled — just as for months to come, every boat in existence would be called into service to bring food and building materials as well to the city.

A soot-grimed, weary fisherman pointed down the wharf. "There's the Lavette boat."

"He's alive?"

"He's dead," the fisherman said. "The kid's alive."

"God be praised," Cassala whispered. "God be praised."

He ran down the length of the wharf, and there was Lavette's thirty-two-foot powerboat, tied up, secure and safe, and in the cargo well, sprawled out and sound asleep, Daniel Lavette. Cassala climbed down into the boat, so moved by the sight of young Lavette, asleep and sound with three days of beard on his face and no sign of hurt or injury, that he could have embraced him and kissed him as he would his own son. It was the sleep of total fatigue, and the boy had not even bothered to take off his heavy boots or his jacket. Cassala recognized this; on the other hand, this was no place for an exhausted, grief-ridden boy to sleep, here on his boat and alone. And for all Cassala knew, he had not eaten during the three days since the earthquake.

Cassala shook him. "Danny, Danny, wake up."

"You won't wake him easy, Tony," a voice said. Cassala

turned around, and there on the wharf was Mark Levy, the chandler whose store was at the end of the wharf, and looking down the wharf, past where Levy stood, Cassala saw that his shop had survived, scorched at one corner and tilting somewhat, but otherwise whole and undamaged. Levy was only twenty-six years old, skinny and long-nosed, an easygoing and competent young man who had taken over the chandler shop five years before when his father died. To Cassala, who had come into this place again and again to buy small gifts for the Lavettes, the Levy store was a veritable wonderland, selling every conceivable item a boatman or fisherman might need, nets and rope and lanterns and compasses and sails and oars, a tangled, jumbled general store of the sea.

Now Levy looked at Cassala curiously, the general question that was being asked everywhere in the city left unspoken.

"Not harmed," Cassala said. "The fire don't reach us, no harm, thank God. But poor Lavette and Anna, they are dead, no?"

"That's what the kid said. He said he woke up about four-thirty, maybe a little earlier, and went down the hill to make the boat ready. He left them both asleep. He was at the boat when the quake came, and then he ran back but the house was in flames. He went a little crazy, and Jeff Peters, who was with him, said he had to hold him down on the ground to keep him out of the house. My wife, Sarah, found him sitting in the boat a few hours later, just sitting there and crying like a kid. Do you know what he's been doing for the past three days? Ferrying people to Oakland. They just poured into the boat and shoved their money at him. This is the first time he's slept in three days."

"We wake him up and I take him home with me," Cassala said. "He can't sleep there. It's no good. He got to eat. He got to be with his people."

It was like waking a drugged man, but the two of them got Dan Lavette on his feet, where he stood swaying, his eyes half closed, his long-limbed six-foot-two-inch body looming over them, staring at Mark Levy and at Anthony Cassala without recognition.

Softly, in Italian, Cassala said, "It's me, Danny, Tony, and I know about your grief. Your father was like a brother to me, and you will be like a son. Now, come home with me."

"My boat," the boy said, clinging to the only part of his life that remained. "I can't leave my boat."

"I'll take care of the boat, Danny," Levy said. "Go with him now."

All the way back to the Cassala house, Dan Lavette remained silent, and wisely enough Anthony did not urge him to speak or to share his grief. Only when he was seated at the kitchen table in the Cassala house, with a dozen people welcoming him back from the dead, with the two Cassala children staring at him in wide-eyed wonder, and with a great plate of spaghetti in front of him, did he come to life, and suddenly ravenously hungry, he began to stuff himself with the food.

"Slow, slow, Danny," Maria Cassala said. "There's plenty food. Eat slow."

The boy finished the plate and then another plate. He drained down a tumbler full of red wine — and he smiled, slowly, tentatively.

"Thank you, Tony, Maria — "

"You be all right, Danny."

"The city's gone — mom and pop gone. I'll be all right. I got the boat."

"Sure."

"I'll be all right, Tony. I'm just tired."

"Sure. You sleep now."

The boy reached into the pockets of his jacket and his hands emerged with fistfuls of bills. Again and again, he dipped into the big pockets of the jacket, piling paper money, gold coins, and silver dollars on the kitchen table. A sudden silence fell over the crowded kitchen, and the men and women and children gathered around the table, watching the pile of money grow. It came from his jacket, from his trousers, from every pocket. Then, when his pockets were empty, he pushed the pile of money toward Cassala, who sat across the table from him.

"I no understand," Cassala whispered.

"I didn't steal it, Tony," the boy said. "They wanted to go to Oakland. They were like people gone crazy. They emptied their pockets and gave it to me, and then they climbed over each other to get into the boat. It wasn't only me — all the boats. Ten dollars, fifty dollars, a hundred dollars — it didn't matter they were so crazy with fear. For three days I have been taking the boat across to Oakland and back, and this is the money they gave me. So take it and keep it for me."

Cassala stared at the boy for a long moment, and then he

nodded. He counted the money carefully. "Here, Daniel Lavette," he said formally in Italian, "is the sum of four thousand and seventy-three dollars and twenty cents. I accept the custody of this money in your name. It is like a deposit in a bank. When you need it, it will be yours, whatever part of it you desire or all of it. Meanwhile, I shall pay you six percent interest and use the money — if that is agreeable to you?"

"I think I understand you," Dan said, "but my Italian is not so good."

In broken English, Cassala repeated his proposal. Now Dan could hardly keep his eyes open. He grinned and nodded, and said, "Sure, Tony — whatever you say."

"Maria," Cassala said to his wife, "make a bed for him where he can sleep. Let him bathe and rest." And to Stephan, "Bring the ledger here."

That, more or less, is how the Bank of Sonoma came into being; the business process was less romantic. A year later, with the advice of an attorney, Anthony Cassala issued and sold a hundred thousand shares of stock at ten dollars a share. A new, incredible, and vibrant metropolis was rising out of the ashes of the old city, and a part of it was a small but dignified storefront on Montgomery Street that bore the legend THE BANK OF SONOMA.

PART ONE

Fisherman's Wharf

Perhaps never before in history — or since for that matter — did a new city arise from the ashes of the old as quickly, as hopefully, as vitally as San Francisco. Almost five square miles in the heart of the city had been turned into blackened timbers and ashes. For seventy-two hours, men, women, children, firemen, soldiers, and policemen fought the flames, and shortly after seven o'clock on Saturday morning, the twenty-first of April in 1906, the fire was brought under control and its advance was halted. Already families were making their way up Howard Street and Folsom Street, clambering up California Street and Washington Street and all the other avenues and streets within the wasted area. Regular army soldiers and National Guardsmen tried to bar their way — having maintained looting rights to themselves over the past three days, but not even the threat of guns and bayonets could deter the homeowners from claiming their particular bit of ashes.

In the Tenderloin, saloon operators, pimps, and prostitutes picked among the ashes looking for coins or cashboxes that might have survived the holocast, for there not a building had been spared. The tall hills that only a few days before had sparkled with light and reflected the rising sun so cheerfully from their thousands of white clapboard houses were now somberly black, but not dead; indeed they had taken on a strange and grim majesty, and the still half-naked citizens, soot-blackened and homeless, greeted the ruin as they had always greeted their city. Had the world ever seen such a sight before? Go elsewhere? Live in another place? Be damned if they would!

The next day, it rained, and the fire was out for good. A week later teams were hauling the rubble down the steep hills and dumping it into the bay. Tents sprang up on the blackened lots. Thousands of ordinary citizens joined in the effort of clearing the rubble, and cots appeared in the foundations of burned houses with makeshift lean-tos to keep out the weather. Men who had never handled a hammer or saw before turned carpenter. For almost nine weeks, the shattered city, known not only as the "Queen of the Pacific" but as the "queen of larceny" as well, entered into a period of benign brotherhood, common effort, good humor, and good will; and during this time, crime almost disappeared from the streets of San Francisco. Money in the form of relief as well as paid insurance poured into the city, and every out-of-work carpenter and mason from a thousand miles around descended upon it. Ships loaded with food made the journey across the bay from Oakland and from Southern California and from the states of Washington and Oregon, and the common kitchens and the breadlines were orderly and good-humored.

And then, as the rebuilt city began to take shape, people reverted to the habits of civilization. The total destruction of Chinatown had given the Oriental population of the city a brief respite from that peculiar racial hatred that marked this city. For a matter of weeks, whites were kind to the Chinese. That came to an end. For three weeks, San Francisco was a city without saloons or prostitutes; that too came to an end, and nowhere in the city was that marvelous American aptitude for organization and construction better exhibited that in that area which had once been the Barbary Coast. Within three months after the great fire, almost a thousand saloons and whorehouses had risen phoenixlike out of the ashes. At the same time charges were brought against Abe Ruef, the city boss, and Mayor Schmitz, his friend and co-worker, that, in taking advantage of the earthquake and fire, they had granted monopolies in transportation and utilities in return for enormous bribes.

Life had returned to normal in San Francisco. City planners had drawn up splendid projections for the rebuilding of the city, holding that never again would a city such as this have such an opportunity to rebuild from ashes. The people ignored the plans; they wanted homes, not utopia, and if they were warned against the consequences of pushing a million tons of rubble into the bay — well, where else could it go? The city mushroomed. Rebuilding became a race, and the area around Powell and Market earned the name of the "uptown Tenderloin" with an overnight, jerry-built creation of saloons, restaurants, and music halls. The cable cars were put back into service, and once again they crawled up and down the steep hills. A month after the earthquake, the Orpheum Theatre opened, a month later the Davis Theatre, on McAllister near Fillmore; and then in reasonably quick succession, the Park Theatre, the Colonial, the Novelty, the American. During the following year, there were seven strikes, the opening of six new banks, and the sentencing of Mayor Eugene Schmitz to five years in San Quentin for corruption. The city lived again.

And with the passing of the next two years, one might walk from East Street to 20th Street, from Van Ness to Bryant Street, and see no sign or indication that this area had once encompassed the greatest civic tragedy ever to strike an American city.

The year 1910 began with a month that saw the laying of the cornerstone of the American Music Hall Theatre, on Ellis Street between Stockton and Powell, and in the same month, four other new theaters opened their doors, causing the San Francisco *Chronicle* to boast that no other city except New York could rival the number or variety of San Francisco's theaters. The newspaper did not boast that according to the most recent count, there were over two thousand saloons of one description or another and half as many whorehouses.

Well, that too was a sign of life and vigor. Once again, the great jewel of a city sat white and gleaming upon its great hills, with the magnificent blue expanse of the bay beneath it and around it.

For two hours, Feng Wo, a Chinese man in his midthirties, had been waiting on the wharf. He was a slender man, of medium height, and neatly dressed in an ancient black suit that had been carefully patched and repaired in a dozen places. He wore a white shirt, very clean, and a black tie, and his cracked shoes were polished until they glistened. His dark felt hat was somewhat large for his close-cropped head, but he wore it with dignity and held himself very straight. He carried a folded newspaper under his arm, and inside he was filled with a desperation that was almost like a sickness. He had not eaten for two days.

He had stationed himself early that morning in front of a

two-story shanty built of wood frame and siding and standing out from the wharf on piles. For all of its crazy-quilt construction, the shanty appeared to be in good repair, and the door of the building, polished redwood with bright brass fittings, gave it an odd distinction. During the two hours since he had arrived there, Feng Wo had studied the building until he felt that he knew every board and beam in its construction.

Now the fishing boats were coming in and tying up and unloading their catch. Feng Wo watched them, glancing from the shanty to the boats and then back to the sign above the door, where in polished brass letters was spelled out: DANIEL LAVETTE FRESH FISH AND CRABS. During the two hours he had been there, on the busy wharf crowded with buyers and sellers and fishermen and commission men and market owners, he had spoken to no one and asked no questions. That was only common sense and reasonable caution. This was 1910 and San Francisco, and he was Chinese. He lived and breathed and walked and talked by sufferance, and there was no moment in his life when he was not alert and wary.

Now his eye was caught by three boats coming into the dock in precise, triangular formation, sloop-rigged and under sail with their motors quiet. In the lead boat, a massive hulk of a man, standing in the bow, his black, curly hair blowing in the wind, gave the signal to drop the sails and then leaped onto the wharf with remarkable grace and agility. He was a very young man, no more than twenty-one or twenty-two, Feng Wo decided, but with a total air of authority and a sense of knowing precisely what he was about. He made no wasted motions, and as the boats tied up, he issued a few terse orders, paused to watch the beginning of the unloading of the catch, and then strode past Feng Wo to the shanty. He carried his oilskin jacket flung over one shoulder and walked with a slight, rather unselfconscious sway and swagger. He had a large head, a heavy face, a small nose, and a wide, sensual mouth — a face of contradictions, Feng Wo thought, a face which defined him at one moment thus and the next moment as something else entirely.

At the door to the shanty, he paused and glanced at Feng Wo. Their eyes met. He studied Feng Wo carefully from head to foot, then took keys out of his pocket, opened the door, entered, and closed the door behind him.

Feng Wo sighed deeply and thought, "No use. No use at all." Still he had spent better than two hours here and he had no other place to go. He went to the door of the shanty, took off his hat, and knocked.

Silence; then steps; then the door swung open and the tall man stood there, towering over Feng Wo.

"Well?"

"You are Mr. Daniel Lavette?"

"Yes."

"Please, sir, with all humility, may I announce that my name is Feng Wo. I am thirty-four years old and in good health, and I am a bookkeeper."

"What the hell — "

"Please, sir, please do not send me away without hearing my argument. Here in the *News*" — he held out the paper — "here I read your advertisement."

"The ad says four P.M."

"And I am Chinese."

"You sure as hell are," Lavette agreed.

"And if I appeared at four, as the advertisement says, there would be ten Caucasians here. Then who would hire a Chinese bookkeeper?"

"Only a horse's ass, which I am not." He turned away, beginning the process of closing the door in Feng Wo's face.

"Please, Mr. Lavette, I beseech you. I have not eaten today or yesterday." The words flooded out. "I have a wife, I have a daughter of thirteen years. Give me a chance. I am honest. I will work any hours you choose. Pay me what you will. Please, please, I beg you."

The door opened again, and Dan Lavette stood there, staring at him. Moments passed. Feng Wo was acutely conscious of all that his world contained, the warm sun, the salty wind from the bay, the fishermen hawking their catch and calling their prices, and the tall young man in front of him.

"What did you say your name was?"

"Feng Wo, Mr. Lavette."

"Where did you learn to keep books?"

"I taught myself, sir."

"Do you know what a ledger is?"

"Yes, sir, I do."

"Do you know what double entry is? Have you ever worked with a twelve-column analysis book?"

"I am not stupid, sir. I can learn anything you wish me to."

"I ought to have my head examined," Lavette said. "I swear I ought to. All right, come on in."

Feng Wo followed him into the shanty, trembling now, unable to believe that it was actually happening. Inside the door was a single large room, a rolltop desk, a kitchen table and chairs, a three-drawer wooden filing cabinet, and a rack from which hung two big sea slickers, to which Lavette added his oilskin jacket. On the walls a calendar, an enormous stuffed fish, an old-fashioned whaling harpoon, and a shelf of canned goods. A small gas stove and a coffee pot completed the furnishings. A narrow staircase led up to the second floor.

"I live up there," Lavette said, indicating the staircase. "This is the office." He pulled a chair out from the table. "Sit down. What the hell do I call you?" he asked as Feng Wo seated himself. "Feng — Feng Wo?"

"As you wish, sir."

"Feng — all right, Feng then." He pulled open one of the file drawers and took out a plate and a fork and spoon and a can opener. "I don't know what a Chink eats. How about canned beans?"

"I am not here to eat. Please, sir, I am here to work."

"Bullshit," Lavette said, as he opened a can of beans and set it to warm on the gas stove. "You're shaking like a leaf. You ever work for a white man before?"

"Yes, sir."

"Where did you work?"

"I did coolie work on construction, pick and shovel. Then I got sick. I hurt my back. I tried pick and shovel again — I can't."

"I'd give you beer, but that's no good if you're starved. Can you drink coffee?"

"Yes, sir."

Lavette emptied the half-warmed can of beans into the plate and set it in front of Feng Wo. He poured him a mug of coffee, and then sat down to face him as he ate. The beans were like honey in Feng Wo's mouth, and he fought for control, fought to eat slowly and politely, recalling with each mouthful that his wife and daughter had also not tasted food for two days.

"So you want to be a bookkeeper," Lavette said. "Well, screw the lot of them. Why in hell shouldn't I hire a Chink? Let them burn their asses. But let me tell you this, Mr. Feng — I'm no soft touch. If you can't do it, I'll boot you out of here on your yellow backside. I may look young and innocent, but I take no horseshit from anyone. I got three boats and eleven men on my payroll, so this job is no cinch. Now I want you to shape up here at eight o'clock tomorrow morning. I'm not going out with the boats, and if you are what you say you are, we'll spend the day trying to make some sense out of my books."

Feng Wo had finished eating. He rose, picking up his hat and his newspaper. "I would try to thank you, Mr. Lavette, but I don't know what to say. I am so grateful."

He turned and started for the door.

"Hold on!"

He paused and slowly faced Lavette, who said to himself, My God, the poor bastard's terrified. And then aloud, "Don't you want to know what I pay?"

"Whatever you pay will be sufficient."

"Twelve dollars a week to start. That's not the best, but it's not the worst." He got up, reached into his pocket, and took out a wad of bills, peeling off two fives and two singles. "Here's a week's pay in advance. Get your kid some food. But if you don't show here tomorrow, I'll peel your yellow skin off, and remember that."

At thirty years of age, Mark Levy's wife, Sarah, still had the appearance of an ingenuous girl of eighteen. She had flaxen hair which she wore tied in a tight bun at the back of her head and wide, pale blue eyes set far apart. She defied all the stereotypes of a Jewish woman; she was slender, small-breasted, and long-legged, and she gave the appearance of being perpetually startled. She had been born in the city of Kiev, in Russia, and brought to the East Side of New York City at the age of seven, and she still had a slight foreign accent, which her husband felt enhanced her slow throaty speech. This together with a certain vagueness in her manner gave people the impression that she was a dull and phlegmatic person, an impression that was far from the fact; and indeed her husband, who worshipped her, took a peculiar comfort in the fact that her imagination and passion were so well concealed. She was a second cousin once removed or something of that sort — Mark was never entirely clear about their family relationship — and they had come together through an arrangement between his family and her family, done in the old European manner without their ever seeing each other before they were pledged — after which Sarah was shipped across the country, three thousand miles by rail and coach, a girl of seventeen tagged and addressed for all the world like a parcel. For two months before the wedding, she had lived in his father's house — which was four rooms behind the chandler shop on the Embarcadero — and during that time, Mark fell totally and romantically in love with her. For her part, she accepted him with the same easygoing tolerance with which she accepted all else that befell her.

Now, married almost thirteen years, with the older Levys dead and buried, she was contentedly mistress of the chandler shop, the four rooms behind it, a son, Jacob, who was eleven years old, a daughter, Martha, who was five, and a husband who took her advice and asked her advice without ever truly understanding that either was the case. Even when she once casually suggested that he use copper rivets to reenforce the pockets of the heavy cotton trousers he sold to the seamen and the fishermen, and thereby tripled his business, he was not certain that the idea was not originally his own.

Now, with the five-year-old Martha clinging to her skirt, she was engaged with her husband in their annual and fruitless attempt to take inventory in the shop, he calling out the items, she writing them down, when Daniel Lavette entered the store. They stopped what they were doing and stared at him.

"I want four new nets," Lavette said, "and I want the Massachusetts stuff and not the garbage they make out here. So if you haven't got them, order them for me."

Still they stared at him.

"What the devil — "

"That suit doesn't fit you, Danny," Levy said.

"It fits." He unbuttoned the tight jacket of the blue serge suit he wore and pulled in his stomach. "It fits. I haven't had it on for a year or so. Maybe I filled out."

"The sleeves are two inches short. The pants are short."

"Let him be," Sarah said. "He's grown."

"I haven't grown. I'm twenty-one years old. You don't grow at twenty-one."

"When did you buy the suit, Danny?"

"Two years ago."

"Well, you've grown. I don't think I ever seen you in a suit before. What's the occasion?"

"It doesn't look right, does it?" he asked Sarah.

"It's all right."

"Sure, it's fine. I'm only going to have lunch with Thomas Seldon at the Union Club — that's all. God damn it to hell, I look like a monkey!"

"Take off the jacket," Sarah said gently. "I'll lengthen the sleeves. It won't take more than a few minutes, and I'll press out the creases."

"Seldon? You mean *the* Thomas Seldon?"

"That's right." He was staring at his cuffs.

"Oh, take it off, Danny," she said.

He pulled off the jacket and handed it to her. Levy, riffling through the pages of a catalogue, said, "That Massachusetts netting is up twenty percent. It comes from Fall River. Seldon — come on."

"Look, Mark," Lavette said, bristling, "to me Seldon's another guy — that's all."

"He only owns the second biggest bank in the city, that's all."

Sarah, small Martha still clinging to her skirt, had taken the jacket inside. Levy motioned for Lavette to follow. "Come on, I'll feed you a beer."

"I don't want any beer on my breath. In one hour, I'm with the nabobs at the Union Club."

They sat around the kitchen table. Sarah cut and stitched with speed and skill. Dan Lavette, grinning like a small boy at Levy's disbelief, told how it had come about. He had walked into the Seldon National Bank, identified himself, and asked for a loan of thirty thousand dollars. He didn't get the loan, at least not yet, but he was introduced to Thomas Seldon himself and invited to lunch at the Union Club to discuss it further.

"That's chutzpa," Levy said admiringly, "pure, unadulterated chutzpa."

"What's chutzpa?"

"Yiddish for gall, nerve, arrogance — whatever. Anyway, what on earth do you want with thirty thousand dollars?"

"The *Oregon Queen*'s for sale."

"So?"

"They're asking a hundred and fifty thousand. I can get her for a hundred, twenty thousand down and ten thousand more to put her in shape."

"Danny, the *Oregon Queen*'s an iron ship. She's a dead-lost experiment."

"Like hell she is. She's rusty and she never had a fair shake, but her hull is good and her engines are good. There's money in the lumber trade. This city eats wood like crazy, and there's no end in sight. I can ship enough timber in one year to pay her off, and from there on it's pure gravy."

"Danny, you got three boats mortgaged to the hilt."

"And I'm a fishmonger and my father was a fishmonger."

"What's wrong with that?"

"It stinks of fish and it stinks of the Embarcadero. We're down here and the nabobs are up there on Nob Hill."

"You're an ambitious young man," Sarah said. "Mark isn't. Try on the jacket."

"Why didn't you go to Tony Cassala?" Mark asked him.

"Because Tony can't say no to me, and if I asked him for his blood, he'd give it to me. I don't want any handouts. I'm not asking for charity. This is a risk, but it's a risk that makes sense." He pulled on the jacket. "How does it look?"

"It's better. Take it off and I'll press the sleeves."

"Suppose the whole thing blows. Seldon can afford it. Tony can't."

"Don't underestimate Tony," Mark said. "Look, loosen your belt and drop the pants. It looks better that way. And for God's sake, if you're moving up to Nob Hill, get yourself a decent suit of clothes."

At the door, leaving, Dan turned to them and said, "Funny thing happened today. I hired a bookkeeper."

"It's time."

"He's a Chink."

"What?"

"You heard me. I hired a Chink. What do you think of that?"

"I think it's all right," Levy said.

After he had left, Sarah asked her husband, "Why does he try so hard to act tough and mean?"

"Two reasons," Mark replied. "First, because a part of him is tough and mean, because if you're going to run fish and crab out of the wharf and not be run out of the place yourself, you got to be a little tough and a little mean, and secondly because he's just a kid. I like him."

That night, at dinner in his home, Thomas Seldon was not quite certain whether or not he liked Daniel Lavette. Of course, his value judgments were not in terms of liking or disliking; in his world, a man was sound or unsound, reliable or unreliable, solid or shaky; liking had nothing to do with it. "Interesting chap," he said to his wife and daughter. "Big — too big for the clothes he wore — and young. Twenty-one." He sat at one end of the great mahogany table in the Seldon dining room, his wife and daughter on his left and right respectively. Fully set, the table held sixteen; and even though there were only three of them at dinner, Seldon liked the feel of its size and substance. There was much substance if little taste all through the dining room, the half-paneled walls, the Victorian bastardization of Queen Anne furniture, the heavy beams across the ceiling, not even shaken by the earthquake, a curious and uninspiring marriage of Spanish Colonial and Victorian, but nevertheless a solid place of substance.

Seldon had built the house for his bride, Mary, who was an Asquith from Boston before her marriage. Thomas Seldon, Senior, dead these twelve years past, had come to California in the late forties, not to mine gold but to care for the gold that others mined, and the present Thomas Seldon presided over the bank his father founded. Now, at fifty-five, a solid, handsome, substantial man with iron gray hair and a firm chin, he found every prospect pleasing except that his wife, Mary, had seen fit to present him with one daughter and no sons. Mary had other virtues; she was calm, coldly beautiful, even at age fifty-two, and made few demands upon her husband, who found Madam Sigeury's bordello on Beale Street a more comfortable outlet for his waning sexual energies than his wife's bed. And if she had presented him with only a single child, a daughter, that daughter was nevertheless known and accepted as the most beautiful woman in San Francisco, providing you also accepted the fact that the choice in such matters was confined to the two hundred or so families that "mattered."

But even in wider circles, Jean Seldon would have been considered to be unusually beautiful. It was bruited around town that Charles Dana Gibson, who had established the ideal of upper-class beauty in his drawings and paintings, had sketched her while in San Francisco, and had thereby come to his Gibson-woman stereotype, and while Jean herself knew this to be untrue and indeed wondered whether Gibson had ever actually been in San Francisco, she did nothing to dispel the legend. She was a tall woman, five feet eight and a half inches in her stocking feet, well formed, with wide, straight shoulders and strong, long-fingered hands. Her face had the same chiseled quality as her mother's — referred to on the society page as "classic" — her eyes were deep blue and her hair of a pale honey color which in certain light took on a golden sheen. She had dutifully undergone twelve years of schooling of a sort at Miss Marion's Classes, but she had little intellectual curiosity and in common with most of her women friends no desire to be college educated.

Nor was she very musically inclined. After ten years of piano lessons, she was capable of playing a Beethoven sonata from the music, correctly if rather woodenly; but in all truth, music bored her. She played tennis competently and rode competently, but did neither with devotion or passion. She wore clothes splendidly and loved shopping, and the trying on of the long, awkward dresses of her time was something she delighted in. She was frequently photographed, and when the first upper-class charity fashion show was held in the city, the *Chronicle* noted that "the occasion was made memorable by the costumes displayed by a bevy of local beauties, and in particular by the classic beauty and regal manner of Miss Jean Seldon." That was two years ago, when Jean was not yet nineteen. Now, she was if anything even more handsome and certainly more discontent, a fact which puzzled and disturbed her parents. She took so little interest in most things that her interest in her father's luncheon guest was rather unusual.

"You say his clothes didn't fit him," she said to her father, "and he didn't even know which fork to use. That's wonderful."

"Why?"

"He sounds like one of Jack London's heroes."

"Who is Jack London?"

"Daddy!"

"I just can't understand why you invited him here," Mary Seldon said.

"You did? When?"

"Friday next. Mary," he said to his wife, "this is a most unusual young man, believe me. He can't be more than twenty-one or twenty-two, uncouth — yet not really. He walked into the bank as if he owned the place, demanded to see me, talked his way in, and cooly asked for a loan of thirty thousand dollars. And believe me, instead of throwing him out, I was taken with him."

"And you'll give him the loan?"

"Good heavens, no. He's a crab fisher."

"What!"

"You heard me, a crab fisher."

"I still don't understand why you asked him to dinner," his wife said. "The way you describe him — well, who on earth could we ask with him?"

"Why won't you give him the loan?" Jean persisted, intrigued with the image her father evoked.

"Because he has no collateral. He owns three fishing boats that are heavily mortgaged, and he operates with a cash balance of about a thousand dollars, when he has it. Also, he's young — too young for the crazy notion he has of buying a coastal steamer."

"Then, as mother says, why did you invite him here?"

"For the same reason I asked him to lunch with Al Summers and myself at the club. I suppose it's his youth and vitality. They tell me his folks were killed in the earthquake — I think he's half French and half Italian, but you don't brush off a kid like that. He'll amount to something some day, and when he does, I want him to come back to our bank."

From a cousin who worked as a teller at the Seldon Bank, Anthony Cassala got the news that Lavette had come there for a loan. He told his wife, Maria, that it made him sick, sick to his heart, as he put it. "To say to me, you, you who are like a father to me — I don't want your help. How can he do that to me?"

"Ask him."

"Not that he gets the loan. That cold Irish bastard would take his heart's blood first."

"The Seldons aren't Irish, Tony."

"The same thing. Who are his people, the Seldons?"

The next day, unable to contain himself, Cassala drove his gig down to the Embarcadero. Dan Lavette's boats were unloading, and Dan himself was raging at a commission merchant.

"Rotten fish! So help me God, you say that word again, and I'll spread you over this dock! Who the hell do you think you are, coming up here from San Mateo to tell me my fish are rotten! Where's your ice? You cheap bastards skimp on the ice and then tell us we sell rotten fish! Look at my fish — they're half alive. I sell my catch when we dock, not the next day. Ah, get to hell out of here. I don't need your business."

He caught sight of Cassala then, turned on his heel, and stalked over to the gig.

"Danny, Danny, you got a short temper," Cassala said. "That's no way to do business. You make enemies."

"Screw the bastard! I don't want his business."

"You don't want mine either, do you, Danny?"

"What are you talking about?"

"The loan you go to Seldon for."

"So you heard about that. From that loudmouth Angelo who works at Seldon's bank."

"That's right. And what for you go to Seldon? Who lend you the money for the fishing boats?"

"You did, Tony, and I'm into you up to my neck. I got this crazy scheme to buy a coastal lumber ship. Suppose I come to you, and you got to say no — and even if you were dumb enough to go along with me, I wouldn't take it. Tony, believe me."

"I believe you, Danny. But come to me, yes?"

"We'll see."

Dan strode over to the dock, where his men were unloading the catch of crabs into bushel baskets. He picked up one of the baskets of crabs and then walked back and stowed it in the boot of the gig.

"Danny, you are a crazy man," Cassala said. "Who can eat a bushel of crab?"

"Your wife, your kids, your relatives — I never seen less than ten at your table."

"Then you come to dinner, Danny."

"Tomorrow. But no business talk. Just forget about that whole Seldon thing."

Cassala drove off and Lavette walked down the wharf to his shack. Upstairs and downstairs, the place was spotless. Feng Wo had taken over, not only as bookkeeper but as houseboy and cook. The smell of fresh coffee permeated the place, and as Dan entered, Feng Wo leaped up from his place at the desk.

"Lunch in ten minutes, Mr. Lavette. As soon as you change and clean up."

"Listen, Feng — you don't have to cook my lunch. That's not in the deal."

"Please, I enjoy it. You eat hash and beans out of cans, Mr. Lavette, and you'll ruin your digestion. My word, you bring in hundreds of tons of fresh fish, and you never eat a piece of fish yourself."

"I hate fish."

"I'll cook you a Chinese omelet. It won't take but a few minutes. Yes?"

"Suit yourself."

The omelet was delicious. Dan ate quickly and hungrily, getting rid of the food rather than savoring it, and then, as he left the place, he told Feng Wo that he would be back in an hour or so. He walked down the Embarcadero to Market Street, and there he entered the first men's tailoring establishment he came to.

"I need a suit," he told the tailor. "A good suit — a suit with some class and some distinction. Do you know what I'm talking about? Forget what I look like now. I'm a boatman, and these are my working clothes. I want a suit for Nob Hill, quiet — no fancy checks or stripes, just quiet class. And I want it to fit me."

"My name is Pincus," the tailor said.

"Lavette. Now do you get my drift, Mr. Pincus?"

"I think so, Mr. Lavette. I'll show you the cloth and you can pick out the material and the style."

"Wait a minute. I need it in three days."

"Three days? Impossible."

"Nothing is impossible."

"Three days — it's got to cost."

"How much?"

"At least a hundred dollars. Depends on the material you select."

"I paid six dollars for the last suit I bought."

"Ready-made." Pincus shrugged.

"All right — three days. Let's get to it."

At the age of seventeen, when his father and mother died, Dan Lavette abandoned all thought of school. During the two years that followed, he came to know the fishermen on the wharf, not as a kid who rode his father's boat as crew but as one of them. He was the youngest of the lot. They liked him; they helped him; they got him drunk for the first time and they took him to his first whorehouse, and they accepted him as one of them, and when they tried to bully him, he fought them with a ferocity that won him his place as a man in a rough, crude man's world; yet he never became a fisherman as such. He won his place but maintained himself as an outsider. The fishermen were Italian and Portugese and Mexican and Yankee, and some of them owned their own boats and others worked on shares, but they all had in common the fact that they were fishermen and they grew old as fisherman, their hands brown and horny, their brown faces as lined and tough as old leather.

He was nineteen when he came to the decision that the difference between Nob Hill and the Embarcadero was the difference between those who owned the boats and those who worked the boats. He decided that life was a plan and a schedule, just as a day's crabbing was a plan and a schedule. He rented the shack on the waterfront, fixed it up, and moved out of the Cassala house, quieting the woeful fears of Maria Cassala that life with the bums and whores on the coast would destroy him. He had no intention of being destroyed. A few months after he moved in, he bought the shack that he had made his home and his office for a thousand dollars in cash against a mortgage. He learned to keep a set of books. He borrowed from Anthony Cassala's bank, mortgaging his boat to buy a second boat, and then mortgaging that to buy a third. He stopped drinking after a dozen drunken sprees, not because he was afraid that he couldn't handle the liquor and not for any moral reasons, but because drunk in a whorehouse, he had been rolled for two hundred and forty-five dollars in cash that he had in his pocket, and then decided that profit and loss did not match. The Barbary Coast, he decided, was a sucker's game, a stupid delusion for kids in the bodies of adults; there were no paths from there to Nob Hill, and at nineteen he had had his fill of wasted, middle-aged whores and maudlin drunks and cheap con men, and fishermen who worked their backsides to the bone six days a week and then blew it all for one night on the Coast. He knew what he wanted; he wanted Nob Hill.

And this night, he was on the Hill, dressed in a gray sharkskin suit that fitted his massive bulk, wearing new black shoes, black socks, a white shirt, and a tie of midnight blue. He saw and observed and learned, and as he walked through the gateposts and up to the front door of the Seldon house, he examined and assessed the place, a Victorian mansion of redwood and gray stone. He was impressed yet not unaware of the gaudiness and ugliness of the place; and he felt that if he had put the same kind of money into the building of a Nob Hill castle, he would have done it differently. How he would have done it, he didn't know; but the very fact that he sensed an aspect of vulgarity gave him assurance.

The butler who opened the door raised a brow. "Your coat, sir?" He was hatless and coatless, indifferent to the weather. He made a note of his error, as he glanced around the foyer, the big staircase leading up to the second floor, the double doors on either side, the view through the glass doors at the back of the foyer to the potted plant wilderness of a conservatory, the dark bronze sculptures in the foyer, the marble floor and banister, the huge, almost awesome crystal chandelier hanging overhead, the two enormous ugly Gothic chairs on either side the staircase, he felt impressed yet not deflated; more as if he were in a store and taking stock. He neither approved nor disapproved; he simply filed an impression for a time when his judgment would allow him to assess it.

The butler, a portly, middle-aged man in livery, opened one of the double doors on the right. Since he had not asked for a name — somewhat surprisingly, for Dan had visions of his reading a formal announcement — Dan concluded that he had been expected and described. He stood for a moment awkwardly, looking at a brightly lit living room, a grand piano, a harp, two enormous couches, overstuffed chairs, a huge Persian rug and five people: Seldon, who came forward to meet him, two older women, a man in his fifties, and a young woman who Dan, with only a glimpse of her face, felt was the most beautiful girl he had ever seen.

Seldon shook his hand. "Delighted, Lavette. Glad to see you. Welcome to my home." He then made the introductions: "This is my wife, Mrs. Seldon — Daniel Lavette." A tall, handsome woman; not friendly, simply courteous with a touch of the dubious as she extended a limp hand. "And Mrs. Whittier." No hand at all this time, just a nod from a stout, tightly corseted woman, whose white satin gown was sewn over with hundreds of small pearls. "And this is Mr. Whittier. Mr. Daniel Lavette." A small man with a waxed mustache; he, like Seldon, wore a dinner jacket and a black tie, a fact of which Dan was now painfully aware. He examined Dan with interest and curiosity and shook hands heartily.

On Dan's part, he was unable to tear his eyes away from Jean Seldon, who sat in one corner of one of the great couches, her blue gown intensifying the pale blue of her eyes, watching him, just the faintest flicker of a smile on her lips. "My daughter, Miss Jean Seldon. And this is Daniel Lavette."

He tried to think of something to say, something he had read, something he had heard — pleased, delighted, overwhelmed, he felt a sick, empty pit in his stomach — or simply how do you do; yet no words would come, and he said nothing. Then she gave him her hand, a large, shapely, long-fingered hand yet lost in his own. He held it a moment and then let go.

"I've heard so much about you, Mr. Lavette," she said. "You made quite an impression on my father. I can see why."

He took it as a compliment and mumbled a thank you. The smile turned to light laughter. Was she laughing at him? The butler appeared at his elbow and asked what he would like to drink. He would have refused a drink, but the other men were drinking, and after a moment's hesitation, he said that he would have a whiskey and soda. Jean Seldon watched him intently. He was conscious of her scrutiny. "Why don't you sit down and tell me about yourself, Mr. Lavette?" she asked. Her manner of speech, her ease, so different from the easy intimacy of the dance-hall girls or the stiff shyness of the girls he met at Cassala's house, was marvelous and new and intriguing. But now Seldon had taken his arm.

"Dan — you don't mind if I call you Dan, I'm old enough to be your father — Whittier here's the President of California Shipping. He's too fat and rich. He needs some young competition."

Jean Seldon smiled at him and watched. The smile relinquished him for the moment, but it also established her proprietary interest for the evening. It said, you're released for the moment, but only for the moment; and he nodded slightly, the thought flashing through his head that this was what he had been looking for and dreaming of, this and nothing else.

"I hear you're planning to buy the *Oregon Queen,* young man."

"Yes, I am."

"She's been nothing but trouble and bad luck since Swenson had her built. Oh, I'm not against iron lumber ships. I've ordered three to be built for my own flag, but it takes time and research and planning. Swenson jumped into his, and it's been nothing but trouble and disaster. That's why he docked it and that's why he's trying to sell it."

"I've seen the ship," Dan said. He addressed Whittier, but he was talking to her. She smiled and listened.

"What do you know about iron ships?"

"Not much. I know the *Queen* is two hundred and forty feet long, and I know her twin screws are out of sync and I think I know what has to be done with them. She's eighteen hundred gross tons, and she'll carry a million and a half board feet of lumber. She blew a boiler and her engine room's a mess, but her engine's good. I'll put new boilers on the main deck, abaft the engines, two boilers instead of one, and they'll never blow again."

"Boilers on the main deck?" Whittier exclaimed. Jean Seldon was smiling now, her father listening intently. "She'll be top-heavy. You'll lose her the first time out."

"No, sir. My arithmetic's nothing to write home about, but I've done the calculations, and she will not be top-heavy. Also, when I take out her boiler, I'll have cargo space for another hundred and fifty thousand board feet."

"I'll tell you this, Mr. Lavette," Whittier snapped. "You'll not have me for a passenger."

Unable to keep from grinning, Dan told him he was not thinking of passengers yet. "That's in the future, sir. I'm thinking that an iron ship can take a deadweight cargo, cement, salt, sugar, sand, so I'm not bound hand and foot by the lumber season or the lumber barons. And I'm not tied to the Redwood Coast. I can take cargo from as high up as Oregon."

"You seem damn sure of yourself for a man your age."

"I'm as old as I can be at my age," Dan said. "I don't know very much, but I know the water."

The butler entered to announce that dinner was being served, and Mrs. Seldon interrupted to say that the very least they could do would be to save their business discussions until after they had dined. Watching, wary of error, Dan waited. Seldon took his wife's arm, and Whittier his wife's. Dan waited. Jean rose. "You will take me into dinner, Mr. Lavette?"

He nodded and took her arm. The easy flow of words that had poured out talking to Whittier dried up now. He simply did not know what to say. "You were splendid," she whispered to him.

"Oh?"

"No one, but no one ever talks to Grant Whittier that way. They scrape and bow and agree with everything he says."

"It was wrong?" he asked uncertainly.

"It was right."

He didn't know what to say to that and entered the dining room in silence. He was seated at her left, with Whittier across the board from him and the Seldons at either end of the big table. He had never sat down to such a table before, three forks to his left, two knives and three spoons to his right and a third knife at the top of his plate. The plate itself was gold-edged with a gold monogram in the center. He saw Whittier move his wife's chair in behind her, and Dan did the same with Jean's chair. He touched nothing until he saw them pick up their napkins, and then he followed suit carefully, conscious of the fact that the girl on his left was watching every move he made. One large goblet, three smaller goblets. The butler was pouring water into the large goblets. His throat was dry and he desperately wanted a drink, and now he became conscious of the fact that he had carried his whiskey with him. How had the others disposed of their drinks? He set it down on the table, relieved when the butler removed it. The Seldons and the Whittiers were chatting, a kind of small talk he had never encountered before, and his own silence began to fill him with oppression. Jean Seldon came to his rescue, and he wondered whether she had any notion that never before in his life had he dined with people like this in a room like this or a house like this.

"How on earth do you know so much about ships?" she asked him.

"I don't."

"But of course you do."

"Well, about the *Oregon Queen,* I guess a little. I know more about boats. I been in boats most of my life, I guess."

"And a ship isn't a boat?"

Whittier heard this. "No, indeed, my dear," he said. "A boat is not a ship, although some say that a ship is a boat." His small joke amused him, and he chuckled over it.

"A ship is large, a boat is small. That's about the difference," Dan said. At least he was talking to her, sitting alongside of her. A maid placed a plate of crab meat and mayonnaise on his service plate and the butler poured white wine into the outside goblet of the three that were lined up before him. He had no taste for crab meat, and he wondered whether he would be offending them if he did not eat it. Jean was only picking at hers; he had no way of knowing that her appetite had fled with his presence there.

"Could be off one of your own boats, Lavette," Whittier said. "The crab, I mean." Whittier was hostile, contriving his hostility in witless remarks. Dan said nothing, only thinking that if this small, pompous, foolish man, so uninformed about the essence of his own business, was a measure of the hundred tycoons who ruled the hills of San Francisco, then his own way up would be none too difficult. It came down to money; if you had the money, you functioned and you could do without guts or brains; and if you had money, you saw a girl like Jean Seldon more than once, more than by accident. He took the outside fork after the other had picked theirs up, and he forced himself to eat the crab meat.

"I'd like to think that it is," Seldon said, taking the edge off Whittier's remark. "Young Lavette here owns three crabbing boats," he explained to Mrs. Whittier, "and that's quite an achievement for someone his age."

"When most young fellows are still in college," Whittier said.

"Eating out of their daddy's pockets," Jean said sweetly, smiling at Whittier. "John's in his last year at Yale, isn't he?"

"That's right."

Mary Seldon looked at her daughter disapprovingly, but Jean refused to meet her eyes. The maid was picking up the fish plates and the butler was serving a clear soup. Trying not to look at her directly, Dan watched Jean.

"And then he'll go into your business, Mr. Whittier?"

"Of course."

"What a pity he can't start a shipping line of his own, as Mr. Lavette intends to do. But then he wouldn't know how, really, would he?" she added, with a smile.

Dan watching, listening. Match their spoon. They dipped away instead of toward them. She turned to him and smiled.

"That's hardly called for, Jean," her father said. "Why on earth would John want a shipping line of his own?"

"Do you like the soup, Mr. Lavette?" Her question abandoned the rest of them.

"Why — yes."

"You don't like crab?"

He found himself grinning at her. His nervousness had disappeared, and suddenly he had a sense of his own size, his physical strength, his own brains and being. Four years, he had earned his own bread and keep, fended for himself, had not only remained alive and well but had put together a small fishing fleet of his own, and kept it alive and functioning and fought the wind and the weather and met a payroll for eleven men in his crews — and be damned with the lot of them if he'd go into a funk over which spoon or knife to use.

"Neither would I, if I were in your place, Mr. Lavette," Jean said. "I would hate fish and I would hate crabs — ugly little beasts."

He found himself talking to her, and he found himself enjoying the challenge of this strange and somewhat incomprehensible dinner. After the soup, a plate of roast beef and potatoes was substituted for the gold-rimmed, monogrammed plate that had been in front of him. Then a salad with cheese. Then an ice. Then a small plate of what he guessed was rabbit stew, highly spiced. His only comparison were the dinners he had eaten at the Cassalas and the Levys, and he felt that both families ate better food and more sensibly. But he would learn the ritual; he would learn every damn thing that existed in Jean Seldon's world.

After dinner, the butler passed cigars and brought out brandy. The women rose to leave the room. Jean Seldon said to her father, "Dear daddy, let me take Mr. Lavette and show him the terrace. I'm sure he doesn't smoke cigars. Do you, Mr. Lavette?"

"No, I don't."

"There. May I?"

Her mother watched coldly as she took Dan's arm, and without waiting for an answer, Jean Seldon guided him out of the room.

"I'm spoiled," she said to him as they stood on the terrace behind the house, with the great, splendid sweep of the bay and the city beneath them. "You must understand that. I am the spoiled only child of a very rich man who adores me, and that's why I do shocking things and get away with it."

"Shocking things?"

"Dragging you away like this and out of the clutches of that stupid Grant Whittier." She watched him. "You don't think that's shocking."

"No."

"Yes. No. You talked your head off with Grant Whittier, Mr. Lavette."

"That was different."

"Why?"

"I don't know what to say to you."

"Of all the silly things I ever heard! There, I've hurt your feelings."

"No." He shook his head, trying to find the proper words. "I don't know what to say to you. I never knew anyone like you before."

"How old are you, Mr. Lavette?"

"Twenty-one."

"And I'll be twenty-one in six — no, five — months. So we're the same age, but every boy of twenty-one I ever knew was a little boy — not in size, mind you — but just a kid. You're very different. Do you know that?"

"No, I never thought about it."

"Do you always say exactly what's on your mind?"

"I don't know. I suppose I do."

"Daddy described you as a sort of roughneck, in clothes that didn't fit you. You're not a roughneck at all."

"This is a new suit."

"That's not what I meant at all. You are provoking."

"I don't mean to be, Miss Seldon."

"My name is Jean, Mr. Lavette. You may call me that. I shall call you Dan. We have been formally introduced, so it's perfectly all right."

"I want to see you again," he said slowly.

"Oh?"

"Will that be all right? I told you I've never met a girl like you before. I've never been to a house like this before. You might as well know."

"Indeed." She looked at him thoughtfully — tall, slender, elegant, coldly and incredibly beautiful. Then she closed her eyes while he waited. Then she opened them and smiled at him. "Yes, Dan, you may see me again."

When he left the Seldon house, he walked quietly for a dozen paces, and then he let out a howl and began to run. He went down the hill like a loping steer. When he reached the wharf, he leaped into one of his boats, prowled through it, and then sat in the stern staring out at the fog that lay upon the bay. He had no desire to sleep. The whole world was new and wonderful and incredible.

Maria Cassala gave birth to a stillborn child. Dan went to the hospital and stood by her bedside, while she clung to his hand and wept. At thirty-four, Maria had already left her youth behind her. She was stout, her once lovely face puffy and blotched. She clung to his hand with a kind of frantic desperation. The doctors had told her that she would never have another child. She was a simple woman, illiterate, and she made no attempt to learn English. In spite of her husband's success and growing wealth, she would have no servants in the house. She did her own cleaning and cooking, but now the doctors told her husband that she must spend at least five weeks in bed.

"But you are my other son, Daniel," she told him through her tears. "You will always be my son, and when Rosa is older, you will turn to each other."

"You get well. Just get well, Maria."

"My child was a son," she moaned. "Daniel, Daniel, he was taken from me before I ever touched him."

Outside, in the hospital corridor, Anthony embraced him. Dan was shaken by the depth of the man's emotion and grief; after all, the child had never lived. "You turn to people you love," Cassala said. "Money — my whole life is money. You are my son, Danny. I lose one son. Not you, Danny."

Away for most of the morning, Mark Levy returned to his shop to find his wife, Sarah, close to tears. Her annoyance was out of character. "How can you find anything here? How can you ever find anything in this mess?" Martha took the cue from her mother and began to wail. "Where were you?" Sarah demanded as she picked up the child and quieted her.

"I was only gone a few hours. I went to look at the *Oregon Queen.*"

"Jenson was in here, shouting at me. He says the oakum you sold him is no good."

"He's crazy."

"He dumped it all behind the shop. I gave him his money back." Mark started to say something, then swallowed his words. "Oh, I hate this whole thing," she cried out. "I hate being a storekeeper. I hate it."

"You never said that before."

"I'm saying it now. Isn't that enough? I'll feed Martha and get your lunch."

"I'm not hungry," Mark said. He began to prowl around the store, straightening a shelf of goods here and there. "I didn't know you hated it. It's pop's store. Hell, it's given us a decent living. Chandlering's not the worst thing in the world."

"I'm sorry." She sat down with the child in her arms and began to weep.

"Why are you crying? The hell with Jenson. You gave him his money back. He has no kick coming."

"I'm not crying over that. Maria Cassala's child died."

"What? Who — Steve or Rosa?"

"No, the baby. It was stillborn. Danny Lavette was in here and he told me."

"Yeah, that's rotten. But you don't have to cry over it. It happens."

"Yes, it happens."

"She'll have other kids."

"She won't. The doctor says no." She dried her eyes with her skirt and pressed Martha to her bosom. "I'm just miserable." She went into the back room with Martha, and a few minutes later Mark heard her singing to the child. "If I were only like that," he thought. "In and out of grief that easily."

"Why did you go to look at the *Oregon Queen?*" she called out to him.

"To see if Danny is crazy."

"Is he?"

"No."

"I have cold fish for your lunch. Will you eat it?"

"I'll eat it," he said with resignation.

Feng Wo's knowledge in a variety of areas was amazing. "What would you wear," Dan asked him, "to take a girl driving? Not a tart. This is a girl with class."

Feng Wo thought about it for a moment. "I think, Mr. Lavette, white ducks, a white shirt, and some kind of jacket sweater that buttons down the front. You can buy that at Lords. Maybe those canvas shoes they call sneakers."

"Just that? Not flannels?"

"I worked for such people once. It is true they wear white flannels for their amusements. But you're a man of the sea. Ducks would be appropriate, I think."

But once at Lords, he bought the white flannels and a blue boating jacket with brass buttons. White sneakers. The shoes were all right, but he felt like a fool in the boating jacket, and at the last moment he pulled on an old gray sweater. At least it was clean and did not smell of fish. At Peek's livery stable on Jefferson Street, he rented the newest, brassiest gig that Jesse Peek owned, with a fretful, nervous brown filly to pull it. "If I had any sense, I'd give you an old nag," Peek said, "because you don't know beans about horses, Danny, and she's lively, lively. So keep her in check but don't hurt her mouth. She's a dandy."

It was six dollars for the day, but worth it, Dan decided. Nor was his mood dampened by the frigid welcome Mrs. Seldon gave him when he arrived to pick up Jean. She came downstairs wearing a pale green blouse, a white cardigan sweater, and a loose plaid skirt that fell to just above her ankles. Her honey-colored hair was tied at the back of her head with a green ribbon — and to Dan she was totally, unequivocally the most beautiful and desirable creature that had ever existed.

"If you will excuse us for a moment, Mr. Lavette," her mother said, taking her into the living room while Dan waited in the foyer. "Jean," she said, "I simply do not understand you."

"What is there to understand, mother?"

"To go unchaperoned with a person like that in an open gig for anyone and everyone to see — I don't understand it. I simply do not."

"What do you mean by a person like that?"

"He has no background, no family, a crude, pushy — "

"Stop that, mother."

"You know exactly what I mean."

"Are you forbidding me to go?"

"No, I won't have a scene. You'd go anyway."

"Yes, I would." She flung open the door, strode into the foyer, took Dan's arm, and steered him out of the door.

They drove for a few minutes before she said, "I had a scene with my mother. I'm not cross with you. I'm upset. You might as well know. I have a beastly temper."

"About me?" he asked.

"Yes, about you."

"That's all right," he said placidly. "I'm not your kind. If I was in her place, I'd probably feel the same."

"You are the most astonishing young man. Doesn't anything bother you?"

"Sometimes. But right now, the way I feel, nothing could bother me. Where should I take you?"

"First to see your boats. I am absolutely intrigued with them."

"They're just dirty, smelly old fishing boats. Now if this was twenty years ago, it would be different."

"Why?"

"Because that was the time my father began to fish here. All the Italian fishermen rigged their boats with the same lateen sails they had used in the Bay of Naples and off the coast of Sicily, and they were something to see all right."

"What on earth is a lateen sail. You see, I know nothing, absolutely nothing."

"It's a triangular sail. It hangs forward on a low mast and a rake angle. You know that artist who paints those purple and blue pictures of ladies on swings with a lot of old Greek columns around them — "

"You mean Maxfield Parrish. What a wonderful description."

"That's right. Well, he has that kind of boat in his pictures."

"Of course. I remember. They're wonderful."

"They're gone now, all of them. Nothing but stinkpots — I'm sorry — oil burners. All right — the wharf."

He drove the little gig onto the wharf amidst the confusion of the boats unloading their catch, the filly prancing and nervous at the crowds and the smell of the fish. Pete Lomas, his chief mate, caught sight of him and stalked over, so preoccupied with his own anger that he apparently never noticed the girl alongside of Dan, and burst out, "Danny, that motherfucking sonofabitch Trankas robbed our traps again, and so help me God I'm going to kill that whore's pup next time I see him!"

"Pete!"

He saw Jean and began to apologize, this big bearded man in a wet jersey and rubber boots. She burst out laughing. Dan tried to apologize. Lomas stood there woefully. When they drove off, Dan tried to explain. He stopped the gig in front of his shack and told her, "He didn't see you. I don't know what to say."

"Dan, he was marvelous. Do you talk the same way when you're with them?"

"Sometimes — I guess."

"And this is your place," she said, looking at the shanty.

"It's just a shack." He was suddenly ashamed, cowed by her. Why had he been stupid enough, senseless enough, to bring her down here? He drew a contrast between the leaning, off-center shanty and the magnificent house on Nob Hill, and he felt a sickening emptiness in his stomach.

"You live here too?"

He nodded.

"Show it to me. Please, Dan."

"It's nothing. It's just an old shack I use for an office. I got a sort of bedroom upstairs where I sleep."

"Please show it to me."

He sighed, put the iron hitch down for the horse, and helped her out of the gig. They went into the shanty. Feng Wo stood up, smiling as they entered, and Dan said, "This is my bookkeeper, Feng Wo. Feng Wo, this is Miss Jean Seldon."

She stiffened. The smile disappeared and the beautiful face became a mask. Outside, she was silent, and as they drove off, he tried to understand what he had done wrong. "I told you it was just a rotten little place," he said.

She was still silent, her face set.

"All right. Everything went wrong today, everything. I'm sorry. You have a right to be angry."

"You don't know why I'm angry?"

"Yes — no, I don't."

"How could you introduce me to a Chink?" she burst out.

"What?"

"You have no sense of what is right or wrong or fitting or unfitting."

"I haven't?"

"No, you haven't."

He stared at her, and suddenly her anger left her and she smiled. At that moment, he would have laid down his life for her smile.

"You're like a little boy who has been scolded and spanked," she said, and then she leaned over and kissed his cheek, lightly and gently.

Eight years before, in 1902, Jack Harvey, a young captain, twenty-nine years old, with his wife and his daughter, Clair, sharing his cabin, had sailed the clipper ship *Ocean Breeze* around the Horn and up the coasts of two continents to San Francisco Bay, where the owners pulled her out of service, berthed her, and let her rot, finally breaking her up for scrap wood. Her day and the day of all the other magnificent Yankee Clippers was over forever. Harvey got drunk and stayed drunk for nine months. His wife, who had been a dance-hall girl before she married him, working in a sailors' joint in Norfolk, Virginia, and who hated him, the ship, and the sea through every day of the journey to San Francisco, walked out on him and disappeared, leaving her two-year-old daughter in his sodden custody. After that, he stopped drinking, except for an occasional bender, and found a living on the lumber ships that plied the Redwood Coast between the bay and Mendocino City. He kept his daughter with him, because he could find no other solution to the problem of raising her; and since this was not a situation the shipowners found to their liking, he would have periodic layoffs, which he filled with whatever odd jobs he could find. Clair's schooling was spotty, but she learned to read, and since her father had a passion for novels and since she adored him, she had at the age of ten read everything available to her, from Ned Buntline to Dostoevski.

When Lars Swenson laid up the *Oregon Queen* — his "stinking iron scow" as he called it — he offered Harvey the job of caretaker, with the cabin of the ship as his living quarters and a wage of thirty dollars a month. Since Harvey had no berth at the time, and saw this as an opportunity to put Clair into school and keep her there for a while, he accepted the offer.

When Dan first chanced upon the *Oregon Queen,* regarding her more as a curiosity than anything else, it was Harvey who enticed him onto the ship, invited him for a drink in the cabin and expanded upon the possibilities of an iron ship. Harvey took a fancy to the tall, good-looking young man, and Clair, a skinny, long-legged, freckled, redheaded girl of ten, was immediately enchanted. She had spent the best part of her young life at sea, and she could scramble up the masts and the rigging like a monkey. Dan became her beau ideal, the personification of a medley of fictional heroes who peopled her world, and he in turn would bring some special gift for her, a model clipper, a dress, a jar of jam, each time he visited the ship. In due time, Harvey told Dan about Swenson's desperation to be rid of the ship, and it was Harvey's guess that Swenson would accept an offer of a hundred and fifty thousand dollars. Clair, meanwhile, counted the days and the hours between Dan's departure and his promise of another visit.

She was thus devastated to see him pull up to the dockside one day and help a beautiful young woman out of a fancy gig. Clair Harvey had neither the anticipation nor the comprehension of the possibility that skinny, long-legged, redheaded kids may evolve into very lovely women. For the first time in her life she engaged in a sexual comparison, herself against this tall, perfect creature whose hand Dan Lavette held; and having made the comparison, she fled into hiding and did not emerge again while Dan and Jean remained on the ship.

Harvey, a week's red beard on his face, barefoot in dirty duck trousers, mumbled his apologies and his pleasure and excused himself to look for his daughter, whom Dan had spoken of and whom Jean expected to see. Like his daughter, he disappeared. Jean walked gingerly around the deck, seeing only rust, peeling paint, grease, oil, and varieties of filth that included two foul-smelling cans of garbage — but listening meanwhile to Dan's dream of a fleet of iron ships and fighting an inner impulse to flee from this strange, crazy boy-man-adolescent who was like no other boy who had ever come into her life. On the other hand, there were compulsions that overran her fears. Since the day she had first seen Dan Lavette, she had been unable to get him out of her mind. She made him the center of her fantasies; she visualized him touching her, making love to her, his sunburned two hundred and ten pounds of bone and muscle pressed down on her white nakedness; and to this fantasy she would respond with a mixture of terror and desire.

Now he was a king in his own castle. "What do you think of my ship?" he demanded exuberantly.

"It's not yours yet — Dan."

"If you're thinking about your father," he said, misinterpreting her expression of distaste, "don't worry. I know he won't give me the loan."

"Then how can you buy the ship?"

"I don't know. But I will."

"But why?" she wondered. "There are people who live without ships and boats — you see, I remembered the difference."

"Without ships — " He shook his head. "No. No. I know what my life is. I always knew."

In Mark Levy's store, while Mark waited on another customer, Dan assembled a pile of supplies, boat hooks, lanterns, traps, cordage. When the other customer left, Mark turned to Dan and regarded the growing pile of supplies. "I need everything," Dan said. "God damn it, Mark, I haven't got the cash for this. You'll have to give me credit — at least until the end of the month."

"Your credit's good here. But why? You never wanted credit before."

"I'm spending money like a drunken sailor. I guess I can afford it, but I'm running low."

Mark studied him thoughtfully, then went to the door, hung up a "closed" sign, and turned the lock. "We'll have a beer and talk." Dan followed him into the kitchen. Sarah was peeling potatoes. Martha sat on the floor, happily smearing crayon on a coloring book.

"Where's Jake?" Dan asked.

"At school. That's a pretty girl, Danny," Sarah said, watching him.

"You saw her?"

"Everyone on the wharf saw her. Who is she?"

"Her name's Jean Seldon."

"Seldon?" Mark said.

"That's right."

"Wait a minute."

"She's his daughter."

"That's a lot of class, Danny. Where'd you meet her?"

"At her house."

"And you took her slumming?" Mark grinned.

"Mark — Sarah — look. Don't laugh at me. I'm in love. I don't know what hit me, but ever since I've seen that girl, there's nothing else in the world. I want her like I never wanted anything in my life."

"Danny, she's a nabob."

"Leave him alone," Sarah said to her husband. And then to Dan, "Look, kid, how serious are you?"

"Serious. I'm going to marry her."

"You're crazy," Mark said.

"Maybe he's not so crazy. But what's she like, Danny? The top of that hill's a thousand miles away."

"I don't know what she's like. I don't care. I just know that this is it."

"How does she feel about you?"

"God knows. I think she likes me. We've been driving twice. I been to her house. I dry up there — the place gives me the chills. But when we're out in the gig, I can talk to her. All right, just give it time."

"O.K. — put your love life aside for a moment," Mark said. "Sarah and I have a proposition for you."

"What kind of a proposition?"

"Just sit back and listen. The other day, I went out to the *Oregon Queen* — "

"I know. Harvey told me. You won't sell Swenson anything. He's fed up with the ship, and all he wants is to dump it."

"I didn't go there to sell Swenson anything. I went there to look at the ship."

"What do you know about ships?" Dan demanded.

"Not much, but maybe as much as you do, Danny. I'm a chandler — I been in this all my life. All right, just listen. I agree with you. It's a damn good ship. Harvey told me about your idea of putting two boilers on the main deck, and I think that will do it. She has to be scraped and painted and overhauled. Her winches are O.K. She needs new rope, but the engine is good and her generators are good. She's built to be fired by coal, but we can change that and convert her to automatic oil firing — "

"What do you mean, we?"

"Will you just listen. If she's converted to oil, there's a fortune in that ship."

"How do you know she can be converted?"

"I don't know. I think so. Anyway, that's the future — oil burners. Now Sarah and me, we been talking about this; I guess we talked ourselves dry. Here's the proposition. The store and the building here are worth maybe sixty, seventy thousand dollars. It's unmortgaged. You and me become partners. We go to Tony Cassala and get a line of credit against my store and stock and building — up to fifty thousand dollars. Maybe we won't need that much, but we'll feel safer with something to fall back on, so we ask for a line up to fifty thousand. Then we buy the *Queen,* fix her up, and we're in the shipping business. We draw on the store for supplies, and that'll cover another two, three thousand dollars. What do you say?" He leaned back and looked at Dan, who was staring, first at Mark and then at his wife.

"You'd do that for me?" Dan asked softly.

"For us," Sarah said.

"No. It's a gift. You're out of your mind. This store is your life."

"I hate this store," Sarah said.

"You put up your store and building — what do I put up?"

"You."

"What do you mean, me?"

"I can't do it," Mark said. "It scares the hell out of me, the thought of running a ship. I can sell the cargo space, I think, but I can't operate a ship. I'm not built that way."

"What makes you think I can?"

"I know you can. I watched you operate your fishing boats."

"That's different."

"Not so different. And Danny, there's a fortune in it. You know that, and I know it."

"No. No, I can't take it from you. I never took gifts from anyone in my life. I can't."

"All right," Mark said, after a long moment. "Throw your boats into the deal. We'll become partners right down the line."

"The boats are mortgaged. You know that."

"There's still an equity. Just think about it, Danny. You got something, we got something. We put it together."

Minutes passed. Dan sat in silence, staring at the table. Sarah finished peeling the potatoes and put them on the stove to boil. "You want a beer, Danny, or coffee?"

"Just coffee."

"Black?"

He nodded, and, almost woefully, he asked, "Why are you doing this for me? I don't understand."

"Maybe we love you," Sarah said, smiling and putting down the coffee in front of him. "You want a piece of cake, Danny?"

He shook his head.

"Well?" Mark asked him.

"I don't know. There's maybe ten thousand dollars of equity in the fishing boats. That gives you eighty percent of the deal."

"Fifty, fifty or nothing."

"I don't know how to work out something like this. We'd need lawyers."

"Tony knows how, and he's got lawyers."

"My shack's worth five thousand. That has to be thrown into the pot."

"Then it's a deal?" Mark asked.

"It's a deal," Dan said. They shook hands. "Get a bottle of wine," Mark cried. "We got to drink to this."

Sarah opened a bottle of wine and filled three glasses. Raising his glass, Mark said, "My dear wife, my dear friend, Danny, this is a historic occasion. I offer this toast to Lavette and Levy, shipowners!"

"No," Dan said. "Levy and Lavette. That sounds better. Jesus God, Mark, I'm twenty-one years old, and I'm scared."

"So am I. Levy and Lavette if you want it that way. Bottoms up!"

At the age of thirty-six, Anthony Cassala had shed his youth. He would still awaken at night, covered with sweat, caught in the nightmare of being a penniless, hungry, ragged urchin in the slums of Naples. The fact that he had lived through the transition that had turned him into a banker did little to dispel the unreality of the situation. He had experienced not a single day of schooling; he had taught himself to read and write, first in Italian and then in English. He had learned arithmetic under the tutelage of his son, Stephan, who was now fifteen, and still he pored avidly over Stephan's books to comprehend the mysteries of percentages and fractions. He arose each morning at six o'clock, and before breakfast he read the *Chronicle* from cover to cover, as well as the *Wall Street Journal,* four days late, but still to be studied and treasured, and all of this before he touched food. He would then shave, shine his own black shoes, put on his carefully pressed striped pants and a black frock coat, and then on foot and by cable car go to his office at the Bank of Sonoma on Montgomery Street.

He always paused outside of the bank to read the gold-leaf letters on the plate-glass window, just as he paused at the door to his office, where small black letters, outlined in gold, bore the legend: ANTHONY CASSALA, PRESIDENT. For all of his wit and intelligence, he was essentially a simple man. When someone flattered him for hard work and its rewards, he shook his head uneasily. He knew what hard work was, recalling all the years he had worked as a laborer and a mason; this was luck and the grace of God. He was a deeply religious man, and at confession he always dwelt on his guilt. Who was he to deserve this? What had he done to make him any different from any other Italian laborer?

Now, for a whole hour, he had been sitting behind his desk questioning Dan Lavette and Mark Levy. "It is not the money," he said again and again. "The money is nothing. If I had to empty my pockets, I would find the money for Danny, and such a loan you ask, it's well secured. But you are boys."

"I'm thirty," Mark said. "That's not a boy, no, sir."

"Danny's a boy."

"To you, maybe," Dan said. "Tony, we know what we're doing."

"You need organization, office, books, insurance. This Chinese you hire, Danny, he got a head on his shoulders?"

"Feng Wo's smarter than I am. He can do anything."

"That's good, fine. You come back tomorrow, ten o'clock, I have Sam Goldberg here. He's my lawyer, from Goldberg and Benchly — honest man. He draws up the partnership, and you sign the papers."

They shook hands then with great formality. Cassala brought out a bottle of brandy and glasses, poured the brandy, and said, "*Buona salute, buona vita, buona fortuna e compassione.*"

They drank, and then they shook hands again and left. Out on the street, Mark asked Dan what the toast meant. "Good health, good life, good fortune — and I think he said we should have compassion for each other. *Compassione,*" Dan said.

"That's peculiar."

"Well, that's Tony. But we got the money, Mark, and we'll have the ship. How do you feel?"

"Good."

"Not nervous?"

"A little nervous."

"I tell you how I feel," Dan said. "I feel like we got the whole world in our hands. God damn it, Mark, the whole fuckin' world — right here!" Holding out his two hands and staring at them, and then bursting into laughter. "Levy and Lavette. How does that sound?"

"Good. Sounds good."

"Marcus, old buddy," Dan said, "you and me — I got a notion we were made for this partnership. You are sane and sober, I go off half cocked given the slightest chance. But we both of us got brains, and that's what counts. A year ago I would have rushed out and gotten myself laid to celebrate. Now I'm in love. Maybe. I think I am."

Mark grinned. "It's a long haul, Danny."

"We got all the time in the world. Let's get drunk."

"Sarah'll peel my hide off."

"Hell, it'll grow back."

They went to Maguire's Bar and matched each other with rye shots and beer chasers. Mark was not a good drinker, and when they left the place, Dan's arm kept him on his feet. Dan guided them down to the wharf. It was late afternoon, the boats in, the catch disposed of.

"Let's sail," Dan said. "Clear our heads and calm our souls."

"No. Danny, you can't handle those boats alone. Anyway, you're drunk."

"You're drunk, buddy-boy. Don't worry. That blue water's my mama and papa. I was raised up on that bay. Shit, I could sail the *Oregon Queen* alone if I had to. I can sail any goddamn thing that floats. Now you just set yourself in there and I'll take care of things."

Nodding his head trustingly, Mark climbed into the boat. Dan untied the ropes and kicked off from the dock. Sprawled out in the hold, Mark was vaguely aware of the strong odor of fish. Dan turned over the engine, and as it caught, he took the wheel and guided the boat out into the bay.

The water was soft, smooth, and glistening gold in the light of the setting sun, and above them the hills of the city glistened like jeweled tiaras. Except for an old lumber scow in the distance, the bay was empty, a slow, gentle tide running toward the Golden Gate. Already, the eastern slopes of Marin County had turned a somber black, and a thousand swooping gulls screeched farewell to the day.

Dan set the throttle low and strapped the wheel, and then he sprawled out alongside of Mark. They were moving out away from the city, holding it in clear view.

"Up there — right up there to the top of Nob Hill, that's where we're going, old buddy, because it's our city, and they are going to know it. They sure as hell are."

Since the first guest had arrived, Jean Seldon had not taken her eyes off the entrance to the room, waiting for him. Her mother watched her. Did her mother know? That would come later in the evening, when her mother would demand to know who had invited him. "I did," she would say. "Why?" "Because I wanted him here." "And you knew I did not want him here?" "But I did." Or perhaps not precisely in those terms. Her mother never screamed or lost her temper; her weapons were silence, cold fury, scorn; and all of these were weapons Jean understood and could use in kind. Her father would simply accept it. She had the feeling that he regarded Dan Lavette with amused respect, and if he dared challenge her, she would point out that if he could have Mayor McCarthy and Police Chief Martin as guests in his house, she could certainly invite Dan Lavette.

Yet she was nervous, sufficiently so for her mother to say to her, "Jean, what on earth is wrong with you? The Brockers said you ignored them. You're not ill?" "I'm just fine, mother." Mary Seldon could not pursue it. There were fifty guests expected, in what was more or less a tribute to the new mayor, Patrick Henry McCarthy, who had been swept into office by the Union Labor Party, and here he was already to meet the kings and the pashas and the nabobs, his sworn enemies during the campaign and now the convivial recipients of his charming Irish brogue, the Brockers and the

Whittiers and the Callans and all the others who ruled the city and so much of the state; and Mary Seldon was totally preoccupied with the business of being a hostess. As for Jean, she turned a deaf ear to the three or four young men who had been asked as her friends, in particular Alan Brocker, who had courted her for the past two years. When he complained that she had not given him two minutes of her attention, Jean, who never minced words, informed him that two minutes were sufficient to bore her to tears.

Her nervousness was due in part to the fact that she was by no means certain that Dan Lavette would appear. She had told him that it would be a formal affair and that he would be expected to wear a tuxedo. He had none. He had never worn one. But now, watching the door and listening to the chatter of her friend Marcy Callan, she saw him come through the wide double doors, tuxedo and all, wearing his dinner jacket as if it had been molded to his enormous body, looking for her over the heads of the others.

"Who is he?" Marcy Callan asked her. "Oh, no, he's not your fisherman?"

"He is. And if you go near him, I'll claw your eyes out." Then she went to him, quickly, avoiding the eyes of her mother, who had also seen him, and took his arm. "Oh, Danny, you were so brave to come."

"You are goddamn right," he whispered to her. "What in hell am I doing here?"

"Being handsome and charming and witty and brilliant — which is exactly what one would expect from the man who intends to marry Thomas Seldon's one and only child." She took his arm. "Come, let me introduce you to the royalty."

Looking at her, Dan would have allowed her to introduce him to the devil himself. She wore a gown of peach-colored crêpe de Chine, and her honey-colored hair was piled like a crown on her head. On her high heels, she was only a few inches shorter than he, and the two of them together became the target for every eye in the room. She felt the keen edge of her triumph; her mother and father could do nothing now but be as pleasant and engaging as host and hostess should. The whispers began, Jean's fisherman, the Tenderloin brawler — she's been seeing him for ages, but who can blame her? Smiling serenely, she introduced him to James Brocker. "This is Daniel Lavette, my friend." She whispered to Dan, "The other bank. He and daddy have all the money in the world."

Whittier shook hands with him coldly. "Bought your ship yet?"

"Just about."

Joe Callan, a heavy mountain of a man, studied him thoughtfully. "So your Seldon's fisherman," he said. Marcy, his daughter, clung to his arm.

"I'm nobody's fisherman, Mr. Callan," Dan replied. "Not even yours."

Jean ignored Marcy and steered Dan away. "You've just insulted the richest man in California. Do you know who he is?"

"The hell with him."

"I adore you. And this is our new mayor. Mayor McCarthy, this is Dan Lavette."

They shook hands. McCarthy's blue eyes twinkled. "Ah, lad," he said, "you got the prize of the evening."

"I have."

"And I hear you're a plain man, like myself." He leaned toward Dan. " 'Tis a den of thieves that we're in. Watch your step, laddie."

"What did he say?" Jean wanted to know.

"That I'm in a den of thieves."

"Delicious." She faced her mother, who nodded coldly to Dan.

"Mr. Lavette."

"Thank you for asking me to come here," Dan said.

"Yes." Mother and daughter exchanged looks, and Jean steered Dan away.

"What was that all about?"

"Nothing. Here's daddy. Be very nice."

He shook hands with Seldon. "Glad to see you," Seldon said. "We'll find time for a chat later."

The introductions went on: heavy-jowled men who smelled of power and success, stout bejeweled women who smelled of fine French perfume. Names Dan had heard about, names that were in the newspapers; he nodded, smiled, took hands that were offered to him, and then breathed a sigh of relief when Jean drew him out of the crowd into the solarium. There, sheltered by the palms and ferns, Jean said, "You don't like us very much, do you?"

"They don't like me."

" 'Granddad worked in the placer mines, Daddy's on Nob Hill, if it weren't for Sutter and Sutter's gold, I'd still be sucking swill.' I learned that when I was five. It used to enrage mother. She's from Boston. The fact is that you are the envy of every woman in the room. I love your dinner jacket."

"We got the loan, Jean. Mark Levy and I are buying the *Oregon Queen.* We've been fighting over the price with Swenson for two weeks and now we made the deal. It's just the beginning. I swear to you, it's just the beginning." He took her in his arms.

"Danny, someone will see us."

"To hell with them!"

When Dan left — the party still in progress — Jean went directly to her room, and it occurred to her that one way to deal with this would be to go to bed and turn off the lights and give her parents until morning to cool off. But she was too stimulated, too alive, too excited to go to sleep or to lie in the dark and pretend she was asleep, as she had done so often as a little girl. Indeed, a part of her wanted the encounter and looked forward to it. She changed into a dressing gown of pale blue velvet and Alençon ruffled lace, picked up her copy of *Vanity Fair,* stretched out on her chaise, and waited. She tried to read, but the words were meaningless, and she let herself float into fantasy. It was about an hour later that they knocked at the door.

"Come in. I'm awake," Jean said.

Her mother entered, followed by her father. He temporized immediately. "I think this should wait for the morning, Mary."

"I don't," his wife said.

"I don't know what all the fuss is about," Jean said mildly. "You gave a party. I invited a friend. I've done that before."

"I told you I did not want him in this house," her mother said icily.

"I thought it was my home too. Or was I mistaken?"

"For heaven's sake, Mary," Seldon said, "he came here first as my guest. If Jean took a fancy to him, it's my fault." And to Jean, "All the same, you showed poor judgment asking him here."

"Why?"

"Because I don't like the idea of your going with a man like Lavette. There are enough decent boys of decent families."

"You said it." Jean smiled. "They're boys. He's a man."

"He is nobody," her mother said. "Your father looked into his background. His folks were Italian immigrants. He has no family, no education, and no position. He lives in a shack on the waterfront, and he is certainly the last person in the world for you to spend your time with."

"His father was French," Jean said calmly, "if that makes any difference. And he's better educated and better read than half the people downstairs tonight. He's kind and generous, and he loves me."

"Oh? And just what do you feel about him?" Seldon asked.

"I love him and I intend to marry him."

"You are quite mad!" her mother exclaimed. "The whole thing is insane! You're talking like a child."

"I am not a child, and I will not be treated like a child. I am almost twenty-one."

"Jean, dear," Seldon said quietly, "your mother is surprised and upset. It's late, and I don't think this kind of an argument will get us anywhere. I suggest we all sleep on it." He fairly dragged his wife out of the room, and once in their own bedroom, he said to her, "That was the worst thing you could have said."

"And what did you say?"

"There is nothing I could say tonight, because she's right. She's been running around with kids. That's a man."

Mary dropped into a chair and stared bleakly at her husband. "I will not have it."

"She'll be of age, and if that's what she wants, we'll have it, whether we like it or not. I have one child, and I will not disown her or drive her out of the house."

"You could stop it."

"How?"

"Buy him off. Give him money."

Seldon shook his head.

"Don't just shake your head at me."

"My dear Mary, your daughter's a better judge of men than you are. You don't buy him off. I had a talk with him before he left tonight. I told him that he could have the loan he wanted, and in return I'd expect an end to his attentions to my daughter."

"What did he say?"

"He just looked at me at first. I would not want to have that kid as an enemy. Then he smiled and said that considering both our positions, he had no intention of responding with anger."

"And just what did he mean by that?"

"He said he didn't give a damn about my money, but he cared a great deal about my daughter."

"And her money, I assure you."

"I don't think so. I really don't think so, Mary." He took off his jacket and pulled at his tie. "I don't know what we can do about it," he said slowly. "I have a feeling that Dan Lavette will get what he wants."

"What are you telling me — that my daughter will marry a Catholic and that there's nothing I can do about it?"

"Now hold on. We haven't come to that yet."

"And when we do come to it, Thomas?"

"We'll cross that bridge then."

"You're not listening. You didn't hear a word I said. The man's nobody, an Italian fisherman and a Catholic. Have you ever thought about Catholics, Thomas? Have you?"

"I've thought about them."

"Have you? Have you indeed? Do you know what they are? My father would turn over in his grave at the thought. I will not have my daughter thrown to the dogs!"

"Mary, I'm tired. Too tired to go on with this. Let's sleep on it."

"She doesn't know her own mind. Her head is spinning, and she's infatuated with that hoodlum. I think she ought to go away for a while."

"Don't misjudge her either," Seldon said wearily. "She will do as she pleases. Our daughter is quite a woman."

The *Oregon Queen* was berthed at Hunter's Point, and it was Anthony Cassala who decided that the signing of the final papers should take place on the ship. Swenson, a tall, sour-visaged man of seventy-six years who had the reputation of never having been known to smile, agreed reluctantly. Maria Cassala prepared two enormous baskets stuffed with red wine, fresh bread, salami, ham, red peppers, cheese, and fruit. The two Cassala children, Stephan, a dark-skinned, serious boy of fifteen, and Rosa, approaching her fourteenth birthday and already in the full bloom of womanhood, her breasts round and ripe and enticing, were dressed in their Sunday best. Anthony hired a carriage, and the family drove from their home on Folsom Street to the berth at Hunters Point. Maria, still overcome by fits of grief for the stillborn child, had fantasied a situation where eventually Dan would marry her daughter, Rosa. She had the firm conviction that the best marriages were arranged, and even though her husband became irritated when she tried to discuss this with him, she felt that Dan would understand and she was determined to bring up the subject today.

When they reached the *Oregon Queen,* the others were already present, with the exception of Sam Goldberg. He arrived a few minutes later, a fat man who puffed his way up the ladder from the dock. Mark and Sarah Levy, in an equally festive mood, had brought their kids with them, and their son, Jacob, eleven years old, long-legged and as blond and blue-eyed as his mother, was already scrambling in the rigging with Clair Harvey, oblivious to his mother's pleas. Jack Harvey had cleaned the deck and hosed it down and brought out chairs from the cabin. He spread the white cloth Maria Cassala provided on the hatch cover and helped her empty the baskets, smacking his lips over the food and showering her with compliments. Dan, wearing his hundred-dollar made-to-order suit, was being assured by Mark Levy that he had been swindled and that a suit of equal excellence could be made for forty dollars. Even Feng Wo was present, in a new black business suit — six dollars ready-made — with a briefcase full of papers.

"You'll stay and have some lunch with us, Mr. Swenson," Mark said to the tall, cadaverous Swede.

"I got delicate stomach," Swenson replied, eyeing the food dubiously. "This is damn good ship," he said to Dan. "You got good buy, young fellow. I am sick of ship — yust too goddamn old for ships. But you got good buy."

"I'll be as kind and gentle to her as if she was my mother," Dan said.

"Don't like yokes about ship."

Anthony Cassala joined them and said that the papers were ready. Goldberg nodded, regarding the rusty ship unhappily. Swenson was studying Dan thoughtfully.

"You a hard worker?" he asked.

"Me and Mark here," Dan replied. "We're the hardest workers you ever saw."

"So don't be young snotnose with me. I like serious boys. I like you, maybe. I tell you something. I got two steam schooners, wooden ships, six hundred tons each, and contract with City of Oakland hauling garbage. I pick up garbage and dump it at sea, and I got contract price eighty-five cents a ton. I'm sick and tired of whole lousy business, and I think I move to Los Angeles, live with my sister. Ships worth fifty thousand dollars each, I sell you both ships for price of one, fifty thousand and throw in contract. You make twenty thousand dollars' profit first year."

"Garbage?"

"You think it stinks, huh? It stinks with money."

"It sounds good, Mr. Swenson," Mark said. "But we don't have that kind of money."

"Cash. You want fifty thousand cash?" Dan asked.

"Hell, no. You give me ten thousand cash and notes. You pay me ten thousand a year — you still got good profit."

Dan turned to Cassala, who shook his head. "Too big, Danny — too much."

"Hell, price ain't too much!" Swenson snorted.

"The job is."

"What's the crew?" Dan asked.

"Twelve men on each ship."

"Christ," Levy whispered to him, "we miss one payroll and we're out of business."

"But we make it, and we got the goddamndest business on this waterfront."

"In time, Danny," Cassala said. "Go slow."

"Just don't go away, Mr. Swenson. Let me talk to Mr. Cassala about this. Have some wine and cheese and ham." He drew Mark and Cassala aside. "Tony — we can't pass this up. Tony, we can't."

"You never even see the ships, Danny."

"I know the ships. I seen them. I tell you, Tony, this crazy Swede is giving them away."

"What do you think, Mark?"

"I think we can do it. I don't know — garbage. I never thought of anything like garbage. But I think we can do it."

Goldberg was unenthusiastic; he disliked ships, felt uncomfortable about them. He insisted that there was a difference between a mortgage on a ship and a mortgage on a piece of real estate. Mark argued that if a ship were insured, there was no damn difference whatsoever. They argued about it, and then marched over to where Swenson was munching cheese and drinking wine and began to question him.

Dan beckoned for Feng Wo. "Get out that Chinee harp of yours!" Feng Wo took his abacus out of the briefcase, and as Dan threw figures, interest rates, and percentage points at him — eighty-five cents times twelve hundred times three hundred and sixty-five — he shuffled the little black and white beads marvelously, jotting down the results on a pad.

The others watched in awe. The children gathered around Feng Wo, and Maria poured wine and cut bread and cheese and meat and pleaded with them to eat. Swenson was taken with Maria. "You remind me of my Annie," he said. "I like a strong woman." Cassala and Goldberg went to the other side of the hatch to caucus and pore over the figures, and Maria, pressing a plate loaded with cheese and meat and red peppers on Dan, said to him, in her soft, southern Italian, "Just look at my Rosa, Danny — so sweet, so gentle, so willing. She will make a wonderful wife for a wonderful man." "I'm sure she will. She's a good girl," Dan said, and then for the life of her, Maria could not think of another thing to say. It was the way Dan spoke, not even looking up from the figures he was studying.

He asked Feng Wo, "What do you think, Feng? Are we crazy?"

"I think it's a remarkable opportunity."

"Could you handle it?"

"I could handle it."

"All right. If Tony agrees and we're in garbage as well as lumber and fish, your wages go up. Eighteen dollars a week, starting Monday."

"Thank you, Mr. Lavette," Feng Wo said.

Cassala called them. "Danny, Mark, come over here." The tone of his voice spoke of decision. Mark and Dan walked over to join him and Goldberg. The two women stared at the little cluster of men. Jack Harvey, as fascinated by the abacus as the children were, was disappointed when Feng Wo put it back in his briefcase to turn and wait for his fate to be decided. Only Swenson, apparently indifferent, continued to eat and admire Maria.

"Danny, Mark," Cassala said, "we make the decision. You buy the garbage boats. Goldberg works out the mortgage, overriding on the whole thing, and we give you one hundred thousand dollars line of credit. You no pay interest, only on what you draw — six percent."

"The line of credit remains in force," Goldberg added. "You understand, this is not a loan but a standing credit situation that can be canceled without penalty by ninety days' notice on the part of either party. It is backed by an overriding mortgage on your entire operation, and we will require monthly statements of your cash position. We include the Levy property, the Lavette property, the fishing boats, this ship, and the two garbage ships — in other words, the total assets of the partnership. You pay interest only on what you draw from your line of credit. There's no other bank in the city that would do this for less than eight percent, but Mr. Cassala's the boss. I'll draw up the papers next week."

There was a long moment of silence, then Mark said to Dan, "Well, Danny, we got a tiger by the tail, haven't we?"

"We sure as hell have," Dan replied, grinning. "We sure as hell have. But, old buddy boy, we are going to let go of the tail and climb on its back and ride it straight up to the moon! Because this beautiful sonofabitch is ours — ours."

He couldn't contain himself. He raced down the deck, halting to caress the rusty winches. He vaulted onto the roof of the deckhouse, standing there where he could survey his new iron empire — while the others watched him in amazement. Then he had to dash down into the hold and look at the engines again. Mark went after him and found him standing in the captain's cabin, a wide, childish grin on his face.

"It's beautiful," Dan said. "It's just so goddamn beautiful I could cry."

A week later, calmly polite in the face of Mary Seldon's cold stare, Dan picked up Jean and took her to dinner at the newly refurbished, reopened Palace Hotel. Wearing his dinner jacket, he helped Jean, in a simple white satin gown, out of the cab and escorted her into the Grand Court, conscious of and totally happy in the fact that every eye was on them. It was not his first visit to the Palace; he had come there the day before to prowl through the place and to admire its opulent Victorian grandeur, and so arrive with Jean as something less than an oaf. At least he could point to the Maxfield Parrish painting and remind her of their discussion of lateen-rigged boats, even though Jean informed him that Maude Adams had posed for it and he didn't have the slightest notion of who Maude Adams was. He was becoming increasingly adroit at covering his areas of ignorance. He listened with pleasure to Jean's story of how her mother had met Oscar Wilde at the preearthquake Palace, but did not feel any necessity to inquire who Oscar Wilde was. Instead, he stored the tale away for his own future telling, with a notation to ask Mark Levy about Oscar Wilde.

At least he knew something about food. He had learned that at the Cassalas and at places like Trigger Joe's on the Embarcadero, where a dollar bought you food no chef at the Palace could equal. Now he ordered mushroom soup, brook trout with butter sauce — which he barely tasted — broiled mushrooms on garlic bread, and a saddle of venison with a sauce of wild plums. The meal went on endlessly, dish after dish, yet they were without appetite and only nibbled and pecked at the food. A salpicon of fruits au rhum, quails in nests of purée of chestnuts, English walnuts and celery in mayonnaise, Roquefort cheese and lettuce, nut pudding, ice cream praline.

"Don't they stop?" he asked her.

"You ordered the dinner, Danny."

He wondered whether she saw through him or not. It didn't matter. He ordered a second bottle of wine and forgot the food, let the dishes come and go untouched. Her usually pale face was flushed now, and he was content to sit and look at her, and thus he was fulfilled and all his life was present before him. Not yet twenty-two, he was where he had dreamed of being, sitting in the restaurant at the Palace opposite the most beautiful — and without doubt in his mind — the most desirable woman in San Francisco, and still it was only the beginning. He told her about Swenson and the garbage ships and the line of credit they had obtained from the Bank of Sonoma.

"Garbage ships, Danny?"

"They're ships — six hundred tons each, steam schooners. My God, Jean, I'm not tied to garbage, and sure as hell I'm not touching it with my hands. I keep the crews and fulfill the contract. Then the ships are mine. Then we got the iron ship, two wooden ships, and three fishing boats — six vessels. Mark and

I figure to clear fifty thousand dollars the first year, and that's only the beginning."

"Danny, what do you want?"

"You know what I want. I want the biggest fleet of ships that sails out of this port. I want to be up there on Nob Hill with a house as big as your father's, and I'm going to do it myself, with my own two hands. And I want you. Jesus God, I want you like I never wanted anything else in the world, and there's no other girl in the world for me."

"I know that, Danny. But you're so young."

"Young? What is young? When you were never a kid, how old are you? They can afford to be young up there on Nob Hill, I can't. I shipped out on my father's boat when I was nine years old. I watched him work and scrimp and I watched my mother work her fingers to the bone for them to buy that first boat. Do you know what poverty is — a disease, a stink."

Wide-eyed, fascinated, she listened to him. She desired him most when he was like that, filled with the passion of his wants, his hunger, his whole body alive with a sense of power. She had never known another man who gave her such a feeling of power, of the intensity of his will. He had no lust for money, and somehow she sensed this; it was power, and the ships were living symbols of power. She felt alive, drunk with his own strength, when she was with him, and she had never felt this way with anyone else.

When they left the hotel, she begged him to take her out on the bay in one of the boats.

"The fog's in. Anyway, the boats stink of fish. Be patient. I got my eye on a little sloop. In six months we'll own her."

"I want to go to the wharf," she insisted.

"All right — if that's what you want."

They drove down to the wharf, where the boats lay like ghosts in the fog. Hand in hand, not speaking, they walked along the wharf to Dan's shack. He hadn't planned it that way; he had never touched her breasts, never kissed her with his lips parted; the virginity he endowed her with was as sacred as her beauty and her station in life; it defined the difference between Jean Seldon and the hustlers on the Barbary Coast. In his mind's eye, he never undressed her; his fantasies were otherwise; and even now he was not sure that he wanted what would have to happen. Yet he couldn't stop. He had reached the point where she became flesh and blood. He felt her grip on his arm tighten as he unlocked the door to his office. A word from her would have changed it, but she said nothing. He flicked on the lights. She led the way upstairs to the bedroom, and there they stood and watched each other.

Still, he could make no move, and, as if she sensed this, she began to unhook her dress, let it fall around her legs, and then stepped out of it. The corset was a redundancy; she was slender and firm of flesh; she reached behind her slowly, deliberately, loosened the laces, and let the corset drop. Then she pulled the camisole over her head and stood naked in front of him, glowing pink and white, her small breasts perfectly formed, the hard nipples like tiny buds of pink roses, the triangle of pubic hair the same honey color as the piled hair on her head, which she now loosened and let fall to her waist.

He pulled off his jacket, ripped his shirt open. He was struggling with his pants, his fingers shaking, and then he tore the pants open to the crotch. The violence of his action terrified her, and she crawled back on the bed, covering her breasts with her hands. He ripped his underwear as he had his trousers, and with the torn trousers still clinging to his legs, he flung himself upon her.

"Danny, darling," she whimpered. "Don't hurt me, don't hurt me. Don't you understand? You're the first one. I'm a virgin."

Momentarily, he came to his senses, propped up on his arms, staring at his erection as if it were a stranger to him. Her hands fell away from her breasts and she spread her legs. "Do it," she cried, "do it, do it, fuck me, god damn you!" Then he drove inside of her and she screamed with pain, and he exploded, as if her cry had washed away all that separated her from the whores in the Tenderloin.

He lay beside her then, cradling her in his arms, trying to stop her tears. "I'm bleeding so much," she said. "Look at your bed." "It's all right." "What happened to us, Danny?" "I don't know. We made love." "That's what they call it?" "It was the first time."

He still wore his shoes. "Oh, take your shoes off — please," she said.

"I didn't know."

"How do you feel about me?"

"What do you mean?"

"You know what I mean. Jesus Christ, get me a towel or something to wipe this blood off me."

He got up, stumbling over his torn trousers, then pulled them off, went into the bathroom, wet a towel in hot water, and returned and began awkwardly to wipe the blood from her crotch.

"Oh, let me do that."

"I love you," he said, as she wiped herself clean. "You know that."

"You damn near raped me."

"I didn't rape you."

"What would you call it?"

"I never even thought of you that way."

"What way?"

He groped for some explanation. "Naked. Then when I saw you, something happened to me."

"Yes. It certainly did."

He leaned over and gently kissed her shoulder. "Does it hurt?"

"What?"

"What I did?"

Suddenly, she began to laugh, half hysterically.

"What is so funny?"

"Tearing your pants to shreds." The laughter stopped as suddenly as it began. She was staring at him as if she had never seen him before.

"Will you still marry me?" he asked.

"Suppose I'm caught?"

"It doesn't happen that easily."

"It can."

"I'll never hurt you again, I swear," he begged her.

"I'll marry you, Danny," she said. "I don't know what else to do."

PART TWO

Russian Hill

It was in August of 1914, soon after the birth of their second child, that Dan and Jean Lavette moved into their new house on Russian Hill. For the first three years of their married life, they had lived in a rented house on Sacramento Street, just a short distance from the Seldon mansion, which, along with James C. Flood's gigantic million-and-a-half-dollar brownstone palace, had survived both the earthquake and the fire which followed. While the new Lavette house could have been fitted into a single wing of the Flood mansion, and while it could not compare to Thomas Seldon's home, it nevertheless ran to a final cost of one hundred and ten thousand dollars. The first plans the architect had drawn for Dan added up to a cost of only seventy thousand dollars, but that called for a wooden front and Jean protested bitterly that she would not live in a house with a wooden front. White limestone was substituted; a solarium was added; and at Jean's insistence, the two rooms in the servants' quarters became three. With the library, the living room, the dining room, four bedrooms, and an entryway floored with marble, the price increased by forty thousand dollars.

Jean was impressed by the fact that Dan never complained about the cost of anything. Whatever he felt about the making of money, he was indifferent to spending. She had been the recipient of a princely wedding gift on the part of her father, stock in the Seldon Bank to the value of one hundred thousand dollars and ten thousand dollars more in cash — princely considering Thomas and Mary Seldon's bitterness at the match — but Dan would not touch the money. It was hers and it would be hers.

His worship of the beautiful woman he had married had not

dissipated, but it had changed enormously in quality. The two pregnancies had been difficult for Jean. The first resulted in the birth of a son, a healthy boy of nine pounds, whom they named Thomas Joseph Lavette for both grandparents. Dan would have preferred that the Joseph take preference, that being his father's name, but he deferred to Jean, as he did with their second child, a girl, whom they agreed to name Barbara, since Jean disliked Dan's mother's name — Anna — and Dan protested naming the child after Jean's mother. If Jean had insisted, he would have given in, but Jean did not insist. Two weeks after the birth of the second child, they moved into the new house on Russian Hill, and for the next eight weeks after that, Jean rejected Dan's sexual advances with one excuse or another. She was polite, amiable for the most part, totally occupied with the new house and its furnishing and decoration, withdrawn, reasonably devoted to her children — for whom she had hired a live-in nursemaid — and apparently quite content to exist without sex. At the end of the eight-week period, she finally submitted to Dan's fervent attempt to make love to her. She accepted him without emotion and without response. When it was done, she accepted his almost servile plea for an explanation in much the same manner, without emotion and without response.

Dan flung himself out of bed and stalked through the dark house, downstairs and into a library full of books he had never read. In four years, he had not looked at another woman. "God damn it!" he pleaded with himself. "What did I do? It's like screwing a corpse." He sat in the dark and then he dozed and awakened with the first flicker of daylight. It was just after five o'clock. The dawning was still early now in the middle of July. He was filled with hurt and anger and frustration — the hurt bursting out of him in an irresistible need to inflict it elsewhere. The middle of July meant that the crabbing season was almost over, and he sat there brooding over the fact that during the past three weeks five of his boats had been highjacked out of their catch, traps robbed; a new breed of young thug had grown up and was out on the bay. Christ, how he hated the whole thing, fishing and crabbing and fighting for the pennies with the commission men! He and Levy owned eleven fishing boats now, and he'd just as soon have the whole fleet at the bottom of the sea.

He leaped to his feet suddenly, went to the closet where Jean had piled his fishing gear into a wicker basket, and put on boots and oilskins for the first time in two years. Where the devil had Jean put his old Colt .45? He found it in a desk drawer in the library, and his shotgun was in a closet in the same room. He checked the cylinder of the revolver. It was loaded. He loaded the shotgun, put the revolver in one pocket of his jacket and a handful of shotgun shells in the other. It was five-thirty in the morning when he left the house for the wharf.

At the dock, Peter Lomas, his fleet captain, stared at the shotgun and made a crack about duck hunting.

"Duck hunting, hell!" Dan said. "I'm going to get that son of a bitch who's been stealing our crabs."

"I know the boat," Lomas said. "But my God, Dan, you can't go out there and kill a man. Not over a load of crabs."

"Let's just go."

"Dan, I don't like it."

"You can take what you like or don't like and shove it up your ass."

Lomas, a big, burly man, fifteen years older than Dan, looked at him steadily and then nodded. "All right. I'll take that. I don't know what's eating you, but it's in your gut."

The boats were pushing off, backing slowly into the fog that lay like soup on the bay. Lomas leaped into his boat and Dan followed. "I'm sorry. Forget it," Dan said. Lomas nodded silently. They didn't speak as the boat nosed its way through the fog.

An hour later, the fog had lifted. "Just keep looking," Dan told Lomas. "Forget the crabs. You say you know the boat?"

"I know it. White launch with a black stripe. He's got one of them new diesels, powerful bastard, he can outrun anything. He's from somewhere in San Pablo, they say Pinole."

It was nine o'clock before they found the white launch — or it found them. Dan stood at the bow, the shotgun at his feet. "Don't be too eager," he told Lomas. "I'm going to open her hull. Then take off."

"Suppose the crew can't swim."

"Fuck them."

"They got pistols."

"Screw their pistols. Tell Billy and Ralph to keep their heads down."

"O.K., you're the boss," Lomas said. He stood at the wheel,

letting the fishing boat run along, as if they had taken their catch and were heading home. The white launch lifted a wake on a course that would cross their bow.

"When I open her hull," Dan shouted, "put us hard abeam and head back. They're dragging a dinghy, so they won't drown."

The white launch cut its motor and swung into a course alongside the fishing boat about twenty feet away. There were four men in the launch, two of them boys of sixteen or seventeen, two of them older men. One of the older men stood in the bow, waving an automatic pistol, shouting for them to cut their motor. Dan bent, picked up the shotgun, and let go with both barrels at the hull of the launch at the water line. The man with the pistol fired wildly. Lomas spun the wheel and kicked in all the power they had. There were two more shots from the pistol that hit nothing, and when Dan steadied himself and looked back, the launch was already sinking.

The following morning at the breakfast table, Thomas Seldon said to his wife, "Mary, listen to this — from the front page in today's *Chronicle:* 'San Francisco shipowner raises the ghost of vigilanteism. Taking matters into his own hands after a series of pirate raids on crabbing boats, young Daniel Lavette, owner of a fleet of eleven fishing boats, rode shotgun on one of his own vessels and sank an alleged fish pirate in San Pablo Bay. For the past month local fishermen have complained to the authorities that they were being robbed of their catch. All to no avail. Yesterday, the owner of the largest fleet of fishing boats on the waterfront took matters into his own hands, and armed with a double-barreled shotgun sought out and sank the launch *Dazzle,* owned by Henry Slocum of Pinole. The launch was hulled by buckshot and sank in a few minutes. According to the Sheriff of Contra Costa County, Slocum denies any wrongdoing and claims that the attack by Lavette was entirely without provocation. On the other hand, he refuses to press charges against Lavette, claiming that an ordinary citizen of Pinole could no more expect justice in San Francisco, where the shipowners interests are at stake, than he could, to quote Mr. Slocum, "from the Emperor of China." Mr. Lavette and his partner, Marcus Levy, operate, in addition to the fishing vessels, a fleet of ships that hauls garbage from Oakland and a coastal lumber ship. Mr.

Lavette is the son-in-law of the prominent banker Thomas Seldon.' " He put down the paper and looked at his wife. "Front page," he added.

"Why? In God's name, why?"

Seldon shrugged. "I suppose he was fed up and decided to do something. I wish he hadn't done it this way."

"The whole thing makes me ill. Riding shotgun. Garbage boats."

"He's had the garbage ships a long time now."

"Not in print. Not on the front page of the *Chronicle.* I don't know how I'll face anyone after this."

"Most people won't mind it a bit. It's a rather romantic action."

"I hardly agree. I don't know why we ever went along with that marriage." Seldon was reading his paper again. "You really don't care how I feel about it, do you? If you think Jean is happy, you're wrong."

He put down the paper. "What has she said?"

"It's what she doesn't say. We don't talk anymore. She's indifferent. They've been there weeks without drapes, and when I asked her about them, she just stared at me."

"That's nothing to worry about. She told me she's having them hand-woven in San Jose or some such place."

"I just can't understand a house on Russian Hill. Jean's not artistic," she complained in what appeared to her husband to be a non sequitur, but in her mind referred to the artists and writers who were moving to Russian Hill. "And a family now. There's room enough in this house. Not that I want *him* here — "

"Mary," her husband interrupted, "you ought to stop that. For one thing, Dan Lavette is making money hand over fist. He denies her nothing. And for another, Jean will do as she damn pleases. You know that." He went back to his paper. "You know," he said, "there's going to be a war in Europe. The handwriting's on the wall."

Two weeks later, on the second day of August, Dan burst into the offices of Levy and Lavette, waving a newspaper and yelling for the presence of his partner. The fact that Mark Levy was there in plain sight made no difference; Dan was filled with excitement and exuberance and it suited him to shout, and when he was that way, Mark saw him as a kid, an explosive kid whose own excitement and energy had to be communicated. It never irritated Mark; and when it irritated Sarah, he explained that Dan was like his brother only more than a brother — something she never entirely understood, not then and not in later years.

It was just about seven months since Mark and Dan had sold both the shack on the wharf and the chandler shop on the Embarcadero, renting instead a large brick warehouse between Battery Street and Sansome Street. Part of it was turned into a larger shipping supply depot; one wing in the back was devoted entirely to the manufacture of the metal-cleated denim trousers that Sarah Levy had devised; and the rest of it, half of the ground floor of a two-story building, twenty-five hundred square feet of space, had become the offices of their burgeoning enterprises. Finally evicting themselves from the rooms behind the store, the Levys had purchased an old Spanish Colonial–style house on a hillside in Sausalito. The house was run down and badly in need of repair, but it was all Sarah Levy had ever dreamed of, and she convinced her husband that seven thousand dollars for the tile-roofed, tile-floored house with its long cool, pillared galleries and the seven acres of land around it was a tremendous bargain, even if they had to put twenty thousand more into renovation. The figure came to a good deal more than that in the end, but Mark had no regrets about the house. It was true that now he would be a commuter, his life at the mercy of the cross-bay ferry, but the incredible beauty of Marin County more than compensated for that; if he had second thoughts, they were mainly fixed on the partnership he had entered into.

He was a slow-speaking, easygoing man — enchanted with the driving force of Dan Lavette and very often not a little terrified by it. It was Dan who had talked him into mass production of the denim trousers. Sarah wanted no part of it, and once they had purchased the place in Sausalito, she retreated there, with the flat statement that the house and the children were sufficient. "I want no part of business with Danny," she said, to which Mark replied, "But you talked me into that. You were all for it." "And I was right. But I want nothing to do with it. I hate business. I hated it when we had the store. I hate it more now." "Then you hate what I do with my life!" he cried angrily, and she protested, "No, no, no — I love you, and you are doing what you must do."

All of which was reasonably unreasonable, and, anyway, she adored Dan, who could do no wrong. She didn't have to face his explosive energy, his endless schemes, his need to gamble and drive them to the edge of disaster, his crazy adolescent arithmetic that said that if six garbage ships made so much money, twelve would make twice as much, his argument that by fighting the pirates he was saving the fishermen whose losses drove them to sell their boats — and then his petulant and increasing hatred for the fishing fleet and the detail its operation involved.

"Danny will grow up," Sarah argued. "Give him a chance. So far he's been right."

"Right because we've been damn lucky and because with half of his crazy schemes I put my back to the wall and fight him tooth and nail. But I can't go on doing that."

Here it is again, Mark said to himself, as Dan shouted, "Mark, this is it — the big bomb! I told you, I told you!" Mark was bending over Feng Wo's desk, reading a row of figures, and Feng Wo smiled gently and understandingly. Now Feng Wo had the title of office manager; he had a bookkeeper assistant and two lady typewriters, as they were called.

Dan grabbed Mark by the arm and fairly dragged him into the part of the partitioned warehouse floor that constituted his office, furnished so far only with a desk and three chairs, the partition wall decorated with a great map of the Pacific Ocean and its bordering land masses. Once inside, Mark turned to Dan, spread his hands, and said, "No. Whatever it is, I don't want to hear it. We took a beating on the crabs and the season is over. You got forty-five fishermen on the payroll and less than five thousand dollars in the bank."

"The hell with the fishing boats! Will you listen to me? Did you see the paper?"

"What paper?"

"The newspaper, Mark, the newspaper." He spread it out on the desk. "Read it. Germany has declared war on Russia, and the smart money says that this is only the beginning. Within a week, England and France will be in this. I phoned Tony from the house. He's had half a dozen cables from Italy, and he says that in Europe there's no question about what's going to happen. Italy will fight Austria and Germany, and then it's France and England."

"All right — granted. The world's gone crazy. Thank God we're here in America."

"You don't see it, do you?"

"See what?"

"Just look at the map." He pointed as he spoke. "Germany has the largest submarine fleet in the world, and England's spread all over the goddamn map, Hong Kong, Australia, Singapore, Malay, India. Do you know what that means? It means that we're the lifeline, the West Coast, San Francisco — it's going to make the Gold Rush look like a kiddy bank. We're heading into a war that's going to make every shipowner rich as God."

"Danny," Mark said tiredly, "we got one ship and it's a coaster."

"And five years ago we had no ships."

"We're overextended, we're short on cash, we've both of us been spending like drunken sailors — and anyway I'll be damned if I can celebrate this lunacy that's going on in Europe. Even if it was possible, which it isn't, I don't want to build a fortune out of blood."

"Why? You got moral scruples? How many millionaires came out of the Civil War? And that was our own flesh and blood. We didn't make this war."

"That doesn't make it an occasion for celebration."

"Come on, old buddy. Don't get sore at me. Just sit down and listen. I haven't been so wrong, have I? We been in clover — you got to admit that. We had problems, we got problems. We solve them. I got ten suits and a house on Russian Hill, and Sarah's got her hacienda. So maybe we didn't do so bad for a Dago fisherman and a sheeny storekeeper." He grinned, pushing Mark gently into a chair. When Dan was like that, Mark couldn't resist him. "You going to listen?" Dan asked.

"You crazy bastard — O.K., I'll listen."

"Now I'm not saying we do this. Just think about it. We sell everything, the fishing boats, the garbage ships — and believe me, old buddy, the contract alone's worth seventy, eighty thousand dollars — the coaster, the pants business — everything."

"We're making money on the pants, good money."

"The hell with it! Levi makes better pants. They'll buy us out and that's better than having them kill us. Their patent was in first and sooner or later they'll take us to court."

"All right," Mark sighed, "we sell everything. What then?"

"Then we got a cash base. We borrow a million dollars, and we buy or build a string of freighters."

"Just like that — we borrow a million dollars."

"Why not?"

"Because the whole thing's insane, Danny. Who's going to lend us a million dollars? Tony? We couldn't ask him. He's a small banker. He can't put out that kind of money, not in a deal like this, and we just couldn't put him in such a spot."

"I know that."

"Then where would the money come from? — and that doesn't mean I buy this scheme."

"We're just talking."

"Like hell we are. I know you."

"Mark, buddy, I'm not trying to con you. You're the best friend I got in the world. But I'm sick and tired of what we're into. *Perdo tempo.*"

"What's that?"

"Time wasting. Ships are real."

"And where do you get the million dollars?"

"From Seldon."

"You're kidding. That old bastard wouldn't give you the right time."

"Maybe — but I never asked for anything. Not one nickel. I'm not going to ask him personally. This is a banking proposition. Either he sees it that way or not. But I got to have you behind me, not looking at me like I lost my mind."

"I guess there's only one thing to hope for," Mark said.

"What?"

"That England and Germany don't go to war."

Dan got up, walked to the wall, and stared at the map. "Mark," he said, "you remember the way the city looked after the earthquake and the fire?"

"Who forgets a thing like that?"

"Well, that's the way the whole fuckin' world's going to look a year from now."

When Calvin Braderman, bearded, with velvet jacket and a black beret, returned to San Francisco after five years in Paris, he brought with him a local corner on Fauvism and names like Matisse, Derain, Vlaminck, Marquet, and Camoin — names which he let drop with authority and intimacy, the suggestion being that if he had not actually shared studio space with these men, he had supped at the same board and quaffed at the same trough of ultramodernism. He also brought with him several dozen of his own paintings and two Derains and a Vlaminck, traded, as he casually informed the people of the press, for his own work.

Even a less-talented artist than Braderman — himself only an average draftsman and colorist — would have been welcomed in the city that already considered itself the Paris of the West; and Braderman was lionized. Jean met him at the opening at Scoffers' Gallery.

Mary Seldon was wont to say, with a sort of perverse pride, that Jean was not artistic. In Mrs. Seldon's circles, a commitment to the arts smacked of pornography and associated indecencies; but in all truth Jean, while possessed of little artistic talent of her own — she had done only middling well in her drawing lessons at school — was utterly fascinated by the world of artists. Her eye was still untrained, but she loved color and motion in a painting. Also, she was in the process of building walls against Dan. As her initial infatuation for her husband withered, her own sense of self-esteem lessened. She fought to create in herself a series of interests that would restore her self-confidence, and instinctively she chose areas that she felt were outside of her husband's ken.

A half a dozen new galleries had opened in San Francisco, and Scoffers' was one of the most prestigious. Marcy Callan and her fiancé, Johnny Whittier, had persuaded Jean to go with them to the opening. Watching young Whittier stand dour and silent while Marcy gushed over Calvin Braderman and his paintings set Jean to thinking. Johnny Whittier refused to reach into his pocket for a Braderman painting, but Jean selected a canvas of a group of dancing nymphs and wrote out a check for five hundred dollars on the spot. Hans Scoffers, the gallery owner, immediately turned into a worshipful, overwhelming salesman, and a half-hour later Jean had signed a second check for a thousand dollars and had become the owner of a landscape by Vlaminck, who, Scoffers assured her, was a great and honored artist. At which point Calvin Braderman directed all his charm to Jean, informing her that she was the most beautiful woman he had ever met and that he would not rest until he had painted her. Nor was the gaiety of the occasion marred at all by the fact that two days before German troops had invaded Belgium, after Germany's declaration of war against France, and in response to this England had declared war against Germany.

Braderman, five hundred dollars richer, insisted that he convey Jean and the paintings to Russian Hill, and they entered her house flushed and delighted with the exchange of compliments, money, and produce. Dan was upstairs, and hearing Jean, it occurred to him that this was the first time in a long while that he had heard her laugh. He came downstairs from the nursery, where he had been admiring the baby, Barbara, to find his wife and a strange bearded man admiring two paintings that were propped for viewing on a couple of dining room chairs.

"This is Calvin Braderman," Jean informed him. "And this is my husband, Dan."

Dan shook hands dubiously. He had never seen a man in a velvet jacket before.

"A pleasure to meet you," Braderman said heartily. "You have a beautiful home, sir, and a beautiful wife — and now a Braderman and a Vlaminck. I won't tout the Braderman, but the Vlaminck is a beauty, isn't it?"

"What the devil is a Vlaminck?" Dan said.

Jean and Braderman burst out laughing. They were laughing at him, Dan realized. For some damned idiot reason, they were laughing at him because he had asked what a Vlaminck was. Jean saw the expression on his face and said quickly, "No, no, Danny, we are not laughing at you. It was just the way you said it — and the three glasses of sherry I had at the opening. Look. That one" she pointed — "that's the painting by Maurice Vlaminck. He's one of a really daring school of painting, and they've broken all the rules and they call themselves Fauvists, and they're all the rage in Paris now — "

"Well, not really now, my dear," Braderman interrupted. "Now it's cults, Expressionism and Cubism, and the Philistines say that Fauvism is over. That's like saying that Impressionism is over and sunlight is a thing of the past."

"You are so right, Mr. Braderman. I declare myself a Fauvist — I love it. And the next time anyone asks whether I am a feminist, I shall reply, no indeed, a Fauvist. And that one," she said to Dan, "is a composition of dancing nymphs — one of Mr. Braderman's. You know," she confided to Braderman, "we inherited two Frederic Remingtons. Daddy adores him, and I never dared even intimate that I don't like cowboys, and we do need paintings so. What do you think of them?" she asked Dan.

Dan stared at the paintings without replying.

"Well, I must be running along," Braderman said. "A thousand thanks. Enjoy them. Delighted to have met you, Mr. Lavette."

Jean took him to the door. When she returned, Dan was still staring at the paintings, his face set grimly.

"Oh, you're so angry because I laughed at you."

"God damn it, I'm not! I was so happy to hear you laugh that I raced downstairs. Do you know how long it is since I heard you laugh?"

"I know."

"Who is he?"

"He's a brilliant young painter. He's been in Paris for the past five years. Studying."

"Where did you meet him?"

"I don't see why you're questioning me like this. I met him at the opening. Marcy Callan introduced us."

"And he calls you 'my dear.' "

"Danny, it's only a way of talking that artists have. Of course I'm excited. I bought two paintings that are my very own. Aren't they beautiful?"

"What did you pay for them?"

"What difference does it make? It's my own money. If you must know, I paid a thousand for the Vlaminck and five hundred for the other one."

"I don't think they're wonderful. I think they're ridiculous," Dan said. "And if that's the best that fop can do, he ought to get out and find some honest work."

"What a rotten thing to say!"

"You asked me."

"And he's a fop. Because he isn't a brawling hoodlum?"

"Meaning that I am?"

"Dan, I don't want this to degenerate into a quarrel," she said coldly. "I don't think we ought to discuss it further."

"Christ Almighty," he whispered, "I love you so much — I love you so much, I want you so much it burns in my gut. I don't want to fight with you. You can buy a hundred paintings

— what the hell do I know about paintings? I got sore because you were both laughing at me and the way he patronized me."

"Dan, we weren't laughing at you."

"O.K. — sure. It's all right." He moved toward her, embracing her clumsily, pressing her to his body. First she stiffened; then she relaxed; when he tried to kiss her, his lips parted, she said, "Don't, Dan. Don't force it, please. Not now."

"When?" he yelled, pushing her away from him. "When?"

"When I'm ready."

Jean felt that Manya Vladavich was the most fascinating and interesting woman she had ever met. Miss Vladavich, whose age was somewhere between thirty and forty, was dark, full-breasted, and, as Marcy Callan described her, totally outrageous. In Paris, she had modeled for Matisse and Manguin — and by her own testimony engaged in affairs with both of them — and now modeled for and lived with Calvin Braderman. She wore dotted veils, flowing crêpe de Chine, and feather boas; and Jean, lunching with her and with Marcy Callan at the Fairmont, found her a little frightening and totally enchanting.

"Darling," Manya said to her — she pronounced it *dollink* — "one does not buy art, like you buy a dress or a dish. One relates. One becomes a part of it. You are beautiful woman. You are art alive. You buy a canvas, it becomes a part of what is inside you. You understand?"

Jean nodded.

"She bought *the Dancing Nymphs,* you know," Marcy said. "It's so lovely."

"Ah, yes, yes," Manya shrugged. "Pretty. When Braderman paints without passion, he is pretty. When he paints with passion, he is magnificent. You saw a painting called *Orgasm?*"

Jean glanced at Marcy.

"Obviously no," said Manya, watching Jean intently. "You know what is orgasm?"

"I think I remember it," Jean said.

"You think," Manya said gently, and Jean felt she had sinned in some way she only vaguely comprehended. "So tell me the truth, beautiful woman that you are, you know what is orgasm?"

Marcy giggled.

"I don't really know what you mean," Jean said.

Manya looked from one to the other and sighed. "Ah, American woman — so young, so beautiful, so innocent. Orgasm, my darlings, is what happens when a man and a woman make love."

"You mean — when the man — " Marcy began tremulously.

Jean felt a curious surge of excitement. She had never talked about these things before, never used the words. She was titillated, alive suddenly. She had never known a woman like this, so intense and so open at the same time.

"No, foolish girl," Manya said. "Not when the man, when the man like you say. What is with the man? An ejaculation, and then it is over, like a monkey. Orgasm is what happens with the woman, not with one little part of her but with the whole body and soul."

Marcy was blushing. Jean could see the flush creeping into her cheeks, and then she realized that her own cheeks were burning. She was frightened and embarrassed, and she fought an impulse to flee, to excuse herself, to find sanctuary in the powder room. She felt that everyone in the resturant was watching her, the waiters, the people dining at the other tables.

"Poor, innocent children," Manya said. "Enough. I make you uncomfortable. We talk of other things. We talk about this beautiful city of yours. It is inspiring, no? Day and night it inspires me. I think I never go away from it." She turned to Jean. "You are in new house. Braderman says is beautiful, on top of Russian Hill. I am born in Saint Petersburg, so Russian Hill pluck cord inside me."

"It was designed by Arthur Brown," Jean said, her words sounding inane to her. "He's very talented. Have you heard of him?" She felt stupid.

"Who has not?"

"You should see it," Marcy said. "If you like Russian Hill, you must see it."

"Yes, sometime. You must come."

"Now is best time. I have whole afternoon free."

Marcy left them to meet her mother and shop for a bridal gown. It was a beautiful, cool afternoon, and Manya spread her arms, as if she were embracing the whole city, filling her lungs with air. "You do not breathe, you Americans. The air is so clean and sweet but you do not breathe."

Watching her was like watching some lissome animal. Jean,

trying to think of some reason why Manya should not accompany her home, was confused and troubled, not by fear, but by her own fascination. She found herself wanting to reach out and touch the other woman, and again she felt her cheeks burning.

"With color, you are divine," Manya said. "You pretend to be made of — what is it, like the snow in Saint Petersburg? But in flesh and blood, you show the truth."

At the house, Manya took over, prowling through room after room, exclaiming, praising, criticizing. She wanted to see the children. Jean explained that at this hour they were outside with the nurse. Then she must see the rooms upstairs. "A room is like a costume you wear. I see the room with the ships and the pictures of ships — so I know your husband. It is his room, no?" They went upstairs, into the nursery, the guest rooms, and then her bedroom. She crooned over the flowered wallpaper and the lush pink bedspread.

"So feminine — you pour out passion on things, things! But inside, you do not allow it. Am I wrong?" Suddenly, she stretched out on the bed, stretching her arms above her. Then she pulled off hat and veil, smiling at Jean. "I frighten you, snow lady, don't I? Why are you frightened?"

"I'm not frightened," Jean said slowly, feeling that she was in a dream, feeling drunk. But on a single glass of sherry. What's wrong with me, she wondered.

"Sit here by me." She sat down on the bed, and Manya took her hand. "You're trembling. Why?" Manya stroked her hand, and then dropped her own hand to Jean's thigh and began to stroke it, very gently, very softly, her fingers like feathers, yet every touch of them sending chills through her body. Jean closed her eyes and sat motionless, while Manya's fingers continued their featherlike dance, higher and now touching her Venus mound and resting there.

No, Jean told herself, this is not real, this is not happening to me, this is insane and impossible. Still, she did not move as Manya's hand slid up her body and cupped around one breast, gently again, feeling, exploring, raising to life the hard point of her nipple. She felt her nostrils close, her breath come pantingly through her open lips, her body beginning to burn in a way that she had never experienced before.

And then she heard the door downstairs open and close, the

squeal of two-year-old Thomas' anger, and the spell broke. She leaped to her feet, her whole body trembling, while Manya lay there, watching her and laughing lightly.

"Poor snow lady."

"You must go. Now. Please."

She went down the stairs swinging her veil and hat, humming to herself and throwing sidelong glances at Jean. "Such beautiful children!" she cried. "Oh, such beautiful children!" Miss Jones, the English nurse — or nanny, as Jean liked to think of her — frowned in disapproval and hustled the children to the stairs. Jean opened the door.

"When do we meet again, snow lady?" Manya asked.

"Never!" Jean exclaimed. "I have forgotten what happened! I have forgotten it completely! I trust you will too."

"Perhaps. Who knows?" Manya said.

Dan Lavette was leaving his office, earlier on the same day, when Feng Wo stopped him. "Please, could I have a word with you, Mr. Lavette?"

"A quick word. I'm walking into a den of lions, so don't say anything that will rattle me."

"Only a moment. My wife, who has heard me speak of you for so long now, begs me to extend an invitation to you and Mrs. Lavette. We humbly ask you to take dinner with us at our home on this Friday next. However, I must add that I will understand if there are circumstances that prevent your accepting."

"Is your wife a good cook?"

"I would say so. Yes."

"Then I'll be there — with bells on. You count on that."

"But Mrs. Lavette may have accepted another engagement."

"I don't think so."

But a few minutes later, walking toward the Seldon Bank Building, Dan realized that an invitation for Jean to come to a Chinese household for dinner was by no means a simple matter. Well, there would be time to worry about that; meanwhile, it was more important that he be clear in his mind as to what he would say to Seldon and Seldon's board of directors. He had made a few notes and rehearsed the facts and figures in his mind at least a dozen times, and his arguments appeared, to him at least, to be reasonable and cogent. A few minutes later he reached Montgomery Street, walked past the modest front of the Bank of Sonoma, and entered the impressive eight-story Seldon Building. A hydraulic elevator brought him smoothly to the eighth floor and the board room. He was a few minutes early.

Five of them faced him around the big mahogany table, Thomas Seldon, Alvin Sommers and Martin Clancy, both of them vice presidents, Rustin Jones, who was president of Sierra Insurance, and Grant Whittier of California Shipping. They were all of them men past fifty, solid, substantial men, with a net worth of many millions among them.

As Seldon introduced him to those he had not met, Dan realized that they were all watching him, studying him as if he were a particularly interesting form of life they had not encountered before. Their faces were impassive and controlled; he remembered such faces from poker games, not on the wharf where the fishermen played poker loose and easy with each other but in the Tenderloin where the pros sat around the tables in their shirt-sleeves and vests with eyes as cold as hard steel. Well, he had not come here to be wined and dined and to be told what a brilliant young man he was. He had come here to ask for a million dollars.

"You gentlemen know what the situation is," he began, standing at one end of the table. "England, France, Germany, Belgium, the Austrian Empire, Italy, Russia — damn near every country in Europe is at war. It's the worst, bloodiest war this world ever saw, and it's only beginning. England is an island with the biggest empire in history, and most of that empire is at our back door, if you think of the Pacific Ocean as our back door. Now already Germany's submarine fleet is nibbling away at British ships. They're going to sink every damn ship they sight, and the British colonies are going to live or die with what we ship over to them out of the West Coast. Now I know that the Panama Canal is going to change things, but chiefly in lower rates from the East Coast to here. As far as the Pacific passage is concerned, rates are going to go up and the sky's the limit. Mark Levy, my partner, and I have been operating a fleet of ships four years now, and I know what kind of money there is in shipping — just as I'm sure Mr. Whittier knows. I'm here to ask for a loan of a million dollars, to underwrite the purchase of five ships of five to six thousand tons each. I know where the ships are and

I know they can be bought. They're cargo carriers in first-rate condition. So I think that such a loan as I propose is reasonable and secure."

"I think I know the ships you're talking about," Whittier said. "Your figures are off. A million's not enough."

"We're aware of that," Dan agreed. "We intend to liquidate all our holdings, our ships, our fishing boats, and our factory. We have an equity of almost a million."

"I know your holdings," Sommers said. "You're heavily mortgaged."

"We have equity," Dan argued. "I'm talking about a good market. I should have said at least a half-million and possibly a million."

"That's quite a spread," Clancy observed, smiling slightly.

"How old are you, Lavette?" Rustin Jones asked him.

"Oh, I don't think that's to the point," Seldon put in.

"Twenty-six," Dan replied, pushing it onto the coming year. "If you're looking for age, I can go out on the street and bring you a dozen men over fifty."

"Take it easy, Dan," Seldon said. "Tell me something about those ships."

"They're steel ships, turbine engines, twin screws, none of them more than three years old, four of them made in England, one in Holland, good condition."

"You see the war only in terms of profit?" Whittier asked.

"I see the war for what it is — a bloody, stupid game they're playing. We didn't make it. It ain't our war. But that's no reason not to carry cargo and take a profit. If I don't do it, a hundred others will."

"May I read you something, Mr. Lavette," Rustin Jones said, his voice a calm contrast to Dan's heated assertions. This is from President Wilson's message to the Senate. I quote, 'The effect of the war upon the United States will depend upon what American citizens say and do. Every man who really loves America will act and speak in the true spirit of neutrality, which is the spirit of impartiality and fairness and friendliness to all concerned.' So speaks the President, Mr. Lavette, yet you propose a very considerable loan primarily for trade with the British Colonies."

Dan shook his head and tried to contain his temper. "We're a Pacific port. Do you want me to trade with Germany? Just tell me how, and I'll be happy to oblige."

"Mr. Lavette," Clancy said, "Mr. Jones made reference to your age. We have children still at school and not a great deal younger than you. Not too long ago, the newspapers carried an account of a shotgun attack you personally made upon what you claimed was some sort of fish pirate. You took upon yourself the responsibility of sinking a boat. Fortunately, the people on the boat survived, but it might have been a disaster. Now you ask us to entrust a million dollars to your judgment."

"I've said my piece," Dan told them, and, taking a sheaf of papers from his pocket, he threw it on the table. "There are the facts and figures, gentlemen. As for fishing, I'm not asking for your instruction. I'm here for a loan, and you can grant it or not, just as you please."

With that, he pushed back his chair and stalked out of the room. Seldon followed him.

"Dan!"

Dan paused in the outer office, the secretaries and bookkeepers watching curiously. Seldon walked with him into the corridor. "You're being unreasonable," he said. "You can't blow your stack that way."

"I will not be treated like some hoodlum kid from the Tenderloin."

"No one is treating you that way. We're a bank. We have our ways. Now give this some time."

"I've given it some time," Dan said.

Jean was changing her clothes when Dan got home that evening. He had time before dinner to play with his son, Thomas, and he rolled on the floor with him, swung him high in his arms, and growled at him, while Miss Wendy Jones looked on without approval. Miss Jones was a shapely, plump Welsh lady of thirty-five who rarely smiled and who never ceased to regard her present circumstances as those of one cast into a primitive wilderness. She had lied about her antecedents, having worked in London at several homes as a housemaid and not as a nursemaid, but she came to realize that such distinctions were not terribly important among the elite of San Francisco. Her present employer fascinated and frightened her — this enormous, impulsive young man, who walked with a rolling gait and whose manners, to her way of thinking, left much to be desired — an odd match for the beautiful young woman who was his wife. On the other hand, Dan, who still could not comprehend the role of servants, treated her with easy good nature and slapped her behind occasionally, if only to enjoy the outraged reaction it elicited. His periods of sexual abstinence were increasing, and he toyed with the notion of seducing Miss Jones. But the opportunities were few and he was still romantically and adolescently in love with Jean.

Now, as so often, playing with the blond-haired, blue-eyed little boy who was his son, he wondered what the hell he, Daniel Lavette, son of a French fisherman and an Italian peasant girl, was doing in this improbable mansion on Russian Hill? Nothing in it gave him the feeling of being his, of belonging to him. The ship models and the sea paintings in the library — which Jean referred to as his room — were gifts from her parents, with the exception of a splendid Winslow Homer that the Levys had given him as a wedding present; the shelves were filled with books he had never read and had no intention of reading, and the furniture there, as in the rest of the house, had been selected by Jean and her mother. It was true that a Packard touring car that he kept in a garage on the Embarcadero was his own selection, but it was bright yellow, and Jean felt it was vulgar, and that if they had a car, it should have been a limousine of some dark and proper color. And Jean's friends, the second generation of nabobs and the increasing mixture of artists, writers, and musicians who were moving to Russian Hill, were as alien to him as the furniture, rugs, and knicknacks that had poured into the new house in a steady stream since it was completed.

"You mustn't excite him too much before his bedtime," Miss Jones said. "Really, Mr. Lavette."

"You don't approve of excitement before bedtime."

"Emphatically not."

"Oh?" Dan grinned at her. "Try it sometime. It's got its points."

At dinner, Jean appeared more withdrawn than usual, and Dan decided to say nothing about what had happened at the bank. He had made up his mind that they would deny him the loan; and if, on an outside chance, they were willing to give him the money, he was no longer sure that he wanted it from the Seldon Bank. He felt that it had been a mistake to approach Seldon in the first place, and Mark agreed with him, telling him, after he had reported what had happened at the meeting, "You do Tony an injustice when you shy away from him. The Cassalas are bankers. Tony needs people like us. If the shipping venture is a mirage, we should drop it. But if it's real, let's go to Tony and talk to him. He deserves that."

Both Dan and Jean sat in silence. More and more, they would eat in silence, and, still, when he looked at her he felt that he was entitled to no complaint, that the fact of her accepting him as her husband was all he could ask, and that the privilege of sitting opposite her and basking in the perfection of her beauty was enough in itself. Time would change things. She had accepted him wholly once; she would again.

Finally, he said, "It was a damn beautiful day, wasn't it? I hope you went out for a while."

"I wish you wouldn't swear, Dan."

"Yeah — I'm sorry."

"I went to lunch at the Fairmont," she said. "With Marcy Callan."

And then she added, "We went to Borsin's and picked out material for the drapes. I'm going to do this whole room over in pastels. I'm so tired of Oriental rugs and this ridiculous period furniture. It's not Chippendale and it's not Queen Anne; I really don't know what it is or why I bought it. I think that if we are going to have antiques, we should have real antiques. We can certainly afford them."

Dan nodded. He was still trying to place Marcy Callan.

"She's marrying Whittier's son, right? A kid by the name of John or something."

"We'll have to have a party for her. She's one of my dearest friends."

"Sure. Nothing I like better than having the Whittiers over here."

"You'll endure it."

"Talking about parties and things," Dan said, "Feng Wo — he's my office manager you remember — he'd like us to have dinner with his family."

"You're not serious?"

"He asked me today."

"With Chinks?" she said incredulously.

"Chinese. Don't call them Chinks, Jean."

"Why not? You do. I heard you use that word a hundred times."

"Not lately. Sure I used it. Everyone does. I don't like it. It's like calling Mark a sheeny."

"I don't think so, and I don't think you're ready to instruct me on the language."

"Jeany," he said gently, "let's not fight. People think I'm some kind of crazy financial genius with what Mark and me built in four years — but there's no way we could have done it without Feng Wo. He's the one who keeps us out of bankruptcy and juggles the books and puts the brake on when I want to blow the whole thing. This is the first time he ever asked me to his home. What can I tell him?"

"Did you accept the invitation or did you tell him you would discuss it with me? It's very simple to tell him that we have a full social schedule for the next two months. We have, as a matter of fact."

"I accepted it."

"Then you'll go alone," Jean said. "I'm very sorry, Dan, but I have no intentions of dining with a Chinese, as you put it."

When Jack Harvey heard that Dan and Mark intended to sell his beloved *Oregon Queen,* which he had commanded since its first voyage under their flag and which was his darling, his home, his passion, he got drunk for the first time in more than three years. He did not simply get drunk; he was not a social drinker; he went on a mighty bender and disappeared for three days into the maw of the Tenderloin. It made no difference that Mark and Dan assured him that he would take over the first of the new ships. He refused to believe them, and he saw the one glorious period of his life going down the drain.

For three days, his daughter, Clair, now fifteen, searched for him. She had grown into a long-legged, oddly lovely young woman — with green eyes, a bronze skin, and a high-arched, imperious nose — very much her own person, independent, five feet, seven inches in height at fifteen, with a great mop of carrot-colored hair. Alone, she prowled through the Barbary Coast, poking into every dive she had ever heard her father mention — and then, in despair, turning to Dan and Mark. Mark joined her, and in the small hours of the fourth day, they found Jack Harvey in a whorehouse on Grant Avenue. Mark took him and his daughter to his home in Sausalito.

Mark put Harvey to bed, where he slept for the next twelve hours, while Sarah, who had always regarded Clair as that "poor, motherless child, living with that witless father of hers," fed the poor, motherless child eggs and pancakes and oatmeal and cream. Jacob Levy, almost sixteen, and his ten-year-old sister, Martha, sat at the kitchen table, watching with fascination as the skinny, redheaded girl consumed everything placed in front of her with an appetite that was apparently insatiable and a stomach that incredibly held everything put into it. "Eat, darling," Sarah said, placing a second plate of scrambled eggs in front of her. "Poor darling, to have to go through something like that. You'll have more pancakes?"

"All right, please."

"Good, good. Now eat, and after that, you'll sleep."

Jacob never took his eyes from her. He had seen her last some two years before, and now he was trying to comprehend the miracle that had turned a skinny, freckled kid into this tall, almost regal woman, with high, firm breasts and straight flaming hair that fell to her waist. Martha nudged him with her elbow and whispered, "Don't stare at her. It's not nice."

Clair said to Sarah, "I'm not tired. It's funny, I know I should be, but I'm not." She turned to Jacob and said, "Don't you ever say anything? You haven't said a word."

"No."

"That's a word. You mean you never say anything?"

"He's shy," Martha said. "He's afraid of girls."

"I am not," Jacob said.

"You finished your breakfast," Sarah said to Martha. "Outside. Go."

Martha stuck her tongue out at her brother and then raced out of the kitchen. Mark came in and told Sarah that he was returning to San Francisco and that probably that afternoon he and Dan would drive down to San Mateo to see Anthony Cassala.

"He asked us to dinner," he explained, "and we'll talk about the loan. I'll be too late for the ferry, so I'll either stay there or at Dan's if we drive back."

"I'd love to see Tony's place. What's it like?"

"It's in Hillsborough, so what would you expect? Stone and redwood. Funny, Tony always lived so simply — you know, Maria did the cooking and they always ate in the kitchen. This place has sixteen rooms. The bank took it over on a mortgage default, and it was such a bargain I suppose Tony couldn't resist it. They brought over a girl from Italy to help with the housework, but Maria treats her like a daughter and still does most of the work herself. Maybe Stephan pushed him into it. The kid's working at the bank this summer. He's a smart kid with all kinds of ideas." He drew her with him out of the kitchen and said softly, "Keep Harvey and his kid here. Tell him I said he has to stay until Dan and I come back, and don't let him get at the whiskey and the wine."

"And how do I do that?"

"You'll figure it out. He's always liked you. Make him understand that he's not going to be beached."

"You know, I'm getting scared, Mark. This big house scares me, and when I think of five oceangoing ships — how did we ever get into this?"

"Very simple. You hated living behind a store. Now don't worry. I'll be back tomorrow."

Meanwhile, Clair finished her second plate of scrambled eggs and Jacob stared at the tablecloth.

"You got a saucy sister," Clair said.

"Yeah, I guess."

"You can look at me if you want to. I don't mind."

Their eyes met and they both grinned.

"Do they call you Jake?" she asked.

He nodded.

"You like it?"

"I like it better than Jacob. That's a dumb name. It was my grandfather's name."

"I like Jake. It's a great name. There was a logger up at Mendocino City who's name was Jake, and he was the biggest, strongest man I ever seen."

"Bigger than Dan?"

"Way bigger than Dan. Six-foot, seven inches. I'd grab his fist and he'd lift me up with one hand. How about that?"

"Can you swim?"

"Of course I can swim!"

"Do you know what a catboat is?"

"Well what do you think?" she demanded indignantly. "I practically spent my life on ships and you ask me if I know what a catboat is?"

"I didn't mean it that way."

"Well, what did you mean?"

"I got one."

"What?"

"A catboat."

"No. You're kidding."

"Swear to God. My own. I bought it myself with money I made working at the warehouse after school. Forty bucks — but it's a beauty. I scraped it, caulked it, and painted it."

"How long?"

"Twenty-two feet."

"Oh, grand! Grand! Twenty-two feet. That is absolutely the nuts."

"You want to sail?"

"Where is it?"

"Down at the marina."

"Oh, absolutely, absolutely!"

But once they were out on the bay in the catboat, her explosive energy succumbed to the past three days of sleeplessness. Unable to keep her eyes open, she curled up in the bottom of the boat. "Just to rest a little," she explained. "I'm so tired, Jake."

"Sure. I know. You had a rough time."

A moment later, she was asleep, her long red hair cast over her shoulders like a burning shawl. There was just the slightest breeze, just enough to move the boat through the placid water with hardly a ripple. Jacob sat in the stern, his hand on the rudder, watching the sleeping girl, totally happy, totally content.

The breeze picked up, and Jake steered the catboat across Richardson Bay past Angel Island. Now he had a full, clear view of San Francisco and its hills, the swelling lumps of land with the streets mounting to the sky, the houses piled one on top of another, and all of it laced across with the last shreds of the morning fog, a lattice through which the morning sun sprinkled the city with gold. If he had seen the city a thousand times before, this was nevertheless and mysteriously the first time he had seen it truly — or was he seeing some magical wonderland that the presence of this strange redheaded girl had created? He stared at the city in silent awe, a flood of emotion rising in him, tears welling from his eyes. He didn't quite know why he felt the way he did, but it was the best feeling he had ever experienced.

He knew that. It was all magic, and all very right and as it should be. He knew that too.

With the help of Gina, the young girl they had brought over from Italy, Rosa and Maria cleared away the remains of a dinner of salad and soup and pasta and veal, stocking the table instead with bowls of fresh peaches and plums and grapes and pears and black Italian coffee for the men. Then the women vanished, excusing themselves with low murmurs of sound, leaving around the table Anthony Cassala, Stephan, and Dan Lavette and Mark Levy. Anthony pressed fruit upon his guests, poured coffee for them, and offered them cigars. Mark smoked a pipe. Dan accepted cigars when they were offered and was beginning to acquire a taste for them.

"Well, what do you think, Danny and Mark?" Cassala asked them, waving a hand at the baronial spaces of the dining room. "You like my house?"

"It's great," Mark said.

Dan puffed his cigar and grinned at Cassala.

"You laugh at me, huh, Danny? All right. In the morning I shave and I look at my face, and I say, Who are you? What for? You are plain Neapolitan bricklayer. I tell you something, Danny, you know where all this come from? I tell you, from the four thousand dollars you give me after the earthquake."

"Never," Dan said. "You're dreaming."

"Am I? You know what a bank is built on? Confidence. I bought confidence with that money. A few dollars here, a few dollars there — but people ate and drank and they remembered. I don't have that money, my whole life is different."

"Come on, Tony, what you did you did."

"Maybe, maybe not. I got one regret — my saintly mother in heaven, she never had a day in her life without hunger, hunger from her children, hunger from my papa, hunger from cousins and brothers and sisters. Always hunger. Now I get fat. I got a paunch. What do you think of that?"

"On a banker it looks good," Mark said.

"Papa," Stephan said, "it's almost ten o'clock. Let Danny and Mark talk."

"Do I keep them from talking? Talk," Cassala said. "Only one thing, Danny, I got to say. Your mother was a good Catholic. She sits with the Blessed Virgin now. When last you go to a mass? When you go to a confession? Don't get angry, please, Danny — I talk to you like my son."

"It's all right, Tony. I know how you feel. I'm married to a Protestant. I can't do something I don't feel."

"Papa," Stephan begged him.

"All right. Talk."

"Tony," Mark said, "we have to talk kind of in circles, because the only way you will make sense of what we're going to ask is if you see it our way."

"You want money," Cassala said. "Tell me what you need. We'll find a way."

"No, no," Dan protested. "You got to understand what we're after, Tony."

"Let me start with the canal," Mark said. "Last month, the first ship to come through the Panama Canal and dock at San Francisco tied up here. That changed the world, Tony, believe me. What it means in plain terms is that we have cut about eleven thousand shipping miles off the cargo exchange between here and the East Coast. That in itself changes the future of California, but let's look at it in terms of this lunatic war they're fighting in Europe. Say a ship sails out of the bay westward. Let's just say it carries cargo for Japan, and it coals at Hawaii and Japan. Suppose it picks up cargo at Japan and sails to Australia, and then to South Africa. Then to the East Coast. With the canal, the profit from the East Coast back here — considering what is happening to the rates — pays for the whole voyage, and the rest is gravy. Otherwise, the ship would have to go around the Horn and shave its profits for fuel. And there's no cargo in Africa or Australia that they're pleading for here. We need East Coast cargo and the British need it desperately in the Pacific, and before this war is over, San Francisco is going to be maybe one of the most important ports in the world."

"So you want to buy a ship," Cassala said, nodding. "That makes sense."

"Wait a minute, Tony," Dan said. "Maybe you're thinking about the *Oregon Queen.* No. This is something else. We sold the *Oregon Queen.* As a matter of fact, we're selling everything. We sold the garbage contracts and the garbage ships the other day, and next week we're selling the pants business and the fishing boats. And maybe we'll dump the chandling business too. Everything."

"What!"

Dan glanced at Stephan, who was listening intently and saying nothing.

"That's right," Mark agreed. "All of it."

"Why? You got a wonderful business and you sell it. Why?"

"Because," Dan said slowly, "we're going to buy a fleet of ships and we need every dollar we can lay hands on. Three six-thousand-ton ships and two five thousand tons. Steel ships. Beautiful ships. We need at least a million and a quarter in cash, and that's why we're here, Tony. We want a loan of a million dollars."

Cassala stared at him; then he sighed deeply, closed his eyes, and leaned back. Stephan was nodding, smiling slightly. Mark and Dan waited. Maria came into the room with a platter of pastry. In her plain black dress that fell to her ankles, she reminded Dan more and more of his own mother. "You're not eating the fruit," she cried out in Italian. "Why? Fruit is good. Fruit cleanses the system. In America no one eats with joy, only to fill the belly. Look at those peaches. They are so ripe they plead with you. Eat fruit and eat pastry. I bring you cheese."

Cassala still sat with his eyes closed, his hands clasped in front of him. Mark looked at Dan inquiringly.

"Eat some fruit," Dan translated. "Otherwise, Maria will be angry."

"If he says no," Mark whispered, "we're finished."

"Did I say no?" Cassala snapped. "Did I say no? So why you whisper? Eat some fruit and let me think." He turned to his son. "You're listening, Stephan?"

"I'm listening, papa."

He turned to Dan. "What about the submarines?"

"The Germans haven't sunk an American ship yet. Maybe they won't. We can get insurance on the ship — not on the cargo but on the ship. Tony, the profits are so big we can afford to lose a ship."

"And the ships are fast," Mark added. "According to what Dan tells me, we can outrun any U-boat."

"It's a first mortgage on the ships, Tony. Cross collateral, if we lose one, you got it on the others. When the insurance pays off, you got first call, regardless of the cargo. An absolute priority."

"And Dan and I will go on the notes to the full extent of our personal property," Mark said.

"Why?" Cassala demanded, annoyed. "Did I ever ask such a thing?"

"Neither did we ever ask you for a million dollars."

Cassala turned to his son. "Well, Stephan, what do you think?"

"Papa, in the fifteenth century in Genoa, five ships would set out for the East. If one of them returned with a cargo of spices and the other four were lost or sunk, the one ship that returned paid for the others and a profit too."

"I am not asking about Genoa in the fifteenth century."

"I'm only saying, papa, that shipping has always been a thing of great profit. If Danny and Mark say they can do it, they will do it."

"If they say they fly to the moon, will they fly to the moon?" He took an apple and began to peel it. "Eat a piece of fruit," he said to Mark. "Eat." Maria came in with a platter of cheese. "Now you bring the cheese," he said. "Why not tomorrow?"

"Tony," Dan said, "if this is impossible — "

"Impossible is what I can't do," he interrupted. "You think I send you away from here without it? But we're a small bank. I never made a loan of a million dollars. Well, first time. How soon you need it?"

"It's a question of getting the ships before someone else moves in."

"Three days?"

"Wonderful, Tony."

"I don't know how to thank you," Mark said.

"Don't thank me. Talk. Stephan, get a pencil and a notebook. I want to know everything, who owns the ships, who built them, what kind engines — everything, because about ships I know nothing. You don't just buy a ship. You pay a crew. You pay rent for a berth. You buy fuel and food. You pay longshoremen. So this is what I got to know, and what kind of cash you got on hand. So we talk."

It was past midnight when they finished, and Cassala persuaded them to stay with him overnight. Maria took Dan to his room, kissed him, and said plaintively, "Light a candle for your mama, Danny. Go to mass. My soul will rest easy. I pray for you always — always."

Walking down the hill to Grant Street and then into Chinatown, Dan reflected that he had never actually thought of Chinese as people with homes and families; but perhaps in that he was no different from most of the population of San Francisco. In all truth, he had never, before knowing Feng Wo, seen Chinese as individuals, as human entities, as people with feeling, with pain and joy and suffering — participating in an agony that was part of mankind. A Chinese beaten did not hurt, wounded did not bleed, and dead was without meaning. In the annals of the San Francisco Police Department, a dead Chinese was statistically different from a dead Caucasian, and in the eyes of the white population, a dead Chinese was good riddance to bad rubbish.

Now, on his way alone to have dinner with Feng Wo and his family, he walked slowly, lost in his own thoughts, trying to understand how Jean felt and what were the origins of her anger, her rage at the thought of spending an evening with Chinese. Yet how could he condemn Jean, thinking back to his own first meeting with Feng Wo, his patronization of the man, his own contempt for anything Chinese? It was as much in his blood as in Jean's. Did he have the vaguest notion of where or how Chinese lived? In Chinatown — of course — he had an address on Grant Street, where he was now bound. Chinese lived in Chinatown; like rats, they had tunnels and burrows into which they disappeared at night to emerge again in the daytime. But homes that were actually homes, families, children — when had he ever credited them with the amenities of even the poorest and most wretched Caucasians?

He found the address, a wooden building divided into apartments, not so different from the building he had lived in as a boy, not so different from a thousand other narrow, three- and four-story wooden buildings that lined the streets of San Francisco. He walked up two flights of stairs in a dimly lit hallway to a door that was marked 2F, and he knocked. Feng Wo had apparently been waiting close to the door, because it opened immediately, and there he was, nervously smiling and nodding.

"So very glad to see you, Mr. Lavette. You honor my poor home and my unworthy family."

Dan had assumed and discarded half a dozen complex stories to account for Jean's absence. Now he simply said, "That's very Chinese, Feng Wo, but my wife has a sick headache and I'm sure your family is pretty damn worthy. Anyway, I'm glad to be here."

"Please to enter," Feng Wo said. He led the way through a short and narrow hall, and then drew aside a curtain of beaded strands for Dan to pass.

The room Dan stepped into was evidently the family room, dining room and living room combined, a black table and chairs at one side of the room, a door to the kitchen, and opposite it a tiny hallway with doors off it to the bedrooms. There was a Chinese screen, quite lovely, but constructed of cheap Chinese printed paper pasted on a frame, and there were three nondescript easy chairs. The floor was painted deep red and polished with many coats of wax, and there were framed prints on the wall, Japanese rather than Chinese, but in keeping with the rest of the room. For some reason Dan did not entirely understand, the room, a hodgepodge of so many things, came together and gave him a feeling of comfort and intimacy. It was not familiar but neither was it strange; and across the room, facing him, a young woman stood, giving the place a final touch of magic, of Oriental wonder that transformed it from a melange of the cheap and ordinary to a place of mystery and excitement.

She was not a beautiful girl, certainly no more than eighteen or nineteen at the most, very slender, wearing a straight black dress that fell from her shoulders to her ankles; her skin was ivory, her features small and regular, her mouth well formed, and on her face there was an expression of great pleasure, a slight smile, a look of eager anticipation combined with childish and worshiping innocence. Or perhaps, wondering whether any other woman had ever looked at him like that before, simply a Chinese girl, hands clasped, bowing.

"I am so happy to meet you at last, Mr. Lavette," she said, her voice low and musical."

"My daughter, May Ling," Feng Wo said.

"So you're May Ling. Well I've certainly heard a lot about you," Dan said awkwardly, a little less than the truth, since Feng Wo had rarely mentioned his daughter.

"And I about you, Mr. Lavette. Please sit down and make yourself comfortable."

"Please," Feng Wo said.

Dan dropped into one of the chairs. May Ling disappeared into the kitchen. "You must excuse my wife for the moment," Feng Wo explained. "She knows that you are a very important guest, and therefore she felt that she must prepare an important meal. I'm afraid it requires all her attention at the moment."

May Ling returned now with a tray that held a tea kettle and several small cups. She placed it on a small table, which was flanked by the easy chairs, and then, kneeling in front of the table, she poured green tea and handed a cup to Dan and another cup to her father. Feng Wo sipped at it and said softly, "Peace and harmony among those we know and touch." Dan drank the hot, acrid tea. May Ling refilled his cup.

"Do you like Chinese food, Mr. Lavette?" May Ling asked. "My mother is a fine cook."

"No, no, indeed," Feng Wo said hastily. "A very ordinary cook."

"Chinese food?" Dan said. "Aside from the Western omelets your father used to cook up for me, all I know is chop suey. It's all right. Sure, I like it."

"Well, we shall see." She rose, went into the kitchen, and then returned with a platter of small, steaming dumplings. "Sau mai," she told him.

"Oh? And what does that mean?"

"It means small, steamed dumplings, Mr. Lavette. You can pick them up with your fingers or you may use chopsticks." She made a face and shook her head. "No, don't use chopsticks."

"My daughter, you see," Feng Wo said, "is a product of American civilization. She speaks when she is not spoken to. She voices opinions which are not asked of her, and she chatters in front of the men in her family."

"There is only one man in my family," May Ling said gently, going to her father and kissing the bald spot on top of his head. "I do chatter in front of him. He is quite right. I am entirely without graces."

Feng Wo's wife, who had been in the kitchen during this, called out something in Chinese.

"We must go to the table now, Mr. Lavette," Feng Wo said. "You know, Mr. Lavette, there is a rather strange thing about the Chinese people here. I myself am the third generation in America. My grandfather was brought here in eighteen fifty-one from Kwangtung Province, yet until I was five years old I spoke only Chinese. We were actually afraid to speak in English. But my wife is a woman from the old country, from Chekiang Province, which is well to the north of Canton — and so much confusion." He sighed. "Such very bad Chinese and she learns no English at all."

"You sit here, Mr. Lavette," May Ling said, indicating one end of the table. "I will join you, because after three generations in America, as my father said, we have succumbed to customs of the barbarians. But not my mother. She would die first. So I am afraid you will just have to accept the fact that she will serve us. She is a lovely lady and a marvelous cook."

"We can wait for praise," Feng Wo said. "We need not invite it," he added, looking at his daughter severely; but she merely giggled and looked knowingly at Dan. "Just you wait and see," she whispered. He was not disappointed. A small, sad-eyed Chinese woman entered from the kitchen bearing a large urn and in it a great melon. As she put it down, Feng Wo held forth in Chinese, pointing to Dan, and the sad-eyed woman nodded and smiled with pleasure, and then stood there, in front of Dan, her eyes cast down, but the expression on her face explaining that she would have embraced him and kissed him were that at all proper. Then she remembered the melon and burst into a flow of Chinese directed at her husband.

"They both speak different dialects," May Ling said, "but somehow they understand each other. I really think my mother understands more English than she admits to." Now So-toy, Feng Wo's wife, was spooning fragrant soup out of the melon — pieces of the flesh of the hot melon and ham and bamboo shoots and black mushrooms. The first bowl of the steaming soup was placed by May Ling in front of Dan.

"You don't wait," she told him. "You taste it immediately, lick your lips, and tell my mother how delicious it is."

He did so. "Great — best thing I ever tasted! What do you call it?"

"Tun qua nor twai ton — or winter melon soup. So you see, Mr. Lavette, it's not all chop suey, is it?"

"Truly," Feng Wo said, "I apologize for my daughter. That is enough, May Ling."

"No," Dan said, "let her instruct me. By all means. Only tell me," he said to May Ling, "when you are not lecturing on Chinese cooking, what do you do?"

"I am a librarian," she said. And then, getting no reaction, she asked, "Does that shock you?"

"That you're a librarian? Oh, no."

"But a woman with a profession? My father is not quite certain it's proper."

"I think," said Feng Wo, "it is the quantity of your opinions that shocks Mr. Lavette."

"You see Mr. Lavette every day," she said calmly. "I have been waiting almost five years to meet him. Eat your soup, father, and you too, Mr. Lavette, because," she told him, "you do not understand Chinese cooking. My mother is preparing five extraordinary dishes which will all be ready at the same time. How that is accomplished is a secret we guard with our lives — " She halted and began to giggle again, and Dan caught it from her, and the two of them burst out laughing, while Feng Wo stared at them in amazement, finding absolutely nothing humorous in their exchange. Dan tried to stop but could not, caught in a fit of boyish foolishness that he had never actually experienced before, and May Ling finally leaped up and bore the tureen of soup into the kitchen. Dan tried to apologize to Feng Wo. "Please, forgive me," he said.

"For laughing?" Feng Wo asked in astonishment.

"Well, it's a silly kind of laughing."

Feng Wo had never seen Dan Lavette like this, relaxed, easy, laughing. Dan asked his host for permission to remove his jacket. "But you are in my house," Feng Wo said. "Please, feel free to do anything that will make you comfortable." Dan took off his jacket and loosened his tie.

May Ling and So-toy came back now, bearing covered dishes which they set down on the table. So-toy served the food, and May Ling said, "Now you must forget that you ever ate chop suey, Mr. Lavette, which in English is 'begger's hash.' You see, my mother is Shanghainese — "

"Not really," Feng Wo interrupted. "She comes from a tiny village to the south of the city. My grandfather was from Canton, and not only is the language different but the cooking too. I taught her to cook Cantonese, but her best dishes are Shanghainese."

May Ling exploded her breath. "I said nothing. It would be disrespectful if I did."

"You are disrespectful beyond belief," Feng Wo said. "My

ancestors shrink in their graves in horror." Then he spoke in Chinese to his wife, who was still piling food onto the plates, and she smiled and nodded.

In all the years he had worked for Dan, he had never spoken this much. "Please eat," May Ling said to Dan. "You see, my father is a very educated man, and from his father, he learned Mandarin, otherwise he could not speak to my mother at all, since in her village they spoke Shanghainese and she would not understand a single word of Cantonese."

"You mean they speak more than one language in China?"

"Oh, many more than one language, Mr. Lavette, except that the educated people everywhere speak Mandarin, and my father is excellently educated, and when you have left, he will lecture me for at least an hour on my unmaidenly lack of modesty. But I am liberated — not at all easy for a Chinese woman."

"You are certainly liberated," Feng Wo said. "To my sorrow."

She was laughing, and again Dan found her laughter irresistible. Then Feng Wo and May Ling both began to speak in Chinese to So-toy, who covered her mouth to suppress her giggles.

"You speak Chinese," Dan said to May Ling in amazement.

"Do you think I grew up without ever talking to my mother? I was speaking Shanghainese and Mandarin before I ever knew a word of English. But I can't speak Cantonese very well."

"What am I eating?" Dan asked her. "It's delicious. I never ate anything like this before. God, it's good!"

Feng Wo spoke to his wife, who nodded in delight and heaped more food on Dan's plate. "That's stewed beef with tara root, wine, and sugar," May Ling said. "We call it hon sau yo zo, and the fish is whitefish, with tomatoes, green pepper, pineapple, ginger, green onions, and shrimp. Tan soan yo. The shredded pork is sauteéd with Chinese stringbeans — that's a peasant dish that they eat everywhere — don't they?" she asked her father.

"I guess so. It's a simple peasant dish, but very good. It's called tzal do tzu zo."

Dan tried to pronounce it, and So-toy giggled and covered her mouth again. "And this?" Dan asked.

"Bean curd," Feng Wo said. "You never tasted it?"

"Never. But I like it. I thought it was some kind of custard."

"It is, sort of," May Ling said. "It's made of soy beans, and they used to import them from China. But now some Chinese farmers down on the Peninsula have started to grow the beans, and they're much cheaper. It's very hot and peppery, a real Shanghai dish, made with tomato sauce, red pepper, and garlic."

"Ma paw do foo," So-toy said with pride.

"I like Mexican food," Dan said. "It reminds me of that."

So-toy filled a side dish with cabbage, and May Ling said, "That's my mother's pride and joy. Kai yan bai tzi, sautéed cabbage with sweet cream and chopped dried shrimp. So if you just keep eating it and eating it, her day will be complete."

"May Ling!" her father said disapprovingly, and then translated for her mother, who again covered her mouth to hide her laughter. Dan emptied his plate, and So-toy filled it again. He ate without shame, great quantities of food, washing it down with cup after cup of the green tea. "Tsa foo," he ventured, May Ling laughing at his attempt to pronounce it. "Better if you just say green tea." When So-toy came in from the kitchen bearing a royal mold of what May Ling described as eight precious rice pudding, or ba bau fa, he threw up his hands in despair and pleaded, "No more, no, please. I'll never walk out of here."

"But everyone said you are so brave, Mr. Lavette, fighting the pirates and sinking them with a shotgun, and now you surrender. You know, really, this is the triumph of all. I must sound like a Chinese cookbook by now."

"You do," her father agreed.

"Good," May Ling said. "Mother and I will clear and do the dishes, and that will give your stomach a chance to empty itself. Aren't you pleased? Look at it — sweet rice, sweet red bean paste, raisins, ginger preserve, orange peel, lotus seeds, cherries, pineapple, kumquats, almond paste — oh, when you were a little boy, Mr. Lavette, did you ever eat the banana split supreme at Bundy's ice cream parlor on Sacramento Street? I never did. I always dreamed of it, but we were much too poor then, but this is a sort of Oriental version — "

Feng Wo rose. "I have matters to discuss with your mother." He looked at his daughter as if he had not seen her before.

"You're a dear sweet man," said May Ling, and then told Dan, "I am the most improper, badly bred Chinese daughter in this entire city. I manipulate my father and I avoid household duties that are the ordained lot of a woman. I am a feminist. Do you like feminists, Mr. Lavette?"

Dan nodded, grinning. "If you're one, yes. I'm pretty ignorant, May Ling. I never went back to school after the earthquake."

Both her mother and her father were in the kitchen now, with the door closed behind them, and May Ling leaned over to Dan and said softly, "I don't always behave like this, Mr. Lavette. Let me explain. We never had a Caucasian in our home before. My father, poor man, was terrified. He worships the ground you walk on, and so do I, believe me, and I'm speaking quite seriously now. You are the great hero of my life, and I've heard stories about you for the past four years, so I feel I know you very well. My mother and father planned and discussed this evening for weeks, and I have been talking my head off to put them at ease. They both feel that I am a bona fide American product, a true barbarian, which is not true at all. You cannot grow up as a Chinese girl in San Francisco and deceive yourself into imagining that you are American. But perhaps I am more at ease with Caucasians since I work in a library. What I am trying to say is just that we all admire you and love you, and we want you to feel relaxed here and happy."

"I don't remember a better evening," Dan said.

A week later, at breakfast, Mary Seldon said to her husband, "It would appear that your son-in-law has a habit of making the front page of the *Chronicle.*"

"He's your son-in-law too."

"Shipping line sold," she read. "The firm of Levy and Lavette, local ship operators, has purchased the five cargo ships of Transoceanic Freight. The selling price is said to be upwards of three million dollars. For some months now, there have been rumors of the impending bankruptcy of Transoceanic — shall I read more?" she asked.

"No. I know all about it."

"Where did the money come from?"

"Cassala, I expect," Seldon said. "Of course, the cash payment must have been considerably less. You know, he came to us for the money first."

"Did he? And you turned him down?"

"Not at all. We wanted time to consider it, but he stalked out in a high dudgeon. I think it was the sight of Grant Whittier that he couldn't tolerate."

"What does he have against Grant?"

"Ah. You would have to understand Dan to answer that — which you don't."

"But you do?"

"Somewhat, I think. I like him, but he's a young bull and he can't bear to be crossed. Sooner or later, he'll stumble, I'm afraid. He has a habit of biting off more than he can chew."

In 1906, before the earthquake and the fire struck San Francisco, literate residents of the city could boast that they possessed the finest public library west of the Rocky Mountains. If the railroad kings and the placer kings had done little reading, no one could accuse them of lacking a veneration for books. By 1878, Andrew S. Hallidie, who invented the cable car, and Henry George, the economist, got together with nine other prominent citizens and established a public library and reading room. Starting in a rented meeting hall, by 1906 the library had mushroomed out into an entire wing of city hall, one hundred and forty thousand volumes and almost thirty-two thousand library card holders. And all of it, the dreams and efforts of book lovers, went up in flames in a few hours. Undaunted, a library committee organized itself within weeks after the earthquake. Forty thousand dollars was appropriated by the city, and a frame building was constructed between Van Ness and Franklin on Hayes Street. Almost immediately, twenty-five thousand books were donated, and in the decade that followed, the temporary frame building filled to overflowing.

All of this May Ling told to Dan, making the point that to be a librarian in San Francisco was a little more than simply being a librarian.

At first he had no thought or intention of seeing her again. Fourteen hours a day were simply not enough hours to do what he had to do: put five oceangoing ships into operation. Mark took over a good deal of the work, booking cargo, dealing with the British and French trade commissions, working through the legalities of what could and could not be done as a neutral in a world at war; but that still left Dan with the problems of operation and crew and supply and loading and coaling and a thousand other details that he had neither anticipated nor provided for. He thanked God for Feng Wo, who could do almost anything, and he rose at six in the morning and stumbled into bed at ten or eleven at night — and found himself increasingly a stranger to his wife and his children.

Yet his thoughts turned more and more frequently, not to Jean, whose aloofness had become a fact of his life, but to the Chinese girl and to the single evening of laughter and joy that he had experienced with her. Then, one day at three o'clock in the afternoon, he dropped everything and walked out of the warehouse that contained their offices and shipping depot, got into his car, and drove over to Van Ness and Hayes. He sat in his car and brooded a while, telling himself that what he intended was pointless and senseless. Then he went into the library.

A stout, friendly woman at the checkout desk looked at him with interest and informed him that May Ling Wo could be found straight back, all the way back, and then to the right. He went straight back, all the way back, picking his way through the stacks, and then to the right, and at a tiny desk hidden in a cave of books, he found her, scribbling onto a pad with an enormous open book in front of her. He waited until she looked up, asking himself, "Will she be annoyed, angry, provoked?"

No one of them. She looked up and smiled. "Mr. Lavette. What a pleasant surprise!"

"I got no reason to be here," he blurted out. "I just wanted to see you again."

"That's a reason, isn't it?"

"Yes, I guess so."

"This," she said, motioning to the limits of her little cave, "is the Oriental Reference Department. That's such an imposing name, and I am it, and if you were wondering how the City of San Francisco became so liberal as to hire a Chinese, well, that's the answer. They simply couldn't find a Caucasian who could read and write Chinese. I would love to ask you to sit down, Mr. Lavette. They promised another chair weeks ago but never delivered."

"That's all right. I won't stay."

"Please. Don't let me drive you away. If I were a proper

Chinese lady I'd give you my seat. But as you know, I'm not."

"Sure. Look, May Ling, when do you finish work?"

"At five, when we close. Why?"

"Well — look, I don't know how to say this — "

"Just say it," she said gently. "You want to see me after I finish work?"

"Right. I'm parked outside. It's not much more than an hour. I'll wait there in my car, and then maybe you'd go for a drive with me and have dinner? Only if you want to."

"I know that."

"I mean I want to talk to you. I just want to talk to you."

"All right."

"You don't have to go home?"

"I can telephone my mother. But you don't have to sit there for an hour. You can come back at five."

"I'll be there. It's a yellow car. You can't miss it." Then he made his escape, so that she would not have time to think about it or change her mind. He sat in the car, rehearsing in his mind what he would say to her and looking at his watch, the minutes dragging endlessly, feeling increasingly the fool, trying to understand what he was doing, what drove him; because it was not sex; he had not even thought of this slight, flat-chested girl in terms of sex; and he was not in love with her. He was in love with Jean; he never had Jean and he wanted her; nothing would change that; he kept telling himself that nothing would change that.

And then, suddenly, she was there, standing by his car in her black dress, a pink shawl around her shoulders, the oval-shaped face tilted, her dark eyes inquiring. He got out of the car and opened the door for her.

"I'm really very excited, Mr. Lavette," she said. "I've never been in an automobile before."

"It's safe enough. You mustn't be afraid."

"I'm not. It's hard to be afraid with you. You're a very reassuring person."

She watched with interest as he swung the crank and started the car. "We'll drive across to the Presidio, if you like that, and there's a place where we can park and get a good view of the ocean."

"I would like that."

He began the drive across town toward the ocean, groping in his mind for words, explanations, subjects, May Ling all the while sitting silently beside him, until at last he said desperately, "I'm trying to think of what I should say to you, and I can't."

"You don't have to think about what to say to me. Can't we just talk?"

"That's it," he muttered.

"Well then," she said, "I shall deliver a short lecture on the birth and history of the San Francisco Public Library." And when she finished, she said, "There, Mr. Lavette. We are not simply librarians. We inherit a tradition."

"Will you please call me Dan!" he snapped at her.

"Are you angry at me?" she asked, puzzled.

"No, no. I'm not sore at you, I'm sore at myself. May Ling, can I talk to you, I mean, can I really talk to you? I mean I never talked to anyone — about what I feel inside — I never had to or maybe I never could, I don't know."

"You can talk to me, Dan. You can say anything you want to me. Anything. Because what I owe to you, I can never repay."

"That's bull."

"It isn't."

"God damn it, May Ling, I don't want you to be grateful to me."

"Then what do you want, Dan?"

"I don't know," he said miserably. "I'm married. I think I love my wife. She isn't there."

"I don't understand."

He drove on in silence for a while, and then he muttered, "I never whined about anything in my life."

"You're not whining, Dan."

"I haven't looked at another woman since I'm married."

"Dan — will you listen to me?"

He glanced at her.

"Will you listen to me? I think you're the finest man I ever knew. I have my own reasons for thinking so. Now I agreed to spend this evening with you. I don't want you to apologize and I don't want you to feel that you have to explain anything. I want you to try to feel the way you did when you came to our house for dinner. So no more explaining, because I am very happy. I am spending an evening with a man I honor and like. Now, have you ever read Charles Lamb's 'Dissertation on Roast Pig'?"

"May Ling, I never read anything. I'm as ignorant as the day is long."

"Are you? Well, I know it by heart, and while you drive, I shall repeat it to you, slightly abridged, and you will understand why the Chinese are such excellent cooks."

They reached Sutro Heights as the sun was setting, and they sat there, watching the dull red orb sink into a golden sea, the hills black and lonely in the distance.

"I liked that story," he said.

"Thank you, Dan."

When it was dark, she said, "The quiet of a wise man is not simply quiet, not made by him, but just as strong as he is."

"That's — that's very beautiful," he said. "I'm not sure I understand it."

"I'm not sure either. I didn't make it up. It was written by a Chinese philosopher whose name was Chuang Tzu. It's my own translation, so I'm not sure it's much good."

"Are you hungry?"

"So much for Chinese philosophy." She sighed. "No, not very."

"Do you like Italian food? We can go to Lazzio's."

"Where you'll be seen by your friends."

"We're doing nothing wrong."

"And when your wife asks you what you were doing having dinner with a funny-looking Chinese lady, you will tell her that you were arranging to have your laundry done?"

It was the first time she had said anything that had taken him aback, and he replied indignantly, "I would never say anything like that. Anyway, you're beautiful."

"I must never tease you. Dan, we're out here. Let's eat at the Cliff House."

"It has no class. The old place did, not now."

"I don't care. No one will see us. I don't want to make trouble for you."

That was the beginning. He saw her three times more during the next two weeks, always meeting her outside the library. He did not know what she told her parents, nor did he ask her, nor did Feng Wo's manner toward him change in any way. He was expecting a change, looking for it, but there was none. Their relationship remained the same. When he kissed her, it was on the cheek, lightly, and there was no other physical contact. He simply knew that when he was with her, the churning, angry discontent within him disappeared. He realized that she possessed a perceptiveness and an intellect that was quite beyond him, but she never patronized him. She talked about books and philosophy and history, and he listened always with a sense of wonder that was turning into a kind of worship, frequently without understanding, yet hanging onto every word, grappling with it. She began to give him books to read, *The Call of the Wild* by Jack London and *Huckleberry Finn* by Mark Twain. It did not occur to him that she chose simple, readable books, and he read them, staying up half the night, not because he enjoyed reading but because he felt a desperate necessity to talk about something other than ships and the process of making money. Yet he found himself enjoying the stories.

Jean did not question his absence during the evenings he was away. Apparently, she accepted the fact that he worked long hours, and he felt that she was relieved by his absence. More and more, she was becoming a part of the Russian Hill circle of writers and artists. She gave a party — the first really large party in the new house — for Willis Polk and Bernard Maybeck, the two brilliant architects who were working on the Panama-Pacific International Exposition, scheduled to open the following year. It was an invitation that no one could refuse, and James Rolph, Jr, the mayor, long and deeply involved in shipping and navigation, was apparently the only one who noticed Dan's absence and asked for him, telling Jean, "I am indeed disappointed. I looked forward to a talk with this young tycoon of yours." But there were sufficient luminaries there that night, and no one else asked for Dan. Jean was rather relieved by the fact that Dan was elsewhere; she could never be sure of what he would say and whose feelings he would bruise; and her new friends were used to his absences.

It happened to be a very special night for both of the Lavettes. One evening, a week before the party, Dan said to May Ling, bluntly, which was very much a part of his approach to any subject, "You know by now that I care for you. You have become a very important part of my life."

"But you still love Jean."

"I don't want to make love to Jean, if that's what you mean. That happened being with you. I want to make love to you."

They were sitting in a little Italian restaurant on Jones Street, near the wharf. Gino's belonged to Gino Laurenti, who had been a friend of Dan's father. It was a tiny place, frequented by the Italian fishermen, a place where they were comfortably unseen and where they had come often.

May Ling looked at him thoughtfully, without replying, and he said, "You do understand me?"

"You're a strange man, Danny. You never even kissed me on the lips."

"That doesn't mean I didn't want to."

"I don't understand."

"How do you feel about me?"

"Don't you know?" she asked in amazement.

"No, I don't."

"You are absolutely the strangest man. Do you know that if you put me into that yellow automobile of yours and informed me that we were to drive across the ocean to Hawaii, I would go. I really would."

"That makes no sense."

"What do you want me to say, Dan? I love you. I loved you from the moment you walked into our apartment and stood there, a little frightened, I think, in that spooky place in Chinatown, and so abashed, like an enormous little boy — "

"Why? Because I helped your father? Because I hired him?"

"Oh, you are stupid sometimes!" she cried, the first show of anger he had ever seen in her. "No! Not because you helped my father. Because you are you."

Then he was silent, staring at his plate.

"Danny?"

He looked up at her now, still silent.

"Don't you believe that anyone could love you?"

"I'm no good with women," he muttered.

"Thank heavens."

"Well, what do you mean by that?"

"I'm teasing you. I know I promised not to, so you must forgive me. Let's finish our dinner."

"I'm not hungry."

"Neither am I. Let's go somewhere."

"Where?"

"Any place you say."

They got into his car, and he drove to a little inn in Broadmoor. He registered under the names of Mr. and Mrs. Richard Jones, and since they had no luggage, the night clerk demanded the rent in advance. He felt cheap and stupid, and he told her so, but May Ling only shook her head and smiled and said that it made no difference at all. He locked the door to the room, and then they sat on the edge of the bed, looking at each other.

"Do you know, Danny," she said to him, "I have never been with a man before, so this is going to be much harder for you than for me. But it's also going to be beautiful. I know that because I know you. You still haven't kissed me truly. Don't you think you ought to?"

He took her in his arms and kissed her, and then they stretched out on the bed, and he kissed her again and again, her lips parted, welcoming him. He lay there, looking at her, touching her face, her arms, her tiny breasts.

"We'll undress, Danny," she whispered. "We'll be naked."

It took only moments for her to slip out of her dress and her underthings, and while he struggled with his clothes, she took the spread off the bed and turned back the sheets. Then she let down her hair and it fell to her waist in a great black flood. Dan could not take his eyes off her. Her figure was slender and firm, her belly almost flat, her breasts small and firm, the nipples like budding roses in nests of old ivory. Naked like that, out of the straight, shapeless dresses she always wore, she appeared to Dan as the loveliest creature he had ever seen, not as another woman as his wife was a woman, but something out of another world and another time and place — an almost unreal person.

She walked over and stood before him, tiny against his huge, muscular bulk, and he clasped her in his arms, pressing her to him. Then he lifted her and carried her to the bed.

"Good God," he said, "what do you weigh?"

"A hundred and five pounds. That's enough, isn't it?"

"I'm two hundred."

"Good. You're a proper man."

He lay down next to her and cradled her in his arms, and she pressed up against him, smiling with delight.

"It doesn't bother you that I'm married?"

"No, but I don't want you to talk about it. I just want you to make love to me."

It was two o'clock in the morning when they closed the door behind them and walked downstairs. Dan tossed the key onto the desk and said to the clerk, "We decided not to stay, buster."

May Ling curled up against him as they drove back to the city. They were silent for a while, relaxed, content, connected, and then May Ling asked him, "Do you still think you're no good with women?"

"Maybe."

"You were terribly good with me, and I'm just a skinny little virgin. I mean I was a virgin. Not now. You deflowered me, Dan Lavette."

"You are the goddamndest girl."

"Why?"

"The things you say. Anyway, you're not skinny. You're the way you are, and that's right."

"Thank you."

"Weren't you afraid?" he asked her.

"Should I have been?"

"That's what they say."

"I was once."

"When was that?"

"When we walked into the place. I half expected the clerk to say that they don't take Chinks." She touched his cheek. "If he had, Danny, what would you have done?"

"I would have killed the sonofabitch."

"You're still a roughneck, aren't you?"

He thought about it for a while before he answered. "No, I'm learning. I read books. I don't say ain't much anymore, and I'm learning how to make love to a woman."

Quite simply, Sarah Levy adopted Clair Harvey. It came about without prior planning or arrangement. Dan and Mark both liked and trusted Jack Harvey, who had been with them since they purchased the *Oregon Queen;* he had his captain's papers; he was a good sailor and fiercely loyal; and when finally the *Oceanic,* the first of the new fleet of ships that Lavette and Levy had acquired, took off under their house flag, Harvey was in command. There was only one problem — what to do with Clair, and Sarah solved it by asking the girl whether she would like to stay with them at Sausalito? The ship was on a Western passage that would take it in due time entirely around the world, and it would be months before her father returned. Her strange childhood existence as a schooner brat on the coasters had come to an end; she could not live alone; and aside from her father she had no relative in the world. For all that she was amazingly independent and capable, and she was still only fifteen years old. Harvey put the problem to Sarah, who replied indignantly that she had never questioned the matter. Still, it had to have Clair's agreement, and Jack Harvey had vaguely discussed the alternative of a girl's boarding school.

Clair had stayed with the Levys for three weeks after her father's enormous bender, and then she had returned with him to their apartment in San Francisco when the school term began. One Saturday, Sarah took the ferry to town, and she and Clair had a long luncheon, just the two of them being very posh and ladylike at the Fairmont. Sarah saw herself in the long-legged, freckled, redheaded girl — the same fierce independence, the same kind of calm and certainty, withal a great pity for someone so totally alone in the world. Bit by bit, she drew out the story of Clair's life, the shabby rooming houses between the voyages on the redwood lumber schooners, the intermittent schooling, the long waits at night for her father's return. Finally, she made her proposal:

"Mark and I have decided to ask you to live with us. You see, my dear, your father's life is going to be very different now. He'll be gone for months at a time."

"I know that," she said. "But I can take care of myself, Sarah. Believe me, I always have."

"I'm sure you can. But your father's worried sick."

"Jack worried?" She laughed. "He never worried about me before. He found some dumb girl's school that he wants me to go to. Not on your life."

"Don't you like our place in Sausalito?"

"Like it? It's like heaven. And Jake is great. I love Jake. But I can't plant myself on you. I can't. I just can't."

An hour later, Clair agreed. Sarah reached across the table to take her hand, and Clair said, "My goodness, you're crying. Please, please don't cry. I won't be any trouble. I'll be a help to you, truly."

*

Marcy Callan persuaded Jean to join the Women's Exposition Committee. Her election to that very select body was no problem, for as Marcy said, the thought of the committee without a Seldon upon it was impossible. While not a member of the committee — for obvious reasons — Manya Vladavich was frequently present at committee meetings. Her opinions were never uncertain, and while a number of the women resented her flamboyance, there was still in San Francisco at that time enough worship of anything that smacked of Paris for them to tolerate her. It also gave Manya the opportunity to spend time with Jean, and while Jean still experienced curious prickles of excitement at the very touch of Manya's hand, she never again asked Manya to the house on Russian Hill, nor did she succumb to Manya's pleas that they spend an evening together.

Still and all, she found herself including Manya in the small "business" lunches that she and Marcy and a few other members of the committee held regularly. Manya was outspoken; she had opinions, of which she was certain; the others also had opinions, but with no conviction.

At one of these lunches, at the Palace Hotel, Manya held forth on the subject of the Tower of Jewels, which she described as an "obscenity." The Tower of Jewels, then still in the process of construction, was to be the central symbol of the 1915 exposition. The exposition itself had for its theme "The City of Domes," projecting a dream city that would represent all nations — or at least a good many nations. The Tower of Jewels was an attempt to root the exposition in the culture of Mexico, and, in a vague way, it was planned as an Aztec tower which would be four hundred and thirty-three feet high when completed.

Jean was inclined to agree with Manya's definition of the Tower. The architect's drawings, published widely in the newspapers, reminded her of nothing so much as an artist's imaginative representation of the Hanging Gardens of Babylon, which she had seen in *The Book of Knowledge* years ago; and she thought it unlikely that Babylon and Ancient Mexico had that much in common. The enormous Tower began, from the ground up, as a sort of Arc de Triomphe, with an overly ornate wing of the Louvre fastened onto each side of the arch, and then on top of the arch a series of colonnaded structures, for all the world like some gigantic wedding cake decorated with neoclassical sculpture and fierce winged birds.

"Eet is hideous and we must destroy it!" Manya announced. Marcy Callan, already an admirer of Manya's, nodded eagerly. The two other women present looked at Jean.

"It's half built," Jean said. "How do you propose to destroy it?"

"With a petition. With ze publicity," Manya declared.

"That makes no sense," Jean said. It was the first time she had ever directly rejected an opinion of Manya's.

"Maybe you think it is beautiful, dear Jean," Manya said caustically.

"I do not think it's beautiful, but it's all right."

"So now you are expert on architecture. You have seen so much in the world — yes?"

"Manya, don't be a fool!" Jean snapped. "There's no way in the world that we can stop the construction of the Tower of Jewels. But even if we could, I'd be against it. Do you know what we've gone through for this exposition? After pouring millions into its preparation, this wretched war in Europe had to start. Well, thank God, now the European countries are only too eager to send us their treasures. At least they won't be blown up by shell fire."

Dorothy Maclane, who was president of the Garden Club and thereby its representative on the Women's Committee, said that, after all, it was the gardens not the Tower that defined the exposition, thirty thousand cypress, spruce, and acacia trees, forty-seven thousand rhododendrons, cineraria, and azaleas — "and chrysanthemums — well, one doesn't count the number. And when you consider that there will be a hundred and thirty-five thousand jewels hanging from the Tower — "

"Bravo!" Manya interrupted. "Will you also count daisies?"

"Perhaps."

"You are a very stupid woman."

"And you're a bitch, Manya," Jean said — at which Manya rose and stalked out of the dining room.

There was a long moment of silence. Then Marcy Callan sighed and said, "She's right about the Tower."

"And I'm right about her being a bitch," Jean replied.

From there on, Manya was absent from the committee lunch

meetings, and, in all truth, Jean was relieved. She also had the good feeling that in some way she had contributed toward the success of the Panama–Pacific International Exposition. Due in part to the intervention of Dorothy Maclane, she was put on the steering committee, and for the next year, the exposition became the focus of her life. If it drew her still further away from Dan, it also created in her a sense of being a vital part of the artistic life of the city. She felt possessive of the Tower of Jewels — mentally embracing its flamboyance — and when the exposition closed at last, after ten months and nineteen million visitors, she felt an awful letdown that was akin to despair.

A few weeks later, with hardly more than an incoherent statement that she was choking and would die unless she could breathe freely, she left Dan with the house and the servants and the children and took off on a visit to her Aunt Asquith in Boston. It was five weeks before she returned; but now her mood had changed, and when Dan met her at the train, she embraced him and praised him for his tolerance and forbearance.

On the twenty-third of March 1917, the cargo ship *Oceanic* was torpedoed fourteen miles southeast of Southampton, England. She was carrying a cargo of food and munitions. The torpedo set off a chain reaction of explosions, and within minutes after the strike, the ship went down with all hands. There were no survivors. On the other hand, the loss of the ship did not even cause a financial tremor in the corporate structure of Levy & Lavette — a condition of international trade that requires explanation. For more than three years, cargo rates had been rising astronomically. By March of 1917, the bulk rate for cotton had climbed 3000 percent. The rate for wheat out of an Eastern port had increased thirty-five times, or 3500 percent, and out of San Francisco the increase was even greater. Dan and Mark had purchased the six-thousand-ton *Oceanic* for $350,000. Two additional ships of somewhat less than five thousand tons' displacement were purchased in 1916, at the cost of $700,000 per ship, and three more in 1917 at the cost of $850,000 per ship. Shipping rates on munitions were higher than the actual cost of the munitions — the money flowing with the same insane mindlessness as the river of blood on the Western Front. No belligerent paused to question shipping costs, just as no belligerent paused to count or be concerned over the number of dead. And in the blood-soaked line of trenches, stretching from the North Sea to the Alps, killing and stalemate evened out in a mindless mass destruction that promised, in the eyes of some, to go on forever.

Dan and Mark received the news of the sinking of the *Oceanic* in their offices on the afternoon of March 24, by cable from their London agent. A British destroyer had been witness to the submarine attack and had dropped depth charges, and the cable indicated that the U-boat had possibly been sunk. At the same time, the destroyer, which remained in the vicinity for several hours, had been able to find no survivors.

Mark was reading the cable when Dan returned from lunch. He was sitting in an oak-paneled office, part of the suite that had been created in their remodeled warehouse the year before. There was a three-thousand-dollar Oriental rug on the floor, a wide window with a view of the bay, and an assortment of period furniture. On the walls were large framed photographs of the *Oregon Queen,* the *Oceanic,* and other ships. Mark's desk was a great antique refectory table, and he sat hunched behind it, his face twisted with pain, looking much older than his thirty-seven years, a small, thin tired man. He handed the cable to Dan without speaking.

Dan read it, and then just stood there, shaking his head. "Jack's dead," he said. "It doesn't seem possible."

"The whole crew — Jack and the whole crew."

"I suppose it had to come, but why the hell did it have to be him?"

"Danny, where the hell is this taking us? It's only the beginning."

"Where we decided to go, I guess."

"For what? We got more money than any person needs."

"We'll be at war any day now. You know that."

"Then every dollar is soaked in American blood. Is that it?"

"Did we make this?" Dan asked him. "Mark, did we make this stinking war? We can sell our ships to Whittier tomorrow. What then? Does it make us virtuous. Can you show me a dollar anywhere in this country today that doesn't smell of blood? We didn't kill Jack Harvey. The Huns killed him, and so help me God, if shipping's going to win this war, I'll make those bastards pay."

"Bastards, Huns — come on, Danny. All right — we're in this

up to our necks, and I don't know what's right and what's wrong. Now I got to go to Sausalito and tell the kid her father's dead. How in hell do you do that?"

Some six months after he had first made love to May Ling in the inn at Broadmoor, Dan purchased a narrow Victorian house on Willow Street, within walking distance of the public library. He bought the house for forty-two hundred dollars and then spent another three thousand on renovations, restoring it to the original condition, retaining the stained-glass windows but doing no decorating. Now, after Mark had left to go to Sausalito, Dan drove to Willow Street, his thoughts going back to the day he first brought May Ling to the place. He had told her that he had a surprise for her. He parked his car then, picked her up at the library, and walked with her to the house. They had often talked about the Victorian houses, and he knew that she loved their style and character; and he opened the door, led her into the empty building, so shining clean and bright, cutting off her questions, leading her through room after room, up the stairs which were bathed in a red-gold glow from the stained glass windows, to the main bedroom where a slanted bay looked out over a greenery-choked backyard.

Finally, he allowed her to speak, asking, "Do you like it?"

"Oh, Danny, it's wonderful. Who's house is it?"

"Yours."

"Oh, don't do that. Don't tease me. That's my prerogative."

"I'm not teasing you. It's yours. I bought it for you. It's a gift. A place of your own. Because there's no way we can go on without you having a place of your own, and if you think I'm ever going to let go of you, you're crazy."

It was another week before Dan persuaded her to accept the house and to allow him to pay for decorating it and furnishing it. How she dealt with her parents he never knew—just as he did not know whether Feng Wo was at all aware of the affair. This was a part of her life she would not discuss with him. "This is a thing that I must do," she would say whenever he brought up the subject, "and I must do it my own way and without destroying what exists between you and my father. So trust me."

And now he went to her with all his guilts and confusions, letting himself into the house with his key—since she was not yet back from work — and dropping into a chair in the parlor, which was the only place he felt secure and content. Sitting there, his thoughts turned to Jack Harvey, and in his mind's eye, he could see him on the bridge of the *Oceanic* when the torpedo struck. It must have hit the hold where the three-inch shells had been stowed, for the *Oceanic* had unloaded and loaded again in Newark, retracing her way across the Atlantic, and then it must have been sheer unimaginable hell as the ship tore herself to pieces. He was awakened out of his brooding reverie by the sound of the door opening, and there was May Ling, her arms clutching bags of groceries.

She smiled happily at him as he took the bags and led the way into the kitchen. "Danny, I didn't expect you. What a good surprise! You will stay for dinner, won't you."

"No, I can't. I wish I could, but I can't. I have to get over to Sausalito tonight."

"But why?"

"We lost the *Oceanic.* She went down off Southampton with all hands. Jack Harvey's dead — the whole crew dead."

"Oh, no! How terrible!"

"I expected it. Jesus, we've been lucky. Hammond lost three ships. Whittier lost two. This is the first one, and it had to be the *Oceanic.* Why this way? Other ships go down and the crews are saved. Why did ours have to be a slaughter? According to Mark, we're murderers."

"Oh, no. He didn't say that, I'm sure."

"Well, that's how he made me feel. God Almighty, May Ling, I know what's going on. I'm a stinking millionaire out of this war. We pick up a cargo of powdered milk, so the kids in England and France won't die, and the cost of the milk is five cents a pound and the freight charge is twenty cents a pound, and the demented part of it is that Mark and me, we're caught in the trap, we don't set the rates, and the government pays the charge and writes it off as loans to the Allies, and they pay the overage on the insurance, and I get rich, and every lousy bastard who's doing the same thing, making the shells or the oil or whatever and shipping it — they're all becoming rich as God, some crazy lunatic God whose running that slaughter in Europe — and me too, me too, and damn it all, when I left the office I found myself stopping to look at our balance sheet — god damn it, the *Oceanic* sinks and Jack is dead, and I look at the balance sheet!"

"Danny," she said gently, taking his hand, "Danny, come with me." She led him into the parlor. "Sit here. I'll make you a drink, and we'll talk about this."

He sat in the single comfortable leather chair among the tufted black horsehair Victorian pieces with which she had furnished the parlor. He was drinking a whiskey and soda, May Ling facing him.

"Danny," she said, "we are going to talk about this. We never have before.

"I thought we talked about everything."

"Not about this, Danny. You know, people become rich out of war, some people, other people become poor and other people die. This is not new. It's as old as war, and you have become richer because of the war. You would have been a rich man anyway, because I think you wanted it so much, and I am not making any moral judgments. I have taken all the things you have given me, so I have no right to make any moral judgments. But now you are trapped in a moral judgment, aren't you?"

"I don't know," he said uneasily. "Maybe I'm just whining."

"Perhaps. We'll both try to be truthful with each other. Are you really a millionaire? I never asked you that before."

"I suppose so, if we liquidated. If I sold the stock and whatever property I have, it might be a couple of million. But there's no way to do that."

"Why?"

"Well, there's Mark — "

"You're stronger than Mark. You always have been. And from what you say about his feelings, he'd go along with you."

"May Ling, what would I do?"

"Danny, you're not even thirty years old. I'm twenty-one. We have our whole lives ahead of us."

"Baby, darling, you don't understand. I have no life apart from ships."

"We, you and me — we're a life apart from ships."

"No, I mean something else. I was out with my father in his fishing boat when I was five years old. You got to understand, May Ling — listen to me. This was going to be a surprise. I bought a cutter, a beautiful thing, thirty-two feet — for you and me. It's being shipped to the marina at San Mateo — "

"Danny, where are you?" she said sharply. "The fact that you bought a boat has nothing to do with this. I'm talking about you and me and Jack Harvey's death and the war in Europe, and the fact that any day now we will be in that war."

"Oh, Christ," he said, "it's all so rotten complicated."

"No, it isn't."

"I'm married. We always forget that."

"I never forget it."

"And you want me to wash my hands of everything."

"No. Only of what hurts you."

"And what about Jean?"

"Tell me, Danny. What about Jean? When did you last make love to Jean — if you ever did?"

He sat there, silent, staring at her glumly.

"God help me for what I'm going to say, Danny, but it's the truth. Do you know why you don't divorce Jean — not because you'd have to give her everything or half of everything, or whatever the price would be, no indeed, but for the same reason you can't see a life with me instead of those ships of yours — because this San Francisco sickness is in your blood and you can't think of yourself married to a Chinese woman."

"No, god damn it, no!" he shouted. "That's not true! I love you! Don't you understand how much I love you?"

"I know you love me, Danny. And I love you, oh, so much, so much, and I don't know why I said all this — unless it's because I'm pregnant."

"What!"

She nodded at him, trying very hard to smile and then giving way to tears. He knelt in front of her, his head in her lap, clutching her; and then she began to giggle through her tears at the sight of his enormous bulk in that foolish position. She stroked his black, curly hair, telling him that it would be all right. "We'll work it out, Danny, some way."

When Mark reached his home in Sausalito that afternoon, he was met by his son, Jacob, and before they saw anyone else, he told him about the sinking of the *Oceanic,* asking him where Clair was and how he thought they should break the news to her.

"She's in her room. But let me tell her, pop."

"I thought your mother should."

"No — no, I must. Do you know about Clair and me?"

"What is there to know?"

"We love each other. Some day we'll be married."

"Just like that?" Mark said.

"I don't know what you mean by 'just like that.' "

"When did this happen?"

"It didn't happen. It was there all the time, from the first day you brought her here."

"All right. Go ahead and tell her. We'll talk about the other thing later."

"There's nothing to talk about," Jacob said.

Mark went into the kitchen where Sarah and Martha — who was almost thirteen now — were setting the table for dinner. The kitchen was a large room, with floors of red Mexican tile and walls of blue tile, all of it brought by ship from Guadalajara. This was their favorite room in the house, full of light and color. Sarah glanced up, saw her husband's face, and asked him what had happened.

"We got a cable," he said. "The *Oceanic* was torpedoed and sunk. No survivors."

"You mean Jack is dead?"

"Jack — the whole crew."

Martha, listening, her eyes wide, suddenly burst into tears. Sarah went to her and held her close. "Does Clair know?"

"Jake wanted to tell her."

"Yes." She held Martha closer. "No hope?"

"It was observed by a British destroyer and they searched the area. Come outside with me for a moment."

They went out of the kitchen door onto the long, columned gallery that ran the length of the house. At the other end of the gallery, Jacob and Clair came out of the house and walked away through the garden. Jacob's arm was around her waist. She was a tall girl, almost as tall as he.

"Poor child," Sarah said.

"Did you know that he and Clair think they're in love with each other?"

"They don't think so, they are," Sarah said, tears running down her cheeks.

Mark gave her his handkerchief. "You mean you knew about this?"

"Of course I knew."

"Why didn't you tell me?"

"Why? Why? Why don't you open your eyes? You're as bad as Dan with those filthy ships." She struggled to control her tears. "If you were here sometimes — "

"I am here."

"Oh, yes, yes." She swallowed and took a deep breath. "Do you remember when you brought Jack here, when he was so drunk?"

"Yes?"

"He was here for three weeks. We used to sit in the kitchen and talk — we'd talk for hours. I think he was the loneliest, saddest man I ever knew. I told him to find a good woman and marry her, and he said that for a sailor to get married was just dumb and asking for trouble, and that anyway the only woman he could imagine wanting was me — "

"He said that?"

"Why not? I'm not an old frump." She was sobbing now.

"You're beautiful."

"How do you know? You never look at me." She wiped her eyes again. "And one day, he tried to make love to me. It breaks my heart to think about it. He was like a kid."

"What happened?" Mark asked.

"Nothing happened, you idiot! But I wish something had — yes, that's what I wish!" And with that, she ran back into the house, leaving him confused and bewildered.

Clair and Jacob sat on the ground under an old, twisted eucalyptus, a vantage point and a favorite place, with a long view across the glistening bay. He held her hand, and for almost half an hour they sat there in silence. Finally, Clair said, "I'll cry later. I have to be alone to weep."

"I understand."

"Anyway, Jake, I always knew it would happen like this. Every time he went up the coast in one of those little redwood schooners. They used to lose one in six. They'd pile up on the rocks. I was just a little kid, and I could never understand why men should risk their lives for some lousy lumber, and I lived my life that way, always sure he was dead and I was alone in the world, and I was so afraid, so afraid. But then I must have realized that

I had to stop being afraid and that I would somehow survive even if he never came back. Only I can't feel that he's dead. He's just not coming back — across the whole world. It's so far away."

"You don't have to ever be afraid, not anymore."

"Jake, he was like a big kid. He wasn't like your father. I don't mean Mark's not great. He is. But Jack was like a kid, always. He used to take me to fairgrounds and amusement parks, and he'd eat the cotton candy with me and stuff himself with hot corn and frankfurters, and he'd go on all the rides with me, and I swear he had more fun than I did, and then on the Fourth of July, if he hadn't shipped out, he'd find someplace where they were doing fireworks and take me there, and fireworks always bored me to death, but he loved them, and even when I was a little kid, I'd say to myself, All right, he likes it. I don't mean he was dumb. He read books, my goodness, he read every book Jack London ever wrote, and he read *The Sea Wolf* at least five times, and he got me to read *Moby Dick* when I was ten years old and I didn't understand a word of it but he made me read the whole thing — oh, my God, you better take me back to the house now, Jake, because I want to sit in my room in the dark and cry. I want to cry the whole thing out of me, please."

It was about seven o'clock that evening when Dan got to his home on Russian Hill. The house was crowded with people. He remembered vaguely that Jean had said something about a reception for Calvin Braderman, who had just completed a mural in a new post office or hotel or some such place. Dan pushed through the crowd, some of whom he knew and others of whom were complete strangers to him. Jean was nowhere in sight. Suddenly, he was confronting a dark, voluptuous, handsome woman, who told him, with a heavy Russian accent, that he must be Daniel Lavette.

"I am Manya," she said. "I am friend of Jean, model for Braderman, worshiper of art, and dying to meet finally the romantic Daniel Lavette."

"Yes. How do you do."

"That is all? You are legend in San Francisco, but indifferent to women. That is so sad."

He was trying to control himself. A dozen times, May Ling had said to him, "At least try to understand Jean and who she is and the people she likes and why she likes them — not to make her love you but at least to live without hate." It was all very well for May Ling to be cool and objective, but whatever he promised her, when he came into the situation his hackles rose and he was tied up in knots of frustration and anger.

Now Jean appeared. "Have you met my husband?"

"We met." Manya shrugged.

Tall, lovely, sheathed in blue silk that matched her blue eyes, Jean moved in command. Eyes followed her. Even in this situation, culminating all that had happened this day, Dan felt his stomach tighten with a kind of desperate wanting at the sight of her. He drew her away from the dark woman and said, "I must talk to you alone."

"Dan, I can't leave my guests."

"For just a moment. It's important."

She sighed and followed him into the library. "Now what is it?"

"Jean, I don't want to screw up your party, but it's been a bad day. We got word that the *Oceanic* was torpedoed off the British coast."

It took a few moments for her to assimilate the facts, to put them apart from where she had been before, and then she said, "How wretched, Dan. I'm sorry. But you are insured, aren't you?"

"There were no survivors. Jack Harvey went down with the ship. I must go to Sausalito tonight. His daughter's living there with the Levys."

"Yes, I suppose so. But Mark is there, isn't he?"

Dan stared at her in amazement.

"Don't look at me like that, Dan. Am I supposed to burst into tears? I don't even know this Jack Harvey of yours. I think I met him once — he was the captain, wasn't he?"

"Yes, he was the captain."

"Well, there is a war, you know."

"Yes. Well, I must go to Sausalito."

"Of course you must. And if it weren't Sausalito, you'd be launching a new ship or spending the night trying to find a crew or out on the pilot boat or at an emergency board meeting, so don't stand on ceremony. Just go." With that, she walked out of the room, leaving him there.

*

A week later, President Woodrow Wilson addressed a special session of Congress, saying, "With a profound sense of the solemn and even tragical character of the step I am taking and of the grave responsibilities which it involves, but in unhesitating obedience to what I deem my Constitutional duty, I advise that Congress declare the recent course of the Imperial German government to be nothing less than war against the government and people of the United States . . ."

A few days later, on the sixth of April 1917, the President signed the declaration of war that Congress had passed, and a little more than a month later, Congress passed the Selective Service Act and the draft began.

It was the beginning of summer and early on a Saturday morning when Jacob Levy received his induction notice. The family was at breakfast in the kitchen and Martha ran out when she heard the mail wagon. Jacob opened his letter and read it to them. Then there was silence, his mother and father and Clair and Martha staring at him, Sarah's face twitching as she fought to control herself.

Then Clair said firmly and quietly, "Jake, I don't want you to go."

"I've got to go."

"You don't have to do a damn thing," she said bitterly. "You can hide. You can take off. You can become a seaman on one of Mark's ships and stay on the run from here to Hawaii. I don't want you to go."

No word from the others. Sarah, Mark, and Martha simply sat in silence and listened.

"No, my darling," Jacob said, just as quietly and firmly. "I have to go."

"This war stinks. It stinks. It's a lousy rotten blood bath and there are no good guys and no bad guys, only a stinking lot of lice who feed kids into the slaughter."

"I know that. I know it only too well. The bread I eat was fertilized with the slaughter."

"That's a hell of a thing to say!" Mark exclaimed.

"It's true."

"It is not true," Mark said. "Can't you see that Clair is right? We can put you on a ship, and that will get you an exemption. You'll still be serving."

"Serving what? Levy and Lavette? The hell with that!" He leaped to his feet and stormed out of the house.

"Oh, my God," Sarah said, choking over the words. "Is this what we ran away from Russia for? First her father, and now Jake."

"Go out and talk to him," Mark said to Clair. "He'll listen to you. You're the only one he'll listen to."

"He's ready to start college," Sarah whimpered. "He's just a boy. Why are they doing this?"

"Talk to him," Mark said.

"All right," Clair agreed, "I'll talk to him. But I know him."

She found him sprawled under the eucalyptus tree, and she stretched out next to him, her head cradled in his arm. He loosened her hair, laying the thick red folds over her face.

"You know how long it takes me to comb it out," she complained.

"I know. You just got to suffer."

"Same as you, you're such a stinking martyr. You think you're going to atone for Levy and Lavette. Well, thank God I can talk freely out here. That's bullshit. Dan and Mark didn't make this war and they're no different from anyone else. There are maybe ten million people in this country who bring home money every week that's decorated with blood, and maybe it would be worse if the ships weren't getting through. Who are you to say?"

"I'm what I am."

"Oh, Jesus, why did I have to fall in love with a crazy Jew? You're all so convoluted and twisted you don't know your ass from your elbow."

"That's some sentence."

"Your guilts are so goddamn precious. Sarah runs the place with guilt and you run your life with guilt — and what about me?"

"What about you?"

"Jake, I love you so much that I swear, I swear to God that if anything happens to you, I'll slit my wrists. So if you want guilt, just wear that around your neck, and if you have to put on that lousy soldier suit to live with yourself, then for Christ's sake become a medic or a clerk or something like that, because if anything happens to you, I'll never forgive you, never, I'll just remember you as the worst unfeeling sonofabitch that ever lived."

"You got a remarkable vocabulary for a sweet young lady."

"I'm not a sweet young lady, Jake. I've been deposited for safekeeping in more saloons than you could shake a stick at, and I had baby sitters who were hookers when I was still teething. So don't think I don't mean what I say."

"Then shut up for a while and just let me hold you."

Stephan Cassala received his induction notice early in August, after his father had left the house for the city. When Anthony returned that evening and heard the news, Maria was gone.

"Well, where is she?"

"At church," Stephan said.

"Since when?"

"Since this morning."

"And you didn't go for her? What were you doing? You didn't come to work."

"I was thinking," Stephan said. "I had a good deal to think about and a good deal to do. Can't you understand? I have to report tomorrow."

"Where's mama?"

"At church, I told you. Rosa went there. I telephoned Clair at Sausalito. Jake's at Fort Dix in New Jersey."

"Both of them go away all day, and you sit here!" Anthony shouted. Then his face broke and he clasped Stephan in his arms. "Papa, don't cry," Stephan begged him. "It's all right."

Then they drove to the church. Maria and Rosa were at the altar rail, Maria a tragic lump of black-clad suffering. Anthony went to her and lifted her up, whispering in Italian, "The blessed mother will watch over him, my darling. Come home now. Together, we'll cook a nice dinner for everyone, like in the old days."

She had been kneeling so long she could hardly walk. Stephan and Anthony put their arms around her, and, followed by Rosa, they led her out of the church.

PART THREE

Sons and Daughters

One day, in August of 1918, over the protests of Wendy Jones, the childrens' nurse, Dan awakened his six-year-old son, Tommy, while Jean was still asleep. By seven o'clock, they were in Dan's new Pierce-Arrow, heading south toward San Mateo, and by ten o'clock they were in Dan's cutter working to windward out in the bay, and Dan was explaining to the excited child the virtues of the cutter design over the sloop, the great weight of lead in the keel, and how in the old days they were used by revenue agents to overtake smugglers. Tommy listened in delight, understanding very little of what his father said, but totally delighted with the fact that he had this enormous, exciting father of his entirely to himself, and thrilling to the rush of wind and spray.

At two o'clock, they were back at the berth, and then Dan drove to the Cassala house, where Maria served them with spaghetti and sausage, two delicious treats that had never been permitted on the Lavette table. Maria and Rosa fussed over the child, and the Cassala dogs, a pair of amiable collies, played with him and rolled him around on the lawn. Dan, meanwhile, telephoned his home with news that all was well, and since Jean was out, he had only Miss Jones to contend with. By eight o'clock that night, he walked into his home carrying a sleeping, dirty, and completely contented child.

He had expected a storm of anger from Jean, and was relieved when her only complaint was to the effect of his having a yacht that was berthed so far away.

"It's more Tony's than mine, and it's just a small boat," he said. "We can have one up here if you wish."

She had come to dislike boats increasingly. "No thank you,"

she said. "I have no desire for a San Francisco Bay complexion. But you ought to awaken me and tell me when the desire to kidnap your own child overtakes you."

Still and all, she was in rare good humor, telling him that she had kept dinner and that if he would clean up and change, they could eat together. He stopped in at the nursery to look at his son, wondering as he so often did how this small, blue-eyed, golden-haired child could be his. Both children were asleep, both of them blue-eyed and fair-skinned, as if denying the heritage of a swarthy, black-haired father. "You mustn't disturb them," Miss Jones whispered to him, and he patted her behind amiably.

"Please, Mr. Lavette," she complained, the prisoner of her whispers.

"You're a fine figure of a woman," he whispered back.

He was always amazed, surprised, flattered when Jean unbent. It did not happen often. She had become one of the leading figures in the New Art Society, an organization which proclaimed its intent to make San Francisco the leading art center of the United States, which had grown out of the Panama-Pacific International Exposition of 1915, and which had coalesced around the drive to save the Palace of Fine Arts and to preserve it for the future. She had made her place among the new elite of art and literature, and since Dan never denied her money and since she had ample funds of her own, she was constantly sought after as a patron and a sponsor of project after project, whether it was a piece of sculpture for the new city hall or a reception for Hamlin Garland, who might or might not be lured to San Francisco. These and other activities gave her a full life which apparently satisfied her. It was several years since she had taken to sleeping in her own bedroom, apart from him; and Dan accepted this not only as a rejection of any sexual advances on his part but also as a normal action in the habits of the rich, whose set of mores were still strange to him. He had fallen into an acceptance of a double life on his part, yet he was unable to cope with the thought that Jean might have a lover. Somewhere in his mind, hardly recognized, hardly dealt with, but there nevertheless, was the notion that Jean's passion for him might reawaken. How he would react under those circumstances he did not know; if he was totally unaware of the woman called Jean Lavette, he was very much aware of the image, cool, tall, beautiful, and totally admired in the circles that knew her; and on those occasions that he was with her, he basked in the admiration, still unable to comprehend that this creature was the wife of a dago fisherman, a kid from the wharf.

Strangely, this feeling lived with his relationship to May Ling. Jean was the illusion, May Ling was the reality and the validity, and to a degree he understood this completely. May Ling nourished him, educated him, adored him, and gave him a sense of himself. If anything happened to Jean — well, life would go on. If anything happened to May Ling — that was a thought he could not deal with. Yet a simple matter of interest and kindness on the part of Jean — perhaps better called a suspension of coldness and hostility — drove the thought of May Ling from his mind. Only Jean could truly accept him as a nabob, sitting opposite him at the dining room table, wearing the jewels he had given her, a pale blue gorget draped from her regal shoulders, her skin so pink and white, her eyes the icy blue that the dark-skinned, dark-eyed races of the earth had regarded for so long as the symbol of beauty and authority. When he sat that way with her, accepted by her, it did not matter a damn that she had closed her thighs to him; she was still his wife, and deep inside of him this was the core of desire.

He was still full of the contentment of the good day with the little boy. "I want him to know how to sail," he explained to Jean. "I sometimes think that's all I can give him. All the rest he gets from you."

"Oh, not at all, Dan. But you spend so little time with him."

"I know."

"I do try to find time for the children," she said, "and I always manage a few hours a day. One must. And now we're putting together a Keith memorial, and you can't imagine how demanding that is."

"Keith?"

"William Keith — lovely, dreamy landscapes, you know, very much in the style of George Inness. For heaven's sake, Dan, we have one of his paintings in the living room."

"Live Oaks," he remembered. He had never made a connection between the painting and reality, and had looked at it only long enough to know what it was called.

"But what great new mountain are you climbing?" she asked him. "I've lost touch completely with the realms of high finance.

All I know is that we seem to become richer and richer until it's almost gross."

"We're still very poor compared to the Seldons," he assured her.

"Still can't accept the Seldons. Daddy's very fond of you, truly."

"No, that's not it. It's a question of what we want to do and how to do it."

"Do what?"

"You know, we're selling out to Whittier."

"No, I didn't know that. I thought you detested him."

"I mentioned it to you."

"I couldn't take it seriously."

"Well, I'm not in love with Grant Whittier," Dan said, "but he wants our ships and he's willing to give us three million dollars for our fleet."

"But why sell them?"

"It's kind of complicated. Mark's kid, Jake, is over there, and he's been through Château-Thierry and Belleau Wood, and it's been a pretty rotten bloody thing, and Mark can't live with making any more money out of this war, and Stevie Cassala got a gut full of shrapnel and they shipped him home — six months in the hospital — and well, Whittier made us this offer — "

"Oh, really splendid," Jean said. "We all think this way, and we just bow to the Huns and explain to them that we just can't bear to make any profits, and therefore they can go ahead and take France and England and come over here too — "

"Come on, Jean, we're not interfering with the shipping. We're just transferring ownership. We've made enough money out of this war."

"It's just so typically a Jew thing. First he makes a fortune out of the war, and then the moment his son is in there, he begins to whine — "

"God damn it, how the hell can you say that!" Dan exclaimed. "There are no Seldons or Lavettes over there in France. I'm thirty — I could be over there. But I'm not."

"You have two children, and your role is vital to the war interests."

"Bullshit! I'm a millionaire, and I don't sail the ships; I own them!"

"If you're going to swear at me and talk Tenderloin, that finishes it."

"Jeany, Jeany," he said, "Why do we have to get into a scrap every time we talk to each other? I'm sorry, believe me, I'm sorry. And what I said isn't the full story, not by a long shot. There's a very basic difference of opinion between Whittier and me."

She stared at him coldly.

"Can I explain?" He reached across the table and touched her hand. "Please."

"All right. I suppose I shouldn't have said that about Mark. But he's such a skinny, sniveling thing."

She is your wife, Dan told himself. She doesn't know any better. She is what she is.

"I know he's very clever," she added. "I know that. They are, you know."

"Well, look," Dan said. "Whittier thinks the war will go on for years. I don't. I think it may end in a matter of weeks. And if I'm right and he's wrong, then cargo ships won't be worth the water they displace. They'll be a glut on the market."

"How can you say that, Dan? The Germans have been sinking everything."

"No, they have not. Do you realize that this country has built over three thousand ships during the past year or so. There's more cargo tonnage in the world now than ever in history."

"But the hunger and the suffering in Europe — even if the war ends."

"We're not carrying food. That's peanuts. We carry guns and munitions and oil and coal. We're feeding a monster that's going to drop dead, and that's why I'm glad we're out of it."

"Then what will you do?" she asked nervously, as if she were suddenly about to be confronted by his presence for the first time.

"There's enough to do." He grinned now. "We bought Spellman's Department Store."

"Spellman's? But what on earth for?"

"It makes sense. Mark talked me into it, but it makes sense. I think he wants something for Jake when Jake comes back. We're going to rebuild it and turn it into the best and biggest department store west of the Mississippi."

"But you in a store? You without a ship? I don't believe it."

"You're right — don't believe it. The store's only part of it. I'm going to build the biggest damn passenger ship that ever sailed out of this bay. We're going to open up the Hawaiian Islands and the whole damn Orient. She's going to be thirty thousand tons displacement, as big as the *Mauretania,* a floating palace, Jean — the ship of the future. How about that?"

"I just don't know what to say."

"Only one catch."

"Oh?"

"I still don't know where the money's coming from."

"But you have so much money."

"Not really. This may run to over ten million dollars." He shook his head. "Well, if you play with expensive toys, it costs."

She was watching him carefully, thoughtfully. "Why don't you go to daddy?"

"I did once."

"Things have changed. The Seldon Bank is the second largest in California. You know that."

"I guess I do," he said.

Roughly, the hole measured sixteen feet across, and it was about five feet deep at its deepest point, and nine men were crowded into it. It was raining lightly but steadily, and the bottom of the hole was a pool of mud and human vomit and nine mud-soaked men who were practically lying one on top of each other. On the lip of the hole was Lieutenant Matterson, or what remained of Lieutenant Matterson, who had been chopped nearly in half by bullets from a thirty-caliber heavy machine gun. For the past half-hour his body had moved spasmodically as the German machine gunner let go bursts at the lip of the hole.

In the hole were seven privates, Corporal Jake Levy, and Sergeant Joe Maguire. It was nighttime. The nine men listened to someone shouting something, but it was not until a pause in the gunfire and the shellfire that they were able to make out the words. The voice came from another hole somewhere.

"Matterson!" the voice was shouting. "Where the hell are you?"

"Who's that?" Maguire shouted back.

"Captain Peterson! Is that Matterson?"

"Matterson's dead."

"Who's in command? What have you got there?"

"Sergeant Maguire! Me, Corporal Levy, and seven men!"

"Well, Jesus Christ, have you set up a fuckin' rest home there! Get rid of that sonofabitch machine gun!"

Maguire looked at Levy; Levy looked at Maguire.

"Fuck him," Jake said.

"Motherfuckin' bastard," said Maguire.

The German machine gun opened up again, and Matterson's body leaped and twisted under the impact of the bullets.

"Maguire, goddamn you, I'll have your stripes and your ass!"

"Fuck you," Maguire said softly.

"What do we do?" Jake asked him.

Maguire looked from mud-caked face to mud-caked face. Levy was nineteen; Maguire was twenty; the other seven were mostly eighteen years to twenty years. The rain increased.

"Anyone want to try?" Maguire asked.

Another burst of fire dumped Matterson's body down upon them. His face had been shot away, and his brains splattered on the men in the shell hole.

"Oh, my God, I shit in my pants," one of the men whimpered.

Maguire and two other men pushed Matterson's body up out of the hole. Levy yelled, "We're pinned down, captain!"

"Who's that?"

"Corporal Levy."

"Well, you get that gun, Levy, you and Maguire!"

"We're pinned down."

"Shit, you're pinned down! Now you listen to me, you sheeny bastard — you get that gun!"

"Sweet man, that captain," someone said.

"All heart," said Maguire, and yelled, "Give us some cover! Where the hell are the field guns?"

"You get that gun!"

"We can go out each side," Levy said. "You take four men, I take three. That gun's not fifty yards from here. Let's try grenades, and then we'll make a run for it."

"Why?" Maguire asked hopelessly.

"God knows."

"So help me God, you motherfuckers," the captain's voice came, "I'll court-martial every last one of you!"

"Let's start throwing," Jake said, crouching, then pulling the pin and heaving the grenade. "Come on — throw!"

They clawed their way through the mud and out of the hole. The German machine gun opened up. Jake fell, got to his feet, ran clumsily in the mud, threw another grenade, and then as a star shell lit up the place, saw the five Germans crouched around their gun. Someone else heaved a grenade at them, and Jake was firing into the burst of flame and mud. Then he and another man flung themselves into the hole and insanely drove their bayonets into the single German who was still alive. They lay there in a tangle of dead, torn human flesh, and then Jake began to yell, "We got them, sarge! Don't shoot! Don't shoot!"

But he never saw Maguire alive again, nor anyone else who had been in the shell hole with him except Fredericks, who had plunged into the machine-gun nest with him.

Ever since their first beginnings in America, it had been a practice among many Eastern European Jews to christen — if indeed such a term can be applied to Jewish naming — their children in duplicate. In other words, the rabbinical birth certificate would bear a Hebrew or Biblical name, while the civil birth certificate would bear an Anglo-Saxon version or a name which might be considered American. Mark Levy, on his rabbinical certificate, was Moses Levy, named after his paternal grandfather. In naming his son Jacob, he abandoned the practice, although at Sarah's insistence his daughter, Miriam, became Martha. For some reason, Sarah abhorred the name Miriam.

Rabbi Samuel Blum, who remembered Mark's father as one of the founders of his small orthodox synagogue, called Mark "Moishe," which is the Hebraic pronunciation of the name Moses, and now he said to him, "It's been a long time, Moishe. You've changed. And you've prospered. Tell me about Sarah and the children."

"They're well. Jacob's alive and unwounded, thank God."

"He's in the army?"

"God help me, yes. Very much in it. Now he's on leave in Paris. They gave him a decoration and a field commission of lieutenant, and God willing, this cursed war will be over before he goes back."

"God willing."

They sat in the rabbi's study, a small room crowded with books; and now they sat in silence for a while, the rabbi, a short, bearded, tired man of seventy-one years, waiting for Mark to speak again, his blue eyes watching him thoughtfully, set in nests of wrinkles. He had been rabbi of the congregation ever since it came into being in 1880.

Finally, Mark took an envelope out of his pocket and handed it to the rabbi.

"What's this?"

"Guilt, I suppose."

The rabbi opened the envelope and stared at a check for two thousand dollars. "A princely gift. Are you that rich?"

"Yes."

"How old are you, Moishe?"

"Almost forty, if you count the years."

"And how long since you came to the synagogue? I'm not reproving you," he added hastily. "I'm curious."

"Ten years I suppose. We live in Sausalito now."

"And is this for your son's life?" the rabbi asked, holding up the check, smiling to take the sting out of his words.

"No, for my own guilt, like I said."

"Well — most contributions are. We can use it, and I am very grateful."

"I'm confused," Mark said.

"It's a normal state." The rabbi shrugged. "When was life not confusing?"

"I don't know who I am," Mark said, forcing the words. "I have become rich out of this rotten war. I lie awake every night in terror thinking about my son. I lost my wife somewhere — oh, she still loves me and I love her, but somewhere we lost each other, and I'm afraid of death."

"We all are."

"And my son is in love with a Christian."

"Ah."

"Otherwise, everything is fine."

The rabbi smiled. "Of course. Tell me about the girl."

"She's a fine, beautiful girl."

"And your son is determined to marry her?"

"My son is in France."

"Yes, but the girl. How does she feel about your son?"

"She loves him."

"She does not mind the fact that he is Jewish?"

"No."

"Well, Moishe, I'm a rabbi. I don't like to see our people marry outside of the religion."

"What should I do?"

"What does Sarah say you should do?"

"She says I should keep my nose out of their business."

"Ah. Tell me, is there an Orthodox synagogue in Sausalito?"

"I don't know. I don't think so."

"If you can find ten Jewish families, you can start one, and then come to me and I'll find you a rabbi. This won't take away your confusions, but it will be very good for your guilts."

"You still did not tell me what I should do about my son."

"Love him. Help him. What else can you do with a son?"

"And the girl?"

"Listen to Sarah. I could tell you to trust in God, but unfortunately that's not enough. He has given us too much free will. We have to do a little something on our own. You're almost forty. That's a good time to become Jewish."

"I was born Jewish, rabbi."

"So you were. And again, speaking for the synagogue, I thank you for this princely gift."

The doctor was very specific about Stephan Cassala's diet. He was discharged from the army hospital after Dan's visit with his son to the Cassala place at San Mateo. His father drove him down the Peninsula in the Cassala limousine, somewhat in awe of this thin, pale wraith of a man, so unsmiling and depressed. Maria wept and embraced him and crooned over him. All of which troubled the family doctor who came to see him that same day.

"I know you will want to feed him and see some flesh on his bones," the doctor said. "But his stomach has taken a terrible beating. Cream of wheat, warm milk, boiled eggs, soft, some well-cooked green vegetables, but no cheese, no spices, no sausage, no meat, no green pepper — " He was trying to remember what else came into the Italian diet.

"But he will die with such food," Maria pleaded.

"No. He will get well with such food. Now mind what I say."

In any case, Maria had to beg him to eat, and whatever he ate caused him pain. For the first few days that he was home, he said almost nothing. Stephan had always been gentle and soft-spoken; the gentleness remained but he was turned in on himself. When the weather was good, he would sit on the lawn, gazing into the distance; and once Rosa had seen him like that — herself out of sight — with tears rolling down his sallow cheeks. She told her mother and then regretted it, for Maria burst into tears herself and could not be consoled. She spent more and more hours in church at the altar rail, and when one day Stephan smiled at her and said, "Mama, I'm going to be all right. So stop worrying," she was convinced that her prayers had overcome the hideous American food that was destroying her son.

Dan drove down to see Stephan, this time with May Ling and their ten-month-old child, called Joseph after Dan's father. His relationship with May Ling was becoming increasingly complex. Neither of them had wanted to face the fact of abortion; both of them had wanted the child desperately, May Ling because it was Dan's child and Dan out of his need to cement a relationship that had become in some strange way the bedrock of his existence. But to have the child in the secrecy that surrounded their lives together was impossible. May Ling had to have a place to go — and therefore over a year ago Dan had gone to Cassala and poured out his heart.

Having told his story, Dan was ready for anything — rage, disgust, contempt — anything but the long, thoughtful silence that followed. Finally, Cassala said, "Danny, I got two sons, you and Stevie. You love this Chinese woman?"

Dan nodded.

"Feng Wo, he knows this?"

"I think so. He must. We never said one word about it."

"And when Jean finds out? What then?"

"I don't know. Why should she find out?"

"Danny, Danny, you talk like a child. You marry a Protestant woman who has no love for you. God forgive me that I, a Catholic, should say this, but I must. For two people to live without love is no good. We can get an annulment. I have enough influence."

"I can't. It's not being a Catholic. I'm a rotten Catholic."

"Why? For what you must give her? Give it to her."

"Tony, I don't know why."

Cassala pressed it no further. Danny needed a home for a pregnant woman; that was enough. At the library, May Ling had already told them that she was married and expecting a child. For the last two months of her pregnancy, she was at San Mateo with the Cassalas. Curiously enough, both Maria and Rosa accepted her with warmth and affection, perhaps in part because of their loneliness in a community so alien to them and in part because no one could be with May Ling very long and resist her charm and openness.

Now, driving down the Peninsula, the baby asleep in May Ling's arms, Dan asked May Ling not to mention to Cassala his plans to build the passenger vessel.

"Why not?" she wanted to know.

"Because I'm going to Seldon for the money."

There was a long silence as they drove on. Dan glanced from the road to the sleeping child. He had his father's curly black hair and his mother's ivory skin — his own child, a child he had been permitted to name for his father.

"Why?" she asked at last.

"Why what?"

"Why do you go to Seldon? Why not Tony?"

"Because it's too big for Tony. If I blow it, let Seldon bleed, not Tony."

"If it's that dangerous a gamble, why should the Seldon Bank back you? Or is Seldon buying you?"

"That's a hell of a thing to say."

"I suppose so. You know, Danny, Chinese women are acquiescent. I suppose it's in our blood. I'm also a little frightened. I never was before."

"Of what?"

"Of losing you. I'm not your wife, and sometimes I feel that I never will be."

"You're my wife and that's my child."

"And Jean?"

"Let me do it in my own way, please, baby. I'll leave her. You have to give me time."

"Time or anything else," she said sadly. "You know that I give you whatever you ask, Danny."

At San Mateo, Maria and Rosa enveloped May Ling and the baby with affection. It took very little to bring Maria to tears, and almost as soon as she held little Joseph in her arms, she began to weep. May Ling smiled slightly as Dan fled. He couldn't bear the sight of tears. Since it was a weekday, Cassala was at the bank. Dan walked out onto the lawn, where Stephan was sprawled in a lounge chair. He waved at Dan and got to his feet as Dan pulled a chair up to the lounge.

"Don't get up. Take it easy, Steve."

Stephan embraced him. "My God, it's good to see you, Danny."

He was skin and bones. "How do you feel?" Dan asked him.

"Better, better. I'm going to be all right."

"You're damn right you are."

"Last night I slept through. First time in months without pills. I still have some pain, but the doctor says it's gas mostly."

"Tony's worried sick about you."

"Pop's worried, mama's worried, Rosa's worried — Dan, they're driving me crazy. She looks at me and she cries. She talks to me about getting married. She found a nice Italian girl for me. I want to get an apartment in the city, and every time I mention it, mama begins to weep." His eyes went past Dan to the house. May Ling was coming across the lawn.

"Look, let me explain — " Dan began.

"No need, Danny. I know." He got to his feet. May Ling came to him and took his outstretched hand in both of hers.

"I am so glad to meet you, Steve. Your mother made me feel like her daughter, so I feel like your sister. If you heard Chinese prayers, they were mine. I am responsible for the most confused Catholic priest in the Peninsula, who twice a week would see a pregnant Chinese lady at the altar rail next to your mother. Now I am going to leave the two of you. I'll see you later."

When she had left, Stephan said, "She's beautiful — and charming. What a delightful woman!"

"I know."

"Look, it's none of my business. The thing is, well, you're both here and I'm here, and we're alive. I never understood the virtue of simply being alive. I sit here and feel the sun and the wind, and I keep telling myself I'm alive."

"Was it very bad?"

"You know, Danny, I don't talk about it because there's no sense talking about it. I had lots of time to read these past few months. I read *War and Peace.* Tolstoi says everything said about war is a lie. He's right. I had five days of it before my gut was ripped open. I didn't kill anyone. I didn't do anything except crawl in the mud and watch people die. And be afraid. Oh, shit — the hell with it. What about Jake Levy? Is he all right?"

"As far as I know. He got a field commission. I think they call it that. He's a lieutenant."

"Still there?"

"That's right."

"Poor bastard," Steve said.

The Brockers had purchased some forty acres of land in what would someday be downtown San Francisco. The purchase price was five dollars an acre. Eventually, a single acre was sold by the son of the original Brocker, a placer miner, for seventy-two thousand dollars, and that was before the price truly began to rise. Alan Brocker was the third generation in California, and he had returned to San Francisco from Harvard College to find that Jean Seldon had married a fisherman called Daniel Lavette.

During the seven years since that event, from which Alan Brocker emerged with his heart unbroken, he had been married long enough to produce a child, avoid the draft, and get divorced, had inherited eleven million dollars, give or take a few hundred thousand, upon the death of his father, and had done Europe — as it was put — and with the approach of the war had returned to San Francisco. He purchased a small but luxurious house on Jones Street, kept a sloop on the bay, played tennis, and kept two saddle horses. If not the most sought-after single man in Jean's set, he was certainly one of them, perhaps too tarnished by divorce and reputation for some of the best families but nevertheless eagerly welcomed where a single man was required at a dinner party. In that capacity, he and Jean had been paired off a number of times — on occasions where Dan could not or would not be present. Twice, he had taken Jean home, the second time venturing a kiss on her lips which had turned into a passionate embrace.

During the months that followed, they met surreptitiously at least once or twice a week. He kept his horses at a stable in Marin County, and on occasion they would meet there and ride together. When they lunched alone, it would be in some out-of-the-way restaurant where they would not be recognized. For weeks, Jean brushed aside any serious advances on his part, but they were old friends who had known each other as children, and when he finally suggested an afternoon at his house, she accepted with full knowledge of what might follow. In her mind, she had turned over and over the question of an affair with him. He was a good-looking man, perpetually sunburned, with bright blue eyes, set off by dark skin, and a high, thin nose; he was of medium height and dedicated to keeping himself trim. The question in her mind was whether she desired to have sex with any man; and when at last she allowed him to take her to bed, she was far more amazed than he by the passion it unleashed in her.

Lying naked next to her, touching and caressing her beautiful white body with almost professional skill, Brocker said to her, "You've been starved, my love. What is that oversized fisherman of yours — a gelding?"

"Let us say a disinterested stallion."

"Disinterested? Shit."

"I love it when you're foul."

"Women like you always do."

"That is truly foul. What a disgusting thing to say."

"You don't look horrified."

"You're the second man in my life, Alan. I've been with no one else."

"Indeed."

"Believe it or not — I don't really care."

"Do you care for me?"

"As what?"

"You're a bitch, you know. You're a thoroughgoing bitch."

"No end to your compliments."

"I'll amend it. The loveliest bitch in California."

"That limits it."

"Do you want the world? Let me tell you something, Jean. I've never known another woman like you. Do you realize how long I've looked at you and wanted you?"

"And now that you have me?"

"I don't have you. The fisherman has you."

"He doesn't think so," she said. "Alan, stop petting me. Your hands don't stop and your mind is a thousand miles away."

"Not a thousand miles. I was only wondering how we could be together for a few days."

"Don't be pushy. Suppose I divorced him. Would you marry me?"

"No," he said flatly.

"You really thought about that. Why?"

"I would never marry again, not you, not any woman. I have all the money I need and I have you."

"Don't be so goddamn sure about that!"

"Ah, the fangs show. I'll bet you're something when you lose that temper of yours."

"Perhaps."

"You'd like me to say I love you?"

"No. Because I'm not a bit sure that I care very much about you."

"But you do, even if the fisherman still has a foot in the door."

"Now you begin to bore me, Alan."

But the excitement of the affair overrode the fact that he was indeed a boring man. Dan talked about everything, the war, his ships, his dreams — at least he did when she permitted a conversation to take place. Alan talked only of the people he met and the food he ate — and horses. Jean was interested in neither food nor horses. Yet he made love to her, and that did not bore her.

A few weeks after they had been to bed together, Jean said to him at lunch one day, "I want something, and I don't know how to get it. Perhaps you could help me."

"Perhaps I could. What do you want?"

"I want to know who my husband has been sleeping with."

"Oh? Why?"

"Reasons."

"How do you know he's been sleeping with anyone? You tell me he's your willing slave when you want a slave. Could be the beast is satisfied with beauty and his gonads are quiescent."

"Don't be disgusting."

"You like it in bed."

"We're not in bed. Whatever else Dan is, he's very much a man. Now can you help me or not?"

"You want to open a can of worms. My dear Pandora, let it lie. Right at this moment, we have a very good thing going, and if your fisherman is banging a filly, why it's simple justice. Quid pro quo, as the lawyers say."

"I told you not to be foul. And don't call me Pandora. I can't abide your wretched metaphors."

"The hell with my metaphors. If you do find out in the affirmative, what will you do? Divorce him?"

"No. Seldons do not divorce."

"Well, there's a statement of principle."

"Will you help me or won't you?"

"All right. Your husband has a secret liaison, and you want to know. The only thing I can suggest is that you hire a detective."

"Do they do that kind of thing?"

"Their bread and butter, my dear."

"I can't be involved in this," she said uncertainly. "I can't go to a detective agency. You do understand that, don't you, Alan?"

"I suppose you can't."

"Will you do it for me, please?"

"All right. Be it on your head. I'll go to the Pinkertons. They're very good at this kind of thing."

"How do you know?"

"My wife hired them. You're not the first one to think of this, bless you."

Clair Harvey had come into ten thousand dollars' insurance money when her father died. She had not known about the insurance, a company plan which Dan and Mark had instituted; as for savings, Jack Harvey had none. He spent what he earned, easily, sometimes grandly, often eloquently. When Clair first came to live with the Levys, she sought work in Sausalito. Until she found a part-time job at Grundy's Hardware Emporium, she tried to do enough cleaning and chores around the place to pay for her keep — resisting all of Sarah's arguments that simply to have her there was reward enough. When the insurance was paid, she gave up the job at Grundy's, which she disliked intensely, and after much argument persuaded Sarah to accept ten dollars a week for her board. She and Sarah were both strong-minded women, and both of them became somewhat hysterical before the matter was settled. Sarah's rationale was to put the money in a jar — whence it would some day be returned as a gift.

Clair, however, was far from idle. Not only did she continue to help with the housework, but she dedicated each day to the preparation of a history, anywhere between five and ten pages, of the past twenty-four hours, both in and out of the Levy establishment — a history that was folded, addressed, and dispatched to France the following morning. When this was finished, she had sixty-one letters from Jake, to be read and reread. While occupied thus, she had the adoration of Martha Levy, who at age thirteen was being transformed by the action of numerous ductless glands from a chunky child into a round-limbed, lovely, and gifted young lady.

There was a process in those times called "elocution," which along with music and dancing lessons constituted the extracurricular activity of each properly raised young lady. It consisted of a technique of dramatic recitation, with much expression, of selections ranging from Shakespeare to William Cullen Bryant to Eugene Field and including such gems as "Oh, Captain My Captain" and "Spartacus' Last Address to His Men." Martha reveled in it, and Clair's necessary return for Martha's interest in her letters was to listen admiringly to the current recitation. For all that, the two had become very close. Clair allowed Martha to read some of Jake's letters, and in turn Martha would listen raptly to Clair's current news report to Jake, as for example: "Dan says that the people who run the Overseas Shipping Company are out of their minds because they have just built and launched a ship made of concrete. Martha's cat died."

"Put in his name," Martha said.

"The cat's name was Frederick. Did you know that street cars are now running through Twin Peaks Tunnel? And speaking of cats, this weekend Martha and I are going to caulk and paint your catboat. Yellow with a black horizontal stripe. Billy Adams put it in the sling and took it out of the water for us. I have been reading *Spoon River Anthology.* It's beautiful, and I sent you a copy yesterday, but who knows whether you will ever receive it. Dan saw Steve Cassala at San Mateo, and he says that he, I mean Steve, is all right now with his wounds all healed except that he still has trouble with his stomach. Sunny Jim (you know I mean Mayor Rolph) came over to Marin County yesterday for a meeting with Mark and Dan. I don't know why they couldn't all meet in the city, but Mark says that Sunny Jim likes Marin County and he likes to ride the ferry every chance he gets. I think he likes tugboats most because that's all they talked about — according to Sarah — when they were in the kitchen eating. She made them gefilta fish, but I don't think I am spelling it right, and Dan who hates fish so much ate it anyway. It's the only fish he will eat — "

"Do you think he likes all that junk, the way you mix it up?" Martha asked. "It's very nice, Clair, but I don't know."

"He seems to like it. I used to tell him how much I loved him, but that made him feel rotten. It's only natural."

"Why?"

"Because we can't do anything about it, and it just makes him feel rotten. I still tell him, but not as much."

"I suppose you know what you're doing. Can I practice now?"

"Which one?"

"The quality of mercy."

"O.K." She stretched out on the bed. "Give it a lot of zip."

"It's better if you watch."

"I'm watching. Look. I'm propped up."

"Is anyone downstairs? I want to be real loud. Dameon says that if the second balcony can't hear it, it's no good."

"Who on earth is Dameon?"

"Dameon Fenwick. He's our dramatic teacher. He's beautiful."

Clair was convulsed with giggles.

Hurt, Martha said, "I don't think it's funny."

"But darling, no one has a name like Dameon. Dameon Fenwick, it's just impossible."

"You just wait until you meet him. You'll swoon. He says I have talent."

"So do I. The second balcony?"

"That's where the important people are, the people who don't have any money but love the theater. They must hear every word."

Clair rose and closed the door to her bedroom. "Right. Now go to it. *The Quality of Mercy,* by William Shakespeare."

"That's not the name of the play. That's Portia's great speech in *The Merchant of Venice.*"

Coming into the kitchen one day, Clair found Sarah in tears, a letter in her hand. Clair had missed the post, and since the letter in Sarah's hand was obviously from overseas, Clair experienced an electric shock of terror. "What happened?" she cried out. "What happened to Jake?"

"He's safe. No more fighting. They made him an instructor, and he's been transferred to a training base near Nantes. Can you imagine? He's out of it. Oh, thank God, thank God!"

The two women embraced. "You frightened me so," Clair said. "My heart stopped. Why do you cry when you're happy? That's a terrible thing to do."

"I know, I know. Sit down, darling, I'll make coffee. Tell me, where is Nantes?"

"I'll get the atlas."

She ran for the book, while Sarah put the coffee on to boil, and then they pored over the map of France. "Here," Clair cried. "Oh, good, good. It's miles and miles from the fighting. They must keep him there, they must. Let me read it." The letter was disconnected, full of passages the censor had inked out. "He doesn't like being an officer. Well, I like it. He feels guilty. Oh, Jake, you're such a fool!"

"Who is this man Maguire?" Sarah asked her.

"Do you know, I think they find the stupidest men in the army and make them censors — or generals. Maguire was his sergeant. He was killed. Jake didn't go into any details, but he writes a lot about Maguire."

"If they only keep him there."

"Sarah, Dan had lunch with General Oglethorpe at the Presidio and the general says that all the very smart gentlemen in Washington say the war will be over in another month. He even let drop some hints that the Germans had put out peace feelers."

"God willing." She poured the coffee. "And when Jake comes back, you'll be married?"

"If he still wants to."

"What nonsense!" She paused and Clair looked at her inquiringly. "Well, I don't know how to say this. Mark is becoming Jewish again, ever since Jake went to France."

"Wasn't he always?"

"Yes and no. You know, I was born in Russia, in Kiev. I came here when I was seven years old, to New York. My marriage to Mark was arranged by his father before I ever saw him — well, that's the way they used to do things. It worked out all right. I suppose it might have been better but it also could have been a lot worse, believe me. Anyway, I grew up Orthodox, which means all kinds of rules and rituals which I won't bore you with — "

"I know," Clair said. "Kosher food and that kind of thing."

"Yes. Well, when we were first married, I used to argue with Mark and I was hurt and frightened by the way he ignored everything religious. A lot Mark didn't know and mostly he didn't care. His father came to America from someplace in Poland in eighteen sixty-nine, and he got a job with a wandering peddler. Would you believe it, just with a wagon and a mule, he and his wife wandered across the country from New York to San Francisco? It took them two years, just buying and selling pots and pans and cloth and anything else you could think of, and finally they ended up here. Mark's father still had some feelings about being Jewish, and he was one of the people who started a synagogue in San Francisco, but Mark let go of it all until now, and now he's decided that he's Jewish again. Which is all right, you understand — "

"But he doesn't like the notion of his son marrying a Christian?" Clair said softly.

"Mark loves you. You know that." She looked at Clair curiously. "Darling, I never asked you before. What is your religion?"

"Heaven only knows."

"But you must know."

"Sarah, the truth is that I don't. Oh, I'm sure I'm some kind of Protestant. Jack never spoke about my mother, and as far as Jack was concerned, he hated preachers so much he used to froth at the mouth when he met one. He would never set foot in a church. Poor darling, he told me once that when he died he was to be cremated and have the ashes scattered up the Redwood Coast, because that's where all his buddies were."

"Didn't it ever bother you, not being anything?"

"No, because I'm myself."

"Do you believe in God?"

"Sarah, I never gave it much thought. Oh, when Jake and I would be out on the bay in the catboat, with the wind blowing and the sun in the sky, then I'd just feel that everything was all right and the way it should be, but with this lousy war—do you believe in God, Sarah?"

She nodded. "Not that I don't get angry with Him. I'm just not clever enough to understand how He does things. Clair," she said, "if we asked you to become Jewish, would you?"

Clair thought about it for a while, her brow furrowed. Then she shook her head. "No."

"But why not—if you're not anything else that's important?"

"Because I have to be what I am, whatever it is. Jake and I talked about that, about what we are. It never made any difference to me that Jake was Jewish. I hate to say this, Sarah, but I don't think you and Mark understand Jake one bit. Mark thinks that Jake will come into that big department store that he and Dan are building, but you know that he won't. It wouldn't make any difference to me if I did what you and Mark want, but I think it would make a lot of difference to Jake."

"How? How could it make a lot of difference to Jake?"

"I can't explain that. I wasn't just keeping company with Jake when he went overseas. We're like one person. I have to be what I am. He has to be what he is. That's the only way I can explain it."

In October of that year, with an appetite whetted but not satiated by the endless slaughter in Europe, death went to work with something called influenza, for want of a better name. In the army, more men died of influenza than in battle, and in the cities the undertakers, until now separated by an ocean from the windfall of death, began to reap their share of the bloody harvest. The hospitals filled to overflowing, and day after day weary horses dragged the hearses up the steep hills of the city. Without justice—explained by the physicians as the action of a thing called antibodies—some were chosen and some were spared. In the house on Russian Hill, good health prevailed, but one day in his office, Dan received a frantic call from May Ling.

"Please come as soon as you can."

When he reached the little house on Willow Street, the doctor had just departed, shrugging his shoulders wearily and telling May Ling, as she informed Dan, that she must keep the child cool with damp compresses and try to get him to drink as much liquid as possible. All the rest of that day and through the night, the boy's fever rose, reaching one hundred and six degrees, while May Ling and Dan sat by the bedside and prayed and waited. Dan watched May Ling weep. That had never happened before. They sat there, wordlessly, helplessly observing the agony of an eleven-month-old bit of human flesh named Joseph, something out of their loins and love, dying, as they saw it. They touched hands. When they embraced, it was because in the dark terror of the night, they had been reduced to nothing, impotent specks in a gigantic, senseless universe. And then, as the first gray image of dawn appeared through the windows of the child's room, the fever broke.

Dan went downstairs, mixed himself a stiff drink, tasted it, and pushed it away. An hour later, the nurse Dan had found arrived, and May Ling was able to leave the child and come downstairs.

"Do you want some breakfast?" she asked Dan.

He shook his head.

"I think we should both eat something," she said. "It will help nothing if we get sick. Joey will be all right now. The nurse says that's the pattern it takes. She says children take it better than older people. You've been away all night, Dan. Should you telephone them?"

"The hell with it."

"You have a family and children."

"Have I? I think I only have you and that kid upstairs. That's the whole world. The rest of it can fuck off and be damned."

"You're all right now." She smiled. "But no such language in front of the nurse. She's a prissy little lady."

May Ling went into the kitchen, and a little later Dan's nostrils were awakened to the smell of frying bacon. He ate hungrily, three eggs, six strips of bacon, buttered rolls, and two cups of coffee.

"You know," May Ling said, "you're putting on weight."

"First you beg me to eat — "

"If I don't tell you, who will?"

"I put on a few pounds. I'm two hundred and ten. I'll take care of it."

"Do you know, Danny," she said, "do you know what I thought about mostly last night?"

"What I thought about."

"No. Well, yes, I thought that he would die, and that was like a hot iron cutting into my heart. But more than that, I kept thinking about how much I love you. Danny, here is something I promised myself I would never say. I'm going to say it. Never leave me — never leave me, Danny."

"Now don't cry again."

"I won't. I'm not. I'm so tired." She was falling asleep at the table. Over her protests, he picked her up in his arms and carried her up to the bedroom and laid her on the bed. She was asleep as he pulled off her shoes. Then he went into Joseph's room.

"How is he?"

"He'll be all right," the nurse said.

"My wife is sleeping. Let her sleep as long as you can."

"That Chinese lady is your wife?"

"Yes, ma'am, she is." Dan took out a roll of bills and peeled off fifty dollars. "This is a bit extra — for you. The kid means a lot to us. Take good care of him."

Lying came easily, or was it a lie? In his own mind, May Ling was his wife. Then, God help me, he would ask himself again and again, what am I doing with Jean?

He left Willow Street and came home. It was ten o'clock in the morning and he had not slept; he was unshaven, and his clothes were wrinkled. A single day without shaving brought a blue black mask to his face, and when he came into the house on Russian Hill, Jean regarded him with a mixture of disgust and anger.

"You bastard, where have you been?" she exploded.

"In Oakland. We had trouble at the pier there. A cargo net broke, and two of the men were injured."

"And you never thought to call?"

Lies, lies, lies — it screamed in his mind. What in God's name am I doing? "I sat all night with death," he said slowly, his face contorted with his inner agony. "I tried to push it away."

The statement was unlike him, not his words nor any way of thinking Jean had ever known him to engage in; it was as if he were quoting. Her anger washed out. "Mother is very sick," she said. "I'm sorry I got so mad. You should have called."

"I should have. What is it, the flu?"

"Yes. I'm going over there now."

"I think I have to sleep," he said, very slowly. "I'm tired. A few hours."

"I'll call you later," Jean said, and then she left.

Stretched out on his bed, Dan slid into a nightmare. First he tried to remember what he had just said to Jean. His lies were becoming so thoughtless and facile that the moment after they were spoken they slipped away. He had completed the deal with Whittier a week ago. Did Jean know that the ships were no longer his? What did he tell her? A cargo net had broken. Well, it would still be his responsibility; the agreement said that Whittier would take possession only after the ships discharged cargo at New York, Newark, or San Francisco; but was there a ship due in at Oakland? He thought so, but his mind refused to function properly. The *Anacreon* was due in from Hong Kong. To hell with it! Let her find out. He dozed off trying to remember what the name *Anacreon* meant, if it meant anything. Then, in his dream, he was on the dock, under a bulging cargo net, and it broke. A warning bell was clanging in his ears, but it was too late, and slowly as if they were held in transparent molasses, the great crates were descending on top of him.

The telephone awakened him. It was Hemmings, the Seldon's butler, and he asked whether this was Mr. Daniel Lavette.

"Yes, yes."

"Mrs. Lavette asked me to telephone, sir. I bear unhappy tidings. Mrs. Thomas Seldon has just passed away. Mrs. Lavette will remain here until you arrive."

Dan stripped and showered and shaved, angry at his own lack of pity or grief or remorse. But then, he had hardly known his mother-in-law. During the seven years of his marriage, she had remained safely behind her rigid barrier of class and family pride, never forgetting for a moment that while she lived in California her family, the Asquiths, were from Boston and could claim relationship with the Adamses and the Lodges. He could count on one hand the times he had been suffered to kiss her cool cheek, and while she had never been nasty to him, he could not recall that she had ever been kind.

Thomas Seldon opened the door of his home for Dan, and said chokingly, "Good to see you, my boy. You'll have to take care of things. I'm in no condition to think, and poor Jean is devastated. The whole world breaking up — she was too young too young."

Two days later, the funeral services for Mary Seldon were held in the Founders' Crypt of the still-unfinished Grace Cathedral, within sight of the Seldon residence. In spite of the fact that the crypt was inadequate for the numbers who would have come to the proceedings, Thomas Seldon specified to Dan that he desired it to be there and no other place. A small piece of property which his wife had owned on Nob Hill had been willed to the cathedral. In this decision, Seldon was following his wife's wishes; and during the two days after his wife's death, he talked to Dan at length about this and other matters. Dan realized with some surprise that Seldon was clinging to him desperately, that one of the three or four richest and most powerful men in San Francisco was to all effects utterly alone in the world with no one else he felt he could turn to. Dan took care of all the arrangements. Bishop Nichols gave the funeral oration, commending Mary Seldon as a woman whose graciousness and beauty would long be remembered and whose generosity had contributed so unselfishly to the great Episcopal cathederal that would someday rise over this crypt.

A few days later, Dan and Jean and Thomas Seldon gathered in the library of the Seldon mansion for the reading of Mary Seldon's will. There were a few bequests to various charities. The bulk of her estate, ten thousand shares of stock in the Seldon Bank, various other stocks and bonds as well as some fifty thousand dollars in cash, went to her daughter, Jean.

Training recruits to crawl on their bellies, their heads down, their guns sliding in front of them, Lieutenant Jacob Levy was informed that he was wanted at the post headquarters. There, Colonel Albert Broderick said to him, "I'm sorry, Jake, but the honeymoon's over. It's open season on lieutenants. Jones is cutting your orders. You go up to the front tomorrow morning. I wish to hell we had some other replacements. You had your lumps."

"Maybe I'll be lucky," Jake said.

"I hope so."

But he had no faith in his luck; he had used it up. He had made friends, good friends, dear friends, the kind of friends who clutch you and look at death through your eyes, and they were all dead. Even Steve Cassala had been torn open, ripped apart, and he thought of Steve now as his command car lurched and swayed over a rutted, muddy road through the Argonne Forest. A misty rain had been falling; then the sun broke through to reveal the tortured, blackened sticks that had once been trees in this demented landscape.

When he reached his unit, there was no welcome. Lieutenants were in the nature of condemned men, and the men who were only half condemned looked at him with blank, tired, bearded faces, their eyes dead already. His captain nodded at him, took his papers, told him to keep his head down, and led him to his dugout.

"Get some sleep," the captain said. "It's been too quiet. Tomorrow, the shit hits the fan."

But it was quiet all that night. Jake didn't sleep. He lay there, thinking. He let the pictures flow through his mind, pictures of things he was convinced he would not see again, the sun on the water of Richardson Bay, the catboat slipping past San Pedro Point on that long, long sail he had taken with Clair through the narrows to Petaluma Creek, the stillness while they drifted for hours, becalmed and content, the old Spanish house at Sausalito, his mother and his father. He pictured them all, and lay awake in his pool of melancholy. Perhaps he dozed. The voice of his captain came out of the blob of daylight that marked the entrance to the dugout — without rancor, strangely gentle: "Levy, you lucky sonofabitch."

He sat up, pulled on his shoes, and stared at the captain.

"Listen."

It was quiet. There were voices outside, but otherwise it was quiet.

"I think it's over," the captain said uncertainly.

Jake went outside into the trench. The men were leaning high on the parapet, staring out over the ruptured, wire-strewn earth that separated them from the enemy. No gun fired and no shell exploded. The stillness was unearthly, incredible, not broken by cheers or tears or any sound except the low voices of the men, speaking to each other almost in whispers.

That afternoon, word came through that Kaiser William had

abdicated and that Prince Maxmilian of Baden, the Chancellor of Germany, had resigned.

The war was over.

In San Francisco, Mark stood at the window in his office over the department store, staring out at the wild celebration below, people in a vast parade, twisting, dancing, embracing strangers, hundreds of them wearing gauze masks to protect them from that silent death of influenza that had slid out of the trenches and across the whole world. When Dan entered the office, Mark didn't move.

"This calls for a drink," Dan said.

"Get out, Danny."

"What?"

"Get out and leave me alone."

"Jesus, Mark, it's over. Over!"

Mark turned to face him, blinking his eyes to keep back the tears. "What's over? Is Jake alive or dead? Tell me what's over. I was on the phone with Sarah for an hour. Tell her it's over."

"Jake's all right."

"How the hell do you know?" Mark demanded.

Dan walked over and put his arm around him. "Come on, old buddy. How many times you told me the kid's a survivor? He's all right. You know what, we'll have a few drinks and then we'll find Jim Rolph and put him on the telephone. There are ways to find out what's with Jake. And Sunny Jim owes us. Mark, bad news comes home and damn quick. All we got now is good news, so let's find a bar and put down a few."

Stephan Cassala had been a quiet, studious boy, very gentle, very unaggressive. If anything, these qualities were accentuated in the man. He returned to work at the bank. He was only twenty-three years old, but he had the lined, thin face of a much older man. He was tall, slender, good-looking. His father adored him, and thanked God every day for his recovery; and more and more, he came to lean on him and to turn to him. While the Bank of Sonoma was still a small institution, it was nevertheless substantial and in the process of growth. When Anthony Cassala wanted to buy a piece of property on California Street—since they were bursting through their seams in the small space on Montgomery Street — it was Stephan who persuaded his father to remain where they were and to erect a nine-story superstructure over their heads while they continued to do business. Montgomery Street was the place to be, regardless of the cost.

In such matters, Stephan could be decisive. In other ways, he appeared to have no will of his own. Dolores Vincente was a countrywoman to Maria, and she had a daughter of seventeen years whose name was Joanna. The Vincentes lived in the city, where Ralph Vincente owned a grocery store. Joanna Vincente was a quiet, placid, rather pretty girl, with large, dark eyes and a mass of fine black hair. For years, Maria Cassala and Dolores Vincente had been plotting a match between son and daughter, and now Joanna became a guest at the Cassala home in San Mateo. Her shyness and gentleness appealed to Stephan; he was not in love with her, but indeed he had never been in love with any woman; there was no force within him that impelled him toward marrying her, but then again there was no force that impelled him away from such an action.

Certainly, she was a comfortable person, unassuming and making no demands whatsoever. Both Rosa and Maria loved her, and she fell into the life of the big house at San Mateo, causing scarcely a ripple. Weekends, the house would fill with guests, and they were all exorbitant in their praise of Joanna. Maria saw her as the perfect daughter-in-law, and Anthony as well indicated to Stephan that it was time he married and settled down.

In all truth, it simply happened and Stephan let it happen. The wedding ceremony took place in St. Matthews Catholic Church on Notre Dame Avenue, where Maria's tears had wet the altar rail so many times, and afterward there was a reception at the Cassala home. Cassala had erected three enormous striped pavilions, one with a dance floor, the other two crowded with tables, chairs, and great mounds of food. More than two hundred guests were invited. Jean Lavette begged off with the understandable excuse that it was too close to her mother's death, and on a public occasion of this sort, May Ling could hardly be present. But Dan came and Mark and Sarah Levy, bringing with them Clair Harvey and Martha Levy. Just turned fourteen, Martha was budding into full womanhood. She was an impetuous, bubbling, effervescent young lady, so filled with life and energy and excitement that people who caught sight of her found themselves seeking her out again and again as the party continued.

Stephan danced with her, and then he found that he kept looking for her, trying to find her in the crowd. When he glimpsed her, he would feel a pang, a kind of forlorn excitement.

She said to him at one point, "Oh, Stephan, your bride is lovely! She's like a Madonna!"

And in reaction to that, he experienced a sense of loss, of awful, poignant loss.

Alan Brocker had been one of the people present at Mary Seldon's funeral, but he had not spoken to Jean on that occasion. He waited for a number of weeks after that, expecting to hear from her, and, when he did not, he telephoned her and made a luncheon date. She was neither warm nor cool, but simply matter-of-fact, and she suggested lunch at the Fairmont. "The easiest way to hide a relationship, Alan," she explained, "is not to attempt to hide it."

When they were seated at their table, Alan looked at her thoughtfully and observed that she had changed since her mother's death.

"Have I? How?"

"I don't know yet. Did you have a rough time?"

"I loved my mother. It's not easy."

"And now?"

"Quite capable of facing the world."

"Am I permitted to say that you're more beautiful than ever?

"Thank you. What is the champagne for?" An iced bottle had arrived.

"I use every opportunity. We are going to have Prohibition, my dear. This will all be a dreamy memory." The waiter filled their glasses, and Alan raised his. "To the living. I don't want to sound callous, my dear, but I have an aunt and three friends who died of the flu. Welcome back."

"Don't be so damned sure of yourself. Just once, show some trace of humility."

"I do, Jean dear. I run errands. You appear to forget."

"And what does that mean?"

"Pinkertons. The report on your errant husband." He took a

folded sheaf of papers out of his pocket. "Six hundred dollars' worth. Don't mind that. It's a gift, but not a paltry gift."

"I had forgotten all about it. I'll pay for it. Don't worry."

"I told you it's a gift."

She opened it and glanced at it. "Did you read it?"

"I could lie and tell you that honor triumphed and that I did not."

"I don't blame you," she said. She wanted to put it away unread in her purse, but she could not resist. Her eyes picked it up in the middle of the page: "From September 16th to September 28th, the subject made seven visits to the house on Willow Street. On September 16th, he arrived at 1:00 P.M. He was observed to embrace the Oriental woman who opened the door for him. On said day, he departed the premises at 2:45 P.M. On September 18th, he arrived at said premises on Willow Street at 7:20 P.M. Surveillance was maintained as per contract until midnight, at which time the subject had not departed. Surveillance began the following day outside subject's Russian Hill residence, from which residence he was observed to depart at 8:12 A.M.—" She broke off reading and stared at Alan Brocker.

"You can go on reading if you wish. I don't mind."

"You're so generous."

"I could have ordered twenty-four-hour surveillance. That would have doubled the price, and I don't think you would have known any more."

"Thank you." Unable to control herself, she was leafing through the pages.

"I don't know whether to commiserate or not," he said. "It depends on how you look at it."

"I don't need sympathy," she snapped.

"Oh, for Christ's sake, Jean, cool down. What did you expect? You haven't been sleeping with the man. He's evidently not a eunuch."

"Can't you be quiet."

"As you wish. Shall I order lunch for both of us?"

"I'm not hungry."

"I'll order anyway." He called the waiter and gave the order for both of them. "Chops and salad," he told her. "Very simple."

She folded the report and stuffed it into her purse. "About the child," she said slowly. "Do you suppose it's his?"

"Possibly. There are ways to find out if you desperately have to know. Do you know who this Chinese lady might be?"

"I can guess."

"You're furious, aren't you?"

"I'm not exactly delighted."

"On the other hand, you are in possession of what might be called an invaluable weapon."

"I am aware of that."

"Do you intend to face him with this?"

"That is none of your business."

"Still, as a friend of the family, I am curious."

She observed him shrewdly. "My dear Alan," she said. "I will satisfy your curiosity. At some time, which I alone will decide, I shall discuss these matters with my husband. That time is in the future. Do you understand? The future. Meanwhile, you are not to imagine for one moment that you too have a weapon. If one word of this gets out — one word, mind you — I shall tell Dan that you are the originating source. And do you know what he might well do?"

"Latins are quite temperamental."

"Yes, he might kill you. And not pleasantly either."

"I should think you could trust me."

"I like you, dear man," she said, smiling. "I like the way you look and the way you make love. So we'll remain friends and not discuss trust. Agreed?"

"Agreed." The waiter brought the food now. "Do eat your lunch," Alan said. "One always feels better afterwards."

She began to eat with excellent appetite. Brocker watched her in silence for a while; then he said, "Dear lady, only one thing. Why won't you divorce him?"

"Do you know any divorced ladies you don't feel sorry for, Alan? I don't. And no one is to feel sorry for me. May I tell you something else? One day, Dan Lavette will be the richest and the most powerful man in this state. He'll own California. But, dear man, I shall own Dan Lavette. Think about that."

The opening of the new L&L Department Store, the largest, the most splendid, and the most stylish store west of Chicago, was, in Mark Levy's words, "a historic occasion for this queen of all American cities." It is true that the planned principal beneficiary of Mark's labors was still with the American Expeditionary Forces in occupied Germany, but since he was alive and well, his absence did not in any way interfere with the gaiety of the occasion. The two enormous and malignant forces of death, the World War and the influenza epidemic, were both in the past, and while an unpredictable thing called Prohibition was settling down on the nation, this was still the beginning of a new era of light and hope, a time when the reborn nations of the earth would embrace in a mighty league to end war forever and to institute the community of man. Of course, there were certain disturbing factors, such as the emergence of a man called Lenin leading a Bolshevik Revolution in Russia — but that was only a temporary phenomenon. The Hun had been driven into his lair, and the war to end all wars was over.

As the main speaker at the reception, held in the street floor of L&L, Mayor Sunny Jim Rolph emphasized all of the above points, and then he joined in the singing of "Smiles," not only his own theme song but in a sense one of the theme songs of the AEF. "There are smiles that make you happy, there are smiles that make you gay," his fine baritone boomed out above all others.

Mark Levy, gray at the temples and almost bald now in his fortieth year, had labored long and carefully over his own small speech. "A store such as this," he said, "is not simply en emporium where things are sold to the public; it is a hallmark, a symbol of the civilization which we have built here on the shores of the mighty Pacific Ocean. Our fathers and our grandfathers came here with only their bare hands and the clothes on their backs. All of us were immigrants together. We worked and saved and built. And on the counters of this great store will be the products of this great and industrious nation. No store like this one ever existed in the great State of California, and every inhabitant of the Bay Area should take pride in its present existence."

Dan was careful and patient in his approach to his father-in-law. He was not in any hurry. By the war's end, the price per ton for the building of first-class passenger tonnage had gone above five hundred dollars, raising the cost of a ship such as he envisaged to over fifteen million dollars. But no one was building passenger ships. Every dockyard in the nation was frantically creating cargo vessels — and then the war ended. Meanwhile, Dan waited. He no longer had one ship in mind, but two — the beginnings of a mighty fleet. He hired Alton Jones, the best naval architect on the coast, to begin work on the plans. With the sale of the cargo ships, he had plenty of time on his hands but no desire to be involved or to interfere with the operation of the new department store. He left that entirely to Mark and Feng Wo. He invested in some tracts of land in Daly City and purchased some property near Lincoln Park. He pored over each new set of drawings for the ships, and he studied the plans of such great liners as the old White Star *Oceanic,* the Cunard *Mauretania,* and the North German Lloyd's *Crownprince Cecilie.*

Much of this he did at May Ling's house, and those days there were the happiest he had ever known. He would sometimes arrive there in the morning, spread out his blueprints on the floor, and then pore over them while his son, Joseph, did his best to crumple and tear them; and then the two of them would roll over on the floor, Dan growling and woofing like a huge bear and Joseph shrinking away in mock terror.

"Do you ever play like that with Tom and Barbara?" May Ling asked him one day.

"No — no, I can't say that I do."

"Why not?"

"I wouldn't dare. Wendy Jones would hand me my head."

"But they're still your children, Dan."

"Jean's children."

"Danny, what kind of a life are you living? You're the father of two children, and you don't even dare play with them. You live with a woman you haven't had sex with in years, without love and without companionship. I don't want to nag you, Danny, and you know that I haven't mentioned this for months — yet you're so filled with guilt and fears that you don't even share my bed for the night. And what kind of a woman is she that she doesn't care?"

"Baby, just give me a little time."

"For what, Danny?"

"I am going to leave her. I told you that, May Ling."

He bought an enormous doll, with eyes that opened and closed and a head of silky yellow imitation hair, and he brought it into the nursery with the determination to conquer the small, gray-eyed child who always greeted him with an air of bewilderment. Barbara was in bed already, and her face lit up at the sight of the doll; but Wendy Jones interposed herself.

"Well, not now, Mr. Lavette, really. Not at bedtime."

"Why not? I brought a doll for her."

"And the excitement will keep her awake for hours."

"Why?" His voice became hard and cold without his realization. This bitch, he thought to himself. Christ, how I hate her!

"Because she's a child."

He pushed Miss Jones aside roughly, and the smile vanished from the child's face. He held out the doll. It had gone wrong, it always went wrong. "Don't you like it?" he asked Barbara. Miss Jones stood there, her face tight with anger, and Barbara began to cry. He laid the doll down beside her, stood there irresolutely, turned to look at Miss Jones, and then stalked out of the room. Downstairs in his study, he dropped into a chair and sat there, asking himself why — why were there walls between these two children and himself? He had thought about the doll and the way he would present it; he had worked the whole thing out in his mind; and then that Jones bitch had destroyed it. Or had she?

"God Almighty," he whispered, "what am I doing here? I'm in Seldon's house. I've always been in Seldon's house."

About the same time that the Congress of the United States was overriding President Wilson's veto of the Volstead Act and making Prohibition the law of the land, Lieutenant Jacob Levy disembarked from a ship in Hoboken. Two days later, he was mustered out of the United States Army, and on the first day of November in 1919, he stood on the deck of a ferry, crossing from New Jersey to New York. People who noticed him would hardly have believed that he was still weeks short of his twenty-first birthday. His face was lined and drawn, the bright blue eyes — so like his mother's — sunken, his whole frame lean and spare. The ferry was crowded with servicemen, but he stood alone, silent and unsmiling, turned in to his own thoughts and memories. Yet he was intrigued with the great river, the shipping, the mighty bulk of the city, the sound and sight and energy of this place that was the near edge of his native land, the smell of the salt spray, the screaming of ships' horns and the great skyscrapers reaching up to the sky.

A few hours later, he boarded a train in Grand Central Station and began his journey westward. He had written briefly to Clair when his orders first came through in Europe, but not since then. There had been too many letters; he had no more to write or say in letters. In Chicago, there was a five-hour layover, but he felt too dulled and depressed to go out into the city and spent the time in the railroad station with his luggage, reading newspapers and magazines. But westward from Chicago, he began to experience the land and a sense of homecoming, especially when the plains gave way to the mesquite-covered hills. The emotion welled up in him, and now his apathy turned into a consuming eagerness. He counted the miles and the hours. He found himself smiling and talking politely to people who desired to show their respect and admiration for his uniform — instead of ignoring them and turning away. His sense of separation from and annoyance with these men and women who talked so glibly of war and who had not the faintest notion of what war was ebbed away; and he began to accept the fact that to chatter nonsense with neither knowledge nor perception was the ordinary manner of mankind. He listened to platitudes without disgust, and he began to create conversations with Clair in his mind.

Strangely, it was hard to form a picture of her. He could define her, her long legs, her freckled skin, her red hair, but the woman eluded him. His desire for her grew like a sickness, and in the last stage of his journey, motion reduced itself to a frustrating snail's pace. It seemed to Jake that he had been traveling forever, through Germany into France, through France to Cherbourg, from there to Southampton, and then eleven endless days across the ocean to Hoboken, and then time without end across the country, and now in a ferry that was taking an eternity to cross over from San Francisco to Sausalito. He had no eyes for the wild beauty of that morning, the fog licking through the Golden Gate, a splendid wand of sunshine striking down onto the bay, the blue water choppy and dancing with whitecaps, and ahead of him, Marin County, which he and Clair had specified so often as the most beautiful place on God's earth, its dark hills thrusting up above the fog — all of this was meaningless because inside him was a whimpering, forlorn plea to be home.

A rattling, creaking taxicab drove him from the ferry landing to the Spanish Colonial house, high on the hillside, and again the few miles seemed to take forever. He paid off the cab and it drove away. He stood there, his luggage on the ground next to him. Where were they?

Then he heard her cry, and Clair burst out of the house, ran to him, and clutched him in her arms. It was all as he had dreamed and prayed it would be.

Thomas Seldon asked his daughter to come to dinner at his home. He was very specific about Dan accompanying her. Whatever rumors of their relationship reached him, it was not anything that he discussed with either of them; yet he made the point that he wanted them both present and that he had matters of importance to discuss with Dan. After his wife's death, his sister, Virginia Carter, a widowed lady in her middle fifties, had moved into the house on Nob Hill, taking over the duties of housekeeper and hostess, and when they sat down to dinner, there were only the four of them, Dan and Jean and Seldon and his sister.

Mrs. Carter was properly shocked at Jean's appearance, and she minced no words in stating that in her opinion Jean's costume passed the boundaries of propriety. Jean smiled with delight and accepted it as a compliment. She wore a Directoire, high collar suit jacket of burgundy velvet, a transparent georgette blouse, a black cravat, and a braided skirt that fell to just below her knees. With velvet pumps and black stockings, the effect was such that her father shook his head and muttered that she was just too damn beautiful.

"How can you permit it, Daniel?" Mrs. Carter asked him.

"My dear Virginia," Jean said, "Dan neither allows nor disallows. And if a woman's leg is shocking, then San Francisco will simply have to be shocked. This is a Pierre Lazai creation, and in Paris they're all wearing skirts this length."

"I think it's horrible," Mrs. Carter said.

Dan voiced no opinion. A part of him was totally servile to her beauty, and he agreed with Seldon that she had never appeared more lovely than this evening. He never escaped the enormous badge of permission; whatever she thought of him, whatever distaste she had for his body and his manners and his self, she permitted his position as her husband, and that permission was in part ownership. A man was judged by his ownership; his property was more than he was. He would never set foot in one of the great homes of San Francisco with May Ling at his side; he would never take her to the Fairmont or the opera or the theater. These were the places of ownership, of possession and permission.

When Hemmings, the butler, almost seventy now, had removed the dessert plates and brought the brandy, Seldon suggested that the ladies might leave him and Dan to themselves.

Smiling as she rose, Jean said, "Soon, dear daddy, this antique custom of yours will go the way of the ankle skirts Aunt Virginia so adores. We shall play the victrola. I trust the music will not disturb you."

The women left, and the two men sat down and lit their cigars. "I have twenty cases of that brandy in my basement, Dan," Seldon said, "so don't hold back. What do you think of this Prohibition idiocy?"

"Idiocy. They'll knock it out in a year."

"Who knows? Well, nothing's changed. Except that now they telephone and plead with me to buy good rye whiskey by the case. Do you suppose they'll ever try to enforce that damn law?"

"How? It would take an army. I'm not much of a drinker, but Jean's friends are putting it down like camels. Where we used to buy a case, we now buy four."

"Jean's friends — well, that's nothing I want to talk about tonight. I want to talk about those ships of yours."

"Oh? Has Jean been telling you?"

"Of course she has. And Alton Jones is a member of our club. He's been working on your plans for over a year now."

"On and off — yes."

"What is he charging you? Or shouldn't I ask?"

"An arm and a leg. More than I paid for the *Oregon Queen,* and these are just blueprints."

"Well, you'll never see a nineteen fourteen dollar again. This damned inflation will never stop. By the way, you know that you just about destroyed Grant Whittier?"

"Come on now. I didn't twist his arm. He was so eager to buy our ships that I couldn't fight him off."

"Well, they're worthless today. You can't give away cargo ships of that tonnage. Who would have dreamed that the bottom would fall out of cargo shipping like this?"

"I dreamed it would."

"Yes, you did. Well, I won't weep over Whittier. Let's talk about these luxury liners of yours. Tell me about them."

"It's not a small thing," Dan said.

"No, I don't expect anything small from you."

"We're drawing plans for two liners, each about thirty thousand tons of displacement. I've drawn up a schedule that takes in half the world, New York to Europe, New York to California via the Panama Canal, and San Francisco to the Hawaiian Islands. The whole world's changing now that the war's over. There's been no European travel since nineteen fourteen, and I estimate that this new canal in Panama will open up California in a new way. We'll sell cruises where the ship itself will be a floating hotel, swimming pools on the ship, the best food, the best accommodations. There's a whole army of bloated rich out of this war, and we'll give them a way to spend their money. As far as Hawaii is concerned, my idea is to build a luxury hotel on Waikiki Beach and to tie in the hotel with ship schedules. We'll want docking space in New York as well as here, and I suppose we'll have to open offices on the East Coast. What I've said is just the sketchiest outline of the whole thing, but I think it gives you an idea of what we're after."

Seldon shook his head and smiled. "You're an interesting man, Dan. Here we are in a total shipping depression. There wouldn't be an American cargo vessel afloat if not for government subsidies, and God only knows what the future of American shipping will be. And you come up with a scheme like this."

"I know where I can buy a five-thousand-ton-gross cargo-capacity Hog Island freighter for five thousand dollars. Two years ago, it would have cost almost a million. All it means is that there are too many cargo ships. But there aren't any passenger ships — I mean there are, but nothing like the cargo situation. Ship-building costs went up five hundred percent during the war; now they're going down. This is the time to build."

"All right — suppose I go along with you. How much will you need?"

"In terms of a credit line? Fifteen million dollars. Now a lot of that will be transferable into first mortgages, but that's the kind of backing I need. I have a thirty-seven-page financial prospectus that Feng Wo, my manager, put together."

"Fifteen million. That's not small. Does it include the Hawaiian hotel?"

"Yes. I'm going there next month. The Bishop Bank there is interested in the hotel, and I could probably get considerable backing on the Islands. You're the first person I've spoken to."

"What about Cassala? You've been banking with him."

"It's too big for Tony. You know that."

"Yes, I suppose so. And the Crocker Bank?"

"They've put out some feelers. I haven't spoken to them yet."

"You're still rankled about that meeting with my board, aren't you?" Seldon asked.

"No, I've gotten over that."

"Send me the prospectus and let me think about it," Seldon said. "And now, let's join the ladies."

The fact that Feng Wo now earned a princely wage of fifteen thousand dollars a year and that he supervised the work of fourteen men and women in the offices of L&L Industries, located on the entire top floor of the L&L Department Store, and that he was the source of the mathematical-financial glue that held the growing Levy and Lavette empire together had not changed his style of living. He still occupied the same small flat in Chinatown. He still walked to work each day, carrying a briefcase that he took home each evening, and he still wore suits of black worsted and white shirts and a black felt hat. So-Toy, his wife, had progressed to the point where she could make herself understood in English, but in all truth she had little interest in mastering the language. The conversations she valued were held with her husband and her daughter, and as far as her shopping went, she could meet all her needs at places where Chinese storekeepers had at least a smattering of Shanghainese.

She never thought of her life as being unduly restricted or unfulfilled. She was married to a man who in her eyes was wise and understanding beyond her comprehension. They had become wealthy beyond her wildest dreams, indeed beyond the wildest dreams of any person in the tiny village where she had been born. She still shopped carefully, saving pennies on the food she purchased, but this was only a matter of habit. She knew that they could afford any food she wished to buy, any quality, any delicacy. Her own needs in clothing were very simple, and her only extravagance was in the gifts she purchased for May Ling. She still suffered a certain amount of guilt and remorse over the fact that she was able to bear only a single child for her husband, and that child a girl; and she often recalled her own trepidation when Feng Wo decided to call the infant May Ling, which means "beautiful" in the Mandarin language. Yet all in all, her happiness was marred only by the curious and alien position of her only child.

When she raised this question with her husband, he would respond with irritation or silence; and then weeks would go by before she spoke of it again. And when she did, the talk came to no satisfactory conclusion. Thus it was with some apprehension that she informed him one morning that it was his grandchild's second birthday, and that May Ling and little Joseph would be at their home for dinner that evening and that if possible he should not be late from work.

"I'll be home no later than seven," he agreed.

"I had a thought," she ventured timidly.

"Yes?"

"Mr. Lavette has not been to our home since that evening so long ago. Would it not be pleasant to ask him to attend this small celebration?"

"No."

"But why not?"

"You know that it annoys me to discuss this. I prefer not to." In any case, Feng Wo felt awkward in the Shanghainese dialect. It was difficult for him to express subtleties of behavior, to explain things that he might well be able to explain in English.

"He is the child's father," she persisted woefully. "He is a good man. You tell me that."

"He is not married to our daughter. We are Chinese. May Ling is Chinese. I have tried to explain this to you before, many times."

"I know. I understand."

"No, you don't understand," he said with some asperity. "I try to explain but you don't understand. You know what a concubine is. Let me be blunt. My daughter is a concubine."

"No, no, no. There are no concubines in America."

"Unfortunately, there are. I am not indicting Mr. Lavette. Our debt to him is too great."

"But he loves her. He gave her a house. He gives her everything."

"Everything except his name. I don't want to discuss this because it gives me pain. I am torn sufficiently. You must take my word for it. We cannot invite him here to our house. There are rules about such things. There is a situation which I must pretend does not exist. I have never spoken about it — not to him, not to Mr. Levy, not to any human being. Now let that be the end of it. I must go to work now."

Then he stalked out of the house. But when he returned that evening, his arms were loaded with toys for the child — whom he loved more than he could say, who had become the center and focus of his own existence.

Sarah warned Mark about Jake. "Go slowly," she said to her husband. "This man who came back is not the boy who went away. Something happened to him, something terrible."

"What?" Mark demanded. "What happened to him that didn't happen to the other kids? He wasn't wounded. He was in a war. Well, millions were in this war."

"You don't know anything," Sarah said, shaking her head. "You know about money, and you don't know anything else. You don't know about your son, or your daughter or your wife, and you don't want to know either."

"Oh, wonderful, wonderful!" Mark exploded. "I break my back trying to make a decent life, and this is what I get in return. I dream of creating something for my son, something that will be a source of pleasure and reward for him, and this is what I get — a wife who tells me I'm a sonofabitch."

"I didn't tell you that." She sighed and said, "All I'm asking is for you to leave him alone for a while, let him find himself. That's all I'm asking."

Mark's office had become his refuge. In the twenty-foot-square, walnut-paneled room on the top floor of the department store building, he was renewed and redeemed. He sat behind a polished mahogany desk, facing a large, leather-upholstered couch. There were two big leather chairs to set off the couch and an Oriental rug on the floor. On one wall were two large framed paintings of the projected passenger vessels, still unnamed. On another wall was a sentimental painting of the *Oregon Queen.* The same three paintings were duplicated in Dan's office. Next to his desk was the newest model of a dictating machine, admired but almost never used. It made him too uneasy to dictate into a machine, and he much preferred giving the dictation in person to Miss Anderson.

Miss Polly Anderson had been his secretary for over a year now. She was a large, bosomy, easygoing woman in her early thirties. Somewhere in her life there had been a Mr. Anderson, but they had parted company and she was now alone. This much about her life Mark knew, that she lived alone and that she sang in the choir at the Lutheran Church; about his life, she knew every detail. She overflowed with sympathy; she clucked over him and anticipated his wants; she endured his moments of temper; she was intimate with the members of his family without ever having met them. She understood Martha's desire to be an actress, Jake's withdrawal, Clair's odd position in the family, and of course Sarah's displeasure with Mark's behavior. Not that she ever criticized Sarah or any of the others; but she understood.

The day after his talk with Sarah about Jake, at half-past five in the afternoon Miss Anderson came into his office to ask him whether there was anything more before she left for the day. He looked at her bleakly and shook his head.

"You're miserable," she said. "Isn't there anything I can do?"

"Can you make my son remember that I'm his father? He's been home more than two weeks and he hasn't said ten words to me."

"Mr. Levy, you know he's said more than ten words to you. Give him time."

"That's what Sarah tells me."

"And she's right."

"She's always right and I'm always wrong. What have I ever asked from her? Polly, would you believe it — I have been married twenty-two years and I have never looked at another woman."

"You have looked at me, I hope."

He looked at her now. "How would you like to have dinner with me?" he demanded suddenly.

"Oh?"

"Not oh. Yes or no? Or have you got another appointment?"

"Won't they be expecting you at home?"

"Polly, they don't expect me anymore. They're not even excited when I show up."

"Mr. L, I have a large steak in my icebox, and I'm a good cook, and I have six quarts of real beer that I've been saving, so may I invite you instead to my place."

"You're sure I can't take you to a fancy resturant?"

"Come to my place. It's comfortable. And we can talk better there."

"Give me the address and I'll meet you there," Mark said. He couldn't bring himself to leave with her, and after she had gone, he was filled with a sense of guilt and danger too. But along with the guilt there was excitement and anticipation, and the platitude he fed himself defined her as a kindly and sympathetic woman. It would go no further than dinner and talk.

Her apartment was in a clean, white frame building on Powell Street. It consisted of a tiny kitchen and a fairly large living room that doubled as bedroom. The bed had a flowered cretonne cover and was piled high with cretonne-covered pillows. She sat Mark down with a glass of beer and set about preparing dinner.

"I don't drink much," he told her, "but I love beer. That's what brought me here, if you must know."

"Not myself?" she asked from the kitchen.

"Of course, Polly. As a matter of fact, I know a place where you can still get good beer, but the food is terrible. You know, years ago, when we first started out as partners, Mr. Lavette and myself, we used to sit and put away three or four quarts between us. Well, we were younger then."

"You're still a young man, Mr. L. Everyone talks about how young you and Mr. Lavette are."

"Forty-one, that's not so young."

"Oh, it is. It is indeed."

The dinner was good, and he stuffed himself. He was only slightly surprised when she suggested that the bed was the only comfortable place to sit; and then he felt doubly foolish as he tried to assuage his conscience by allowing her to make all the overtures. He had the feeling that he was clumsy, mawkish in his lovemaking, conscious of his protruding belly as he undressed himself—as if he had only this moment realized that he had developed a paunch. He tried to assume some degree of sophistication, remarking that he was quite aware of the fact that his BVDs were the most ridiculous garment ever invented. Yet she was kind and warm and managed to put him at ease; and then he realized that in all truth she was grateful for his presence and for the makeshift bout of sexual intercourse that he provided.

She said afterward, "Mr. L, I sometimes think I am the loneliest woman on God's earth."

He caught the last ferry back to Sausalito, and standing there, looking at the black waters of the bay, he felt a surge of pity and remorse — not at what he had done, but because for at least a moment he had experienced the monumental sorrow of human existence.

Jake bought a secondhand Model T Ford, and he and Clair explored the dirt roads of Marin County and the Sonoma Valley. Their favorite spot was in the Muir Woods. To Clair, the grove of giant redwoods was like a sanctuary, and she realized that somehow this place eased the anguish that was blocked inside of Jake. He told her the story of William Kent's thirty-year-long battle to save the splendid trees from the loggers. "It's the only church of God I would give ten cents for," Jake said, "and all the while Dan Lavette and my father were fattening on the corpses of the redwoods."

"They weren't the only ones," Clair told him gently. "Half of San Francisco was built of redwood. You know that."

His bitterness against Mark and Dan was something she simply could not comprehend; and she wondered whether it was just an outlet for a knot of nameless anger that he himself could not comprehend. She never pressed him to talk, to let out the worm that was gnawing at him, but one day, sprawled in the catboat that was becalmed out on the bay, the water momentarily glassy and still, she asked him about Maguire, whom he had mentioned so often in his letters.

"Funny about Maguire," he said. "I haven't thought about him for months, and then I dreamed about him last week. Bigoted, stupid sonofabitch — he grew up in Chicago and became a regular army top sergeant. He was drill sergeant in my unit, and he kept after me night and day, Jew bastard this, Jew bastard that — the only proper, prideful thing he had in his life was his hatred of Jews. And then it got to a point where I couldn't take it anymore, and I got him in a quiet corner — we were already in France — and I beat the hell out of him. Great achievement. I was bigger and stronger and younger. He could have had my hide, but he never said one word about it, but after that he kind of worshiped the ground I walked on. Like I was his big brother. He never read a book. All he knew about women were whores. He boasted that he had come through five doses of the clap. He used to tell me about how he grew up in Chicago — a kind of unholy poverty of the body and soul that I couldn't even imagine. He had been twisted and deprived and brutalized and depraved as much as one human being could be and still live. He had intercourse with his own sister at the age of thirteen. She was eleven. His father was a drunk who systematically beat him half to death, and at the age of fourteen he left home and became a spotter for a pimp. That was Joe Maguire, and do you know, we became closer than I have ever been with any man in my life. He was a damn good soldier, but more than that, under all the filth and crap there was something beautiful and wonderful. He saved my life once. Oh, hell, what's the difference?"

"What happened to him, Jake?"

"He died."

"I know that. Tell me how he died."

"Why?" he demanded, almost belligerently. "What difference does it make?"

"Because until you do," she said slowly, "until you let me into that part of you, there's going to be a wall between us, and I don't want any walls between us. Did you ever think about how I grew up, Jake, and what it meant for me to come into that great hacienda up there on the hill with Mark and Sarah? You know you made it possible. I think I fell in love with you the first day I was there."

"Yeah? Well I think I fell in love with you that day I first saw you on the *Oregon Queen.*"

"No kidding? You remember that?"

"Would I forget it?"

"Tell me about Maguire."

He didn't look at her now. A faint whisper of wind picked up, and the limp sail began to flap. Jake leaned over the side of the boat, letting his hand trail in the water. "We were in a shell hole," he said. "Nine of us. Pinned down by machine-gun fire.

Our lieutenant was dead, his body on the lip of the hole with bullets slamming into it. You have to understand that the German gunner knew we were in the hole and he pinned us there. There was nothing we could do, but then some crazy bastard officer in another hole began screaming for us to clean out the gunner. I took half the men, Maguire took the others, and we made a rush for it. I don't know why. For the life of me, I don't know why. We went out in two directions, two clumps, which gave the gunner the choice. He chose Maguire, and he wiped him out with his men, all of them. I never saw any of them again."

"And you, Jake? What happened to you?"

"You want to hear that?"

"Yes."

"All right," he whispered. "We got through, me and a skinny little kid from Palo Alto whose name was Fredericks. The others were killed. There was only one German left alive, a fat, round-faced kid with sandy hair and blue eyes — big, blue eyes. His helmet was off, and he was staring at us in complete terror when Fredericks and I dived into the hole and bayoneted him. My — bayonet — went — into — " He sat up and looked at her. "Into his face, Clair," he said harshly. "I drove my bayonet into the center of his face."

Her eyes met his squarely, and she would not look away. "All right, Jake. I'm glad you told me."

"Are you?"

"Yes."

"Do you know what shell shock is?"

"I read about it."

"It's a euphemism for insanity. In war nothing is called by it's right name. I'm lucky. I was never wounded and my mind stayed together. Fredericks wasn't. His mind went. He's in a vet's hospital and he's finished. I telephoned his mother and tried to explain. You want me to talk about these things and I talked. Do you still want me to talk about them?"

"Yes," she said flatly.

He took a deep breath and reached out for her hand. "You are one hell of a woman, Clair Harvey."

"You're one hell of a man, Jake Levy. Now let's sail the boat. The wind is up."

"Why don't we get married?" he said.

"It's time you asked."

"What kind of wedding do you want?"

"The same kind you want."

"You know my mother and father will never forgive us," he said.

"Sure they will."

Three days later they packed a picnic lunch, drove across the Sonoma Valley to the tiny town of Napa, where they were married by the justice of the peace. Then they drove north through the Napa Valley. It was a clear, cool beautiful day. Small clumps of cloud drifted across the sky, while their shadows raced crazily over the golden hills. They turned off the main road onto a dirt cart-track, the little Ford lumping and bumping its way along. They lunched in the shade of a grove of live oaks, spreading a blanket on the ground, lying side by side and watching the clouds meander across the blue sky.

"What a beautiful stinking world it is," Clair said. "Why don't you make me pregnant. I want to have at least eight kids, so we ought to start right away."

"Here?" He pointed up the road, to where a pair of iron gates hung from two stone gateposts.

"No one's watching. Not that I care if they are. We're awfully good. We could give demonstrations."

"God Almighty, I married a tramp."

"You're damn right you did, and it's time you knew."

Afterward, they walked up the road to the iron gates. Across the top of the gateway was spelled out HIGATE WINERY. A road, lined on either side with weed-grown rows of vine stumps that thrust out a tangle of green tendrils, led up the hillside to two old stone buildings. Tied onto the gate itself, a small sign rather hopefully and somewhat pathetically proclaimed, "Rooms for Rent."

They looked at each other. "This is as close to paradise as we've ever been," Clair said. The valley swept down beneath them to the golden hills in the east. Beyond the stone houses, the mountains climbed westward, covered with live oak and mesquite.

"We'll give it a try," Jake agreed.

They opened the gate and walked through up the road to the house. A small, stout man of about sixty was cranking an old truck that refused to start. He let go of the crank to watch their approach.

"This old sonofabitch is more trouble than it's worth," he said to Jake.

"You get in and work the spark and the throttle. I'll crank," Jake said.

The engine started. The fat man got out of the truck and shook hands enthusiastically.

"We just got married," Clair said. "You're renting rooms?"

"What else with this lousy, rotten, barbarian Volstead Act of theirs? You run a small winery and you're lucky to keep body and soul together. Now they've scragged me, ruined me, destroyed me, driven a stake into my heart — that devil's brew of temperance swine! You're not temperance, are you? Because if you are, I'll not have you dirtying the ground you stand on. I'll drive you away like the devil himself."

"We're not temperance," Clair replied, laughing. "Good heavens, no."

" 'Tis nothing to laugh at."

"I'm Jake Levy. This is my wife, Clair. Our car's down there on the road, and we saw your sign."

Now a small, round, red-cheeked lady came out of the building, wiping her hands on her apron.

"I'm Mike Gallagher," the fat man said. "There's my wife, Mary. We got a clean room for two dollars a night, good bed, three dollars if you want breakfast, four dollars if you want dinner."

"Oh, what an old skinflint you are," his wife cried out. "A dollar for breakfast. That's shameful."

"You leave the business matters to me, old lady."

"We'll take it," Jake said.

As they walked back down the hill to get their car, Clair said, "Oh, what a beautiful honeymoon! Who would have ever dreamed it would come out like this?"

Coming into the house on Willow Street, Dan announced to May Ling, "Well, young lady, I am off to Honolulu."

"Oh, no, Danny. When?"

"Four days from now."

"And how long will you be there?"

"Including the passage, I'll be gone five weeks."

"Five weeks? Oh, Danny, it's too long."

"Not at all."

"And is she going with you?"

"Who is she?"

"The ice lady," May Ling spat out.

"Oh, I do like you when you're mad."

"I am not mad. Only disgusted. You just haven't enough sensitivity to know the difference. I just wish you were in China right now."

"In China? Why?"

"Because then everyone would look at you and be filled with disgust and say, who is that enormous, oversized creature with a huge nose who walks like a man?"

"I didn't know you felt that way about me," he said, grinning.

"Well, I do. Is she going with you?"

"No. She hates ships. She hates boats."

"She also hates you, but you haven't enough sense to know it. Are you going alone?"

"No."

"Well, don't grin at me. Who is going with you? Mark?"

"No."

"Who?"

"You," he said.

"Oh, Danny, don't tease me, don't."

"I'm not teasing. You are going with me."

She kept shaking her head.

"Will you please just listen to me. The passage is all arranged. You are to come as my secretary. Frank Anderson is a friend of mine, and we're going to go on one of his ships, the *Santa Barbara.* She's a twelve-thousand-ton cargo carrier, and she makes her run between here and Yokohama, with a stopover at Honolulu. She has two passenger cabins and a Japanese and Kanaka crew. As far as Anderson is concerned, it's all up and above board. I'm taking my secretary. That makes sense. I have important business in Hawaii. You will get down to Pier Thirty-eight at the Embarcadero at ten o'clock on Friday morning and board the ship."

May Ling stared at him. Then she sat down, still staring at him. Then their son, Joseph, almost three years old now, came into the room and embraced Dan's leg. Dan swung him up into the air, and he howled with glee. May Ling's mouth was open. Tears appeared and ran slowly down her cheeks.

"Now what in hell are you crying about?" He set down the child.

"Don't cry, mommy," the little boy said. She took him in her arms.

"And what about him?"

"He'll stay with your mother. Your mother will love it."

"Oh, Danny, it's crazy."

"Why?"

"I can't. You know that I can't. Where would we stay there? In those islands — "

"Those islands are a very civilized place. For three days, we'll be the guests of the Noel family at their plantation. They're the biggest sugar and pineapple growers in the islands, and I'm hoping that Christopher Noel will put up half the money for the hotel Mark and I are going to build on Waikiki Beach. For the rest of the time, we'll find a hotel or we'll be beachcombers or we'll rent us some kind of craft and sail around the islands. My God, what in hell's the difference? It's you and me, together night and day for five weeks, and that's all I care about." He paused. "Well? Why are you still crying?"

"Danny, I don't know. I'm just happier and sadder than I have ever been in all my life."

In the big tile kitchen of the house that to Clair was always the hacienda, the five of them were seated around the redwood table, Sarah and Mark and Martha and Jake and Clair. Mark was a millionaire, but Sarah would not have a servant living in the house. A gardener, yes, and a woman in to help with the cleaning, but she would do the cooking herself; and now they had eaten her soup and chicken and vegetables, and Jake told them that he and Clair were married. He told it flatly, because he knew of no other way to tell it. Then there was a long, painful silence, until Sarah burst out, "Why? But why?"

"Because we had to do it our way," Jake said.

"When?" Mark demanded.

"Yesterday. The justice of the peace over in Napa married us."

"God damn it!" Mark shouted. "That was a stupid thing to do!"

Sarah looked at him, her blue eyes cold as ice. "Just keep quiet, Mark. Whatever you say now will be wrong."

"Why?"

"If I could tell you why, you wouldn't be what you are."

"And what am I, some animal to be treated this way?"

"Please," Clair said, "I love both of you. Try to understand that we had to do what we did the way we did."

Mark breathed deeply and managed to control himself. "All right. You've been like a daughter to us, Clair. Don't you think I knew that you and Jake would be married some day?"

"Yes, I think so."

"Have we ever mistreated you?"

"Stop that!" Sarah said. "Leave it alone. They're married. You should thank God. There's nobody in the world I'd rather have for a daughter." Close to tears, she rose and went to the stove. "I'll give you coffee and dessert. I have an apple pie. And then we'll talk about this like civilized people."

"Well, I'm glad," Martha said. "I'm glad. I think you're all dumb about this. I'm glad." She got up, ran over to Clair, and threw her arms around her. "You're the best person in the world, and Jake's just lucky."

Choking, fighting the tears as she cut the pie, Sarah said, "Only, I don't know what else this big house is good for except for a wedding. I always thought it would be."

"It still can be," Mark said. "So I got excited — with reason. Well, it's done. But who says you can't be married again — this time with Rabbi Blum."

"The rabbi can't marry them," Sarah said. "For heaven's sake, Mark, don't start in with that again. Clair's not Jewish, and the rabbi can't marry them. That's the Law. That's the way it is, and that's the way it has to be."

"It doesn't have to be that way," Mark said stubbornly.

"Dear Mark," Clair said, "I can't become Jewish."

"Why?"

"Because she is what she is!" Jake cried. "Can't you understand what that means?"

"Don't talk to me like that! I'm your father."

"Please, Jake," Clair said, "let me try to explain."

"No, let him explain," Mark said hotly. "It's time he did some explaining. He's been back two months now, and I can't talk to him. I built that store for him, the biggest goddamned department store in this state, and he won't even look at it."

"It's not for him," Clair pleaded. "Mark, we're not ungrateful, but — "

"I'm ungrateful," Jake interrupted. "It's time I said it. You built your damned L and L empire on blood, and it stinks."

"Don't!" Sarah cried. "That's not fair."

"Like hell it stinks!" Mark shouted. "Without the supplies we carried, you all would have died over there. What are you telling me? That we're rotten because we were patriots? That we're no good because we wanted this country to survive, because we wanted France and England to survive? We didn't sink the ships! That was the same bastards who tried to kill you over there. The same Huns. And then you talk like that to me! What gives you the right?"

Jake leaped to his feet and stalked out of the room. Sarah wept. Martha sat frozen, her mouth open. Mark sat there, his hands trembling. Clair ran over to him and put her arms around him.

"Mark — dear Mark, we love you, both of us. Jake's upset. He's been upset since he came back, terribly upset. You have to understand that."

"What did I do to him?" Mark asked, his voice almost a whimper. "What did I ever do to him? Was I ever mean, nasty to him? What did I ever do that wasn't for him? He's my son."

"It will be all right," Clair said. "Just give him time. We both love you, Mark."

"Go outside to him," Sarah said.

Now Martha burst into tears and ran from the table. Clair followed her. When they were alone, Sarah said to her husband, "Do you know how far I am from home, my husband? From a place called Kiev, in Russia? Maybe eight, nine thousand miles — here in this strange land on the other side of the earth. I'm a lonely Jewish woman growing old. Did that ever occur to you? You want her to be Jewish. You want Jake to be Jewish. But you stopped being a Jew twenty-five years ago. Go to Rabbi Blum and tell him to convert you before you try to convert my daughter. I don't know who makes wars and who makes money, but

I know the best thing that ever happened to us is that wonderful girl he married."

Jean Lavette had often felt — though she would have hardly articulated it — that one of the desirable goals of wealth was an indifference to money. The difference between such a condition and extravagance was subtle but nevertheless real; and her own background was too close to the placer mines and too compatible with banking to achieve true indifference. Dan was openhanded, but hardly indifferent. Alan Brocker was indifferent, in a manner that reminded her of the New York City society heroes in the stories of Richard Harding Davis she had read so avidly in her schoolgirl years. It was not that Brocker was wealthier than the Seldons — although in terms of liquid assets he was a good deal wealthier than the Lavettes — but rather that his wealth was there without compulsion on his part, managed by others and increasing, swelled by the war which he had hardly paid lip service to. Now he paid thirty-seven thousand dollars for a custom-built Leyland touring car. It was unique, the only one of its kind on the West Coast, the first British touring car with an eight-cylinder in-line engine.

The day after Dan departed for Hawaii, Alan turned up at the house on Russian Hill, driving his new mechanical wonder, which could climb any hill in the city at a gallop, dangling in front of Jean an invitation from Douglas Fairbanks and Mary Pickford to visit them at their home, Pickfair, in Los Angeles and to watch their current movie being filmed. Alan knew everyone and had been everywhere, and as he pointed out to Jean, Los Angeles was neither Venice nor the South of France, but only two days' journey south by car.

"We'll stay over at Carmel," he said. "I know a delightful little inn there. It will be a great adventure."

"I am much too old for adventures," Jean protested.

"What nonsense. I'll tell you something else. Let a director look at you once, and he'll be on his knees pleading for a new star — namely, Jean Lavette."

"That kind of flattery is idiotic." And then she added, "What will you tell your friends the Fairbanks — that I'm your mistress?"

"If you wish."

"I do not wish," she said firmly. It was the first time she had ever used the word mistress, even in her own mind, and it left a raw, nasty taste on her tongue. Yet she agreed to go with him, making arrangements with Wendy Jones for the children.

The trip started poorly. She disliked the sun and the wind on a complexion she cherished, and they argued about putting up the top. Finally, she prevailed, discovering that he was so inept with his hands that she had to get out of the car and help him. The road was lumpy and bad, and she prayed that they would not have a flat tire, but her prayers were to no avail, and on an empty stretch of bad road, just south of Davenport, they blew a tire. There was nothing in sight but the rocky beach and the broad, dazzling sweep of the Pacific.

Swearing softly under his breath, Alan got out, removed his pale blue sport jacket, walked around to the back of the car, and opened the tiny boot.

"Do you know," he called out to her, "there's no jack here."

"That's impossible."

"Well, come and see for yourself."

"I don't have to see. If it's not in the boot, it's somewhere else."

"Where?"

"How do I know?" she shouted at him. "I've never seen one of these ridiculous cars before. But if you were stupid enough to pay thirty-seven thousand dollars for a car that has no jack, then you deserve whatever happens."

"That's cheering," he replied, giving up on the boot and coming over to where she sat. "You're a real love."

"Do you want me to get out and find the jack?"

"There is no jack."

She leaned out and pointed to a leather box strapped onto the running board. "What's in there?"

"Who knows?"

"Well, why don't you stop being absolutely stupid and look?"

"Thank you!" he snapped. He opened the leather box, and there was jack and lug wrench. He stood and stared at the tools. "I can't change a tire," he said finally.

"What?"

"It's not as simple as you think. You have to get the old one off the rim, put on the new one, and inflate the inner tube. I can't do it. I'm not a damn mechanic."

"No, you certainly are not."

"Well, what would you want me to do? I'm wearing white flannels."

"So you are. Well, we passed a garage about three miles back. I suggest you walk there."

"Three miles? In this sun?"

What would have come of the argument, Jean never knew, for at that moment a car driving north pulled off the road behind them, and a neatly dressed young man in his twenties got out.

"Trouble?" he asked. "That's a real beauty," he added, admiring the Leyland but looking at Jean.

"I have a flat."

"I'd help you, but I'd hate to try it on that car. Never saw one of those before."

"If you could run me up to the garage? It's about three miles north of here."

"My pleasure."

"I'm not staying here alone," Jean said.

"For a half-hour?"

"No."

The result was that Alan remained with the car, and Jean rode off with the neatly dress young man, whose name was Fritz Alchek, who drove a Ford, who carried a line of men's haberdashery, and who was on his way to San Francisco. At the garage, the owner demanded ten dollars in advance before he would close up and go down the road. Jean paid him the ten dollars and then said to the young man, "Would you mind taking me to San Francisco?"

"My pleasure." He was eager but not inventive.

They were at least five miles north of the garage before Mr. Alchek put his hand tentatively on Jean's knee. "Mr. Alchek," she said quietly, "I'm as tall as you are and quite strong. The next time you put your hand on my knee, I'll break it for you."

At San Gregorio, he pulled up and told her to get out.

"Why?"

"Because it's my car, you bitch."

The local garageman at San Gregorio charged her twenty dollars to drive her home, and three days later her suitcase was delivered by messenger. Curiously enough, the whole experience excited rather than depressed her, and the result was a restless urgency to get out of San Francisco on her own. She wrote to Dan in Hawaii, telling him what she had decided to do.

Then she went to Cook's and made all the arrangements. Her mother's younger sister had married an Englishman, a tea merchant named Vincent Cumberland who lived in London. There was an exchange of cables, and ten days after the incident with the Leyland, Jean, Wendy Jones, Barbara, age seven, and Tom, age nine, were on a train to New York to take ship for England. It was time, she decided, that she overcame her dislike for ocean travel.

On their second trip to Higate, in the Napa Valley, both Clair and Jake had the sensation of returning to a place they knew very well indeed, a place that was familiar, that knew them as they knew it. Jake left the motor of his old car running, while he opened the creaking, rusty iron gates; and then they drove up the rutted dirt road to the house. It was midday, the air undulating gently in the heat, butterflies floating like fat, lazy drops of gold, a saucy lizard sunning itself in the sand. Two white hens scratched at the soil, and as they got out of the car, Mike Gallagher came around the house, leading a milk cow.

"I'm a bloody rotten farmer now," he said. "Hello, kids — you back for the night?"

"If you'll have us," Jake said.

"We're ready to eat, so why don't you join us. Go inside. I'm just putting Bessie out to scrounge, and I'll be with you in a few minutes."

Lunch was homemade sausage meat, fried eggs, boiled potatoes, and fresh milk as thick as cream, and with it Mary Gallagher's home-baked sour bread and home-churned butter. Jake and Clair ate until a sense of shameful gluttony put a stop to it; and then Gallagher poured glasses of a clear amber sweet wine of his own making. "A bit of dessert drinking," he explained, "and a wee opportunity to flout their cursed Prohibition."

The wine was delicious. "You make it?" Jake asked.

"We did," Mary Gallagher said.

"And now the stinking government agents are all over us. I am at the end of my rope, kids, and I'll not make it out of renting a room to a lad and a lass once a month."

"Have you ever thought of selling the place?" Jake asked innocently.

"Oh? And who the hell would buy this turkey?"

"We dream of selling," Mary Gallagher said. "My sister lives in Santa Barbara, and she begs us to come down there. They got a nice little dry-goods store and we could buy into it. We're too old for this kind of thing."

"What have you got here?" Jake asked. "I mean how much land?"

Gallagher regarded him shrewdly. "Ah — are you making conversation, boyo, or are you interested?"

"We're interested," Clair said, smiling. "That's why we came back."

"Well, both buildings are stone. You saw them last time. Oh, I admit they are run-down, and the plumbing ain't what it should be. Roof needs some work. But the buildings are sound. Counting the kitchen, there are nine rooms in this one — not that we use them, but you're both young and healthy, and God willing, you'll plant a few seeds. You've seen the other building. It ain't a modern plant, but it's good. Them fermentation vats and them aging barrels are all good German oak, worth their weight in gold if this country should ever get over this insanity. Now I couldn't give them away. The presses are good. I got a thousand or so bottles — " He spread his hands hopelessly. "Never made fancy wine, just good white table wine. I'm a small man, Jake, that's the truth of it. Well, it's all there. It ain't worth a tinker's damn today, but it's there. The well is good, and it's never gone dry. You can take out a thousand gallons, and it won't go dry. As for the land, I got nine hundred acres, sixty acres in vines, and they're choking with weeds. It's a sorry thing to watch it all perish, believe me."

"Can't you market them for table grapes?" Clair asked.

"Hah! You seen the price of table grapes? They're a glut on the market. I want to be honest with you. I can't afford no labor, and I ain't got the strength to pick them and crate them and market them even if it was possible. Oh, no, kids, they done us in proper. They put a knife in my heart, the lousy bastards, just as if the good Lord Himself didn't lift His glass of wine. And what did they drink at the Last Supper — water? Like hell they did!"

"Oh, don't carry on like that, Mike," his wife said. "You'll have yourself a stroke."

"And good riddance. Now wait a minute, kids," he said, "your name's Levy. You're Jewish?"

Jake nodded.

"Ah. Well, it's the damned Baptists and the damned Methodists that did this shameful thing to us. I never had no rancor in my heart against the Protestants, but it's a shameful thing they have done, a shameful thing."

"We'd like to walk over all the land," Jake said, "and we'd like to look at the buildings again. Then we can talk about it."

"Sure, so long as you realize I'm not trying to cheat you. I've told you the truth."

As Gallagher led them over the great spread of the nine hundred acres, Jake and Clair's excitement grew in leaps and bounds. High up on the hillside was a thick copse of live oak and mesquite. In one place, a dry, rocky bed cut a ravine.

"It runs like the devil himself when the rains come."

"Have you never thought of damming it for irrigation?" Jake asked.

"Sure I've thought of it. Strength and money, lad, strength and money. You could put five hundred of these acres into vines with the proper irrigation. This is the finest wine country in the world, and some day the world is going to discover that — if we ever rid ourselves of this lousy Volstead thing."

They poked through the old winery. "Oh, I love the smell," Clair said.

"I make a bit of squeezing for us, but you got to be careful. Look at these walls. A foot thick. It can be hot as hell outside, and just so cool and pleasant in here. Breaks my heart to look at it."

They went back to the kitchen, where Gallagher poured glasses of a clear, white, dry wine.

"My God, this is good!" Jake exclaimed. "This is as good as anything I ever drank in France."

"Better, boy, better. Truth is, I bought them vines out of a French dealer almost thirty years ago, but there's no weather in France like this and no soil either."

"Is it a Chablis?" Clair asked.

"You cannot name it, because it's all changed with growing here. It's California wine, and there no other wine like it, and when it's good it's magnificent. You don't taste the fruit and you don't taste the sour; you taste an angelic brew. Ah, the hell with it! What am I talking about with what these bastards have done!"

"We'd like to buy," Clair said.

"So if you'll make a price," Jake said, "we'll talk about it."

"All right. There are nine hundred acres. Even in this rotten world of Prohibition, the land's worth twenty dollars an acre, and that's eighteen thousand dollars. With the two buildings, the barn, and the rest of it, I got to have fifty thousand dollars."

Clair and Jake looked at each other in silence.

"How big is the mortgage?" Jake asked finally.

"Nine thousand."

"Why didn't you increase it if you needed money so badly?"

"Because they won't give me a nickel more, and that's the truth like all else I told you."

"I'll be equally frank with you," Jake said. "We want this place. For days, we've talked about nothing else. My wife has about nine thousand dollars. That's insurance money that came to her after her father's death. I have almost four thousand, my army pay and some savings. If we can get a mortgage for the rest — "

"Give it up, my lad. You'll get no mortgage here or in San Francisco. The bastards have put a curse on us."

"You wouldn't take a mortgage yourself?" Clair asked.

"I like you both, kids, but I can't play the fool. You can't come into a place like this penniless. My trucks are tired, tired. If you want to raise cattle, you must buy the stock. I got a cow and a few chickens, that's all. If you're going to raise grapes for the market, you must crate them. That takes money."

"If I give you a check for five hundred dollars," Jake said, "will you hold the place for thirty days?"

"You been a soldier, eh?" said Gallagher. "You go through hell over there, but back here it makes for a kind of innocence. Who the hell is going to want this white elephant? You're the first boarders we had and the first buyers. Keep your money, and if you can get the price, come back. We'll be here."

Christopher Noel's home on the island of Oahu in Hawaii was called by the people who inhabited it a bungalow, but its twenty-two rooms sprawled over half an acre of ground, and it was quite the most magnificent house May Ling had ever entered. The bamboo posts, the hardwood floors, the reed blinds gave her the feeling that at long last she had touched a part of the Orient. She and Dan were housed in a two-bedroom suite with a connecting sitting room and a private porch that overlooked the beach. There, through the palm trees, she could see the magnificent breakers rolling in and listen to the endless thunder of the surf. There was a swing seat on the porch, and sitting there with Dan's huge arm around her, she experienced a degree of happiness and contentment that was almost terrifying. The first evening they were there, a wild black storm swept out of the Pacific. Silent, entranced with the spectacle, they watched it approach and then huddled together on the swing seat as the skies opened and a torrent of rain fell. In a few minutes, it was over, and the setting sun burst through a ragged tracery of clouds.

"I think, Danny," she said to him, "that as long as I live I will remember this as the most perfect moment."

But there had been many perfect moments. For five days on the ship, they had been together morning, noon, and night. Their isolation had been complete; for the only person on the ship, aside from themselves, who spoke more than a few words of English was the Captain, Caleb Winton, a crusty New Englander whom they saw only at mealtime. Dan taught May Ling to play Jack-o-diamonds, a favorite game on the wharf among the fishermen. They played for ten cents a point, and he carefully contrived to lose — with total transparency — so that at the end May Ling's winnings amounted to over a hundred dollars. At other times, as they stretched out on deck chairs, she read to him — something he never had enough of. When she was employed at the public library, she had conducted Saturday afternoon story readings for children, and she realized now that Dan listened to her with the same rapt and total intensity that the children had displayed. She read well, allowing herself to be swept up into the story, and he loved to watch her, to see her dark eyes flash with emotion and passion.

Knowing that there would be no books aboard ship, she had put together a small package, very carefully and thoughtfully. She had selected *My Antonia,* Willa Cather's story of an immigrant girl's experience on the frontier, *Winesburg, Ohio,* by Sherwood Anderson — a book that caused hours of discussion with Dan — and Sinclair Lewis' *Main Street,* which had been a national best-seller for months and which was certainly the most talked about book of the year. Dan loved it, and demanded to know why other writers didn't write the truth the same way. "It's not the whole truth," she countered, "and he writes rather awkwardly, I think." "What difference does that make? It's what he says." There was more discussion, but always in the end he bent to her point of view. "You shouldn't give in to me all the time," she told him severely. "You have a fine mind. Stick to your opinions." But at the same time, she realized that she was for him all that his own life lacked; she completed him; she took away his sense of emptiness, of ignorance, of blundering like a bull through a world he never really looked at or understood while in pursuit of the simple twin goals of money and power.

She also selected and brought with her two books of poems, *The Collected Poems of John Masefield* and *The Collected Poems of Algernon Charles Swinburne.* Neither were to her own taste, but she felt that Dan would enjoy them. She was right about Masefield. He was enchanted by *Dauber* and by the *Salt Water Poems and Ballads,* and when he heard "Sea Fever" for the first time, he exploded with excitement. "That's it, that's it! How can he say it, and I'd never be able to say it myself in a hundred years?" But Swinburne simply annoyed and provoked him. "That poor bastard!" he exclaimed. "He needs a solid week in a cathouse with a couple of girls I knew in the Tenderloin, and maybe that would set him straight." To which May Ling replied that it was certainly the most original criticism of Swinburne she had ever heard.

For those five days, May Ling accepted the dream and the illusion. Dan was hers; it would never be otherwise; and now in Hawaii, she was being treated with courtesy, attention, and respect — and no one appeared to be in the slightest way disturbed by the fact that she was Chinese. This had never happened before.

The first day after his arrival at the Noel estate, Dan had a long meeting with Christopher Noel, his cousin and business associate Ralph Noel, and the largest real-estate developer in the islands, Jerry Kamilee, who was part Hawaiian, part American, and part Portuguese. The Hawaiian part of Kamilee predominated; he was a huge man, taller and heavier even than Dan, brown-skinned, an odd contrast to the slender and somewhat delicate Noels. Dan already knew that nothing large or important in the islands happened without the consent or participation of the Noels. Now he learned that Kamilee was equally important to his project, and it was Kamilee who constantly brought the discussion back to the ships. Could he build the ships, and could he resist the lure of Atlantic passage? There's where the money was. Californians went to Europe. How did he intend to bring them to Hawaii? If they were to put several million dollars of their own money into a hotel and golf links to go with it, how would they fill the rooms? The Islands were just that, islands. Who in his circle of friends had ever been here? Even Dan's own wife — as he had explained — refused to make the trip.

Dan argued and talked and persuaded, brought out his plans and projections, spelled out the wonders of the floating pleasure palaces he intended to create — and at the end felt that he had at least reached them, even if he was yet to convince them. Finally, Christopher Noel put an end to the discussion. "Enough for today, Dan. Tonight we're having a luau in your honor. You'll meet the people in the islands who count, and you'll eat some good food and drink some good booze. Your idiotic Volstead Act has not taken here yet, and we intend to see to it that it never does. So rest up, swim, enjoy, and for heaven's sake, don't blunt your appetite. And by the way," he added, "you'll bring your secretary — if you wish?"

"I'd like to," Dan replied, offhand. "She's a good, hardworking girl."

"Fine. Let me mention that it's a side of you I like, a Chinese secretary in San Francisco."

"Thanks," Dan said. He was wise enough not to ask what a luau was.

After he had left, Kamilee grinned and said, "Secretary my ass."

"Whatever she is, she's a beauty."

May Ling was on the verandah. She had found Stevenson, Jack London, and Mark Twain in the Noel library, and now she was gleaning what she could find on Hawaii.

"We're both of us invited to a looway, looie, or something that they're holding in our honor tonight."

"Your honor, my love."

"What in hell is it?"

"Luau. It's a feast. It began with the old Hawaiians, who worshiped their Gods and celebrated important things with food. Overeating. Very sensible, I think. In the olden days, they only allowed men to take part in the proceedings. Men cooked the food, and no woman was allowed to touch it. Taboo. The women feasted separately. But then one day in eighteen something or other, the king sashayed over to the women's feast — I'm sure the food was better there — and that put an end to the separateness."

"How on earth do you know all that?"

"It's an old Chinese trick, knowing about things. And, Danny, while you were meeting with the big muckamucks, I went into the kitchen for a pot of tea. They have four cooks in the kitchen — would you believe it? — four cooks and five helpers, nine servants just in the kitchen, and one of them is an old Chinese gentleman from Shanghai, and when he found out that I speak Shanghainese, he practically wept, because it seems that all the Chinese in this place, or almost all anyway, are Cantonese, and the poor dear has to speak Pidgin — "

"Take a breath." He picked her up and kissed her.

"No. Put me down and listen, because this is interesting. This whole luau thing revolves around roast pig. Do you remember when I read you Lamb's "Dissertation on Roast Pig"? I kept thinking about it. They were dressing five enormous pigs there in the kitchen, not to mention fifty other mysterious things they were preparing and a great basin of mush they call poi, which tastes just hideous but it's a great favorite with the Hawaiians and also with the haoles — "

"What are haoles?"

"You and me. No, just you. White folk who live here. Anyway, you'll never believe how they cook the pigs. That's why I thought of Charles Lamb. They dig a big hole in the ground. It's called an imu. Then they fill it with rocks and burn a fire on it. The fire has been burning for hours now, and the rocks become red hot. Then they rub the pigs all over with salt and stuff them with hot rocks and put them in wire baskets and lay them on more hot rocks, and then cover the whole thing with leaves and dirt — can you imagine? — and this dear old Chinese cook invited us to come and watch. They begin the cooking in about fifteen minutes, so can we please go and watch, Danny, please?"

"Sure we can go."

"Why are you laughing at me?"

"Because I love you."

*

May Ling's gown was a gift from her father, a black sheath of heavy Chinese silk, embroidered in gold thread with a twisting, descending line of royal dragons. She had gathered her hair at the top of her head, holding it in place with two gold combs Dan had given her, a great black pile that sat like a basalt crown. The gown was slit from knee to ankle. She wore black stockings, and satin slippers embroidered with the same dragon motif. She came out of her bedroom, stood in front of Dan, and asked him whether he approved.

"Jesus Christ," he whispered. "Why don't you ever dress like that for me?"

"Why don't you take me to more luaus? On the other hand, this may be inappropriate for a secretary, and perhaps I should go back and let down my hair and change into a simple black cotton."

"Like hell. Come here."

"Gently. Don't ruin my hair."

Cocktails were being served on the large verandah that covered the whole side of the Noel house that faced away from the sea. The verandah was thirty feet deep, covered with a thatched roof on bamboo posts, and lit brightly with Japanese lanterns. If Prohibition intended to implement itself in Hawaii, there was no evidence of it here. Champagne flowed like water, and two long bars for the dispensing of hard liquor and various fruit punches were set up on either end of the verandah. At least a hundred men and women in evening dress were already assembled when Dan and May Ling made their entrance from within the bungalow.

Dan noticed with appreciation how conversation stopped and how men and women alike turned to stare at May Ling as they entered. Indeed, they made a striking couple, Dan in his white evening jacket, towering over most of the people, his curly black hair just touched with gray at the temples, and, at his side, the slender, exquisite Chinese woman, her face seemingly carved from ivory, the gold thread dragons on her gown glittering in the lantern light, as if they were alive. If Christopher Noel and his cousin had only given her a passing glance when they first met, they made up for it now, and Dan found himself in a circle of admiring men who had eyes only for May Ling and tight-lipped women who had suddenly become conscious of their weight. There were endless introductions that neither of them could remember, and then May Ling was borne away, Ralph Noel on one side of her and Jerry Kamilee on the other.

Waiters were circulating with trays of hors d'oeuvres which Kamilee called pupu, urging May Ling to try the cho cho and the dim sum, saying, "You've never tasted food like this before."

"But I have." She smiled. "Those dumplings you call dim sum are Chinese, you know."

"So they are. Of course. But I forget that you are Chinese."

"A beautiful woman has no nationality," Ralph Noel said.

"You see," Kamilee told her, "there is something we taught the haoles — to rid themselves of their racism. Well, tried to teach them at any rate. They're slow learners. But you know, Miss — what does one say?"

"It would be so confusing. I'll try to explain. In China, the family name comes first, but in America many families reverse it in the American way. My family name is Wo, which means nest. But my given name is May Ling. Oh, it's so complicated. Call me May Ling."

"But Dan introduced you as May Ling," Noel said. "I surely thought it was Miss Ling."

"Just May Ling. No Miss."

"Ah, then, May Ling," Kamilee said, "I was pointing out that this is not the mainland. There is no place on earth where a Chinese can live with as much right and equality as here."

"But there is one place."

"Where?"

"China," May Ling said gently.

"Touché," said Noel. "Enough of such talk. Have some of these."

"Oh, won ton."

"We have no secrets from you."

"But so many," May Ling assured him. "This is the loveliest, strangest place I have ever been. The only place. I was born in San Francisco. This is the first time I have ever been away."

"What a shame! And who keeps you prisoner? That ugly brute you work for?"

"That ugly brute is a handsome and kind and good man."

"Is he now? And do you know that he spent most of today trying to talk us out of a million dollars and the best waterfront land on Oahu?"

"Then you must give it to him," she said primly.

They burst into laughter and now the group around her increased. When it was time for the luau, Dan had to work his way through a crowd to reach her.

Seated next to her at one of the tables on the lawn, the air full of the smell of roasting pork, a great platter of roasted pork in front of them, so tender that it was crumbling, flanked with sweet potatoes and little bundles of meat in green ti leaves, Dan leaned over to her and whispered, "Do you know what Ralph Noel asked me?"

"No."

"Could he take you to dinner in Honolulu tomorrow?"

"And what did you tell him?"

"To ask you. It's your affair."

"And if I go with him?"

"I'll break every bone in your sweet body."

"Would you?" she replied, trying to keep herself from remembering all the nights he had spent with his wife, away from her. "Well, I'll not have my bones broken by some ugly brute."

"Ugly brute?"

"Some people think of you that way," she said, smiling sweetly.

On the third day, Noel's lawyers drew up a letter of understanding that would guarantee Dan a million dollars of initial investment plus thirty-one acres of the best land on Waikiki Beach — the beginning of the process that would turn lovely Waikiki Beach into a sprawling vacation slumland. But that lay in the distant future, and Dan's cables to Mark Levy and to Thomas Seldon spoke only of his immediate triumph.

Dan rented a small sloop, and with May Ling set out to sail among the islands. For eight days, they lived on the boat, built fires on sandy, isolated beaches, cooked the fish they caught, wandered in paradise, watched sunsets of indescribable beauty, and swam naked in the warm tropical water. The world disappeared, and never for a moment did they regret its passing. Sprawled on his stomach on the hot sand, watching May Ling, her body as slender and lithe as the first time he had looked at her nakedness, he acknowledged himself as the most fortunate man on earth. Jean faded from his consciousness, and the memory of how easily he melted at the sight of her immaculate beauty became simply testimony of his own childishness. It was over, and on the way back, running before an easy wind in sight of Oahu, he said to May Ling, "It's over, you know."

"I know, Danny," she agreed sadly.

"I don't mean this. I mean my marriage. When we return, I'll ask Jean for a divorce."

"Danny, I don't want to talk about that."

"I've made up my mind. If I can't be with you like this, my whole life makes no sense at all."

"Danny, you know what they say in the Islands — that there is no mainland, that it's all a dream and an illusion. But this is our dream, Danny, and next week we go back to the mainland, which does exist. I don't want to talk about this here. I want to talk about it when we're back on Willow Street with Joey, when I'm scrubbing the kitchen."

In Honolulu, a letter from Jean awaited him, and May Ling watched him anxiously as he read it. "She's gone to England," he told her incredulously. "Can you imagine? She just picked up both kids and took off for England."

"I thought she hated ships."

"Only ships that I'm on, I suppose."

And please, God, let her remain there, May Ling said to herself.

Lord James Brixton was twenty-three years old, a former captain in the Queen's Own Lancers, a newly appointed director of Vincent Cumberland's tea company — in which he had invested a substantial sum of money — six feet in height, blue-eyed, blond with hair that swept down over one side of his head, pink-cheeked, handsome, an excellent horseman and totally ingenuous. He met Jean at dinner at her uncle's house, took her to the races the following day, the theater the evening after that, and then at a late supper at Simpson's informed her that he was totally and completely in love with her.

"You dear, foolish boy," Jean replied. "I'm old enough to be your mother."

"Hardly, even if you came from that barbarous state of yours called Kentucky, where I hear they bed down at age eleven. I'm twenty-three, soon to be twenty-four. You are thirty-one."

"And how do you know that?"

"I made inquiries."

"Which is hardly polite."

"I have no intentions toward politeness," Lord Brixton informed her. "All is fair in love and war, and you are the most beautiful and the brightest lady I have ever known. So in the words of a famous but rather stupid general in the late war, I attack and attack and attack."

"I am a married woman with two children."

"And a husband indifferent enough to allow you to come six thousand miles without him."

"He doesn't allow me. I do as I please."

The next day it was a cricket match, and a week later Jean was a guest for the weekend at his country place. Her Aunt Janice was troubled about the propriety of the matter, but Cumberland assured his wife that Jean would be adequately chaperoned, not to mention the fact that she was an adult woman who knew precisely what she was about. Cumberland himself was delighted with anything that would make Brixton even more amiable toward the company.

Two weeks after that, a week before their scheduled return to America, Jean missed her period. In a strange country, at her wits' end, she confided in Wendy Jones, who found her a doctor with no connection to either Brixton or her family. She was informed by the doctor that she was most likely pregnant. A subsequent visit confirmed his diagnosis. Her reaction was to tell the bewildered Lord Brixton that she never wanted to see him again, an explosion of anger that brought him pleading to her aunt's home, only to be turned away by a woman as cold as ice. But most of Jean's anger was directed at herself, at her own stupidity. She would have to remain in England, find a doctor who would perform an abortion, go through the whole wretched, nasty business. And for what? For an idiotic British boy who had the audacity to propose that she leave her husband and come to live in this wretched cold country where it rained eternally.

And there was only Wendy Jones to lean on — assuring her that it would all come out very well indeed. As for Wendy Jones — well for a poor girl who had always lived with the specter of poverty and unemployment, it was a welcome thing indeed. She and her mistress had something in common now, a bit of knowledge that was an excellent guarantee of continuing employment.

When Jake and Clair Levy entered his office, Stephan Cassala's face was wreathed in smiles. He kissed Clair and had to hold back from hugging Jake. "You both look wonderful," he said. "It's been so long. Why don't we ever get together?"

"San Mateo and Sausalito. We're at opposite ends of the world."

"Nonsense. That's no excuse for either of us, and I'm as much to blame as you are."

"And guilt," Jake said. "I go through the whole thing without a scratch, and you get torn to pieces."

"No, no. Look at me." He patted his stomach. "As good as new. I can even eat mama's spaghetti. Come down to San Mateo, please. Do you know how much she asks for you?"

"We will. We certainly will. Steve, can we talk to you in confidence?"

"Absolutely."

"All right. We're here for a loan." And then he and Clair spelled out the story of Higate. Stephan listened, and when they had finished, he said, "Can I ask you one question?"

"Sure."

"Why don't you go to your father?"

"I can't."

"You mean you won't," Stephan said. "I know. All right. I heard rumbles. Tony and Mark have lunch every couple of weeks or so, and it drifts back to me. The point is, you want a mortgage on a piece of industrial property whose industry has been destroyed — so in that sense it's worthless."

"We don't look at it that way," Clair said. "We want to buy a home. And it isn't destroyed. There are two good stone buildings, a wooden barn, and nine hundred acres of wonderful land. Jake and I have talked about this and nothing else for days now. We think we can grow grapes for market. We also think we can bottle grape juice and sell it."

"So does every other winery," Stephan said.

"All right. It won't be easy. But the land is there, and we have water. You know what water is worth. We can raise cattle. We can do any number of things."

"Look at it this way. If I gave you a mortgage of thirty-five thousand dollars, the interest would be almost three thousand a year. Not to mention the taxes and the fact that you have to live. How can you possibly make it?"

"Give us a chance," Jake argued. "We'll work our asses off. We think we can do it."

"You say you have about thirteen thousand dollars. You can't spend it all. You need some capital to begin. Cattle cost money, and from what you tell me, the place is probably a shambles. Now I'll tell you what I want you to do. Go back there to the Napa Valley and offer Gallagher thirty-five thousand dollars."

"But we can't," Clair cried. "He needs the money so desperately. They're old people."

"You are babes in the woods — both of you, if you will forgive me. He hasn't the chance of a snowball in hell of selling that place, and from what you say he must either sell or starve. Thirty-five thousand is a fair price. Those structures are worth five thousand if that, so you're paying thirty thousand for the land, and that is a damn good price. You're not cheating him."

"But he won't sell for that."

"Believe me, he will. Then I'll give you a mortgage for twenty thousand from the bank, which can pass by the examiner. I'll also take a personal mortgage, a second mortgage for ten thousand more, which I'll talk pop into. That will leave you, after legal fees and everything else, over seven thousand dollars to get you started. And you'll need it, every cent of it."

"You'd do that for us?"

"Oh, what's the use?" Stephan sighed. "You'll blow the whole thing. I'll tell you what I'll do. I'll take tomorrow off, and I'll get Sam Goldberg, my lawyer, to come with us, and we'll drive up there and set the deal. Only one thing, one promise, neither of you are to say one word until the sale is set. I'm going to offer Gallagher thirty thousand and we'll close it at thirty-five. But only if you sit there quietly and listen."

The following day, after three hours of listening to Steve and Sam Goldberg haggle with Mike Gallagher, Jake and Clair Levy became the owners of the Higate Winery at a sale price of exactly thirty-five thousand dollars.

Dan took his car across to Oakland to meet Jean and the children and Wendy Jones. Their stay in England had turned into a matter of fourteen weeks, during which time Dan's life had come to focus entirely around May Ling and the house on Willow Street. He was indifferent to what the servants in the place on Russian Hill thought of his coming and going. He confided in Mark — to whom it was not news — and one evening Mark and Sarah were guests at Willow Street, partaking of a sumptuous Chinese banquet which May Ling prepared, and before the evening was over, Sarah's tight-lipped disapproval disappeared in the warmth of May Ling's charm. Dan was quite sincere in what he proposed to do; on the other hand, Mark had a number of unspoken thoughts about the fifteen-million-dollar credit line that the Seldon Bank had extended to them.

Jean, somewhat paler than usual, but otherwise unchanged, greeted Dan with some words on the agony of the endless train trip, kissed him dutifully on the cheek, and made no apologies. Dan asked for none. The children were shy and unhappy, as if he were a stranger to them, but Jean assured him that they would have to be angels not to be out of sorts after that awful journey.

During the ferry crossing and the drive home, Jean chatted about England and her aunt and uncle and the various people, titled and otherwise, whom she had met. Wendy Jones maintained a smug silence, and when Jean asked about Hawaii, Dan replied that it had been interesting. It wasn't until they were alone, after dinner that evening, that he told Jean he had something of great importance to discuss with her.

"Can't it wait, Dan. I'm utterly exhausted."

"It shouldn't take very long. I think it's best that we talk about it right now."

"Very well. If you insist," she agreed.

"I want a divorce, Jean."

"Oh? Really?"

"You don't seem very surprised."

"Should I be? And what then? Are you thinking of marrying your Chinese mistress? Really, Dan, it's not done."

"I don't want to talk about that. I've put it to you straight. Our marriage is a joke. We'll both be better off out of it."

"Will we? How can you be so sure?"

"Jean, let's not play games. We haven't slept in the same bed in years. You have your life. I have mine."

"Really. You've worked it all out. But where would you be if you hadn't married me? There's more to marriage than rutting. You'd still be down at Fisherman's Wharf."

"I won't argue. I'm asking for a divorce now."

"I'm sure you understand that in California there's a thing called the Community Property Law?"

"You can have whatever is coming to you, this house, the children, and everything else the law specifies."

"The answer is no."

"But why?"

"Because the Seldons do not divorce. Because I am quite satisfied with things as they are now. Perhaps because I still have enough affection for you not to see you throw yourself away on that little Oriental tramp."

Dan fought for control, contained himself, and managed to say quietly, "I want the divorce, and I will not take no for an answer."

"But of course you will, Danny dear. My father has just given you a credit line of fifteen million dollars. That's a great deal of money, Danny. You've already contracted for the ships, and my father informed me that work is due to start on your Hawaiian enterprise. Will you wash all that down the drain? This is becoming very tiresome. I don't mind what games you play with your mistress, so long as you are reasonably discreet, but there will be no divorce. Now I'm going to bed."

PART FOUR

The Vintage

On the twenty-sixth of August, in the year 1927, the Lavette house on Russian Hill was host to two photographers and a feature writer from the *Chronicle.* In part, the occasion celebrated the fact that Jean Lavette had been the prime mover in the first comprehensive show of French Impressionist paintings to be held in San Francisco; and indeed eight paintings out of her own collection were the nucleus of the show, two Cezannes, three Sisleys, a Pissarro, and two lovely Renoir nudes — all of them to be photographed in her own home before being moved to the Memorial Museum. While it was questionable whether the Renoirs could be reproduced in the paper, the photographer included them. He also photographed various aspects of the house, the living room having just been redone with a Chinese-Chippendale motif, set off by Japanese prints, Mrs. Lavette's most recent passion. And, of course, the Lavettes and their two handsome children, Thomas, age fifteen and Barbara, age thirteen. Thomas favored his mother, tall, slender, blue eyes, and fair skin; Barbara was darker, gray eyes under a mop of chestnut hair — both of them extraordinarily handsome children.

After the pictures were taken, Mr. Lavette excused himself, pleading a business appointment that he could not put off. Jeff Woodward, who was doing the interview for the *Chronicle,* shook hands with the tall, heavy man, whose face revealed neither pleasure nor displeasure, and then gave all his attention to Jean Lavette, by no means the first to fall victim to her charm and beauty. She wore her thirty-seven years with ease and grace, secure in the fact that she was still considered one of the most beautiful women in her circle. She refused to bow to the style of short, shingled hair that had swept the country, and she wore her thick, honey-colored hair in a bun at the nape of her neck. For the interview, she was dressed in a yellow and blue printed voile, long wide sleeves and a cowl neck, and a knee-length skirt relieved by a wide sash. Woodward noted her clothes and reminded himself to check with the fashion editor, remembering that Jean Lavette had been voted one of the three best-dressed women in San Francisco, not at all a small distinction.

"Would it be correct to say, Mrs. Lavette," Woodward asked her, "that your interest in art extended through your entire life?"

"If you mean did I color pictures with crayons when I was six, the answer is yes. In all seriousness, I became a collector only after my marriage, and compared to collectors like Mr. Crocker and your own Mr. De Young of the *Chronicle,* I am the merest tyro. However, I must admit that art is the moving passion of my life. Yet it is not enough to be just a collector."

"Would you elaborate on that?"

"The collector must be a patron. Oh, there's no great trick to buying a Renoir for thirty-two thousand dollars. It only requires that one possess the thirty-two thousand. But to find a young and gifted artist, and to be willing to pay a thousand dollars for a canvas no one else will touch — and thereby give life and sustenance to a talent that may someday be recognized as great as Renoir's — that, Mr. Woodward, is my notion of a proper collector."

"And your husband? Does Mr. Lavette share your enthusiasm?"

"In another way," Jean replied, impressing Woodward with her sincerity and straightforwardness. "His taste is more basic than mine, but nevertheless quite good. You know of his long association with shipping. His instinct is toward paintings of life at sea. He has two Winslow Homers and a Turner hanging in his study. Later, we can step in there and see them, if you wish."

"But basically, you are the collector."

"Oh, yes. Even if my husband was of a mind to collect, I don't know where he would find the time."

"And right now, as I am given to understand, your own portrait is being painted by Gregory Pastore. May I ask why you chose Pastore?"

"Of course. It goes back to what I said before. Pastore is only twenty-seven, but marvelously gifted and unrecognized. He is not one of the moderns. Please let me insist that my taste is eclectic. You will remember — oh, perhaps not, you were so young then — but when the modern artists exhibited in the Sixty-ninth Armory in New York, I talked myself hoarse in defense of Duchamp and Walt Kuhn and the others. I love modern art. But when it comes to my own portrait, well if Thomas Eakins were alive today, I would cast myself on my knees before him and plead with him to paint me — " She smiled ingenuously. "I am a very vain woman, you must understand."

"My goodness, with reason," Woodward said gallantly.

"But, alas, poor Eakins is dead. Pastore painted both my children — very much in the style of Eakins, and so I chose him. I am afraid my husband demands that a portrait resemble the subject. As a matter of fact, I have a sitting at eleven. So I am afraid — "

"Yes, of course. I've already taken up too much of your time. Just one last question. Do your children share your enthusiasm?"

"Thomas paints. Yes. And he is talented. But Barbara — I'm afraid she's very much like me."

Woodward thanked her. It was already almost eleven, and she knew she'd be late. Pastore was furious when she was late, and when she entered his studio, in an old loft at Hyde and Bay streets, he was already pacing back and forth with annoyance. He was a stocky, muscular man, with a full beard, curly hair, and black eyes. In some ways, although he was rather short, he reminded her of the young Dan Lavette. He had the same drive, the same fire.

"Half-past eleven," he spluttered. "You rich women — you do not know what time means. Time is all I have."

"Please don't scold me. It's so unfair. Do you know why I am late — because I was praising you to the sky to Jeff Woodward, who is doing a piece for the *Chronicle.*"

"Who will he write about, you or me?"

"Both of us, I trust."

"Good. Thank you." He pointed to the screen. "Go. Change your clothes." She kept a filmy gown of sky blue chiffon at the studio, her costume for the painting.

From behind the screen, she asked, "Do you ever sweep this place, Gregory? It's filthy."

"I am an artist, not a housemaid. Tell me something, Jean, have you heard of Francisco Goya?"

She came out from behind the screen, barefoot, her hair loose, the blue gown falling almost to her ankles. "What a stupid question! Of course I have heard of Francisco Goya."

"Jesus Christ, you're so goddamn beautiful. He's my hero."

"Who?"

"Goya. You know, he was doing a portrait of the Duke of Wellington. The Duke said something that offended Goya, and Goya picked up a plaster cast and threw it at the Duke. Unfortunately, he missed him."

"You're a bloodthirsty little wretch."

"I am not. Unfortunately, I live in a world where the artist is despised. What do you think Cezanne was paid for those paintings you own? Nothing. He couldn't give them away. Your husband makes more in one hour than I earn in a year."

"Shall we start?"

"One word, and I offend you. Now listen to me, about Goya. He painted a beautiful woman called 'La Maya.' Two paintings — one with clothes, one nude."

"I know the paintings."

"So. I want to paint you nude. I am almost finished with the portrait. One sitting nude. I make the sketch, and then I finish it myself."

"Dear Gregory, you're out of your mind."

"No. Listen to me," he said emphatically. "I am making no advances. I am a professional. You are the most beautiful woman I have ever known. I have drawn from the nude a thousand times. It is nothing, nothing."

She studied him thoughtfully and coolly. The notion was titillating, dangerous. "My dear Gregory," she said, "I don't pose in the nude. I am not an artist's model."

"Nonsense. You posed in the nude for Calvin Braderman."

"And how do you know that?"

"He told me. Not that you could recognize anyone from a Braderman smear."

"If I did, that was a long, long time ago. I'm thirty-seven years old."

"And still the most beautiful woman I have ever seen."

"What would you do with the painting?"

"It's yours if you want it. Or I'll change your face. Or I'll destroy it. It's yours. I only want to paint it."

Still she stood, measuring him thoughtfully. Then she reached up, pulled loose the piping tied behind her neck, shook herself slightly, and then stood naked as the chiffon gown dropped around her feet. Her body was still youthful, her breasts firm and unsagging, her long limbs as unmarred as those of a young girl.

"Well, get to work," she said as he stared at her. "It's cold in here."

Jean's interview had taken place on the second day after Dan's return to San Francisco. He had been in New York City for the past three weeks, with the exception of a trip to Albany, where he spent two hours with Governor Alfred E. Smith, and another quick trip to Miami, Florida. Smith was testing in his own mind and in the minds of others the possibility of his being the Democratic candidate for President in the election of 1928, and he had sent word to the coast that he would be more than receptive to a talk with Lavette.

Dan never thought of himself as a Catholic layman. His religion had died with the death of his father and mother, and he had not been to confession since then. Nevertheless, he had been born a Catholic, and Smith was intensely interested in what observations he could provide concerning the West Coast.

For the first time in a long while, Smith's questions forced Dan to reflect on himself, not simply as a person but as a man in relation to a religion and a society. Was he a Catholic? Was he an Italian, an American, an atheist, a freethinker — or was he driftwood, a rudderless boat? Or was it true that he could never bring himself to force the divorce from Jean because under everything he was still a Catholic? A lost Catholic, a burned Catholic, a failed Catholic — but still —

Smith — the pink cheeks, the bulbous nose, the shrewd, small eyes — was watching him, and he felt like asking, "What kind of a Catholic are you, governor?" A ridiculous question. Did anyone know what kind of a Catholic he was?

"What do they say about it out there?" Smith wanted to know. "I don't know the West Coast. It's another country, another way of thinking."

"It is and it isn't," Dan replied. "Of course, the whole damn thing is different. We don't think the way you think here. We're too new. My father-in-law, who heads up the second largest bank in San Francisco, is the son of a placer miner turned banker, and my own father was an immigrant fisherman from Marseille. My mother was Italian. That might mean something on Nob Hill, but it doesn't mean a hell of a lot anywhere else. Nobody gives a damn whether I'm a Catholic or not."

"And when it comes to voting?"

"It's the New York thing as much as anything else. We've got a different set of prejudices, Oriental and Mexican. The kind of anti-Semitism and anti-Catholic bias you got here just doesn't exist out there, not in the same way."

"Have you ever thought about politics, Dan?" It was Dan from the very beginning. Suspicious at first, Dan melted easily under the governor's charm and flattery. "You're rich and powerful and still young. I don't mean ward politics. But there are people who'd rather have an embassy than a million bucks."

Dan grinned. He had an open, boyish grin that Smith liked. "Ambassador? Hell, governor, I never finished high school."

"You don't get smart in school, Dan. You bring it there. All right, just let it sit a while. We'll be looking for support, and if you can find some respectable money that isn't Republican, make a note of it."

Aside from his trip to Albany and routine meetings at the New York offices of L&L Shipping, Dan's main purpose in the East was to investigate a company called Pan American Airways, which had just gone into operation. Ever since Lindbergh's non-stop flight to Paris, Dan had been intrigued by the notion of air travel. The first Pan American flights were from Key West to Havana. Dan traveled to Miami and took the flight in both directions, and on the sleeper back to New York, he lay awake most of the night, reliving his experience on the big trimotor plane. He was so filled with it that when he sat down with Mark back in San Francisco he could talk of almost nothing else.

"It's the face of the future," he said, "and it's open, Mark, wide open. Do you know how many miles of air transport there are in America right now — fourteen thousand. And not more than a thousand miles of it has decent equipment. We're back a hundred years when the railroad started. Fourteen thousand miles would not even take care of California."

"Dan, don't get carried away. What makes you think people will ride in airplanes?"

"Would you?"

"I don't know. It's a scary proposition."

"Well, I did — Key West to Havana. And it was marvelous. Mark, that place is booming. We think we got something at Waikiki — well, Miami Beach has got it beat all hollow. They're buying and building like people gone mad. They showed me sand lots that went for fifty dollars an acre six years ago, and today it's fifty thousand dollars. It's going to be big, big. It's going to make Atlantic City look like a village when it comes to resorts. As much sunshine as we got out here, and warmer, and only an overnight train trip from New York and Philadelphia. I looked at some beachfront that we could pick up for a song — "

Mark exploded. "No!"

"Easy, old buddy. Why not? Why not think about it?"

"Dan, do you realize how big we are already? I'm almost fifty, and I'm tired as hell. We both of us have all the money we need."

"It's not the money. It's doing it."

"All right, all right. We'll discuss it. Meanwhile, May Ling called here. Did you tell her you were going?"

"No, I didn't think I'd be gone this long."

"Did you write to her? Did you telephone her?"

"God damn it, Mark, what is this, a cross-examination? I'll see her tomorrow."

"It's none of my business, but — "

"You're damn right. It's none of your business."

Mark stared at him, and Dan said, "No, I'm sorry. I shouldn't have said that. I'm tired. I haven't been home yet — I haven't even changed my clothes."

"It's all right," Mark said gently. "We've been together too long to let something like this get to us. Only — "

"Only what?"

"While you were gone, Feng Wo resigned. I think he couldn't face you."

"What in hell do you mean he resigned?"

"Just that. No explanations. He resigned."

At age ten, Joseph, May Ling's son, was a testimony to the virtues of miscegenation. Tall for his age, he promised Dan's height without his bulk. He was long-limbed, slender, his features a refinement of his father's, his black hair slightly wavy. His dark eyes were set wide apart, his skin, where it was not burned by the sun, the deep ivory color of his mother's. He was a quiet, introspective, and thoughtful boy who responded to Dan's boisterous advances with increasing unease. Now, on this day, he opened the door for Dan without greeting.

Dan's arms were filled with packages. He dumped them onto the sofa in the living room before he turned and swept Joseph up into the air. "Damn it, you've grown. But I can still do that, right? What do you weigh?"

Joseph shook his head and shrugged.

Dan, unwrapping the packages, had not yet noticed that there were two crates sitting in the room. He was intent upon unveiling his gifts. "Dumb presents," he explained. "I know you got a catcher's mitt. This is a first baseman's mitt — gives you a choice. These three books, well they got the best pictures Scribner's in New York could provide, *Robin Hood, The White Company,* and *Moby Dick.* Knowing your mother, I bet you read them all."

"Only *Robin Hood,* " Joseph said. He was looking at the books. "They're just beautiful."

"Glad I'm back?"

He nodded soberly.

"Where's mother?"

"Upstairs."

"May Ling!" Dan roared. "Home is the sailor, home from the sea!" Then he noticed the crates. "What the devil!"

Joseph was watching him unhappily. May Ling came down the stairs. He was prepared to take three steps and sweep her up into his arms, but something in her face stopped him. He looked at the crates again. May Ling stood in front of him, her hands loosely clasped, her hair tight in a bun, She was wearing a simple, almost severe Chinese-style dress.

"Your father resigned, walked out." He hadn't meant to say that.

"I know." She said to Joseph, "Go upstairs to your room, just for a while."

The boy walked slowly up the stairs.

"Why isn't he in school?"

"Because it's summertime, Dan. There is no school." She

walked over to him, put her hands on his cheeks, and drew his head down for a kiss. He saw the tears in her eyes.

"Why are you crying? What the devil's going on here? What happened?"

She drew him over to a chair. "Danny, sit down here. We're going to talk."

"Talk? I come here after a month, and you tell me to sit down and talk."

"That's just it, Danny — after a month."

"Darling, I was away. You know that."

"Do I? Or did you forget to tell me?"

"Mark told you."

"Danny, what am I supposed to do? Accept you as if you were a child? Joey is more responsible than you. You were here a month ago, and for three weeks before that I didn't see you."

"I was in the Islands."

"You're always somewhere. But not here."

"Well, I'm here now. Suppose you tell me what's going on. Feng Wo walks out on me — and what the hell are those crates doing here?"

"Danny, I sold the house."

"You what?"

"I sold the house."

"I don't believe you."

"Well, you must believe me," she said slowly. "I came to the end of my rope, Danny. I have a son ten years old — with no name. Who is his father, they ask him? Mr. Wo. Where is Mr. Wo? Ten years old and day and night he has to lie. Will you tell him why his name is not Lavette, why he has a father who slips in and out of here, a father he reads about in the newspapers. Yes, he reads, Dan, and he asks me questions, and one day he walked over to Russian Hill, and all day he stood in front of that mansion of yours — and who is the beautiful lady who lives there and comes out of the house and steps into a chauffeur-driven Rolls-Royce? And who are the young man and the young woman who live there? Well, tell me, who is the Chinese boy who stands in the street and watches? Just tell me that — "

"Now hold on," he interrupted. "Just hold on."

"No. No, Dan. You are going to listen to me, because all this has been bottled up inside of me for years, and now I must say it. Your son is a wonderful boy. You don't know that, but he's a remarkable, beautiful boy. He's not only intelligent, he's wise — wiser than any ten-year-old has the right to be. And more depleted, if you understand what I mean."

"Will you give me a chance to say something, to explain?"

"You've been explaining for years. Well, I came to the end. I sold the house. My father resigned because it became too much for him as well as for me. All these years, has he ever mentioned our relationship?"

"No."

"Because he worshiped you. Because you were the wonderful Dan Lavette who could do no wrong. But that too comes to an end."

"What in hell are you talking about?"

"We're leaving San Francisco. While you were gone, I went down to Los Angeles. There was a job open at the University of California library for someone who could deal with Oriental languages. I got the job. It doesn't pay very much, but it's enough. We rented a little house in Hollywood, close by the campus. My father and mother will live with me — "

"My God, May Ling, why? Why?"

"Dan, don't you understand why? I took the job as Mrs. Lavette. My son will go to school there as Joseph Lavette, whose father is dead. He will be able to stop lying — no, but most of the lies will stop. He'll be able to hold up his head."

"You goddamn crazy woman," he whispered. "I love you."

She fought to hold back her tears. "As much as you can love anyone, Dan."

"You're my whole life."

"No. Not even ten percent of it, Dan."

"I won't let you do this." He leaped to his feet and began to pace back and forth. "To hell with this house. You're right. I wanted you to get out of here for years. There's a piece of property in Marin County, not far from Mark's place. It's big enough for Joe and your folks, if you want them to live with you. I don't see why, but if that's what you want, fine. Two acres of land — that's what the kid needs, to live in the country."

"Dan, you haven't heard a word I've said. It's done. It's over."

He stopped pacing and faced her. Very quietly, he asked, "What's over?"

"You and me."

"No."

Her face crinkled in pain and she closed her eyes. "Don't fight me, Danny. Don't make it any harder. I love you so much."

He went to her and knelt in front of the chair where she sat, taking her hands and pressing them to his lips. "I know how it's been for you. I swear to God I know. I get involved in things. It's not the money. I don't give a damn about money, you know that. But all my life I've been climbing Nob Hill and pushing at those bastards up there. I go to bed and dream I'm still the kid in the fishing boat with the whole damn city in flames. My father, he wanted to buy my mother a gold ring. He put aside the pennies for months, and then the boat was stove in by some crazy bastard and for months there was nothing, barely enough food to live. I don't know, I don't know anything except that you're the only thing in my life that ever really mattered, and I know how it's been, but it won't be that way anymore."

"How will it be, Danny?"

"Different."

"Will you marry me?"

He stared at her, his mouth open.

"Will you marry me, Danny?"

He rose and went to the couch where he had dropped the gifts. He took a slender box, ripped the paper off it, opened it, and revealed a string of matched pearls. "They're for you," he said. "I bought them at Tiffany's. That's the best jewelry store in New York. They're on Fifth Avenue."

"I know where Tiffany's is, Danny," she said coldly. "Oh, damn you and your stinking pearls!"

The word reached him. It was the first time in all their years together he had ever heard her swear.

"I asked you whether you would marry me," she said. "I will not go on this way. I would lay down my life for you, Dan, and you know that. But not because I'm weak. Because I love you. But this kind of love is like a sickness, and I will not spend my life and my son's life being sick."

"He's my son too."

"Is he? What have you given him?"

"I've given both of you everything you need."

"What? This?" She took the pearls from his hand. "This?" She picked up the baseball glove, and then she flung both the glove and the pearls across the room. "Give him your name," she whispered. "Now listen to me, Daniel Lavette. Today is Tuesday. We leave here Friday. That gives you three days. Any time during those three days, come to me and tell me that you have initiated divorce proceedings against your wife, or made up your mind to do so, or discussed it with your lawyers, and I will go with you anywhere on earth or stay with you here in town or live in a shack in the desert if we must, or do anything you decide we should do. Otherwise, it's done, and I won't see you again."

"For Christ's sake, May Ling, you are my wife and that kid upstairs is my son!"

"That's all, Dan. That's all I can say."

During the long eight-hour train ride between San Francisco and Los Angeles, May Ling lived with her own thoughts. Her father, her mother, and her son all respected her silence; they had their own preoccupations. San Francisco had been their world; through the years, they had seen it change from a city filled with fear and hatred and suspicion of Chinese to a place where slowly but certainly Orientals were being accepted as a valid and constructive part of the population. Now they were going into the unknown, to a place they did not know and could not visualize. Dan Lavette had been Feng Wo's rock and salvation. At the end of his rope, his wife and child literally without food and wasting from hunger, Dan Lavette had rescued him, given him food and sustenance, and raised him to a position equaled by few if any Chinese in the city. He did not consider what he had given to Levy and Lavette in return, the wisdom with which he had managed their finances, the battles he had fought when they were on the edge of destruction, the integrity he had maintained through the wild scheming and flights of fancy that were a part of Dan Lavette's empire building. This was only what was expected of him. Eighteen years ago, he had gone to work for Dan Lavette at the wage of twelve dollars a week. When he told Mark Levy that he intended to resign, his pay was twenty thousand dollars a year, probably the highest wage earned by any Oriental in the City of San Francisco.

Now, fifty-two years old, he sat in the railway coach next to his wife and facing his daughter and his grandchild, his face calm and impassive, his heart broken, his soul filled with agony. He had done what he had to do; he knew that. Physically, they would survive; he had lived simply and saved his money, and in Los Angeles he would find work of some sort; but he was leaving behind him a structure he as much as anyone else had created and a man he loved and honored more than any other man he had ever known. Through all that had happened, he would neither say nor hear said a word against Dan. Not from his wife or his daughter or anyone else.

May Ling knew some of what went on in her father's mind. She had made her own decision to leave San Francisco; it was her father's decision that he would go with her, and that meant that at least she would have her father and mother to take care of her son while she was at work.

The three days after Dan had come to the house were the three most awful days she had ever lived through. She had known with absolute certainty that her ultimatum was meaningless, that to marry her was no part of his life and had never been a part of his life; she knew him that well; but she also knew that there had been moments between them as precious and as wonderful as ever existed between a man and a woman, and for that reason, whenever the phone rang during those three days, whenever the doorbell sounded, her heart stopped and there was a crazy moment of hope and belief. On the second day, a messenger brought a letter from him:

> MY DEAR, BELOVED MAY LING:
> I am writing to beg you to change your mind. There is nothing more that I can say that I haven't said. Even if you won't change your mind and remain in San Francisco, this is not the end of us. Just don't believe that. This money is to help out. Please take it. I love you.
>
> DAN

Enclosed with the letter was a check for ten thousand dollars. She mailed the check back to him with a very brief note:

> DANNY:
> I don't want to close any doors. I will write from Los Angeles. Only think about what I said. I have enough money from the sale of the house. Thank you.
>
> MAY LING

Now it was done, as she had known it would be, and she called upon all her reserves of inner strength to blot out what had been. She knew that she had to counter her grief with anticipation. She was the pivot of these four people on the train, this quiet Chinese family that the others in the car kept glancing at so curiously. Her father was no longer a young man. He had saved a substantial sum of money, but it would not last forever. Nor did she know what kind of prejudice existed in Los Angeles. They would have to live frugally and carefully. She had her son to raise, and she was sufficiently Chinese to tell herself that he must do honor to all of them. When applying for a position at the library, she had pretended to know Japanese, but her knowledge was cursory at best. She could read Japanese fairly well, but she would have to master the spoken language to some degree before they discovered her deception.

And as for Dan? She closed her eyes, and there she was with him, the two of them sprawled on the deck of the boat, he with one hand on the rudder, the other hand touching her, the wind in the sails and the taste of salt spray on her lips.

"Mommy, don't cry anymore," Joseph said, touching her. "It will be all right."

"I know it will." She managed to smile. "Of course it will." She pointed through the car window to the rocky, spectacular California coast. "Look there, how lovely it is."

The thing was not to think of Dan — not at all.

For the tenth time since the beginning of the journey he had embarked on, Rabbi Samuel Blum regretted the fact that he had allowed Bernie Cohen to be his driver. Rabbi Blum was eighty; Bernie Cohen was nineteen; and while the distance from San Francisco to the Napa Valley was little more than thirty miles, the journey for Rabbi Blum appeared to extend itself indefinitely. Part of this lay in the profession of Bernie Cohen; he was a self-styled "pioneer," which meant that with nine other young men, he was preparing to go to Palestine and become a part of the tiny community that a handful of Jews had founded there. In the course of this preparation, he and his fellow pioneers were learning how to use the necessary machines, and having very little money, they put things together with what they could find or scavenge. When Rabbi Blum ventured to ask what kind of a car they were riding in, Bernie Cohen replied that most of it was once a Chevrolet. The rest of it had been drawn from a number of places.

Bernie Cohen was a large-muscled, good-natured young man who had been within earshot when Rabbi Blum let drop that he had to go to a place in the Napa Valley. "I will take you there," Bernie Cohen declared. "It will give me an opportunity to observe the irrigation systems."

"As long as you take me to a place called Higate. It used to be a winery."

"I am even more interested in wineries."

They were halfway there when young Cohen, intrigued by the soft drone of sound from the old man, asked him what he was saying.

"I am not saying. I am praying. It may surprise you since I am eighty years old, but I have a peculiar desire to live."

"Oh, we'll make it all right, rabbi. This is a good car when it runs. Anyway, what can happen with a rabbi in the car?"

"That's what I wonder."

The rabbi was amiably surprised when they reached Higate untroubled by calamity, and he briskly descended from what he would always think of as an infernal machine. It was his first visit to the Levy place or to the Napa Valley, and he was impressed by the beauty of the scene, the green hills, the old stone buildings, the cattle grazing in the upland meadows — and also impressed by the lovely redheaded woman who came out of the house to greet him. He remembered Clair from the last time he had seen her at the Levy home in Sausalito, but that had been years ago. Life worked wonders. This tall, long-limbed lady, a child in her arms and two little boys hanging onto her apron, her face red and freckled by the sun, was a delicious surprise, and the old man beamed with pleasure as he regarded her. The older he got, the more it seemed to him that each new generation vindicated his life and his belief.

"How marvelous!" he exclaimed. "I turn my back, and you have three children."

"You turned slowly, rabbi. It's been years. Oh, it's so good to see you. But what brings you here?"

"This one," he replied, indicating Bernie Cohen, "in his infernal machine that he calls a car. He's a nice boy. His name is Bernie Cohen."

"Can I look around, Mrs. Levy?" he asked eagerly.

"Wherever you wish. You may run into my husband. Just introduce yourself and tell him that Rabbi Blum is here. And, rabbi," she said to the old man, "come out of the sun. It's cool inside."

"First I must be introduced to what God has given you. This one?"

"My oldest. He's five. His name is Adam." Adam clutched his mother's leg and buried his red hair and his freckled face in her apron. "This is Joshua — three." Joshua stared at the old man with unabashed curiosity and demanded, "What's on his eyes?"

"Glasses. I'm not as young as you."

"And this is Sally," Clair said. "She's new. Well, not so new. A year old. She can walk if she tries. But what brings you here, rabbi? Of course I'm delighted."

"A small business proposition for your husband."

Clair led the way inside to the kitchen, where she put Sally down in a playpen. The kitchen was cool and comfortable, and Rabbi Blum seated himself gratefully at the kitchen table. Clair poured him a glass of lemonade.

"It's good. Our own lemons. It'll cool you, rabbi."

"If it's not too much trouble, I'd prefer hot tea."

"In this weather?"

"Absolutely. You know, this is a fine place you have here."

"It's been a struggle, rabbi. We do everything ourselves. Jake made these cabinets, and the table too. We both found we can do anything — or almost anything. We have four acres in table grapes, and we sell them. We have forty-one steers and six milk cows, and we've made a cash crop out of plums. And a garden. Last year we broke even for the first time, and this year we expect to make some money. We have to. At this point, we don't have a dime."

"And Jacob's father?"

"Oh, we're friendly, and they come up here and we go down there with the kids, but Jake won't take a penny from him."

"That's a shame. You're denying Mark a very deep pleasure. He's a good man. Why should you hurt him?"

"Jake is Jake. And I think I like him the way he is. Here is your tea, rabbi. Do you want sugar?"

"Three lumps."

The rabbi was thoughtfully stirring his tea when Jake entered and greeted him warmly. "I left your agricultural expert outside complaining that I don't make full use of my irrigation facilities. What is that kid?"

"He's going to Palestine to build a Jewish homeland. He's practicing now."

"Good. Anyway, it's wonderful to see you, rabbi. It's been years. But what brings you here?"

"I could come as a shepherd looking for a lost sheep."

"I don't think Jews look very hard for lost sheep," Clair said.

"Possibly. I come on business, Jake."

"Business?"

"I'll come directly to the point. The point is sacramental wine."

"What?"

"Precisely. I have a suspicion that Clair is as indifferent a Christian as you are Jewish. So I will instruct you. Wine plays a very large part in both religions. Among the Jews, we use wine every Shabbat — you know what that is? The Sabbath — for a prayer called the Kiddush. On Passover, wine is a part of the Seder. On other occasions, wine is necessary from a religious point of view. So we must have wine."

"But what about Prohibition?" Clair asked.

"Ah!" He reached into his pocket and took out a worn scrap of paper. "You see, I come prepared. A rabbi is an assortment of things, also a lawyer and a judge. Ask your father about that. I haven't time to go into it now." He began to feel through his pockets. "My other glasses."

"I'll read it for you," Clair said.

"Good. It's an extract from the Volstead Act, Section Six. Read."

Taking the piece of paper, Clair read: "Nothing in this title shall be held to apply to the manufacture, sale, transportation, possession or distribution of wine for sacramental purposes, or like religious rites . . . The head of any conference or diocese or other ecclesiastical jurisdiction may designate any rabbi, minister, or priest to supervise the manufacture of wine to be used for the purposes and rites in this section mentioned . . ."

Clair looked up at him in bewilderment, and Jake said, "Wait a minute, rabbi, you're not coming to ask us to make wine?"

"Why not? Now both of you listen to me for a moment. We have an association of twelve synagogues. Each year we buy eight hundred gallons of sacramental wine. It's made in the East, and they have been charging us seven dollars a gallon. Now they've raised their price to nine dollars. We don't make profit on the wine, we give it out for the Passover at cost, but even cost is a burden for poor people. So since I am a rabbi in retirement, they appointed me to see what can be done, and since you have the only Jewish winery in the area, I come to you. You will make the wine, and we will pay you seven dollars a gallon." As an afterthought, he added, "And occasionally, I will supervise."

Jake shook his head. "Rabbi, I'm sorry, but you've come for nothing. There aren't any wineries, Jewish or otherwise. They're all busted and closed down. The only one who makes any wine around here is a Basque named Fortas who lives down the road and who makes a few hundred gallons of bootleg stuff, a kind of zinfandel. We buy a gallon from him occasionally, but believe me his days are numbered too. The Feds go up and down these valleys like hound-dogs. As for us making wine, we just don't know how. We never made a gallon of the stuff, and we wouldn't know where to begin."

"Seven times eight hundred is fifty-six hundred dollars," the rabbi said calmly. "Clair has been telling me what kind of a struggle you had. I admire that. You are young and strong and you can work twelve hours a day. What about tomorrow? What about your children?"

"It's impossible," Jake said. "Wine-making is an art, a profession."

"So my mother was an artist, God rest her soul, because she made her own wine. Good wine too. How did you learn to grow plums and raise cattle?"

"It's different."

"Ah! You know the Bible? Three thousand years ago, we raised cattle and we grew plums and we made wine. We used to be called the people of the vine. And now a boy with your education tells me he doesn't know how. Jacob, I speak for only twelve small Orthodox synagogues. What about the Reform Jews? The capacity of the rich is always larger than the capacity of the poor — "

"It's just not feasible."

"Now you hold on, Jake," Clair said. "I want you to listen to what the rabbi is saying and stop telling him it's impossible. We broke our backs over this place when everyone said it was impossible. The only days of rest I've had in the past seven years were when I was too pregnant to move, and we still dream about owning a washing machine and a radio. If the car runs another thirty days, it'll be a miracle. If Fortas can make wine, we can make wine. We got all the equipment out there in the big house, just sitting. Now, rabbi, what about this. I'm not Jewish."

"I suspected as much." Rabbi Blum smiled.

"Well, doesn't that matter?"

"Not as long as you follow my instructions. What I tell you now is only for you to think about. I'll write you a long letter, spelling it all out. Now, we require that the barrels and the presses be cleaned in a certain way. If they have lain fallow for seven years, they can be considered usable. The wine is to be made for the Passover. If it is used before the Passover, it becomes *humotz,* or not usable for the Passover. But once it is used initially for the Passover, it can then be used through the rest of the year, when it becomes humotz and humotz is allowable."

"It's too late to start vines," Jake said.

"Jake, we'll buy the grapes. Heaven knows, there are enough grapes for sale in this valley. Rabbi, what kind of wine is it?"

"Traditionally, Clair, a sweet wine is used, and whatever wine you make, it should be heavy and sweet. In the olden times, the wine came from Malaga in Spain, which was once, a long, long time ago, a Jewish city. The real Malaga is a kind of muscatel, very rich and luscious and full-bodied. What we have been buying is made in New York City from Concord grapes. It is called Malaga, but it resembles Malaga like I resemble you."

"And you trust us to have eight hundred gallons of wine that you can use ready for you by Passover?" Jake asked him.

"Much worse than what we buy from New York it couldn't be," the rabbi said. Bernie Cohen entered the kitchen at that moment, and the rabbi said to him, "Out in the car, Bernie, there's a bottle of wine. Bring it in here. I'll leave it with you," he said to Jake. "It's a sample of what they call Malaga in New York. There's no hurry. You have seven months, and that's time enough. Meanwhile, they'll draw up some contracts and send them to you. Have you enough money to start?"

"We'll find the money," Clair said firmly.

Speakeasys, blind pigs, blind tigers, private clubs — the fact that there were at least a hundred places in San Francisco where liquor was sold made it no easier for Dan Lavette to get drunk. His enormous body resisted alcohol, and going about the matter with cold, sober, and depressed determination did not help. On the day that May Ling left the city, he walked out of his office at half-past four, walked into a place on Battery Street called Madam X's, and put down three shots of what was euphemistically called rye whiskey. The taste disgusted him, and he went to another place called Harry's. Harry's had imitation Tiffany chandeliers and a thirty-foot bar of polished oak. There were four bartenders, and by six o'clock the customers were elbow to elbow.

Harry's attested to the fact that the rye whiskey it served was Golden Wedding, bottled in bond. Dan ordered a double shot and put it down with a beer chaser. The beer was needled. The bartender poured him another double shot, and Dan drank it and then stared at the beer.

"The beer," he said to the bartender, "is needled piss. The whiskey is bootleg swill, and you, my friend, are a motherfucking fraud."

The men on either side of Dan looked at him and then backed away. The bartender put out both hands, palms down. "Just take it easy, mister. We don't advertise. This is a private club. You don't like what we serve, go elsewhere."

Another bartender waved a hand, and two heavyset men moved toward Dan.

"I go where I please," Dan said slowly.

"You're drunk, mister. Better leave."

"When I decide to, buster."

The two heavyset men closed in on him. Each grasped one of his arms. Dan stepped away from the bar and swung the two men together. The move was sudden and unexpected and their heads met with a loud crack. The bartender vaulted the bar and came down on Dan, who staggered and then flung the bartender over his head and across the room. The two heavyset men came at him now, shaking their heads and growling. Dan grabbed his beer mug and crashed it down on the head of one of them. His knees buckled and he went down. The other man was sending hard, driving blows at Dan's stomach. Dan hit him in the face, and the man went down, his nose spurting blood. Now two more bartenders were over the bar, each hanging on to one of Dan's arms, while the first bartender, his fist clenching a pair of brass knuckles, let go at Dan's face and stomach. The blow to his face opened a cheek and dazed him, and the two bartenders dragged him across the room. The third bartender opened the street door, and they dragged Dan out into the street. As the third bartender came at him with the brass knuckles again, Dan kicked him in the testicles. The man went down, groaning and clutching his groin, and Dan flung off the other two. A crowd gathered, and as Dan stood there at bay, blood streaming from his face, his clothes torn, one man down at his feet, the two others circling him warily, the police appeared.

Mark Levy was still in his office at seven-thirty that night when Polly Anderson buzzed and informed him that Inspector Crowther of the San Francisco Police was on the phone and would like to talk to him. Ever since Feng Wo had left, Mark had worked late. They had already hired and fired a replacement, and Mark had come to realize that any valid replacement was out of the question. Feng Wo had traced the intricacies of their operation from the day it began, and there was no one who could step into his shoes and do what he had done. Dan would never stoop to details; everything he did was in the grand manner. If money was needed, he would say to Mark that they needed so much and let it go at that; if money had to be spent, he would spend it. It was up to Mark to plan and connive and juggle.

Now, irritated, he asked what the devil Inspector Crowther wanted.

"He'll only talk to you."

"Put him on, put him on."

Crowther was respectfully troubled. "It's about Mr. Lavette, Mr. Levy — "

"Dan Lavette?"

"That's right, sir."

"Well, what about him? Is he hurt?"

"Well, yes, he's hurt, not too badly. Trouble is, he hurt a lot of other people. He wrecked a speakeasy and he put two men in the hospital. We got him here, and it adds up to aggravated assault, but we didn't want to charge him or book him until we got a better picture, and I think you'd better come down here."

"God Almighty," Mark whispered. "What happened?"

"Well, sir, as near as we can make out, he got drunk and became violent."

"Are there any newspapermen there?"

"Not yet. I understand. We're keeping a lid on it."

"Now listen, please, inspector," Mark said. "I'm going to try to find Mayor Rolph, and if I do, we'll both come down to headquarters. I'll come anyway — right now. But for God's sake, try to keep this quiet, and don't book him. I ask that as a personal favor and I know the mayor will be with me on this. You do that for me, and I'll remember it."

"I'll do my best, Mr. Levy."

Bolting out of his office, he paused to enlist Polly Anderson, who pleaded, "It's almost eight already, Mr. L, and I have a dinner date, which happens once a month — "

"Look, they've arrested Mr. Lavette — "

"Good heavens, why?"

"I'll explain another time. I want you to track down Mayor Rolph and get him to meet me at Police Headquarters, and don't take no for an answer, and I swear I'll buy you the best dinner the Fairmont can put on the table. Will you?"

"I will." She sighed. "I hope it comes out all right. He won't go to jail, will he?"

"I hope not."

At least they hadn't put Dan in a cell. Crowther took Mark to an interrogation room, where Dan sat slumped over a table, his cut cheek held together with a piece of cornplaster, his shirt and suit torn and soaked with blood.

Crowther said, "I swear, I don't know what to do with this one, Mr. Levy. We're just lucky it happened in a speak, because maybe no one will bring any charges. That is, if nobody dies."

"What do you mean, if nobody dies?"

"Well, these two in the hospital. One is a bouncer, whose skull he fractured with a beer mug, and the other is a bartender who he ruptured with a kick in the balls. Jesus God, here's one of the leading men in the city in this kind of a brawl. I never ran into nothing like this before."

"How many were there?"

"Five as near as we can make out."

"Then it's self-defense."

"In a courtroom, Mr. Levy, in a courtroom. And like I say, if nobody dies."

Now, in the interrogation room, Dan stared bleakly at his partner.

"How on God's earth did you get into this?"

"Don't lecture me," Dan whimpered. "I'm sick as a dog. Look at me. I vomited up my guts, and my belly feels like a mule kicked me there. I'm almost forty years old, Mark, and I'm soft and flabby, and I got no business in a fight. Christ, I haven't been in a fight since I was a kid."

"Well, just tell me what happened."

"What's the use? I got shit in my blood — I always have. I'm no better than some lousy gunsel. May Ling's gone. Gone."

"What happened?"

"Nothing happened. I tried to get drunk, and I got in a fight. I felt ugly and I acted ugly. That's all."

The door opened, and Crowther entered with the mayor. Mark was so happy to see Sunny Jim Rolph that he almost embraced him. Rolph was in formal attire, white tie, and tails, and, as always, his shoes were polished to a dazzling shine. He said sadly, "Only for you, Danny Lavette, your poor dumb guinea slob. Look at yourself. A man who should be an example to the youth of the nation."

"I need that," Dan said.

"Five of them, and Danny Lavette puts two in the hospital where they may never see the light of day again. You dumb bastard."

"Thank you."

"The point is," Crowther said, "what do I do?"

"The point is that there is no perpetrator," Rolph decided. "A gentleman is attacked in a speakeasy and beaten half to death. They know that if they open their yaps, we'll close them down. They won't bring charges, and the thing to do with this captain of finance is to get him the hell out of here."

"And if they die?"

"People die. They still won't bring charges."

"There are a dozen cops know he's here."

"Do they know his name?"

"Some of them do — and Sergeant Murphy."

"Then tell them and Murphy they're mistaken."

"And what do I tell Chief O'Brien?"

"Tell him to talk to me. Crowther, I'm due to speak to Rotary in thirty-five minutes. Don't argue with me. Do it."

Mark tried to tell Rolph that he would not forget this.

"Forget it?" Rolph said. "Who the hell could ever forget this? I'll sure put it in *my* memory book."

Driving to Mark's place in Sausalito, Dan asked him what he thought this would cost them. They had already decided that Dan could not go home, and Mark had phoned to have a doctor waiting at Sausalito.

"In time, a lot. Rolph's a gentleman. He won't press. But sure as God, we are the number-one supporters of his next campaign."

"I'm sorry, Mark. God, I'm sorry. If this should break in the press."

"It won't. Rolph put the fear of God into Crowther. What the hell. We been together almost twenty years. You're entitled to at least one grade-A binge."

"And suppose I killed those two clowns? Poor dumb bastards, I had nothing against them. I had a few shots and started to talk loud and nasty and they decided to throw me out. That's their job."

"We'll just hope they live."

"Where are they?"

"San Francisco General. We'll call when we get home."

In the Levys' kitchen, Dr. Frank Saltzman was waiting. He peeled off the plaster and cleaned the cut on Dan's face. "That's a beauty," he said. "What did it?"

"Brass knuckles."

"You live an interesting life, Mr. Lavette."

"More interesting than you could imagine," Sarah said.

"I'll have to take a couple of stiches."

"Be my guest," Dan said sourly.

"Give you distinction."

"Take off your shirt," Sarah told him. "I'll have it washed."

"Sarah, do me a favor. Call Jean. Tell her I been in a car accident. Mark's car."

"She's a rotten liar," Mark said. "I'll do it."

"And make her sick with worry?" Sarah asked.

"Not Jean," Dan said. "Just tell her I'm alive and walking."

Saltzman prodded the black-and-blue marks on Dan's stomach. "You haven't been spitting blood?"

"No. I threw up a couple of times."

"Any blood?"

"No. But it hurts like hell what you're doing."

"It'll hurt more tomorrow. You'll be all right. Wait four days and your doctor can take out the stitches."

The doctor left. Mark took Dan upstairs, where he got out of his clothes and sponged himself. Then, wrapped in one of Mark's robes, which came to above his knees, he sat in the kitchen and drank Sarah's coffee under the fascinated scrutiny of Martha. At twenty-three, Martha had only Dan for a real-life hero. She lived more in the dramas she created than in the quiet house at Sausalito, and she peopled her dramas with an idealized Dan Lavette. She had enrolled in a dramatic school for film acting in Hollywood, and she resented each day that remained before October 1, when the course would begin. Dan, with two stitches in his cheek, a veritable Cyrano fighting off the savage attack of five brutal thugs, was a romantic dream come true. "The scar will make you better-looking, truly, Dan," she assured him. "Not that you aren't good-looking — but it will give you a certain something, I mean — "

"I know what you mean," Sarah said. "I want to talk to Dan very privately. So please leave us, Martha."

"Why?"

"Because I say so."

"I'm not a kid anymore."

"None of us are," Mark said. "Come on, Martha, beat it."

She stalked out of the room, and Dan said, "I know what you're going to say, Sarah. Do me a favor. Let it go."

"No, you don't know what I'm going to say, and even if you do, I'll say it anyway. Mark tells me May Ling left for Los Angeles and took your son with her. Now I'm not even ten years older than you, Danny, but I'm the closest thing to a mother you've had since your own mother died, and if you will permit me, I'll talk bluntly. I think you have done a stupid and terrible thing."

"Sarah, for God's sake!" Mark exclaimed.

"Let her say it," Dan told him. "She's right."

"Then why? Why?"

"I couldn't stop her. It was either that or leave Jean."

"Oh? And why don't you leave Jean?"

"I can't."

"Why?" Sarah insisted.

"Christ, I can't explain it."

"Because she's Chinese."

"No, Sarah, no! Not because she's Chinese. Don't you understand? Everything Mark and I have, everything we built, a whole lifetime of making something that's going to be the biggest thing in this state, maybe in the whole country — and we've just begun, it's just starting to roll. I leave Jean, and she washes it out. She told me this. It's not just a question of community property — we're in hock almost fifteen million dollars to her father's bank."

"Danny, it's just a business. It's nothing. It's a golem that has both of you by the throat. Why can't you and Mark see that?"

"It's not just a business. It's my life. Without it, I'm nothing."

"God help you," Sarah whispered.

"Mark, call the hospital," Dan cried, almost wildly. "Find out what happened."

He left the room to make the call, and Dan sat there, looking at Sarah. She covered her face with her hands and began to cry softly.

"Don't," Dan begged her. "I'm not worth it."

"I'm not crying for you, Danny. I'm crying for myself."

Mark came back into the kitchen, a grin on his face. "Both of them off the critical list," he said. "They'll be all right. Lady luck is with us, Danny."

The next morning, dressed in an old pair of Jake's army trousers — the only pants in the house that fit him — and his washed, mended shirt, Dan came downstairs to be informed that Jean was on the phone.

"How do you feel?" she asked him.

"All right. I have a cut cheek and some black-and-blue marks, but otherwise I'm all right. I look ridiculous. I'm wearing Jake's old army pants. They washed my suit, and if it still fits, I'll be home this afternoon."

"Was Mark hurt?" she asked.

"No, no, he's all right."

"Shall I come for you? I'll have to break a luncheon date."

"Forget it. I'll take the ferry and a cab."

He put down the phone and turned to Sarah, who was watching him and listening.

"She'd have to break a luncheon date to pick me up," Dan said.

Sarah shook her head and turned away. "Breakfast in ten minutes," she said shortly.

At the breakfast table, helping her mother serve, Martha said to Dan, "I wish you'd put *your* oar in. It's absolutely great. We're as rich as God, but my mother won't have a servant in this place. It's bad enough with me here, but in a month I'll be leaving for Hollywood. Then she'll be in this great barn of a place by herself."

"And when that time comes, I'll think about it," Sarah said mildly.

"Hollywood? What for?"

"What does anyone go to Hollywood for? I want to act."

"Can't you act here?"

"Dan, I'm going to school — where the movies are. And films are only in one place, in Hollywood."

"It's a pesthole," Dan said.

"Well, it would be less of a pesthole if you and pop would buy a studio there instead of all the other silly things you do with your money."

"That will be the day," Dan said.

Stephan Cassala's first child, a boy, was born at the end of August in 1927. He had been married to Joanna for nine years before the child came, and those nine empty years had been a source of grief and anxiety and for a time a mystery to all four parents. For Joanna, it was a specific misery, since for the first three years she alone knew that as far as she was concerned, her husband was impotent. Her knowledge came about with such agony and guilt on the part of Stephan that it broke her heart, and she hastened to assure him that she loved him and that this fact would make no difference in their relationship. The second disappointment in Joanna's married life came from an unwillingness on Stephan's part to leave his father's house at San Mateo. Rosa, Stephan's sister, had married a teller in her father's bank, Frank Massetti — who was promptly promoted to assistant cashier — and they had taken an apartment in San Francisco and dutifully produced three children. The great house at San Mateo, with its seven bedrooms, gave Stephan all the room and comfort he required. He had no desire for a place of his own, and Joanna found it increasingly difficult to communicate with him.

He had never fully emerged from the depression that resulted from his army experience, and since that was a time when the name and philosophy of Sigmund Freud was known to few in Northern California and the practice of psychiatry to even fewer, it never occurred to Stephan or to the people around him that his persistent gloom could be an illness or might yield to treatment.

Meanwhile, Maria Cassala and Joanna's mother, Dolores Vincente, discussed the matter woefully and endlessly, brought it to their priests and prayed earnestly. They also put pressure upon Joanna, who had lost weight and become a wraith of a woman from her own helplessness and grief. Finally, after three years, Joanna told them the crux of the problem. She also told them that Stephan had honorably offered a church annulment if she so desired. But that was more than either parent could contemplate, and in a difficult discussion in which all four parents were involved, they decided to do nothing and let time cure the situation.

Time cured nothing. Joanna, a silent, dutiful, sad woman, lived on in the house. Stephan took a small apartment in San Francisco, spending an occasional night there at first and then remaining there more and more frequently. His windows overlooked the bay. He often worked until seven or eight o'clock at night in the bank office, ate alone at Gino's Restaurant on Jones Street, and then went to his apartment to sit and stare out of the window, occasionally contemplating suicide, occasionally fantasying a relationship with Martha Levy — a curious dreamlike relationship that was without sex or passion. Once, with the excuse of illness, he stayed in the apartment for three days, without shaving or eating.

Usually he would spend Friday, Saturday, and Sunday night at San Mateo, but he had conceived an unresolved and unspoken hatred for the church, and he refused to go to mass or confession — in spite of the evident pain it caused his mother. He slept poorly — in a separate room after the first few years — and frequently he would awaken during the night and go downstairs and read.

One such night he went to the kitchen for some warm milk — his stomach still bothered him — and noticed that the door to the housemaid's room was open, a light burning. Gina was twenty-seven now, rather heavy, but full-breasted and firm, someone who had always been there, whom he had looked at a thousand times and never seen. Curious, he stepped to the door of her room and glanced in. She lay in bed, her radio turned so low it was almost inaudible, her nightgown pushed up carelessly, revealing her legs and the edge of the dark triangle of hair in her crotch.Her eyes met his as he stood there; she smiled at him but made no motion to cover herself. He stood there and the minutes ticked by, yet neither of them said a word; and then at last she said, "Come in, Stevey, and close the door behind you."

He stepped into the room, closed the door behind him, and stood there staring at her. He was wearing his pajamas and no robe, and as he stood there, staring at Gina, he felt his desire rise in him like a gush of flame. She held out her hand; he took it; and she drew him down to her and kissed him. Then she touched his penis, and he ejaculated with a force and passion that wracked his entire body.

"All right, all right, Stevey," she whispered. "You see, it's all right. You're a man, you're a wonderful man. You'll never have trouble again." She spoke in soft, liquid Italian.

He made love to her until just before dawn, the Italian words "Sono un uomo" echoing and reechoing in his mind.

When he left her, she said to him, "I must not have a child, Stevey, so you buy some condoms and I will keep them with me. And tomorrow night — or when you wish. I love you very much, and I ask nothing, I swear."

For the next six months, he spent most nights at San Mateo, and the affair with Gina went on, once, twice, sometimes, three times each week. No one knew or suspected. At the end of the six months, Joanna was pregnant, and by common consent of Gina and Stephan, their affair ended. They never slept together again after that, but, in a curious way, they loved each other.

And amidst great joy in the Cassala household, Joanna's baby was born, a fine eight-pound boy they named Ralph.

Fortas was an enormous, large-bellied, shaggy-haired Basque who was always engaged in minor feuds with his neighbors, whose dogs, as he claimed, killed his lambs. He kept a small herd of sheep, and the degree of his anger depended upon how far-ranging the neighborhood dogs were and how dangerous, by his judgment, the breed. Since Jake and Clair owned a pair of gentle mongrels who stayed close to home, their relations with Fortas were on the better side. Now, when they came to him for advice, he greeted them warmly, took them into his kitchen, and poured wine while his wife sliced a cake.

Jake outlined, briefly, Rabbi Blum's proposal. "So we come to you," he said. "We don't know the first damn thing about making wine."

"Jewish wine!" Fortas exploded. "Sonofabitch — you two Jewish?"

Clair grinned and nodded.

"Goddamn! Hey, Sada," he yelled to his wife, "these two kids the same bastard what killed our Lord. First goddamn Jew I ever see."

"Oh, shut up, Fortas," his wife said. "He got the brains of a monkey and the voice of a bull," she said to Clair.

"Ah, hell," Fortas said. "Goddamn long time ago. Who give a shit? You kids want to know how to make wine? Easiest goddamn thing. You crush the grapes and then you got the wine."

"Oh, sure," said Sada. "Easy for you because I make the wine. What does he know?"

Jake produced the bottle of wine that Rabbi Blum had left with them and explained, "This is the kind of wine we have to make."

"The point is," Clair said, "that we wish we could just buy this zinfandel of yours, which is absolutely delicious, but it wouldn't be acceptable."

Fortas nodded. "I know the slop they drink in church."

His wife poured a glass of Rabbi Blum's wine, tasted it, made a face, and handed the glass to her husband. Fortas drank and spat out the wine.

"Goddamn slop!"

"Oh, shut up," Sada told him. "Listen," she said to Clair and Jake, "this is a sweet wine, very sweet. Not so good, I'm afraid, but very sweet. Not even like a good muscatel or Tokay — I don't know what. You want to know how we make the wine, fine, I show you — you still got Gallagher's stuff, the crushers and the vats and the barrels?"

"Yes, we have his equipment."

"Good. Next week, maybe, the weather is good, we begin to pick the first grape. Then you crush. You get the juice —

we call it 'must.' We make a red wine, so we let the skins ferment with the must. You watch, you taste, you strain, you clarify — you got wine."

"But your wine is dry, not sweet."

"Ah, yes. That's another art. You stop the souring, the fermentation."

"Throw in some brandy," Fortas said. "That stop it."

"Brandy, brandy — where they get brandy today?"

The argument went on, the upshot of it being that if you were Fortas and Sada, you made wine by taste and instinct; but for Jake and Clair, the result was only bewilderment and confusion. The following day, they packed the children into the car and drove to Sausalito, where they delivered the children to a grateful Sarah, pulled out Volume 28 of the *Britannica* — a gift for Jake's thirteenth birthday — turned to "Wine," and found the subsection "Malaga."

"Malaga," Clair read aloud, while Jake listened with intense concentration, "is a sweet wine generally, as exported, a blend made from *vino dulce* and *vino secco,* together with varying quantities of *vino maestro, vino tierno, arope,* and *vino de color.* The *vino dulce* and *vino secco* are both made as a rule from the Pedro Jimenez (white) grape. The *vino maestro* consists of must, which has only been fermented to a slight degree and which has been 'killed' by the addition of about 17 percent alcohol. The *vino tierno* is made by mashing raisins (6 parts) with water (2 parts), pressing, and then adding alcohol (1 part) to the must. *Arope* is obtained — "

"Enough, enough," Jake pleaded. "I don't know what in hell they're talking about."

"Neither do I," Clair agreed sweetly. "You didn't think we were going to solve this out of the encyclopedia. I don't for a moment believe that this Malaga wine which is made somewhere in Spain has much connection with what the rabbi wants. There must be someone somewhere who can give us simple and scientific directions for the making of sweet wine — and Jake, believe me, it's worth it. I think that the making of wine is one of the most romantic things in the world. We have nine hundred acres of some of the best vineland in the Napa Valley, and we've broken our backs to own it. This crazy Prohibition thing can't last forever. It's turning the whole country into a cesspool of crime and violence, and sooner or later the people are going to be fed up and disgusted enough to repeal that crazy law. Meanwhile, if we learn how to make this sacramental wine, we have a head start on every other grower."

"So? What do we do?"

"Let's start by leaving the kids with your mother and going over to Berkeley and finding someone on the faculty who can give us some scientific answers. And if we can't find him at Berkeley, we'll go to Stanford — but somewhere there's someone who can say, do this and this and this. Right?"

"O.K., we'll give it a shot."

Professor Simon Masseo was enthralled with Clair. He was a small, rotund, middle-aged man, who obviously adored women and who was completely taken by her height, her splendid, strong body, her pleasantly freckled handsome face, and her great unruly mop of red hair. He could not keep his eyes off her, and insisted that she and Jake lunch with him at the faculty dining room. He was one of those men who derive a simple and total pleasure in being in the company of a beautiful woman; and Clair possessed the open, unfettered quality of making a man feel that he alone mattered. She gave Professor Masseo just that feeling, and he unbent in return.

"Of course you must make the wine," he told them. "Should the art perish entirely because a handful of maniacs have decreed that man's dearest consolation is criminal? I've taught the art of wine-making, among other things. In nineteen eighteen, I had over two hundred students. In nineteen twenty — well, we dropped the course."

"Then if there is no course," Clair began, "how — "

"How? Dear lady, let me begin by assuring you that man does not make wine. Nature makes it; man directs the process. And how did man come to it? Five thousand years ago, he tasted the wine in overripe grapes, crushed them in his mouth, and drank wine. What is wine? Take some grapes, put them in a large receptacle, mash them, and place the pot or whatever in a warm place. Stir the mixture each day — and thus begins that marvelous process called fermentation. Then one sniffs at it. Ah, what a delicious odor! Now it comes alive and begins to move and heave and chuckle with its own voice as you stir it. Then it appears to rest. Now it is time to drain off the must, which is simply the word used for the wine fluid. This is still alive with yeast. We drain it off into a clean container. Then we squeeze the fluid from what remains in the original jug, and we add that to the must. We cover the receptacle this time, but we do not seal it because the wine is still alive, and once again we set it in a slightly warm place. And we watch it — carefully. And then, very soon, it comes to rest. At this point, the increasing alcohol content has halted the action of the yeast. Now we pour the wine into bottles or jugs or whatever, and we stopper it tightly. Place it in a cool spot, a nice part of the cellar, and let it settle. Then we open the jug, pour out the clear liquid, gently leaving the sediment — and behold, we have wine!"

"As simple as that," Clair exclaimed.

"Precisely — or as complicated as one could imagine. Because, dear lady, when you drink the wine — well, you might have a superb wine or a perfectly wretched wine, a bitter wine, a sourish wine, a bland wine, a marvelous wine — who knows? It is the thousand variables and the control of these variables that constitute the wine-makers' art. The yeast is there, in the marvelous waxy bloom on the skin of the grape, but now we must ask, what kind of grapes, and how ripe, and from what district, and what of the stems? The stems contain about three percent of tannin, and it is tannin that give the wine astringency, that delicate puckering in taste — and how much of it do we want? And what of the seeds? They too possess tannin. And what of the skins? It is the skin that makes the difference between a red wine and a white wine, and this coloring substance in the skins is not a simple pigment but a very complex substance somewhat like the tannin yet different — and different in every different variety of grape, mind you, and this is only the beginning of the art of knowing and controlling the variables."

Jake sighed. "I knew it was too good to be true."

"Defeat so soon? My dear boy, I am sure your lovely wife is not discouraged."

"But our problem," Clair said, "is to produce a sweet wine like the wine we brought for you to taste. And that certainly must be very difficult."

"Indeed no — nowhere so difficult as to produce an excellent dry wine, and I'll explain, and if you have an hour to spend in my laboratory, I'll spell out the steps and you can make notes. I'll also lend you a book or two on the subject, and then if you will be so kind as to invite me to a tasting at your place in the Napa Valley, I'll be delighted to come."

"Would you?"

"I would indeed. Now let us consider the wine your friend Rabbi Blum gave you. Not a very good wine. From the taste, I would suggest that it was made out of New York State or perhaps Maryland Concord grapes and sweetened with additional sugar. Now I must explain that in the fermentation process of wine-making we begin with a very high proportion of sugar in the pulp of the grape. Depending on the grape and the degree of ripeness, you can have as much as two hundred and seventy-five grams of sugar in relation to eight hundred grams of water. This sugar, known as grape sugar, consists of dextrose and levulose, and in the process of fermentation, the sugar is converted into ethyl alcohol and carbon dioxide gas. But when the alcohol in the grape juice has reached a level of about fourteen or fifteen percent, the yeast is halted in its process of converting the sugar. At this point, most wines are still rather sweet. Now your problem, of course, is not to rid yourself of the sweetness but to add to it, and there are several ways to go about this. First of all the grape. What kind of grapes do you grow for the market?"

"Zinfandels mostly. We have some Thompsons — "

"Ah, well the color of zinfandels is excellent, but we want a sweeter grape. Next month there ought to be some excellent muscatels and Marsalas available in the San Joaquin Valley. There is no need for you to try to produce a varietal, which simply means a wine produced out of a single variety of grape. What you want is to imitate that stuff you gave me — and improve it. I don't think the rabbi would object to that. Now you want your grapes to be very ripe, indeed a trifle overripe — almost at that stage which in France is called the *pourriture noble* state, or just a bit rotten. *Pourriture noble* is a trifle risky, but table grapes are always picked a bit early. We want something in between, and I can give you the name of a couple of growers in the valley who will know what you are talking about. The point is to select your grapes and contract for them in advance, so that the growers will let them hang on the vines. So much for the grapes, and we will talk some more about that. Now another factor which we must also consider is the addition of brandy, which halts the yeast process while the must is quite sweet — simply by raising the alcohol content to the required fourteen percent. And then there is the use of sugar — oh no, no simple matter this wine-making, but intriguing. We shall discuss it."

When at long last they parted from Professor Masseo, loaded with books, notebooks, confusion, and a mass of uneasy information on wine-making, Jake said to his wife, "Baby, I am scared. Eight hundred gallons of wine. Do you realize how much that is? I have visions of us bankrupt, loaded with tubs of rotten grapes and barrels of sour wine. Heaven help us."

"Rabbi Blum will see to that," Clair said.

Pierre Kardeneaux had opened a small but exceedingly elegant couturier shop off California Street where an evening gown could cost more than a thousand dollars. On her second visit there, Jean ran into Alan Brocker, whom she had not spoken to for years. He sat in one of Kardeneaux's velvet-upholstered chairs, his chin on a gold-topped walking stick, observing a slender blond girl pirouette in a white velvet evening wrap with a white mink collar. Then the slender blond girl kissed him lightly on the cheek, and Jean heard her say, "Oh, please, dear, dear Alan — may I have it? I do love it so."

Smiling, Jean said, "But of course. You can't deny your daughter a little thing like that."

"Oh, but I'm not — " the slender blond girl began.

"But of course," Jean agreed, and swept away.

Brocker telephoned the following day, and Jean said cheerfully, "Dear Alan, how delightful to hear from you after all this time."

"Darling, you are the most incredible bitch."

"Then that lovely child wasn't your daughter?"

"Shall we have lunch?"

"Certainly."

"Tomorrow then. I'll pick you up."

Now why did I agree? Jean asked herself, and could find no other answer except that she was bored and that Alan Brocker was entertaining. He had a quality not too frequently found in men, the ability to gossip and to wet his gossip with acid. She also felt a pleasant sense of superiority. When she had first met Brocker, he was the teacher, sophisticated, knowledgeable, and in command. But nothing about him appeared to have changed very much, whereas Jean had changed a great deal. She saw him now as an ineffectual, permanent adolescent, and she enjoyed the sense of being in command.

"At least he will be amusing," she decided.

At lunch the following day, Jean said to him, "How old are you these days, dear Alan?"

"How old are you, my dear?"

"Thirty-seven. I make no secret of it."

"I'm only forty-three, my love. We are both of us in our prime."

"Then wouldn't you say that child you were squiring yesterday is somewhat underdone? How old is she? Eighteen?"

"Twenty."

"And she's earned an evening wrap. How very talented!"

"My dear Jean, are you moralizing?"

"Heaven forbid! It would become me poorly, don't you think?"

"I'm afraid so."

"Anyway, thank you for accusing me of moralizing and not of jealousy."

"Jealousy? My dear, you cut me out of your life."

"You were never in my life, dear Alan."

"Let's stop being nasty and catch up. What are those two handsome children of yours up to?"

"Children? Yes, I suppose so. Barbara is thirteen. Jazz, films, and horses. There seems to be something valid underneath all that, but when and where I don't know. As for Tom, well, he's just beautiful. Almost sixteen, six feet, and the apple of my eye, if you must know. I adore him. He has brains and character and looks, not his father's, I may say."

"I would say you've found a substitute."

"For whom?" she asked coldly.

"For the fisherman."

"You do hate him, don't you?"

"Don't you, Jean?" he asked her.

She stared at him, shuddering inwardly at the thought of being married to this man who sat across the table from her.

What an aimless, mindless, contemptible creature he was! And how strange that in all the years she had known him, she had never passed judgment upon him. Yet he amused her, and she could talk to him and spend time with him without being bored — and of course she was not married to him, which was the decisive factor.

"Why should I hate him?" she wondered aloud.

"He keeps you prisoner."

"Or do I keep him prisoner? Think about it, Alan."

"Why, I can't imagine. You are still the most beautiful and engaging woman in San Francisco. And by the way, he does occasionally escape."

"Oh?"

"You do know about the incident at Harry's bar?"

"You mean that wretched speakeasy? What incident?"

"As I hear it, your husband wrecked the place a few weeks ago. Became offensive and they tried to throw him out. Five or six of them. He put two of them in the hospital and got himself beat up and arrested. It took Sunny Jim in person to get him out of it."

"And when was this?"

"About two weeks ago from what I hear."

"Two weeks ago," she said slowly, thinking of the scar on his cheek and the supposed auto accident. "Six men — really. My dear Alan, what would you do if six men attacked you?"

"I would not become offensive in a speakeasy."

"No, I'm sure you wouldn't. But if six men — or two men — attacked you?"

"I'd yell for help."

"You would," she said.

Dan sat in front of the fire and stared into the flames. He was sitting in the room that was called a library at times and a study at other times, with a wall of books he had not read, with half a dozen expensive oil paintings on the walls, paintings he had not selected and was totally indifferent to, and he was engaged in a sort of introspection — a process somewhat unusual for a man who was not greatly introspective. His thoughts were confused and aimless, and if he had possessed the concept, he might have been asking himself who he was and where he was. But he lived in a time prior to the public airing of that question, and it never occurred to him that he did not know who we was.

Yet the aching desire simply to be pressed in upon him, and he found his memories in the flames. The moments with May Ling stood out most sharply; they existed; they were etched out of the confusion: the tiny house on Willow Street which exhibited in every corner the imprint of her personality, a day when they walked hand in hand on Ocean Beach, an evening on Telegraph hill, next to Coit Tower, with the whole incredible panorama of San Francisco spread beneath them, the luau in Hawaii and the days on the boat when they sailed in the Islands. The memories stabbed painfully, yet they were real and everything else was an illusion.

He became conscious of someone else in the room, and he glanced up to see Jean. It was quite late, past eleven o'clock. He had dined out and come home to what appeared to be an empty house. Now Jean appeared wearing a pale green negligee under a robe of white lace. He had learned what things cost; the bill for the robe and negligee would be at least five hundred dollars.

"Hello, Dan," she said, dropping onto the couch where he sat. "You look very lonely."

"It's part of being alone, isn't it."

"I suppose so." She reached over and touched the scar on his cheek. "It healed nicely. I think the scar is rather cosmetic."

"I could live without it," Dan said.

"I heard about the fight at Harry's bar. Why didn't you tell me about it?"

"I don't know. A drunken barroom brawl isn't the happiest kind of thing. I guess we're used to lying to each other."

"I haven't had to lie. You never question anything I do."

"Why should I?"

"We're married, Dan. We've been married a long time."

He nodded. "I wonder sometimes how many people are married the way we are?"

"Quite a few."

"It's harder when you're poor. Money greases the skids, doesn't it?"

"I don't know. I've never been poor."

"Were you disgusted with me?" he asked. "Or are you past that?"

"No. I thought it was rather wonderful — six men against one."

"Only five. No, it wasn't wonderful. It was stupid and vicious — on my part."

"The strange thing is, you drink so little." When he made no reply to this, she said, "You know, I found a flask in Tom's room. Filled with that rotgut they sell."

"What did you do with it?"

"I threw it away."

"You didn't say anything to him?"

"You might."

"I barely know him," Dan said bitterly.

"He's a nice boy, Danny."

It was the first time she had called him Danny in years. He looked at her curiously, realizing that until this moment he had not seen her, only a woman in a green negligee and a white lace robe, but not herself. Now, seeing her in the low lamplight, the fire casting its play of light and shade on her face, he remembered her — as if time had never touched her. Yet the longing, the hunger for her, the ache inside of him whenever he looked at her — that was gone. He was married to a strange woman he had never known or caressed or kissed. He was empty, used up and depleted, and his only desire was that she should go away and leave him to stare into the fire.

"Danny," she said softly, "come to bed with me."

He stared at her, unable to conceal his astonishment.

"I know." She smiled. "It's been a long time."

"Just like that — come to bed with me, Danny?"

"How else?"

"Jesus Christ, I don't know. Ask me who I am. Or do you go to bed with strangers?"

"What a rotten thing to say!"

"O.K. I'm sorry. I shouldn't have said that."

"But you did."

"Oh, what the hell! It's going to become a fight, isn't it?"

"Isn't that what you want?"

"I don't know what I want. I'm no use to you, Jean. In bed or out of bed."

"Did it ever occur to you that you're a bastard?"

"It has occurred to me. Yes."

A week later, Thomas Seldon Lavette, age fifteen and a half, was preparing to leave for his second year at the Groton School for boys in Massachusetts. His father and mother were to drive him to Oakland, where he would take the train for the East. His trunk had gone on ahead, and he was sitting in his room dressed in gray flannels and a blue blazer, bolting his tennis racket frame, when his father entered the room. Tom was a tall, slender boy, six feet in height, with blue eyes and blond hair. He had a narrow, handsome face and good skin that had escaped the acne that attacked so many boys of his age. Dan always felt uneasy in his presence, prey to a sense of strangeness and inferiority. It was difficult for him to communicate, and in all truth he had seen little of the boy during the past five years and almost nothing of him during the past twelve months, when he had been either away at school or playing tennis at the club — the San Francisco Golf Club where Dan rarely appeared — or riding with his sister and their friends.

Now Dan stood in his room, awkward, wishing he had not left this until now and trying to work out how to say what he felt he must say.

"Time to go, dad?" Tom asked him.

"Almost. I want to talk to you about something."

"Shoot."

"The flask of bootleg booze your mother found in your room."

"She threw it away. The flask cost twelve dollars."

"Don't you think you're a little young to drink that rotgut?" Dan asked him.

"It wasn't rotgut. It was good whiskey."

"You're not sixteen yet."

"I don't drink that much. All the fellows carry a flask. So I had one. So what?"

"You don't see anything wrong with it?"

"No."

"I do. I think it stinks."

"You would."

"What do you mean by that?"

"Only that your notions of morality are most peculiar."

"I would still like to know what you mean."

"That's all I'm going to say." He went back to tightening the bolts on the tennis racket frame.

"God damn it," Dan said, "when I ask you a question, I expect an answer. Don't tell me that's all you're going to say. I happen to be your father."

"You happen to be."

"Now what in hell does that mean?"

"I should be grateful for that damn flask!" the boy cried, his voice rising to the edge of hysteria. "Without it, a year could go by and you wouldn't speak to me. When did you last talk to me about anything? Why don't you ever tell me I do something right? Why don't you tell me it makes a difference if I'm alive or dead? Because it doesn't make any difference! Not to you!"

Shaken by the outburst, Dan stared at his son, pleading inwardly for the boy's love, thinking, My God, you're my son, my own flesh and blood. Give me a chance. Talk to me with love. Let me talk to you. Tell me how. I don't know how. God Almighty, I don't know how. Every muscle in his body strained toward the boy with the desire to embrace him, to take the boy in his arms, yet he could not, any more than he could find words to say. He stood there for perhaps a minute while the boy held the tennis racket in his shaking hands; then Dan turned and left the room.

During the drive to the railroad station, he was silent, as was his son.

The Marin County Players, an unpaid group of amateur acting enthusiasts under the direction of Dameon Fenwick, presented three performances of *Romeo and Juliet* at the high school auditorium. Martha played Juliet, and Stephan Cassala, who had heard about the performance from Mark, managed to be there for two out of the three evenings. For the first performance, he sat in the audience and watched and then left quietly. The second time, he made his way backstage and managed to have a few words with Martha. He told her in no uncertain terms, with an air of sophisticated backlog knowledge, that she was the best Juliet he had ever seen. It was quite true; he had never seen the play before, so he might have said with equal truth that she was the worst.

Martha, still in make-up, high on her performance and flattered that this handsome friend of her father's, an older man—Stephan was thirty-two—had seen fit to make the trip to Sausalito just to see her perform, threw her arms around Stephan and kissed him.

"What a dear man you are!" she exclaimed. "Did you really think I was good?"

"Splendid. Absolutely splendid."

"Oh, I needed that so badly. You don't know what you've done for me. Ten days from now, I'm leaving for Hollywood, and, Steve, I'm scared."

"Hollywood? But why?"

"Because that's where an actress must be. The only place. There's nothing here. I would curl up and die if I had to stay in this place."

"But you're an actress, not one of those idiots in film."

"Steve, don't you know what's happening? Silent pictures are finished. Everyone says so. In another year or two, every motion picture will be a talkie. And I can talk."

For the next three or four days, Stephan wracked his mind for a valid reason to go to Sausalito. He was filled with guilt and confusion, compounded by the arrival of his infant son and the bliss of his wife, Joanna. She was totally submissive and totally content. She no longer suggested that they move out of the house at San Mateo; indeed, she dreaded the thought of being separated from Rosa and Maria, and, now that she had a son, she felt that her existence was justified. She never questioned the nights that Stephan spent in San Francisco. Her husband was soft-spoken, gentle, and kind to her. She asked for no more, and thereby condemned him to the tortures of guilt.

Yet strangely—or perhaps not so strangely—this tortured guilt brought zest and excitement to his life for the first time. He was in love. He had never been in love before, never idolized a woman, never thought of himself as a man who could complete a woman's life; nor had he ever elevated a woman to an object of total desire and beauty. In all truth, Martha was not very beautiful. She had good features, her mother's sparkling blue eyes, and straight brown hair that she wore in the tight shingled style so popular then. She had a good bust and good legs, but it was her air of excitement, her bubbling enthusiasm for life that fascinated Stephan. He made no plans; the very thought of leaving his wife, as a part of a deeply religious Catholic family, was so complex and preposterous that he could not even entertain it, and it was further complicated by the lifelong relationship between the Cassalas and the Levys and by the fact that he was Catholic and Martha was Jewish. For the moment, it was sufficient that he was in love, that the whole world was different, and that each morning he awakened, not to the dull, featureless prospect of another day but to a day of holding Martha Levy in his mind and his heart.

By the third day after the performance of *Romeo and Juliet* Stephan had worked out a reasonable package of excuses and lies. He manufactured an appointment with a banker in San Rafael that had to take place on Saturday, and since the trip would take him through Sausalito, he asked Mark whether he could stop by for lunch and discuss a matter of business with him. He chose Saturday because Mark would be home that day, but he lacked the courage to ask that Martha be there too. On that score, he would have to chance it.

It worked out well. Anthony Cassala had accepted the circumstances that took L&L into the Seldon Bank, both with its loans and its business, yet Danny and Mark continued to maintain an account of almost a hundred thousand dollars with Cassala. Now, sitting at lunch with Mark and Sarah and, fortune prevailing, with Martha as well, Stephan argued that the money ought to be used for some purpose, put into government bonds possibly. It earned no interest, and both he and his father felt a sense of guilt. Mark pushed his arguments aside. "Too fine a day to talk about it," he said. "Anyway, Dan's committed to this airline thing, so we may get at the money after all."

Sarah blocked her mind where money was concerned. She refused to think about it, to deal with it, or to face it. Forty-seven years old now, her fair hair was already beginning to be streaked with white. She still maintained her slender, youthful figure, but her face had aged. As the men talked, she watched Stephan, noticing that he could not keep his eyes from Martha, who was impatient with all this talk of money and banks. To Sarah, Hollywood was a festering sink of sin and corruption, and her anxiety increased as the day of Martha's departure neared. Now Martha was telling Stephan about the New York School of Acting, where she had enrolled as a student. The school had just been organized under the direction of a man called Martin Spizer.

When Martha first announced to her parents her intention of enrolling there, Sarah kept after Mark to make inquiries and find out something about it. Several phone calls to Los Angeles told him only that it was one of a dozen new schools that had mushroomed in Hollywood with the advent of talking pictures, and that it was apparently no better and no worse than most of the others. Martha chose it because a leaflet advertising it had been handed to her by Mr. Fenwick, her local drama teacher; and the whole subject was so alien and so distant from any area of Mark's knowledge that he was finally content to let her abide by her own choice.

"The trouble with the film stars," Martha explained, "is that they can't talk. Oh, it was just great when all they had to do was prance around and make faces — but now that people can hear them, well, it's just open season for actors. Real actors."

"Providing," Mark said, "that talking pictures ever become anything else but a novelty."

"Father, how can you close your eyes to it? Talking pictures are here to stay. Didn't you see *The Jazz Singer?* And in *Tenderloin,* that ridiculous Dolores Costello, lisping."

"Darling," Sarah said worriedly, "every pretty girl in America is dreaming about Hollywood. And so many of them go there. So many of them."

"But can they act?" She turned to Stephan. "Tell them what you think of my acting, Steve. They'll listen to you."

"Did you ever see her act?" Sarah asked curiously.

"He did. He came to see *Romeo and Juliet.*"

"I saw the notice in the paper," Stephan answered uneasily. "She was wonderful, I thought."

"And Steve's seen half a dozen productions of *Romeo and Juliet,* and he thinks I was the best Juliet of the lot."

"Well, maybe not half a dozen," Stephan said. "But she was great. I think she can act."

He had to be alone with her, if only for a few minutes. Before he left, he told Mark that he wanted to say goodby to Martha, since he might not see her again before she went to Los Angeles.

"You'll find her in the old gazebo, out on the lawn behind the house. She does her reading aloud out there. She can't stand it if anyone comes near the place while she's declaiming, but she might make an exception for you."

As Stephan walked toward the gazebo, he heard Martha. If one could criticize her acting, certainly her voice was powerful and far-reaching. She was doing Saint Joan, from Shaw's play, which had come to San Francisco two years before.

"If you command me to declare that all that I have done and said, and all the visions and revelations I have had were not from God, then that is impossible: I will not declare it for anything in the world." She saw him, and her face bubbled with laughter. "Oh, Steve, you heard me, and my secret is out. But I will be Saint Joan, if I have to wait ten years to play the part. I will. I must. They must make a great movie out of it, even if I have to go to Mr. Shaw and plead myself. I will get down on my knees. I will say, look at me, Mr. Shaw, am I not Saint Joan? No! Of course I wouldn't do anything that silly. Are you leaving, Steve?"

"I'm afraid I must."

"When will I see you again? Will you come to my first talkie?"

"Before then I hope. Martha — "

Her laughter stopped. "Is something wrong, Steve?"

"No. No. Only — well, I have a little present for your going-away. You will accept a present for me, won't you?"

"I love presents."

Stephan reached into his pocket, took out a small, velvet-covered box, and opened it to reveal a diamond pendant on a gold chain. Martha stared as he slipped the chain over her neck.

"Steve, you are insane. This must have cost a thousand dollars."

"What difference does it make what a gift costs?"

"You know what difference it makes. How do I explain this to Mark and Sarah? What do I tell them? And why give it to me? I don't understand you."

"I love you," he said simply.

"No. Oh, God, no. You're absolutely out of your mind, Steve. You're a married man. Your wife has just had a child."

"I know, I know," he said unhappily, taking her hand. "You're right. I never led up to this. You don't just tell a woman you love her."

"You certainly don't. What did I do to let this happen?"

"Nothing. It just happened."

She took off the chain and handed it back to him. "I have to be honest, Steve. I've known you since we were kids. I always liked you, but I'm not in love with you, and I have no intentions of falling in love with anyone."

"I know. That's why I never said anything or did anything. I think it began at my wedding. That stinks, doesn't it, to say that all I could think about at my wedding was another girl? But I didn't love my wife. I never loved her, and the funny thing is that I don't know why I married her. It just seemed to be something that everyone wanted and I didn't have enough guts not to go along with it. I didn't sleep with her for years — oh, Christ, why am I saying all this? I feel like a fool, an idiot, and a louse."

"Poor Steve." She leaned forward and kissed him. "Steve, I think you're the kindest, sweetest man I ever met."

"Will you keep this?" he asked, holding up the pendant. "Please. Don't show it to your folks. But keep it, please. I'm not asking for anything else. You're going away. God knows when I'll see you again. I can accept what you say about your feelings for me. I have to. But what harm will it do if you take this, and then at least I'll know that something I got for you is with you."

"It's beautiful, Steve." She looked at him. His dark, sad eyes pleaded with her, and then she nodded and smiled and said, "All right, Mr. Cassala. I'll keep it, and you must think of me as a little gold digger, and that will break down all your silly notions about how great I am and you'll stop being in love, and then we'll be good, dear friends forever and ever. Agreed?"

"We'll be good, dear friends — be sure of that."

Thomas Seldon had aged quickly in the years since his wife's death. His hair had turned white, and at the age of seventy-three, he showed signs of feebleness. Going into his club with Dan, he walked slowly and carefully, and when he was greeted in passing by John Whittier, he looked at him blankly. "Who was that?" he asked Dan.

"Grant Whittier's son, John."

"Of course. I saw him only last week. What will he think?"

"It's all right," Dan said. "He probably thought nothing of it."

"Well, it gets worse. Forget names, faces — only the old days are clear and bright. I keep thinking about the city, the way it was when I was a kid. Clipper ships as thick as fleas in the harbor, board sidewalks, muddy streets — by golly, I remember the vigilantes, and that goes back a while. Saw a public hanging once, right there on the Market Street wharf. You know, I rode the first cable car on California Street — well, maybe not the very first but it was the first day. The Eighth Wonder of the World. But it's all like a dream. You look at the city now, and it's all like a dream."

Seated in the high-ceilinged dining room, with its paneled oak walls, its white tablecloths, and gleaming silver, among those who in Dan's youth had been called the nabobs and pashas and who were now simply men of distinction and power, Dan felt that his own beginnings were equally dreamlike.

Seldon was wandering again, remembering how the cart horses labored on the hills. "The teamster would get down and put his own shoulder to it, and then the kids would come running. Did it myself — oh yes. We'd all put our shoulders to the cart, and the teamster would shout, 'Gee! gee!' — can't believe it today. Where's Mark? Wasn't he to be here?"

"He'll be here any minute," Dan assured him.

"Good man, Mark. Good man. Good heavens, when I think of it. Twenty years ago neither of you had a nickel — and today. But this, Dan, this airplane business. I don't know. Never been up in one and I never intend to go up in one. If the good Lord intended us to fly — "

"Tom, you could also say that he would have given us wheels if he intended us to ride in trains."

"That's good. I'll listen. Say your piece, and I'll listen."

Mark joined them then, and the waiter came to take their order. "If you want a drink," Seldon said, "I can swing it. The committee disapproves, but they keep a few bottles of good stuff on hand. They serve it in coffee cups, a degrading way to treat fine whiskey, but if you want it — "

They passed on the drinks. "How's that pretty wife of yours?" Seldon asked Mark.

"Fine, Mr. Seldon. Just fine."

"You know, Mark, I kept a bit of company with a Jewish girl once. Oh, she was a beauty. Her father ran a three-card faro game in the Tenderloin. Did well, too. But when my daddy found out about it, he took my head off — "

Dan steered the conversation to his own point, troubled by how easily Seldon's mind wandered. "The basic thing is the airport," he told Seldon, "and now that the Municipal Airport has opened at Mills Field, the future is clear. Mark has been out there, and we bought the franchise. We've rented space for two hangars and office facilities and waiting room. As we see it, the first step is regular passenger service between here and Los Angeles, and we're making arrangements at the Los Angeles airport. I've had a statistical prognosis done, and according to the figures they give me, the growth in Los Angeles will be enormous. Mind you, Tom, we've put all this together in a complete projection. Mark has several copies with him, and we'll leave that with you. Now I just want to fill you in and answer any questions you have."

"The first question is who's going to use this service of yours? I wouldn't."

"Don't be too sure of that." Dan smiled. "You'll have a company pass in any case."

"I'm damn sure. I'd have to have my head examined to climb into one of those stick and fabric contraptions."

"So you would," Dan agreed. "We're not going to run any stick and fabric contraptions. I've made three trips to Detroit, and I've had hours of conversation with Henry Ford, his son, Edsel, and Jim McDonnell. Mostly with McDonnell, his designer and engineer. They've designed and produced a thing called the Ford Trimotor, and it's going to revolutionize the whole industry. And it's no contraption of sticks and fabric. It's metal — a whole airplane out of metal."

"Metal? Iron? Dan, do you mean to tell me you can make an airplane out of iron and get it off the ground?"

"Not iron, no. The Ford trimotor is built out of high-strength Duralumin. That's a light, strong metal, and they coat it with aluminum to prevent corrosion. It's an incredible plane, Tom. It's fifty feet long, with a wingspan of seventy-four feet. The cabin is sixteen feet long. Think of that, sixteen feet, and you can stand up in it and walk around. There are seats for twelve passengers, and it's just about the safest plane in the world. It can take off in not much more than a hundred yards, which means we can go into almost any airport — San Diego, Reno, Tacoma — when we're ready. It's something out of the future. There's never been anything in the world like it. And it will fly at a hundred miles an hour — three motors — and it can land with two of them."

"Dan, a train will go eighty miles an hour."

"Not between here and Los Angeles. That's nine hours, and we can cut the time in half. Leave San Francisco at seven in the morning. You're in Los Angeles in time for lunch. Leave Los Angeles at four and you're back here in time for dinner. No train can come near matching that. We go as the crow flies."

"And what will this cost?" Seldon asked, shaking his head dubiously.

"A million and a half to start the ball rolling — more as we expand. We've taken the first step already and put in the order with Ford for five planes. Tom, you backed us on the ships and other things, and it's worked. Believe me, this is the beginning of something bigger than anything we ever dreamed of."

"What are you into us for now, Dan?" he asked bleakly.

"Mark?"

"Thirteen million, two hundred and twenty thousand. We've been reducing the principal at the rate of ten thousand a month — and we've never been a day behind on the interest. I think that's pretty damn good," Mark answered.

"How's the store doing?"

"We should run a net profit of eight hundred thousand by the end of the fiscal year. That's nothing to be ashamed of."

"I'm not complaining about how you run things, but how much are you going to run? Three ocean liners, the store here, the hotel in Hawaii, and I hear you been buying land."

"Some day that land's going to wipe out every penny of indebtedness we have. You can see how this city is expanding. The land we're buying on the peninsula and in Marin County will be worth a fortune some day. When they build a bridge across the Golden Gate — "

"Son," Seldon said, "I've heard that bridge talk for twenty years. They'll never do it. You say you've put this all down on paper? Let me study it and think about it."

After they had left Seldon, Mark said to Dan, "I think we're making a mistake. Putting everything in one basket, I mean. Why don't we go to Tony Cassala with this? He can handle a million and a half."

"Because, old chum, a million and a half is only the beginning. It's only a hook. That operation you laid out in our prospectus can't work the way it is, and I'm glad it can't. We have to go up the coast to Portland and Seattle. This is only the beginning. We're going to build us the biggest damn airline west of the Rockies, and that's only the beginning. McDonnell says that in two years, they'll have something that can take the Rockies and in five years the airplane's speed will be two and a half times what it is today. Two hundred and fifty miles an hour, and we're in at the ground floor."

"Listen, Dan," Mark said, "even if your dreams are real, we're doing the wrong thing, hanging it all on bank loans."

"What other way do you suggest?"

"I was talking to Sam Goldberg, and he says now is the time to go public, to issue stock and get a listing on the New York Stock Exchange. He says that if we put out half a million shares at twenty-five dollars a share — "

"Hell, Mark, what we've got is worth more than twelve and a half million, a damn sight more, and you know that."

"Let me finish. I'm talking about half the issue. We keep fifty percent. We still have control, and we got a working capital of twelve and a half million dollars. Goldberg says that in this market the shares could double and even triple in a matter of weeks — months at the most."

"No, sir! God damn it, Mark, we built this thing ourselves. It's ours. We've talked about this before. I'm not going to hand it over to the public."

Mark spread his hands hopelessly. "No matter how much we talk about this, I don't seem to get through to you. We're not giving away one damn thing. We pick up twelve million on the issue, and the fifty percent of the common stock we retain is worth another twelve million — that is at the date of issue. Suppose it triples, and with our earnings, it's got to triple in this market. They're selling garbage at fifty dollars a share. We're giving real value. But if it triples, we're sitting on thirty-six million dollars."

"Which we can't touch without relinquishing control."

"Dan, that's absolutely wrong. Sam Goldberg has been in corporate law for years. Hell, we've known him twenty years. According to him and his partner, we can retain control with twenty percent of the stock. But I'm not advocating that. I'm only saying that if we can lay hands on twelve million, we should grab it. We can pay out what we now pay in interest as dividends, or half of it, or nothing at all if we're pressed."

"Mark, I just don't like it."

"Do you realize that we pay Seldon over a million dollars a year for the use of his money. What in hell sense does that make? And suppose he should call his loans?"

"Hell, if he calls, we cover it somewhere else. We could go to Crocker or Wells Fargo. Even Tony could come up with five million if we had our backs to the wall. I'm not worried about that. The old man likes me. He always has. If you want to take a hundred thousand dollars and play this crazy market — O.K. But our own issue — "

"Will you at least give it some thought? Will you at least meet with Goldberg and listen to what he has to say?"

"I'll listen. Why not."

"Good. Now what about the old man? Will he come up with the million and a half?"

"He'll come up with it. Never forget a thing called community property — the curse or blessing of California, depending on how you look at it. Half of whatever I build belongs to Jean. And the old man's absolutely nuts about his grandchildren." He grabbed Mark and swung him around. "Marcus, my lad, you know what's going to run this country some day? The airlines, lad. The railroads had their day. Next, the airlines. And laddie, do you know who's going to run the airlines? Marcus Levy and Daniel Lavette. We're just beginning to crawl onto the top of this golden shitpile they call big business, and once we get there, we're going to stake it out. Placer mining? Shit, lad. That's where the real gold mine is — out there." And he swept his arm around to include the city and the bay and the mountains in the distance.

Of all the things May Ling had to bear, the most painful was to see her father's spirit broken, to watch him grow old and bent before her eyes. Day after day, week after week, he left the house each morning to look for work. He had never learned to drive a car. First, on foot, he exhausted the possibilities of Hollywood; then, still on foot, he exhausted what opportunities might have existed in Beverly Hills; finally he made his way by trolley downtown. He was skilled and he was educated. He knew more about the management of a business than most of the businessmen in Los Angeles and more about accounting than most certified public accountants. He knew more about the financial complexities of a functioning department store than Marcus Levy and more about the financial complexities of shipping than Dan Lavette; but in the City of Los Angeles, in the year 1928, there were only three kinds of jobs open to Orientals: they could be gardeners, they could clean latrines, or they could work in the kitchen of a resturant. This at least was the knowledge accumulated by Feng Wo in his search, and each evening he returned home more defeated, more hopeless.

Until one day when he announced to his family at dinner that he had found a job. But there was no joy and no note of triumph in the announcement, and May Ling regarded him suspiciously.

"What kind of a job?" she asked him.

"It's a job. What does it matter, so long as I work?"

"Because we are not starving, We have enough money. We have savings. So tell me, father, what kind of a job is this?"

"The dignity is in the worker, not in the job. The job is to wash dishes in a Chinese resturant."

"No!" It came out of May Ling like a cry of pain. "No, you will not!"

"My dear daughter," Feng Wo said gently, while his wife, So-Toy, and his grandson, Joseph, sat wide-eyed and silent, "when I was a young man, before I met Daniel Lavette, and you were a little child, I did work that you would consider unspeakable. I cleaned toilets. I shined shoes. I picked up the droppings of the cart horses and sold them to a fertilizer company for three cents a bushel. I dug muck from the bottom of a silted canal. No one in Los Angeles will accept the services of a Chinese bookkeeper or accountant at any price — no, not even if I offered to work for nothing. To wash dishes is decent and honorable labor, and at least I can hold my head up."

At that time, the University of California campus was still on the eastern edge of Hollywood, at Vermont Street north of Melrose. Work had already started on a new campus, to be located in Westwood Village, but it would be at least two years more before the new quarters would be ready. May Ling had found for her family a small, five-room, one-story house about three blocks from the campus, a small, stucco house, the type called a Hollywood bungalow. Its location enabled her to walk to and from work; and the day after her father announced his new occupation, she decided, walking to work in the morning, upon a course of action. This was very much in the nature of May Ling. She was not a victim. During all her years with Dan Lavette, she had acted out of her own will and desire and out of love for a man. When the situation began to take its toll on her child, she had changed the situation. She had a deep, unshakeable love for four people: Dan Lavette, her son, and her father and mother; and she was sufficiently Chinese to regard the family as the core of existence.

Her first step, now, was to see Mr. Vance, the head librarian. He was a small, thin, nearsighted man who was reasonably in awe of May Ling's ability to find her way through the increasing collection of Oriental literature; and when she sat down in his office and informed him that nowhere in the library was there an English version of the writing of either Lao Tzu or Chuang Tzu, he agreed with her that the situation was deplorable.

"Are they important?" he asked.

"As philosophers," May Ling assured him, "they are as important to Chinese thought as Plato and Aristotle are to Western thought."

"Indeed? Then by all means we should order the books."

"We can't. English translations simply don't exist."

"Really? Not even in Great Britain?"

"I presume not. Certainly not in America."

"Then I don't see what we can do about it."

"The problem is," May Ling insisted, "that there is simply no way for a student to approach China historically without these books. If there had never been a Lao Tzu or a Chuang Tzu — well there would not be a China as we know it. They lay down the basis of Taoist thought, and Taoist thought is the rock upon which the whole structure of Chinese philosophy is built."

"But if the books do not exist in English?"

"They are not very long. Five thousand words contains the essence of Lao Tzu. Perhaps twenty thousand words more for the most important writing of Chuang Tzu. Certainly we can afford to have this work translated, and then if we mimeographed even a hundred copies, we would have a veritable treasure-trove — something that exists in no other university in

America. Think of the distinction it would bring upon the library."

Mr. Vance was impressed. "A fascinating notion, Mrs. Lavette, but you know, the university has no press here. The press is at Berkeley. Of course, we could submit it later for publication, as a product of Los Angeles. They tend to sneer a bit at our scholastic achievement. Could you do it?"

"Good gracious, no," May Ling said. "I can read Mandarin — but a proper, scholarly translation, no, not in a thousand years. But I know someone who could do it."

"Do you? And who might that be?"

"My father."

"Oh? Really?"

"Yes, indeed. In San Francisco, when we lived there, he had a notable reputation as both a scholar and a translator." She did not mention that the reputation was limited to his family.

"And what is his occupation now, if I may ask?"

"He's retired," May Ling said, smiling. "He studies, writes. I think he's into Chinese culinary things right now. You know, there is no Chinese cookbook."

"Ah, well, I'm afraid cookbooks are a bit out of our field. However, this notion of yours fascinates me. What would it cost?"

"The problem is to persuade my father to put everything else aside."

"Could you?"

"I think so. The cost is inconsequential. I think that if you were to give him an honorarium of fifty dollars a month, it would be ample."

"For how long?"

"Probably a year."

"That's certainly modest enough," Mr. Vance agreed. "Six hundred dollars, and perhaps fifty dollars more for the mimeographing, since we do it ourselves. Our purchase fund could certainly afford it. I'll tell you what I'll do, Mrs. Lavette. I'll telephone the University Press at Berkeley, and if they're interested, they'll put up the money as an advance against royalties. That might not give your father any more income, but he might be pleased to see his name on a book."

"I couldn't ask any more," May Ling agreed.

A week later, Mr. Vance announced triumphantly that not only would Berkeley be delighted to publish the book under the imprint of the University of California, but they were willing to pay an advance of five hundred dollars against royalties. "A true feather in our cap," Mr. Vance chortled. "And we get a credit logo. Time we had a press of our own, but I suppose that will have to wait for the new campus. Now when can I meet your father?"

"Tomorrow," May Ling promised.

Yet May Ling still had some doubts, and she approached the subject warily at the dinner table that evening.

"I agree with you concerning the dignity of labor," she said to her father. He ate slowly and silently, his weariness apparent, his hands swollen and raw.

"I don't care to discuss it," Feng Wo said.

"No, I suppose not."

"Obviously, you want to say something. Say it."

"My boss at the library, Mr. Michael Vance, would like to see you tomorrow. I made a date for you to have lunch with him."

"You did what?"

May Ling smiled sweetly. "Please do not be angry with me, honorable father. I made a date for you to have lunch with him."

"Stop using Hollywood Chinese. Lunch is when people eat, and when people eat, dishes must be washed. You know that. I also wear work pants and a work shirt."

May Ling sighed. "I'll tell you the entire story, and perhaps you'll be very angry at what I did. But please hear all of it."

"Go ahead," Feng Wo said.

The whole family listened with rapt attention. When May Ling had finished her narration of how she had plotted and won, Feng Wo said coldly, "And is it true that there is no Lao Tzu and Chuang Tzu in the English language? Or did you lie about that?"

"I did not lie!" May Ling said hotly. "As far as I know, it's true. Certainly if Berkeley will publish the book, they did their own research."

Feng Wo nodded his apology, and explained to Joseph, "Lao Tzu means 'the old philosopher,' or perhaps 'the old man of wisdom,' depending on how you translate it. We must spend more time on the language. We are not ignorant people in our family. But at the same time," he said, turning to May Ling, "we are not scholars. How could you dare to presume that anyone like myself could translate Lao Tzu or Chuang Tzu?"

"Because you can."

"How do you know?"

"Because all my life I have known you."

"Well, it's impossible, unthinkable, and you will tell that to your Mr. Vance."

So-Toy had been listening intently, following the English with great attention. Now she broke the long silence that followed Feng Wo's declaration, speaking angrily in Shanghainese, "I am only a woman, and as a woman I have been silent about things that do not ask for silence. Too long. I have watched this idiocy of my husband washing dishes in a worthless restaurant, and I have said nothing. It would appear that the only wisdom in this family has been granted to the women. Your daughter did a wonderful thing, and she will not go back to Mr. Vance and tell him you refuse. You will not refuse. You will write this book, and you will stop being pigheaded and stupid." Then, realizing what she had said, she turned pale and cast her eyes down at her clasped hands.

A long silence followed, and Joseph, who had not understood a word of what she said, looked from face to face in astonishment. This had never happened before. There had never been an argument in the family before this.

Finally, Feng Wo said, "They will want a preface to the book. I am not distinguished enough to comment on Lao Tzu."

"Nothing was said of a preface. The contract with the University Press is only for the translation."

Then, almost humbly, Feng Wo said to his daughter, "Will you help me?"

"If I can. My Mandarin is not terribly good."

Again there was silence, and then Feng Wo said, "I shall have to go to the restaurant in the morning and tell them I am leaving. Then I will come and have lunch with Mr. Vance."

Jake and Clair had done everything humanly possible, and, by working fourteen and fifteen hours a day, much that was inhumanly possible. They had scrubbed and cleaned and painted the old stone winery until it shone. They had exhausted their small bank account in the purchase of grapes and bonded brandy. They had cleaned the barrels and the tubs and scraped the rust off the old presses. Rabbi Blum risked another trip from San Francisco and put his seal of approval on all that had taken place. Bernie Cohen, deciding that some day he might be making wine in Palestine, volunteered his services for a week and proved invaluable in the heavy labor of moving and cleaning the casks. Professor Masseo came twice, the first time when they were ready to crush the grapes and the second time when the must was maturing to a point where brandy would be added.

After the first crushing, the winery filled with the good, sweet smell of the new vintage, Jake and Clair hovered over the tubs like mother hens, still unable to believe that out of this straightforward process, Rabbi Blum's sweet sacramental wine would emerge. Day after day, they watched the life in the liquid heave and gurgle; and then Professor Masseo came to tell them precisely when to halt the fermentation.

Word had gotten around the valley that the Levys were making wine, and one day two cars came screaming up the dirt road to the winery, jolting and lurching, and out of the cars poured eight G-men with drawn guns. Jake and Clair heard the yelling from inside the winery, and they ran outside to find their three children standing curiously between the small army of government agents and Bernie Cohen, who, with more courage than brains, faced them with an ancient, rusty, unusable double-barreled shotgun which he had found in the barn — the G-men roaring, "Put down that gun! This is a raid!" And Bernie screaming back, "Get off this property before I blow your heads off."

Clair ran to rescue her children, and Jake pleaded the legality of his operation, getting out his permits and government license. The G-men departed reluctantly, and later Professor Masseo supervised the pouring of the brandy. Bernie Cohen drove back to San Francisco, to return the following day with Rabbi Blum for the final test. Professor Masseo seized the opportunity to stay overnight and bask in Clair's grateful smiles, and all evening Jake and Clair sat and listened to the professor's instruction on the lore of the wine. They learned that the stem of a cluster of grapes was called the rachis, the individual stem the pedicel, the point where the stem entered the umbilicus.

They learned about the complexity of the tannins, the virtue of diglucoside pigments in the skin, the variables of fortification. And by now they had both read enough to join in a technical discussion.

"Some day," the professor said, as he left for his bedroom, "the Higate label will be known throughout America — perhaps the world. And when that time comes" — he smiled at Clair — "you will allow me to fulfill an old ambition."

"And that is, professor?"

"To supervise your tasting room when the buyers come."

But that day was still in the future. The next morning, Rabbi Blum arrived and was seated ceremoniously in the kitchen and given a glass of the new wine.

He tasted it thoughtfully, stroked his beard, and decided, "Not sweet enough."

The professor stared at him in amazement. "I beg to differ."

"Are you a rabbi?" Blum asked mildly.

"No."

"Are you Jewish?"

"No."

"Then how can you differ?"

"Because I am a professor of viticulture and a connoisseur of wine."

"It's still not sweet enough."

"What do we do?" Clair asked woefully.

"All right. We will do an execrable and unforgivable thing. We will add sugar syrup," announced Professor Masseo.

"God will forgive you," Rabbi Blum said.

Jake shook his head. "We're broke, professor. I've got three dollars — that's all. You can't sugar eight hundred gallons of wine for three dollars."

"A small advance," Blum said quickly. "Not a loan. An advance on delivery."

He took out of his coat pocket an old-fashioned purse and counted thirty dollars in worn bills.

"Enough?"

"Unless you want candy," the professor said.

Bernie Cohen was dispatched for the sugar; meanwhile Clair boiled a pint of syrup from the sugar she had in the house. The professor made the mixture, and the rabbi tasted the sugared wine.

"Ah." He nodded.

"Sweet enough?"

"Children," Rabbi Blum said, "you are now vintners."

"Wine-makers, not vintners," the professor said.

"Whatever. You can begin delivery as soon as the wine is ready. If there is more than eight hundred gallons, we will accept it — at seven dollars a gallon."

And Clair cried out, "My God, Jake — we did it."

Governor Alfred E. Smith telephoned from Albany, and the news of the call ran through the offices of Levy & Lavette. Polly Anderson abandoned decorum and burst into Mark's office with the news. "Governor Smith from Albany. Person to person for Mr. Lavette. They're talking now."

"I'm not impressed," Mark said. He was still smarting from the check he had written for Sunny Jim's campaign fund.

On the telephone, Governor Smith was saying, "Danny boy-o, we're at the starting gate, and we're separating the boys from the men."

Flattered, Dan asked, "How does it look for the nomination?"

"Just fine, Danny, just fine. No declaration of war yet, but we're packing the war chest. I want to know that when I get to the station, I'll have the stuff to buy the ticket."

"I'm with you all the way, governor."

"Damn right. They asked me, who've we got out there on the Coast? Danny Lavette, I told them, and he's one of us. Can I count on you, Danny?"

"All the way to the White House."

"No money yet, just pledges. But when they pass the plate, what can I find there?"

"Well — " He paused as Mark entered his office. "Suppose we say ten thousand to start the ball rolling."

"You're on the list, Danny. Will I see you in Houston?"

"If I can make it, governor."

"You'll get an engraved invitation."

He put down the phone and looked at Mark. "That was — "

"Al Smith. And you just handed him ten thousand dollars."

"Just a pledge, Mark."

"Dan, what in hell has gotten into you? He's playing you for a sucker. If by some miracle he gets the nomination, Al Smith's got as much chance of being elected as I have. He's a Catholic."

"And it's time we had a Catholic president."

"Sure. It's also time we had a Jewish President, but this is the USA and we're not going to have either one. It's money down the drain."

"It's only ten grand."

"It's only ten grand! God Almighty, Dan, can't you see the spot we're in? We're running an operation worth twenty million dollars, and we have no cash. Do you know what our payroll is? Sure, the store is making money hand over fist, but it goes down the drain. The airline won't show a profit for six months, and when a storm holds up one of the ships, we scrape the bottom of the barrel. Your friends in Hawaii scream bloody murder if we don't show a profit out there, and meanwhile we're fifteen million dollars in hock to Seldon."

"Mark — take it easy. I like Al Smith. Do you know what it means to go to Washington and face that cold bastard Coolidge?"

"You are dreaming. Furthermore, you pledged ten grand that we don't have."

"Oh, Christ, Mark, we've got it. Look, I'll tell you what I'll do. For months now, you've been talking stock. All right. Tell Goldberg to go ahead and put us on the market. We'll pick up that goddamn twelve million you keep talking about, and at least you'll stop crying that we're broke."

"Danny, you mean that?"

"I told you O.K."

"Thank God. Twelve million in cold cash — and do we need it."

"And when Al Smith's elected President, you're going to kiss my ass on Market Street at high noon. Right?"

"Right," Mark said, grinning.

Marty Spizer was one of a thousand things that happened when the silent films began to talk. It was discovered then in the New York City theater scene that there was an art that was only fitfully represented in Hollywood, the art of human speech. The rug was pulled out from under hundreds of silent-film actors who had lived by body movement and facial mugging, and there began a very considerable movement of theater people from the East to the West Coast. Properly speaking, Marty Spizer was a theater person only by proximity. In his thirty-three years, he had stage-managed two flops, scalped tickets, served as a leg man for a gossip columnist, done some publicity, and done the best he could whenever he was broke — which was not infrequently. In the course of all this, he had picked up sufficient scraps of knowledge and pieces of talk to feel that the new West Coast bonanza belonged at least in part to him. After two months in Hollywood without anything better than a small coaching job coming his way, he teamed up with another Manhattan expatriate, Timothy Kelly by name, rented an old dance studio on Vine Street, and opened the New York School of Acting. Spizer, dark, of middle size, and reasonably successful with a good many ladies, was glib and adroit and could chatter impressively about Stanislavsky and inner interpretations and deep-seated emotional responses; Kelly, small, skinny, a failed hoofer and vaudevillian, performed as the expert in mime and dance. They began their first semester with twenty-two students, one of whom was Martha Levy.

Marty Spizer was at the beginning of a career, functioning in a small jungle, feeling his way around, getting his footing, as he put it. He was shrewd, nasty, choking with an assortment of deep-rooted hostilities, and wary in this new environment of mesquite-covered hills and stucco-covered houses. The idea of the school was a stopgap, a stake, perhaps a point of penetration into a directing or producing job, and the twenty-two youngsters, who had homed into Hollywood from all over the country, were not difficult to impress. Spizer and Kelly put them through scenes from current Broadway plays, and Spizer played the role of director as he had watched it done in the East. Being somewhat sadistic in nature, he chose to imitate a famous theater director who operated with calculated viciousness. This director would single out one of the actors and make him or her the butt of his anger and hostility, using the poor devil as a negative example. Whatever the results were in the original context, Spizer used the technique senselessly and because it suited his nature; and once the school began to function, he chose Martha Levy as the object of his hostility.

He did not know why he chose Martha Levy, nor did he ask himself why; he was simply not given to self-searching or introspection; possibly she reminded him of a girl he had lived with for a while who had finally turned on him and thrown him out of her house and her life. And while it might be said that Martha's talents left much to be desired, that was also the case with four fifths of the enrolled members of the New York School of Acting.

Spizer was not an originator. His outbursts of critique and direction were couched in precisely the same words the New York director had used. He would lash out at Martha, "Donkey! Donkey — you, Levy, look at me!"

Martha would turn to him, hurt, terrified.

"Why do I call you a donkey? Why not a Shetland pony? Why not a gazelle?"

Martha speechless, embarrassed, trembling.

"Because a donkey brays. Brays. Voice is voice, not braying!"

Or he would shout, "Clowning! You're not acting, toots. You are clowning!"

After two weeks of this, Martha was reduced to a point where she would approach each day with fear and finish each day at the point of tears. The persecution reduced her to a point where she fed it herself, unable to remember her lines, unable to do anything right. She would return to her apartment and weep, determined each day to get out of the school, to leave a place that had become a torture chamber — and then telling herself that she would not quit, not yet, that if this was the way to become an actress, she would endure it and see it through.

And then, after the first two weeks, Kelly said to Spizer, "Marty, maybe you're leaning too hard on that Levy kid."

"She stinks."

"You got a hate on, buddy," Kelly said. "Take another look. She's not a bad-looking broad, and she's loaded."

"What do you mean, loaded?"

"You're telling me you don't know? Is this Marty Spizer or some jerk?"

"Come on, come on, don't play games."

"Her old man is Marcus Levy. San Francisco."

"And who the hell is Marcus Levy?"

"For you, Marty, there is obviously nothing west of the Hudson River."

"Except for this shithole."

"Marcus Levy is one of the L's of a thing called Levy and Lavette, which owns the biggest department store in California, not to mention a shipping line and maybe half the land in California and maybe a few other goodies too."

"You're kidding."

"Like hell I am. Talk to her sometime instead of spitting at her."

"You schmuck!" Spizer burst out. "You dumb mick schmuck! You let me ride her all this time and you never tell me I'm shitting in a pot of gold. Where are your brains?"

"I'll tell you where yours are, you dumb bastard. In your asshole."

That same day, Marty Spizer asked Martha to have lunch with him. She looked at him dumfounded and speechless.

"Say yes, honey," he told her gently. "The initiation is over. You're going to be an actress."

He took her to Musso and Frank's on Hollywood Boulevard, playing expansively the roll of tour guide and knowledgeable citizen. Sitting across the table from her, summoning up every bit of charm he had ever seen or heard, he said to her, "I suppose you wondered why I put you through those two weeks of hazing?"

Her eyes welling with tears, Martha shook her head. "I don't understand it at all. Maybe I am rotten, but I'm no worse than most of the kids."

"Martha," he said earnestly, "you're a damn sight better than any of them. You got a natural talent, a gift, a glow. That is precisely why I leaned on you. I had to shock you into letting go. I had to give you what Stanislavsky calls a sense of your interior. I had to hit you to make you know you are alive, and I may say that you know it, baby."

"Then you don't think I'm hopeless?"

"Hopeless? Are you kidding?"

She was biting her lip, trying to hold back the tears. "I was so miserable — so wretchedly miserable."

"Exactly. You were feeling, you were alive. All right, that's over. Phase one is done. Now we make you an actress."

Gregory Pastore was one of those virtuoso painters who appear to have enormous reservoirs of skill in their hands yet very little in the head or the heart. He completed both portraits of Jean Lavette at about the same time. The clothed portrait, which depicted her in a Grecian type of blue gown, barefoot, her splendid hair loose, evoked echoes of Eakins whom she admired so much — as Pastore well knew — but it had a sleek perfection which Eakins would have found distasteful and dishonest. By now Jean's taste in painting had developed to a point where she was aware of the incipient vulgarity in trompe l'oeil when applied to the human figure; nevertheless, she was sufficiently self-oriented to react to the beauty of the woman in the long canvas. What it lacked in truth, it made up for in sheer perfection, and that certainly did not displease her.

The nude Jean was a better painting, bold and lusty, filled with life and flesh instead of perfection. Pastore had fleshed out her breasts and her hips, bent her head forward so that her features were unrecognizable behind a wave of her fine honey-colored hair, and laid one hand provocatively on the pubic tuft.

"It's a damn good painting," she said when he showed her, finally, the finished product. "What do you want for it?"

"You or three thousand dollars," he replied, grinning with pleasure. "And that's a princely—a kingly—price for any woman."

"What are you talking about?"

"Become my mistress for one month, and it's yours free. Otherwise, three thousand clams."

"In other words, if the price is right," Jean said, not at all disturbed by his offer, "any woman is a whore?"

"I've always thought so."

"Perhaps. Only you don't appeal to me that way, Gregory. And you don't bathe."

"You are a bitch, you know."

"Oh? Anyway, I want it. Bring both paintings to my home tomorrow. I'll have a check for you."

"Three thousand."

"I heard you the first time."

When the paintings arrived on the following day, Jean hung the full-length clothed portrait of herself at one end of the living room between a John Marin landscape and a Charles Sheeler industrial scene. A big Renoir nude that had occupied the same space was moved into Dan's study, to take its shadowy place with the Winslow Homers and the Frederick Remingtons, works by artists whom Jean tolerated grudgingly. A few years before, Jean had enlarged the living room, ripped out all the molding, created plain walls of a pale ivory tint, and installed ceiling spotlights. The Queen Anne antiques went the way of the molding and were replaced by pieces in the Chinese style. She had gone through a period of Japanese prints, but now she tired of them and relegated them to other rooms. Her collection now included over thirty paintings, eighteen of which she felt were as good as any modern collection in San Francisco.

The nude went to her bedroom, where it kept company with a second Renoir nude, a Picasso of the Blue Period, and two Degas ballet scenes. For the two weeks after it was hung, Dan had no occasion to set foot in her bedroom. When finally he did and saw the painting, he stared at it for a few minutes before he asked her whether it was a painting of herself.

"What nonsense! Does it look like me?"

"Yes."

"I'm amazed you remember."

"I remember," he said.

"And if it is me, does that disturb you?"

"It doesn't matter," he said.

Yet it mattered. It chipped away at his self-respect, his shrinking sense of himself as a male creature, and at his confused, anxious, and complex musings on morality. The morass deepened one day when, passing the open door of Jean's bedroom, he saw Barbara standing there staring at the picture. His first instinct was to escape unnoticed. His daughter was fourteen years old, already ripening into womanhood, tall, lissome, and increasingly foreign to him.

He stopped in the hallway, turned, and forced himself to walk into the room. Barbara glanced at him and then returned her gaze to the painting. He was embarrassed; apparently, she was not.

"It's mother, isn't it?" Barbara said.

"No."

She faced him now. "You don't think so? Did she tell you that?"

"Yes."

"Well, it looks like her. I should think you'd be in a perfect pet about it."

"It's not your mother, and I don't think you have any business in her room."

"The door was open," Barbara replied, and then stalked out past him; and he stood looking after her, wondering why every approach to his daughter went wrong.

*

The new line of credit at the Seldon Bank passed two million dollars before the airline — West Coast Air, as they decided to call it — was ready to begin service. New problems kept cropping up: limousines at either end, service within the airplane, sky-high insurance rates, and above all the rumors that another twelve-passenger plane was being developed that would put the Ford Trimotor out of business. Dan spent a hundred thousand dollars on two of the best aircraft designers in the business and set them to work to invent a faster and quieter plane than the Ford. With this and the complexities of terminals, pilots, mechanics, transportation, franchises, and a hundred unforeseen problems that occurred because no one west of the Rockies had ever operated a passenger service before, it was not until mid-1928 that the airline opened for business.

By that time, even Dan's enormous calm had been splintered. He would get to bed night after night at two or three in the morning and then find that he was unable to sleep; he would toss and turn until dawn and an hour later be in his car headed out to the new airfield. In the midst of all this, the *Sacramento,* the largest and newest of their passenger liners, was rammed by a cargo ship in New York City's Lower Bay, and Dan had to spend three and a half agonizing days on the train to New York and then three more weeks seeing the situation unsnarled and the ship into dry dock for repairs.

When at last the great day came and the big Ford Trimotor stood shining in the California sunshine, Dan was miserable rather than pleased or exultant, exhausted, taking part in the ceremony with a kind of dulled indifference. It was a good turnout, all things considered, with almost a thousand people present to watch the great silver bird take to the air and inaugurate a new era. His children were away at school, but Jean was there, as beautiful as ever and the center of attention, not only for the photographers but for Mayor Rolph, Governor Clement Young, her father, and her friends. Both the mayor and the governor spoke, and then Mark, who had declined to be one of the twelve on the first flight — as had Jean — read a short speech that Dan had been too busy to write. A troubled Sarah kissed Dan, hugged him to her, and said, "I wish you weren't going up in that crazy thing, Danny." The Dumphy Marching Band played, people waved and shouted and clapped their hands, and Dan climbed into the plane, along with Sam Goldberg, who had begged to be given one of the seats, Jerry Belton, in charge of promotion and the author of Mark's speech, Toby Bench, the radio commentator, and eight newspapermen and photographers. Dan made his way up to the pilot's compartment, where he told Bill Henley, war ace and his chief pilot, "This is it, Billy, and for Christ's sake, let's give them something to talk about. Smooth and easy."

"O.K., boss." Henley grinned and turned on the ignition. The three motors roared into life, a deafening sound; and back in his seat, next to Sam Goldberg, Dan breathed a sigh of relief and cast his eyes around at eleven, white-faced, tight-lipped people. The passengers partook of so total a sense of terror that Dan burst out laughing, and Goldberg yelled at him, "What's to laugh? Let me out of this deathtrap!"

Jean watched the great silver plane roar down the runway and lift off, so easily and gracefully, lifting up higher and higher, effortlessly, and something caught in her throat and for a moment she regretted that she had declined Dan's invitation to come with him. But only for a moment. As Dan had said, it didn't matter.

Martha, accompanied by a now-devoted Marty Spizer, was in the crowd that welcomed the Ford Trimotor as it floated, light as a leaf, into the Los Angeles airport. There, on a lesser scale, the San Francisco scene was repeated, to the sound of wild cheering at, according to the mayor, "the opening of a new era— a time when we can think of San Francisco and Los Angeles as sister cities."

"That's Danny, the tall man with the black, curly hair," Martha told Spizer excitedly, pushing through the crowd. "Daddy was supposed to be with him, but I don't see him."

"He's one big sonofabitch," Spizer said.

"He's a pussycat, and he's my dear, dear friend. Come on."

As they tried to make their way through the crowd of press and celebrities that surrounded Dan, Spizer said, "What gives between you and this guy? You couldn't wait to get down here."

"He's Danny. I've adored him since I was a kid."

When Dan spotted her, he pushed through the crowd and swung her up in his arms. "Baby, I've missed you."

"Where's daddy?"

"He chickened out."

"And Jean?"

"Same thing. Old Goldberg here was the only one with guts enough to make it. Sam," he said to Goldberg, who stood beside him, thanking God that firm earth was beneath his feet, "you remember Mark's daughter, Martha?"

Martha introduced Marty Spizer as "the director and producer," and then Dan told them not to go. He'd get through the rest of the formalities and they'd all have dinner together. "Whatever you say," Goldberg agreed. "But I'm taking the train back."

"Hold it down," Dan said. "We're in business now."

The four of them had dinner at the Biltmore. By that time, Dan's ebullience had washed out. All that day, under the excitement and the glory of the first scheduled flight, was the knowledge that he would be in the city where May Ling lived. It was now seven months since he had seen her, and during that period he had been to Los Angeles four times, and each time he fought it out with himself and willed himself not to see her, and came out of the struggle sick and lonely and frustrated. And now it was in him again, the same sickness, the same loneliness, the same unbearable hopelessness. Goldberg left to catch his train, and Spizer talked about himself and the film business and talking pictures and the opportunities for investment. Dan listened without hearing. When the dinner was over, he invented a business meeting, and Martha, kissing him, whispered, "You're so glum, Danny. You shouldn't be. It's your day of victory."

Spizer had gone to the men's room. "What about him?" Dan asked.

"He runs the school. He's brilliant. Don't you like him?"

"Just watch your step, baby."

"Danny, I'm a grown woman."

In his room at the Biltmore, Dan sprawled on his bed and stared at the ceiling. He was forty years old, and if anyone ever had, he had surely dreamed the American dream. This was 1928, only forty years since his mother and father had climbed out of steerage onto Ellis Island, in New York Harbor, a French-Italian fisherman with an Italian wife, penniless, without a word of English, bewildered, friendless in the world of New York's East Side. The story of what had happened to them had been told and retold to him, the days of semistarvation in New York, his father recruited into a labor gang for the Atchison, Topeka and Sante Fe Railway, the line over the mountains into San Francisco, the first sight of San Francisco, the golden city on the bay, the struggle to live, to survive, to be, and the day at long last when he and his father put out to work in their own boat — and all of it over in the flaming eruption of the earthquake.

That memory was real and vivid. He had only to close his eyes to taste the salt spray and to hear his father singing out, in his Marseille dialect, "*Rejette les petits, coco!*" Out went the crabs too small to matter. He could hear his father's booming bass voice. He never sang on the way out, but only when they had their catch and were coming in with the wind. He never sang when they used the motor. He despised the motor. "*Le cochon qui fume,*" he called it. But when the wind was in their sails and the boat rode low with the catch, his father's voice would boom out over the water, off-key but powerful enough to be heard across the bay. He tried to bring to mind that one day off San Mateo when he had his own son, Thomas, out in the cutter, but the memory was vague and misty, as were all the memories of his life except those times with May Ling. All the rest was a dream and apparently without meaning, yet as he lay there on the hotel bed, half dozing, he resented and rejected this. He had come out of nothing, and he had made himself a king, a veritable emperor. He ruled a fleet of great passenger liners, an airline, a majestic department store, a splendid resort hotel, property, land, and he dispensed the food of life to hundreds of men and women who labored at his will. True, Mark Levy was his partner and friend, but Mark was like a shadow. It was of his own making and his own doing that he controlled twenty million dollars of property — and how could that be a dream and meaningless? He was welcomed in Washington and in New York; people kowtowed to him, and he was surrounded by servile men who were ready to agree with anything he said, and he lived in a mansion on Russian Hill and his wife was far and widely admitted to be one of the most beautiful women in San Francisco.

Yet he was as alone as anyone on the face of the earth, lying alone and fully clothed in a dark room in the Biltmore Hotel in Los Angeles, so bereft of passion that he had neither the will nor the desire to call a bellhop and give him the twenty dollars that would bring a floozie to his room to warm his bed. He wanted no woman except one.

He fell asleep, and when he awakened, the first gray light of the morning was seeping into the room. He showered and put on fresh clothes. Outside his window, the sky was filled with a turbulence of racing clouds. It had apparently rained all night, and this was one of those rare and welcome days in Los Angeles when the air was clean and cold, the sky silver gray. After he had dressed, he called Bill Henley, asleep in another room at the Biltmore, awakened him, and said, "Take her home nice and easy, Billy. I won't be going with you. Tell Mr. Levy I'll be back tomorrow."

He had eaten almost nothing at dinner the night before, and he was hungry. He made a breakfast out of fried eggs and steak and home-fried potatoes and drank two cups of coffe. At the desk, he asked how far it was to the U.C.L.A. campus at Melrose and Vermont.

"Too far to walk, Mr. Lavette — like everything in L.A. I'll call you a cab."

He felt lightheaded, foolish, wonderful, looking out of the cab windows at the sprawling, strange stucco city. San Francisco was a city of hills, with great open vistas to be seen from the hilltops. This place was precisely the reverse, a bowl surrounded on three sides by hills and mountains, yet for some reason it excited and pleased him. The day was so clear, the air so fine that the great humps of the San Gabriels were clearly visible to the east, while ahead of him, at the end of Vermont Avenue, miles away yet as prominent as a gate at the street's end was the green wall of the Hollywood Hills. He saw and noticed things with the eyes of a delighted child, the huge, clanging green streetcars, the shacks on Vermont Avenue and beyond them, where the land rolled up to end the bowl, candy-cane mansions of pink and white, the profusion of roses and ferns and palms contrasting so oddly with the one-story shabby bungalows — and the cars, so many automobiles of every variety, and beyond the houses the wooden derricks pumping the oil that fed the cars. It was raw, new, different, and it intrigued him, perhaps most of all because it was a place where May Ling and his son lived.

Then he was filled with apprehension and he began to rehearse conversations inside of his head. He was almost trembling when the cab dropped him at the edge of the campus.

He made no judgment of the ugly, cream-colored Art Nouveau buildings, of the small campus with the city blocks of wood and stucco bungalows licking at the edge of it; it was ennobled because May Ling was in some way a part of it. He walked slowly across to the largest building, inquiring of some boys and girls who stood in front of the place where the library might be. They gave him directions, and he walked there in a sort of dream, transported back through the years to his first visit to the San Francisco library, where May Ling ruled the little cubbyhole of Oriental languages. Then he entered the building, and there she was, not different, not changed, sitting at the outgoing desk and stamping some books for a student. He stood there silently until she looked up, stared at him, and then smiled.

"Danny," she said. No reproach. She turned to the librarian sitting beside her and said, rather tremulously, "An old friend. I'll be back in a moment." Then she came around the desk and steered him out to the front of the building.

"May I kiss you here?" he asked.

"Danny, Danny, take me in your arms and kiss me. Yes. Yes."

He took her in his arms, the smell, the feel of her, the touch of her lips — all of it unchanged as if there were no passage of time for them.

"Can we go somewhere, talk?"

"Yes, of course. It's almost ten. I'll take an early lunch at eleven-thirty, and then we'll have a whole hour. Can you wait, Danny?"

"I'm here. Where would I go?"

"That's nice. Yes."

"I'll be on that bench, over there," he said, pointing. "You'll see me when you come out."

"Of course."

"One thing — how's Joey?"

"Big, strong, beautiful."

"And your folks?"

"All right. Good. You wait for me, Danny."

He sat down on the bench, stretching out his long legs, watching the students passing by, basking in his own euphoria, delighting in the sensation of a man of forty in love with all the excitement and fervor of a teen-age boy. Would he wait for her? Just to sit there, facing a building which contained her presence, made his life richer than it had been in months. He was quite content. If she had said wait for me five hours, six hours, he would have been equally content.

At eleven-thirty she appeared, and he took her in his arms and kissed her again, and she said, "You know, we're doing this in public, and if anyone asks me or sees me, I shall simply say that this is my husband. It's time someone here saw the father of my child."

"I want to hear that."

"What?"

"This is Mr. Lavette, my husband."

"You know, you're like a kid, Danny. You pretend like a little boy."

"You're angry?"

"No, no, no. I'm so happy. Now listen, I brought a sandwich, but I left it inside, because I am sure you want a proper lunch, because I remember how you eat."

"How I eat!"

"And we can go to the faculty dining room. It's just a little cafeteria sort of place, but it's all right. We'll find a quiet corner."

Sitting across from each other, ignoring their trays of food, they just stared at each other.

"You don't change," Dan said. "You don't grow older, only more beautiful."

"I'm thirty-four. That's considered quite old in China."

"I'm sure."

"And you, Danny — you're turning gray, and that's distinguished. But I think you're putting on weight."

"Nine, ten pounds. It's nothing. I can carry it. Trouble is, nothing costs money anymore. We have charge accounts in every good restaurant in San Francisco and in New York. So you just eat what you please and sign the check, and that's what I can't get used to. Funny, we got this damned empire, and it's all like a game I'm playing."

"Hopscotch to the top of Nob Hill?"

"But it's the bottom, not the top, and you got to play the game again."

"And the airline is part of the game. I read all about it in the paper. They had your picture there. Joe saw it."

"What did he say?"

"Nothing. I'm never worried about what he says, only about what he doesn't say."

"God, how I miss him. Can I see him, baby — please!"

"What will you say to him if you see him, Dan? You'll come with your arms filled with presents, but what will you say to him?"

"I could tell him I love him."

"I don't think he'd believe you, Dan."

"Do you believe me when I say that I love you — more than anything on earth?"

"I believe you love me. Not more than anything on earth. I think you love the game you're playing more. And that's the strange part of it. You're not like the others, the Seldons, the Mellons, the Crockers, the Hearsts — all those uncrowned kings of this country."

"How do you know I'm not? You don't know them. You only know me."

"There's a way to know things. And sometimes I think I know you better than you know yourself."

"I sent you money four times. Why did you always send the checks back?"

"How did you get the scar on your cheek?"

"I got drunk and smashed up a speakeasy."

"Oh, no — "

"Why did you send the money back?"

"Because I don't need money, Danny. That's the truth. I received nine thousand dollars for the house on Willow Street — which was a gift from you. And during those years we were together, I saved almost four thousand dollars. You always gave me too much money. And my father has his savings. I don't need money, Danny. I need you. I need you because I'm only half alive without you. I've never been with another man, and I don't want to be with another man. There's only you, and it's been that way since the first time we met. And if this hurts you, I'm selfish enough to want it to hurt, and I'm not going to salve your guilt by taking more money from you. Anyway, money is meaningless to you. It always has been. You don't give anything of yourself when you give me money."

"Don't be so damned logical!" he burst out.

"Then what should I do, dear love? I can't be angry at you. I adore you."

"Now look," he began, "my airline is functioning now — "

"Danny, stop! Don't you think I know what you're going to

say? Don't you think I know what you had in mind with this airline of yours. You're going to tell me that you'll come to Los Angeles in four hours now and that we can see each other — "

"Yes, yes. Twice a week, three times a week. And in another year or two, the new planes will be in production, and then it will be two and a half hours — "

"Danny!"

He stopped and stared at her. "What did I say?"

"Oh, Danny, Danny, this is a land where men don't grow up. Don't you understand me? You're not a little boy, working out a way to play hooky and not get caught. I love you. I call myself Mrs. Lavette. My son is registered in school as Joseph Lavette. And I am not playing a game. You live with a woman you hate and who hates you. If there's a shred of sanity on this earth, you are my husband. You are the father of my child. That's the whole of it. Come to me whenever you want to, but come to stay. I don't care whether you divorce Jean or not, and I don't even care whether you can marry me or not, or whether you're the richest man on earth or penniless. But when you come, you have to say to me, May Ling, I will not leave you again. Because I'm strong enough for everything else, but not for the leaving, Danny, not for the leaving."

PART FIVE

The Wind

Sam Goldberg was a sentimental man. After all the years, he still kept a photograph of the *Oregon Queen* hanging in his office. His father, then aged fifteen, had come to California in '52 to dig for gold. He never found gold and settled for a fruit stand in Sacramento, and somehow set aside enough money to send his son to law school. Goldberg had deep loyalties. He was ferociously loyal to and proud of San Francisco, which he never tired of defining as the one and only great city in the United States wherein Jews and Italians and Irish played commanding roles from the very beginning. He also hotly defended it as the only truly civilized city on the face of the earth, and he specified California as the only place on earth fit for human beings to live.

He had the same loyalty to and love for Dan Lavette and Mark Levy — his oldest continuing clients and now his biggest and most important clients. His partner, Adam Benchly, was four years older than Sam, who was now sixty-two. Benchly, whose father had jumped ship in San Francisco in 1850, had run for mayor once, but was defeated, and had served as district attorney some twenty years before. Unlike Goldberg, he was coldly cynical and sourly suspicious. They made an excellent combination. They had worked out in detail the public offering of stock for Levy & Lavette, and now, a pleasant afternoon in April of 1928, they were both of them, Goldberg and Benchly, sitting in Goldberg's office with Dan and Mark.

"The trouble is," Benchly began, "that you two young fellows have been running this operation like a grocery store. No board of directors, no vice presidents, just Dan here running off like some besotted steer, with Mark trying to hang on to him. Well, god damn it, this is no grocery store. You two got yourselves one hell of a big and sprawling operation."

"We've got managers," Dan said defensively. "We've got Anderson in New York and Burroughs at the store, and we've got Sidney Cohen in Hawaii."

"You don't know what you got," Benchly snorted. "When you had that Chinaman running things, you could make some sense out of it. Now — good Lord, Sam and I have been trying to make sense out of your books for two months now. Well, we got them in some kind of order. Do you realize that you've got an operation with maybe twenty million dollars of capital worth and you don't make a nickel?"

"What about our balance sheets? What about our statements?" Mark demanded. "We showed half a million clear profit last year."

"Where is it?"

"In the business. Do you know what this airline is costing us? And we bought that building on Eleventh Avenue in New York. We had a floor of offices that cost us more than the taxes, and we have seven floors rented."

"What Adam is saying," Goldberg put in, "is that you've been very lucky. When you two kids decided to buy the *Oregon Queen,* Adam and I set up a corporation for you and we issued a hundred shares of capital stock, fifty in your name and fifty in Dan's. That stock is still lying in our office safe. Since then, you been flying and lady luck rode with you. But the bitter truth is that you don't own the business. The Seldon Bank is into you for sixteen million."

"We're into them." Dan grinned.

"No, sir," said Benchly. "They are into you. That's something you have to understand."

"Now wait a minute," Mark said. "We're issuing a million shares of stock — which represents twenty million dollars. That takes us off the hook, doesn't it?"

"Yes and no. Like I said, you're not running a grocery store. Sam and I have drawn up a new charter for the corporation. You're in the big time and you've got to play it like the big time. You have to put together a board of directors. You have a responsibility to your stockholders as management and you've got to exercise it like grown men, not like a couple of kids gone hog wild."

"Adam, that's not fair," Mark protested.

"It's fair enough."

"It's not that we don't respect you," Sam Goldberg said. "Our job is to protect you. Right now, if Seldon called his loans, you'd probably be able to cover. Tony Cassala would protect you, and between him and Giannini and maybe with Crocker and Wells Fargo in the picture you'd get out from under. That's because we're sailing on milk and honey these days. But suppose the situation changes? All right, we got Cohen, Brady and Wilkinson to take the underwriting and they're very confident. At this time next week, you'll have ten million dollars, less the underwriter's commission, and you'll be a publicly owned corporation. But if you insist on retaining fifty-one percent of the stock, you will still be in hock to the bank."

"We can carry six million easily," Mark said.

"Not six million. Mark, your idea of paying off ten million of the loan is impossible. We're in an inflationary situation, with prices skyrocketing. There's going to be a longshore strike as sure as hell. You're going to have trouble with your crews. You can't go on operating without money, and you can't keep going to Seldon. Now I hear that Dan is ordering six new planes from the Douglas Company. Where does the money come from?"

"When the time comes — "

"No, sir," said Benchly. "Either you listen to Sam and me, or we're out of this."

"Come on, come on," Goldberg said. "No ultimatums. Boys, please — we've got to play it differently. You're paying Seldon a million and a quarter a year. We want you to put away three million in government paper to cover that, and above all, the debt stays. You don't go into Seldon or any other bank — not until you can show a realistic profit. Otherwise, you're playing roulette."

"That's all right with me," Dan agreed. "God Almighty, we can use that money."

Mark began to protest and Dan said, "Mark, we can't stay still. This whole country is snowballing. It's a new era, a new time, a whole damn new civilization."

"Then we don't retire any of the loan?" Mark asked.

"Sam and I think three million might go to that. Let the rest of it lay."

"I bought a stock ticker," Dan said. "Can you imagine —

never bought a share of stock in my life, and now I got a brand-new classy ticker, all my own."

Jean had left for England again, this time to attend an auction at Sotheby's. She had conceived a sudden passion for water colors, and Sotheby's was selling a wide range, from David Cox to John Marin. Thomas was at school in the East, and Barbara was totally devoted to horses. The year before, Dan had made his daughter a gift of a five-year membership in the Menlo Circle Club, a very exclusive riding club in Menlo Park, just outside of Atherton and about thirty miles down the Peninsula, and ever since then she had pleaded with Jean to give her consent to the purchase of a country house at Menlo Park. But Jean was not only averse to a second home; she also expressed the opinion that Menlo Park had become the haven of the newly rich. There had been a time when Jean rode, if infrequently; of late she had taken a dislike to horses and the company they kept — as she put it. Still too young to drive, Barbara had become a part of a clique of boys and girls, between sixteen and twenty — she was the youngest one of the group — who raced down to Menlo Park at every opportunity that presented itself.

School had been reduced to a chore that kept her from the stables. She was a poor student — not because she lacked intelligence, but out of resentment for anything that kept her from riding. She was a tall, long-limbed girl, five-foot-eight already, very much like her mother in appearance and very much of a stranger to Dan. Not only was he unaware of who she was, but with Jean away, he had no notion of the rules by which she should live. The two of them shared the house with Wendy Jones and the servants. Miss Jones ran the place, planned the meals, and took care of the household accounts with money Dan gave her. With the stock offering that turned Levy and Lavette into a publicly held corporation, Dan's trips to Hawaii, New York, and Detroit became more frequent, and when he was in San Francisco, he would frequently eat dinner downtown and then return to the offices. He saw his daughter only intermittently and salved his conscience with gifts. He took a day off to attend a horse auction in Sonoma County, where he purchased a splendid chestnut mare, which he immediately shipped to Menlo Park. Barbara encountered it the following day at the clubhouse stables but curiously enough did not mention it to Dan or even thank him for it until the two of them met in the house one day a week later.

He had to prod, finally asking her whether she liked the horse.

"Oh, yes. It's a beauty."

"Did you name her?"

"Her name is Sandy," Barbara said. "Didn't you know? You bought her."

"Funny, I never asked her name of anyone. If I did, I forgot. I'm sorry."

"That's all right."

In his mind's eye, he saw her throwing her arms around him, kissing him and thanking him effusively; but the reality was a tall, slender, distant person, properly polite. When had they last kissed or embraced? He could not remember. He said, suddenly, "How about the two of us going out to dinner?"

"Wendy has dinner here."

"The hell with Wendy. She can eat alone."

"I have a party later."

"All right, I'll drop you off at your party."

She agreed without enthusiasm, and when they were in his car, he asked her whether she liked Italian food — aware of how strange the question was, but no stranger than the fact that she spoke not a single word of Italian and probably had never thought of herself as Italian.

"If you wish, sure."

"There's a little place on Jones Street where I eat. It's not very posh, but the pasta is as good as any in the city and better than most — "

"Pasta?"

"Spaghetti, linguini, tortellini." He wondered whether she had asked the question deliberately. Could she conceivably not know what the word meant?

Gino welcomed him with delight, wringing his hand. "Danny, two month I don't see you. Too long."

"I been away, here and there. This is my daughter, Barbara."

"So beautiful," Gino exclaimed. "So tall, so beautiful. I welcome you here. Come, here is your papa's favorite table."

She was stiff and cold, looking around the little restaurant with its checked gingham tablecloths with distaste. Already, Dan realized that it had been a mistake to bring her here. Why had he ever imagined that she would like the place?

Gino led them to the table, pulled out the chair for Barbara with as sweeping and courtly a gesture as he could manage. Oblivious to her reaction, he was beaming with delight. "What do you think, Danny," he said, "Al Smith, he gonna make it?"

"I raised a hundred and sixty thousand dollars of San Francisco money that says so."

"What's he like?"

"He's a smart boy from the streets. I like him. Tell you something, Gino, when he comes out to San Francisco, I'm going to bring him here. That's a promise."

When Gino left, Barbara said, "Why do you let him call you Danny?"

"Because he's an old friend."

"Does mother know you're backing Al Smith?"

"I suppose so. Why?"

"Because she despises him. So does grandpa."

"Well, that's their right, isn't it? I don't think we should talk politics. There are too many other things to talk about, and I don't think you know enough about this election anyway."

"You don't think I know much about anything, do you?"

"Now why do you say that?"

"Well, why did you bring me here? You think I don't know about this place? Well, I do. This is where you go with your Chinese mistress."

"What! What in hell are you talking about?"

"Just what I said."

"How do you know that?" he whispered.

"Mother told me."

He closed his eyes and fought to control himself. Then he said, very slowly, "I don't intend to discuss that with you. We will eat our dinner here, because Gino is an old friend and he would be deeply hurt if we left. There are some things you don't understand."

"I'm sure there are," she said tightly.

"There are no virgins," Timothy Kelly said to Spizer. "I know. I been there. The whole notion is a con invented by some crazed white Protestant-god-merchant. This is me speaking, Marty. I must have humped three hundred broads in my time, and I tell you there is no such thing."

"You been there? Baby, I been there. It was as bloody as the Battle of Verdun. This tomato is twenty-three years old and she's a virgin. Jesus God, I don't want to go through that again. I had to feed her a pint of rotgut in ginger ale — you and your stinking smart ideas. Then when it's over she throws up all over me, blood and vomit and the tears, all mixed up. That's beyond the call of duty. I shoulda given her a shot in the head. No, sir. Not Marty — the last of the good guys."

"You're all heart," Kelly said.

"You're goddamn right. Then she says to me, with the tears, 'I don't know if I can marry you, Marty, I don't know if I'm in love with you — ' "

"That is not a bad idea, Marty."

"You bite your tongue, you little sonofabitch. It just happens that I am married, which is the only protection a guy has in this world. And if you weren't such a miserable little motherfucker, you'd be in the front line instead of me. I don't like that little bitch."

"Don't blow this, Marty. It's the one chance we got to get out from under that lousy acting school."

"There are easier ways to earn a buck."

"You didn't walk out on her?"

"You're talking to a gentleman. I cleaned her up. We took showers. That's one hell of an apartment her old man pays for. I turned on all the Spizer charm. I convinced her that she's going to be a star. Look, just let me play it my own way — give it another few days."

It was the day after this conversation, six o'clock in the evening, that Martha opened the door of her apartment and saw Stephan Cassala standing there. He was the last person on earth she would have expected, and since Marty Spizer had indicated that he might or might not drop by, she had thought that he would be ringing her doorbell. Instead, it was Stephan, saying, "May I come in, Martha?"

"Steve! This is crazy. What are you doing in Los Angeles?"

"Business."

"I don't believe you. Sure. Come in."

"I lied. I wanted to see you."

"Oh, you crazy guy," she said, closing the door behind him. He was looking around. "Do you like it? It came furnished, but I think it's nice. Don't you?"

"Yes, it is nice — if you like Hollywood."

"Well, who does? But that's where the movies are. I was so lonely. I'm glad you came. What a nice surprise!"

"When were you last home?"

"Sit down — there. Three weeks ago. Can I get you a drink? Real honest-to-God imported Scotch. Marty gets it from the best bootlegger in town."

"Who's Marty?" he asked sharply.

"Steve! Steve, I'm not a nun. I do have gentlemen friends. Marty's our coach. He's a director — and a good one. I've learned so much from him. He runs the school with another director, Timothy Kelly. And he's doing a film now for Great Western. That's a small studio in the valley. I mean the San Fernando Valley. It's not far from here. Let me get you a drink." She went to a small ornamental bar and began to mix the drinks.

Stephan looked around. The bright wallpaper, the overornate cheap furniture, the pile of movie magazines in one corner — he had not known what to expect nor did he understand why all this depressed him so. Martha was different. Well, he had not seen her for months, and it was only to be expected that she would change. It was plain to him that she was glad to see him, yet not overexcited, and what good would it do to tell her how he had longed for her? Yet wasn't it only to be expected that she would be immersed in her own career?

"Steve, stop being so glum," she said, handing him his drink. "I really think I'm going to make it. Last week, Marty introduced me to Jack Donaldson. He's the studio head at Great Western. He's going to give me a screen test."

"That's great," Stephan agreed.

"Oh, Steve, you don't know how great it is. This town is the toughest place in the world. What do they say — many are called but few are chosen? Well this is it, and very few."

"I'm glad for you. I truly am, Martha."

"How long will you be here, Steve?"

"Just this evening. I'm taking the sleeper back."

"Not one of Dan's airplanes?"

"The last one leaves at four, and I can't stay overnight. I have a ten o'clock appointment in town. I thought we might have dinner together."

The doorbell rang, and Martha opened the door for Marty Spizer. She resisted the hug and kiss he gave her, and then he saw Stephan. "I told you about Steve Cassala," Martha said quickly. "Steve, this is Marty Spizer."

Stephan saw a surly, good-looking, dark-haired man in his thirties who stared at him coldly. Then Spizer's face changed and he grinned. "Of course. The Bank of Sonoma. Well, by golly, I'm always inspired by meeting a banker. That's the nature of this business. No financing, no movie."

"Marty's the director I was telling you about," she said to Stephan. "He's a dear old friend," she said to Spizer. "We've known each other since we were kids."

"Childhood sweethearts?" Spizer said generously.

"No, just dear friends."

"I did have a dinner date with Marty," Martha said. "If you had only called."

"Not a word more," Spizer said. "I'm taking both of you to dinner. How many real friends do we have in this world? And you don't know," he said to Stephan, "How lucky you are. I mean to have any kind of a relationship to this kid. She's going to be another Joan Crawford, and you can take that from the horse's mouth. I know. She's got talent, and she's got a voice. No more silent pictures, Steve. That day is done. This is the day of the actor, and this kid can act."

They ate at Lucy's, with the great sprawling mass of the Paramount lot as a backdrop. "Good food and good friends, right, Steve?" Spizer said. "Now let me bring you into the picture. That's a good note, the picture. I'll level with you. Great Western is not Metro and it's not Paramount. It's a small studio, and until now their specialty has been horse operas — Westerns in plain English. But sound changes all that. You can't do Westerns on a soundstage. So they got to break with the past and go into something different, and that's where Martha and I come into the picture. Now I don't know what goes between you and this talented kid here, and it's none of my business. Maybe you got a torch for her, maybe not. But we both got her interests at heart. We're both pitching for her, and she's on the way up. So I introduced her to Jack Donaldson, who runs Great Western, and he's impressed, believe me. We arranged for a screen test."

"Which just may not be the greatest thing ever," Martha interrupted, sensing Spizer's direction. "They could decide that I'm a very cold turkey."

"Never! I should just have a million bucks to lay on that screen test. It would be the easiest money that ever came my way. No, sir," he said to Stephan. "I have no doubts about that test. We got the star and we got the story. Let me tell you something about this story."

"I don't think Steve's interested in the story," Martha said. "He's not in the film business, Marty."

Marty Spizer glanced at her, a cold flash, and Stephan said, "But I am. I'm interested in anything that concerns Martha."

"All right. It's a simple story, but effective. Here's a kid, a hoofer. Dancer in English. Sings too. Comes to New York from a small town to make it. Like a thousand kids. She's got talent — but New York's a tough town. Wears out the shoe leather and gets nowhere. Then she meets this guy. Nice guy who knows his way around. He's a hood, mixed up with the booze, bootleggers, you know, the mob. He gets her a job singing and hoofing in this club, a speak, but classy. He's got all the hots for her a guy can have. She knows what he is. Of course, she wants him out of the rackets, but there's no way out for him. Then the rival mob snatches the girl. Kidnaps her. Our guy tracks them down and moves in on them, two guns blazing. He's wounded, but he rescues her and puts half a dozen of the other mob to sleep. She nurses him back to health and he quits the mob. It's got everything, love, excitement, gunplay, action. Everything, and it's soundstage work. When I laid it out for Donaldson, he hit the ceiling with joy — and when I told him Martha's the kid for it, he agreed. He agreed. Sure he wants to see a piece of film on her. But that's just a part of the industry."

"It sounds very exciting," Steve admitted.

"It is, it is, believe me. And I got Chester Morris interested, which makes it one hell of a package."

"You didn't tell me about Chester Morris," Martha said.

"Just happened today. So you can see what we got going, Steve. We got the stars and we got a studio hot as hell, and we got the story and we got the director. One more little thing, and we're off to the races."

"Marty," Martha said, a note of pleading in her voice.

"Listen, kid, Steve's a businessman, a banker. I'm not conning him. I tell him what the situation is, and if he's interested, he's interested. If not — not. Now look, Steve, when they made a silent picture, they'd have some kind of two-bit scenario and go in front of the cameras and shoot. It didn't matter much what the subtitles were, because they could always change them. Today, it's different. Making a picture is like producing a play, only harder, but there's got to be a screenplay and it's got to be good. For that you need a writer. That's the one thing we don't have, a writer who can take my story and turn it into a screenplay. But once we get a writer, we're home, screenplay, director, star. The truth is, we may just tell Great Western to stuff it and take our little package to Metro or Paramount, because then we're king of the hill."

"Steve," Martha said, ignoring Spizer's glance, "we need a lot of money to get a good screenplay — and this isn't your kind of thing. I'm trying to get up enough nerve to go to my father, and I will."

"How much money?" Stephan asked. "There's no harm talking about it."

"Twenty thousand," Spizer said quickly. "It's an investment. We call it front money, seed money. When the studio picks up, the money is repaid, and if we make our deal with Great Western, Tim and me are cut in for maybe fifty percent of the profits. One third of it to you. And the picture could make a million dollars — which is by no means a bad deal for an investment of twenty thousand."

"It sounds interesting," Stephan admitted. "Would one film make Martha a star? I mean, establish her career?"

"You bet your sweet patooties it would."

"Steve," Martha said, "I had no idea we were going to talk about this. It's not fair to put this burden on you."

"Maybe it's not such a burden," Spizer said.

"Well, there are a lot of questions," Stephan said. "I want to think about it."

"You got questions, I got answers," Spizer told him.

In June of 1928 Dan went to Houston at the personal invitation of Al Smith. By his own choice, he was not a delegate to the convention, which was to begin on the twenty-sixth of June, and he spent less than a day in the city; but during that time, he had an hour alone with Smith, in the course of which the governor said to him, "Danny boy-o, this is one hell of a gamble we're taking, and maybe it's not time yet for a Catholic President. I think it is, and I think you and me we got something this country needs. We're a different breed than these cold Protestant bastards who own this country — not all of them, there are plenty like young Roosevelt who can smell the winds of change — and we can't sit back and let it happen. No, sir. So why the hell aren't you in politics?"

"Because all I have is street knowledge," Dan replied. "I never even finished high school."

Smith nodded and smiled. "That's all you have, boy-o. But if I win, I want you in Washington. How about it?"

"To do what?"

"We'll work that out later. Yes or no?"

"I'll think about it."

"Good enough. Now I'm not apple polishing, Danny, and I'm not working you over for money, but where do we go? The Mellons and the Rockefellers hate my guts. I got to turn to men like you."

"I understand."

"I'll be in touch," he said.

Traveling back to San Francisco, Dan thought about it a good deal. He was flattered and excited. It was a long way from Fisherman's Wharf to the White House. Sure he's using me, he told himself, but what the hell, everybody uses someone else. Strangely, politics left him cold. He was obsessed, as he had been for months, with the thought of airlines — airlines that swept across the country from coast to coast. It was five years away, six, ten years away; that didn't matter. It was the way of the future and nothing would stop it, and already he had his edge with the coastal line. But airlines meant franchises, and he was not the only one who saw it coming. The fight for franchises would be a very tough one, and it didn't hurt one bit to have that door to the White House wide open. Whatever he paid now would be money well spent, and he had the money. For the first time, they had all the money they needed, and he admitted to himself that Mark had been right in pressing for the stock issue.

He had left a check for twenty-five thousand dollars with Al Smith, and now he braced himself for Mark's anger.

Strangely enough, Mark agreed with him. The stock ticker in Dan's office had worked its magic. Coming into his office on his return from Houston, Dan found Mark fondling the tape as it ticked out of the machine.

"Well, Danny my lad, where do you think we are today?"

"We're up. I know that."

"That's a safe guess. The stock of Levy and Lavette closed yesterday at thirty-nine and a half. It just passed forty."

"We're sure as hell making a lot of stockholders rich."

"We are rich. Do you realize that the stock we hold is worth twenty million dollars? Our half. It's crazy, but by God, it's a fact."

"I gave Al Smith twenty-five grand. Are you going to chew my head off?"

"I swear, Danny, if there's one thing you never understood, it's money. All right. Tell me why."

"Because if he makes it, we're going to have the pick of every damn air franchise we want."

"He won't make it."

"So we gamble. You're not sore at me, are you?"

"Not while that thing ticks out money. We can afford it." He stared at the ticker thoughtfully. "You know, Danny," he said, "you were always the gambler and I always sat on you, but this market fascinates me. There's no top to it — and with reason. This country's bursting at the seams. I don't think Herbert Hoover's any great brain, but when he talks about a chicken in every pot and two cars in every garage he makes a practical case. We never bought any stock on our own, and I think we ought to have a shot at it. You can go into this market with ninety percent margin, ten dollars on the hundred. What do you think?"

"I'm not exactly broke. Pick out a few, and I'll play along with you."

Thomas Seldon died in August of that year. He was seventy-four years old, and had suffered from angina for the past three years. On the morning he died, he had complained of severe pains in the chest. Old Hemmings, the butler, almost eighty and none too well himself, went downstairs to call the doctor. When Hemmings returned to the bedroom, Seldon was dead.

Jean was in Europe when this occurred. On her instructions, at the end of the school term Wendy Jones had taken Barbara to New York, where they were joined by young Thomas; and then the three of them sailed for England on the *President Jackson,* the L&L ship that was in the Atlantic crossing trade. From England, the four of them, Jean, the two children, and Wendy Jones, traveled in France and then settled down in a villa at Nice for the month of August. They were there when the news of her father's death reached Jean.

Dan was still at home on Russian Hill when Hemmings telephoned him with the news, and he went immediately to the Seldon home. He found himself deeply disturbed. Not since the death of his own parents had anything of this sort touched him so sharply. Through the years, he had moved closer and closer to Seldon, the original mistrust turning into a grudging and then open admiration on the older man's part. As for Dan, he had, without realizing it, come to count on Seldon as a sort of father figure, a feeling buttressed by their enormous bank line at the Seldon institution. Indeed, Seldon had been a sort of mythology in his life, the great mansion on Nob Hill being the first focus of all his dreams and aspirations. Now it was among the last of the big, ornate mansions still standing — anchoring him in some way he did not wholly comprehend.

It was nine-fifteen when Dan arrived at the Seldon house. Dr. Lamont, the family physician, was there, and he informed Dan that he had given a sedative to Mrs. Carter, Seldon's sister, who had lived with him and been his housekeeper since his own wife died. She had been quite hysterical, but now she was resting comfortably. Hemmings told Dan that he would have tried to reach Mrs. Lavette, but he had no idea where she was. Dan called his secretary at the office and told her to cable Jean in the south of France immediately. Then it occurred to him to place a telephone call. It was a half-hour before the call got through, and then he spoke to Wendy Jones, who informed him, as well as he could gather through a very bad connection, that Mrs. Lavette was away for the next three days on Mr. Horn's yacht — whoever Mr. Horn was.

"Is there no way to reach her?" Dan asked.

"Not for three days. She'll be back then."

"Well, try. Tell her that Mr. Seldon died peacefully. I'm taking care of all the arrangements. See if you can't reach her by radio. If there's a harbor there, there must be a harbormaster. Tell him what the situation is." He remembered to ask after his children, and he was informed that they were well. He didn't ask to speak with them.

By now, reporters from the *Examiner* and the *Chronicle* had arrived, and Dan gave them whatever facts he had. The news had spread quickly, and already there was a small crowd of the curious in the street outside. A few minutes later, Martin Clancy, the vice president of the bank, and Rustin Jones entered the house.

They went to pay their respects to Mrs. Carter and then returned to ask Dan what arrangements he would be making.

"The trouble is I can't reach Jean. She's out on a yacht somewhere in the Mediterranean and won't be back in Nice for three days."

"Terrible, terrible," Clancy muttered. "Poor child. Terrible loss. We'll miss Tom."

"The old-timers are going," Jones said. "Terrible loss — for all of us."

Father Templeton, an old friend of the Seldons' who was attached to the Grace Episcopal Cathederal, which was still in construction within sight of the Seldon house, arrived while they were talking. He, too, talked to Mrs. Carter, and then he asked Dan where the body was.

"Upstairs in the bedroom. Dr. Lamont was here, but he left."

Father Templeton shook his head. "A pity I couldn't be here, but Hemmings tells me there was no time. I'll have a prayer said in church. Where is Jean?"

"Right now on a yacht in the Mediterranean. The children are in the house at Nice. I'm afraid we can't reach her for three days."

"What a shame! Poor child. Then how long would it take her to get here?"

"If she gets a ship on the same day — well, seven days on the ship and three and a half days on the train. A fast ship cuts a day off that, but then she would have to make connections in Cherbourg or perhaps in Southampton. The one ship we have in the North Atlantic is coming into New York right now. The truth is, Father — I don't know what to do."

"And the other relatives?"

"Well, his sister, Mrs. Seldon's family — I think there's some family in Boston, not very close. I'll have my office take care of it."

"Tom was only the second generation out here. Didn't give him much time to create family, did it? Well, what do you think we should do, Mr. Lavette?"

"Damned if I know. I'm not an Episcopalian, Father. What do you suggest?"

"You're sure Jean and the children can't get here in less than two weeks?"

"If they make all the connections. If they don't, it might be fifteen or sixteen days."

"Well, there's nothing in the canon that forbids us to wait, but I disapprove of such things. The body is dead. The soul lives, and we don't foster any worship of the body. If you ask me, two weeks is too long. I would suggest that you make arrangements to have the funeral four days from today. That will give you a chance to speak to Jean and explain my feelings. Then when she and the children return, we can have a memorial service."

However, when Jean finally called from Nice, Dan was neither at home nor in his office; and without waiting, Jean and her children and Miss Jones left for Cherbourg. They had a day's wait there for the ship, and when she finally reached Hemmings from Cherbourg, she learned that the funeral was already in progress. She became furious and insisted that her father not be buried until she was home, but there was nothing Hemmings, himself late for the proceedings, could do about it. It was, nevertheless, an impressive ceremony as hundreds of the dignitaries of San Francisco turned out to watch one of the last nabobs of Nob Hill laid to rest. Dan sat with Anthony Cassala and Mark Levy, pashas in their own right, millionaires among millionaires, thinking as he rarely did of the awful finality of death, where a man goes naked and alone, his flesh already putrifying. What was Thomas Seldon that made him any different from Dan's own mother and father? His life was the same lost wisp of a dream, eddying fragments of memories half lodged in the minds of others; and soon that too would be gone, and his great mansion would go the way of the other great mansions on Nob Hill, replaced by a hotel or an apartment house; and already here at the funeral service in the crypt of Grace Cathederal, his own mind wandered, not hearing Templeton's eulogy, not truly caring now that the initial shock was over, but seeking for his own salvation in memories of May Ling. Was it only six months since he had seen her and held her in his arms? Why had he made no attempt to telephone her, to speak to her? Had he decided? Could he live the rest of his life without her, without knowing her or seeing her or seeing his son again? There was overtaking him now a gray and awful grief, a turning of his whole being into ashes, a sorrow so profound that had he been capable of it, he would have burst into tears; yet the sorrow was entirely for himself. Inwardly, he wept for his own death without ever knowing that he was dying.

When Jean returned, eleven days later, she had done with her grief, for what it was, and only a cold, dismal anger remained. She had left Thomas with friends in the East, and the first moment she was alone with Dan, she said to him, "You bastard! You buried my father without me. What a cheap, dirty revenge!"

"That's crazy," Dan said. "That's the last thing I ever thought about. We had the funeral because Father Templeton thought it was best. Why don't you ask him?"

They never spoke about the funeral again, and the day after Jean returned, Dan went to Chicago to meet with Al Smith. He brought with him over one hundred thousand dollars for the campaign fund. He had intended to go on to Detroit, but a call from Sam Goldberg brought him back.

"Foster Thorndyke called me," Goldberg said. "They were going to read the will tomorrow, but I persuaded him to postpone it until you returned. Can you get back here by Saturday?"

"I'll be there," Dan promised.

Thorndyke, a stout little man, bald, with a dry voice and gold pince-nez clipped onto a thin, small nose, sat facing Dan, Jean, and Virginia Carter in the somber living room of the Seldon house. Both Jean and Mrs. Carter wore black, in Jean's case a trim suit of black wool, black stockings, and black pumps. She rarely wore black, yet the costume was becoming; and even now Dan found himself reacting to her beauty. She had lost weight; her cheeks had fallen slightly; yet the strong bone structure of her face preserved her good looks. Her hair was piled under a small black hat, which she did not take off. She had hardly spoken to Dan — aside from the single outburst — since she had returned from Europe. Mrs. Carter kept dabbing at her eyes; she was frightened, having little money of her own, at what the reading of the will might portend for her.

Clearing his throat, Thorndyke pointed out that as Seldon's lawyer, having drawn the will himself under Seldon's instruction, he knew what it contained. "It is an eminently fair and sensible will," he said. "Mr. Seldon had no animosity toward anyone. It must be understood that he loved his daughter Jean without reservation, yet he had to take into consideration that she was already a very wealthy woman married to a wealthy man. He had a strong sense of family, and that too must be understood. I shall now break the seals and read the will." He opened the document he held and read it: "I, Thomas Seldon, being of sound mind, do make this my last will and testament — "

There was the sound of Mrs. Carter sobbing.

"To Fannie Jenson, my cook, who has served me so long and faithfully, I leave five thousand dollars. To Sadie Thornson, my housemaid, two thousand dollars. To Albert Hemmings, I leave ten thousand dollars. This house and property wherein I have lived these many years, I leave to the Grace Cathederal to aid in the building of that great structure, to keep or to dispose of as they see fit; except that all the furnishings and paintings and artifacts it contains, I leave to my daughter, Jean. To my dear daughter, Jean, I also leave what jewels and possessions of her dead mother remain to me. To my sister, Virginia Carter, I leave my Rolls-Royce limousine, so that she may have the comfort of it, and also ten thousand shares of American Telephone and Telegraph stock, to be held in trust for her by Foster Thorndyke, the dividends of said stock to be paid to her monthly, and also a cash bequest of ten thousand dollars. The remaining part of my estate, three hundred and eighty-two thousand shares of stock in the Seldon Bank, constituting the majority of such stock, I leave to my beloved grandchildren, Thomas Lavette and Barbara Lavette, to be held in trust for them by their mother, Jean Seldon Lavette, until the year nineteen forty, when it shall be divided equally between them. Until that day, my daughter, Jean Seldon Lavette, shall act as trustee of the income from said stock, with full power to dispose of said income as she deems right and proper with no restrictions placed upon said disposal of income. I do this, not because I practice a preference between child and grandchild, but to preserve the institution I have created and to preserve my family."

This was followed by a series of small charitable bequests. Mrs. Carter now sobbed openly. Jean did not look at Dan. She stared straight ahead at Thorndyke, her face placid and revealing nothing.

The following day, Sunday, a memorial service was held for Thomas Seldon in the crypt of Grace Cathederal, where Father Templeton announced his large and gracious gift, and the day after that, a meeting of the board of directors was held at the Seldon Bank. Martin Clancy invited Jean to be present. She appeared in a simple but striking suit of black linen that she had purchased in New York on her way back from Europe; and the various members of the board, all of whom she had known for years, wondered why they had not noticed before what an impressive and commanding woman this was.

Alvin Sommers, the second vice president of the Seldon Bank, now in his middle sixties, stout, and pompous, delivered the formal sentiments of the board. He stressed the many virtues of Thomas Seldon, the care with which he had fostered the bank, once a small frontier institution, now among the dozen largest banks in America, his sense of civic responsibility, his love for his family. "No one knows better than you, dear lady," he said to Jean, "in what honor and esteem we held your father. That is why we have invited you here today — so that in this board room" — he might well have said temple — "where your father spent so many of his hours, we, his closest associates might each in turn convey our feelings, the full depth of our sympathy."

"Hear, hear!" said Grant Whittier.

"How thoughtful of you," Jean said. "I'm such a foolish woman. I thought perhaps it had to do with my father's will."

"Your father's will?" Clancy asked.

"I'm sure you've spoken to Mr. Thorndyke. The will was read to the family on Saturday, only the day before yesterday. So perhaps you haven't had a chance to discuss it with Mr. Thorndyke?"

"Of course we have discussed it, Jean," Whittier said. "And we are gratified — immensely gratified that your father, in his wisdom, made provision to keep the bank in the family."

"Then naturally you must have considered my own relationship to this board."

"By all means," Clancy agreed.

"And what will that relationship be?" Jean asked quietly.

"Very close, very close indeed," Clancy said.

"Let me be more specific," Sommers said. "Not only will you receive quarterly reports of the bank's condition, but we shall see to it that the minutes of each and every meeting of the board of directors are conveyed to you. Of course, this does not mean that you must read every report or trouble yourself over the statements. We have a very well-managed bank, Mrs. Lavette, and I don't think you need lose a minute of sleep over its condition and progress."

"That is to say," said Clancy, "that we are well aware of your interest in the arts and in civic affairs. We applaud them, Mrs. Lavette, and we have no intentions of burdening you with the complexities of this institution."

"You all appear to have missed the point," Jean said.

"The point?"

"The point being that for the next twelve years, I am the trustee for the majority of the stock in this bank. I have discussed the matter very carefully with Mr. Thorndyke, gentlemen, and I am under no illusions. I vote that stock, gentlemen. In so many words, for the next twelve years, I own the Seldon Bank."

"Yes, in a manner of speaking," Sommers agreed. "We are well aware of that."

"Not in a manner of speaking," Jean said, quietly but firmly. "In a legal sense. There are no qualifications. For the next twelve years, I have control of the Seldon Bank."

"But no one denies that," Whittier said. "My dear Jean, you can't for a moment imagine that we do not repect your position?"

"Well, there does appear to be a contradiction."

"How is that?"

"As I understand it — and you may correct me if I am wrong — it is the board of directors that constitutes the highest authority of this bank and has the decision-making responsibility."

"Quite right."

"And the board members are elected by the voting stock, which in this case is merely a euphemism. My father appointed this board of directors."

"Are you saying that you are dissatisfied with us?" Clancy asked worriedly.

"No indeed," Jean replied. "I have no reason to be dissatisfied."

"I think," Sommers said slowly, "that Mrs. Lavette is making a point. I think she would like formally to approve our position. I see no reason why she should not."

"No," Jean said. "No, gentlemen. When I came here today, I expected you to take it for granted that I would take my place on this board."

There was a long silence. Then Clancy said, "But, Mrs. Lavette, we have never had a woman on our board. Indeed, unless I am greatly mistaken, there has never been a woman on the board of any major bank in this country."

"I'm sure you are correct."

"It would seem," Clancy said uncertainly, "to be a matter of some impropriety."

"Oh, don't be an ass, Mr. Clancy," Jean said, losing patience. "I don't give a tinker's damn what has been or what is propriety or impropriety. This is nineteen twenty-eight. Women exist. They vote. They are in most respects admitted members of the human race. Now I not only intend to sit on the board of directors, I intend to chair it. I am not denigrating your wisdom or management. I have a great deal of respect for the way the affairs of this bank have been conducted. But the plain fact of the matter is that for the next twelve years, I vote the majority stock of this bank, and I intend to exercise my affairs with knowledge and involvement. And you needn't worry about the time or energy that will be required. I have both. Now there is my position, stated as plainly as I can. If any of you gentlemen have any serious objections to the role I have chosen for myself, I would like to hear them right now." She had lost her patience only for a moment; then her voice was quite calm and matter-of-fact, and when she finished speaking, she looked from face to face.

Again, there was a long moment of silence. They waited for Clancy, who said finally, "You are quite within your rights, Mrs. Lavette. I think I can speak for all the members of the board when I say that we will render you whatever good advice and aid that is within our powers. And simply to formalize it for the record, I will move that the chairmanship of this board be offered to Mrs. Jean Seldon Lavette."

"I will second the motion," Grant Whittier said weakly.

*

Two weeks after he had seen her in Los Angeles, Stephan Cassala telephoned Martha and told her that he would be in Los Angeles the following day. Could she see him and have dinner with him? She tried to dissuade him at first, but when he pressed her, she agreed. He was so easily hurt, and he always gave her the feeling that to reject him would hurt him beyond his tolerance for the pain. She wondered why he appeared so defenseless to her. Surely, he was not defenseless. She knew, from what she had heard at home, that he was the moving force in the Sonoma Bank, that it was he who had built it from a tiny bank that served Italian fishermen and laborers for the most part into a substantial institution; yet she always felt that he approached her with the assurance that she could destroy him, pleading with her not to. She wondered why he could not realize that all the men she was attracted to were almost his opposite in their character.

He was a serious man. Martha's depression lurked under a gaiety that she wore like a favorite dress. The New York School of Acting, for what it was, had closed, and Martha had fallen upon long, endless days of boredom and inactivity. Her mother and father begged her to come to Sausalito for the summer, but she felt that to leave the scene she had chosen would be an admission of defeat. Having enough money to survive without a job, she looked for a role instead, always cushioning her defeats with Martin Spizer's promises. When Stephan arrived at her apartment, he noticed the change in her. Odd corners of her despair had begun to show.

He came to the point immediately. "Before we eat," he said to her. "Before we talk. Before we do anything, you and I have a small matter of business to transact."

"Steve dear, what business?"

He took an envelope out of his pockets, unfolded some documents, and handed her a check for twenty thousand dollars. It was made out to Martin Spizer Productions. She stared at it, then shook her head and burst out in protests. "No, no, this is crazy, Steve. This is absolutely crazy, and I won't have it. Do you know, I haven't even asked my father for this money. Marty keeps after me to ask him, and I can't. And now you hand me this. You're out of your mind."

"Will you calm down," he said to her. "Will you please calm

down and listen to me. This is not a gift. Not that I wouldn't make you a gift of the money if I could. I'm a banker and this is a regular bank loan. I have all the papers here."

She began to protest again, and again he interrupted her. "Why don't you try to think of it as something apart from you. I'm approached for a loan and I decide to grant it."

"Because it isn't apart from me."

"My darling Martha, listen to me. This is all perfectly legal. We make loans every day. This loan will help you. If the loan is a bad loan, we will write it off, as we do with other bad loans."

"Does your father know about this, Steve?"

"My father doesn't question my decisions. Martha, there are all kinds of people. You are someone who will never be happy until you make it in this business. I love you very much. I don't ask much in return, but I do ask that you let me go ahead with this loan. Now I want you to call this man Spizer and have him meet us later. He can sign the documents, and then the film is on its way."

"I don't understand you, Steve, I swear I don't."

"Let's say that I don't understand myself very much. I just seem to be here on earth in a very strange place that doesn't make much sense to me surrounded by strangers. You're one of the few people who is not a stranger."

"I'm not in love with you, Steve. You know that."

"I know. So we won't talk about being in love or not in love. There are plenty of other things to talk about. I'm staying at the Ambassador for the night, so why don't we eat there and have a nice, leisurely dinner, and you call Spizer and have him meet us later, and he can sign these documents and then we're on the way."

"Steve, you're an angel, a complete angel."

Martha reached Spizer in his hotel room, where he was sitting with Timothy Kelly, the two of them finishing off a bottle of cellar muscatel, which they had purchased with what was practically their last ninety cents. Spizer listened to what Martha had to say and enthusiastically promised to meet them at the Ambassador at ten o'clock that evening. He turned back to an inquiring Kelly, grinning from ear to ear.

"Timmy, my lad, the eagle has crapped. Not just crapped, a veritable storm of shit. The brilliance and charm and patience and persistence of Mrs. Spizer's boy has finally paid off. At ten o'clock tonight, we shall be in possession of the incredible, impossible, unthinkable sum of twenty thousand dollars."

Sarah Levy still kept the big Spanish Colonial house in Sausalito without a servant or household help of any kind. On occasion Mark would lose his temper and shout about this. "At present market prices," he once stormed at her, "my stock in the company is worth over eleven million dollars. And I haven't done anything criminal to become a millionaire. I gave forty thousand dollars to charity last year, and I built the synagogue in this town almost single-handed. I got nothing to be ashamed of, and the least I could have is a servant to help my wife."

"And then what would I do?" Sarah asked mildly.

"Enjoy life."

"You mean spend the eleven million? You know, Mark, you've devoted your life to making it. You haven't given much thought to spending it."

"Stop being foolish. We went to Europe last year. I don't deny you anything."

"Then don't deny me the right to clean the house. That's my work," she said bitterly.

Dan spent more and more time at the house in Sausalito. For one thing, Sarah lit up when Dan was there. She cooked special foods for him, fussed over him, coddled him, and lectured him. She was only nine years older than Dan, and as it was with her daughter, Martha, Dan had always been the swashbuckling, romantic concomitant of her life. She approached him as a mother, but also, somewhere deep in her mind, neither admitted nor fostered, as an adoring mistress. Still a year short of fifty, Mark had aged. He had lost his hair, taken on weight, developed a paunch. Dan at forty was erect and youthful. Time had bound the three of them close together, and circumstances cemented that bonding. When Dan came to Sausalito, Sarah appeared to shed her years. She still possessed her trim, youthful figure, and when she laughed, Dan saw the same slender blue-eyed girl Mark had married so long ago.

The one thing Sarah could never comprehend was the relationship between Dan and Jean. With the coming of fall, Barbara had been sent to school in Boston and Wendy Jones, with a bonus and the money she had saved, returned to England. Yet Dan and Jean continued to live their separate lives in separate bedrooms in the house on Russian Hill. They functioned on separate schedules, and Dan was no longer expected to be present when Jean came to a dinner party. When one or another was gone through the night, there were neither questions nor recriminations; and one night, when Dan sat with Mark and Sarah in the big Spanish tile kitchen at Sausalito, Sarah said to him, "Why? Why, Danny? How can you live like that?"

"Because it doesn't happen all at once. It goes slowly, through the years. The truth is, I suppose, that I don't really give a damn. She has her life, I have mine."

"The truth is that you have no life," Sarah said.

"Sarah, don't let's start that again. It's Dan's life."

"Hell, Mark," Dan said, "Sarah can ask me anything she wants to ask me. It's the answers that don't make sense. There are things I can't explain, even to myself, so what's the use of trying to talk about them? Jean and I live what she calls a civilized life. I'm civilized, she's civilized, my children are civilized. That goes a long way. She doesn't bother me. Our mutual dislike has become very tolerable. Anyway, she's plunged head over heels into being a banker. Funny thing is, she is actually running that bank."

"Which also puzzles me," Sarah said. "It would seem to me that now she really owns you. You and Mark owe the bank sixteen million dollars — "

"Not really," Mark said. "The company has the bank loan, and if the Seldon Bank calls it, we could lay it off in a dozen places. It's nothing to worry about. We're in good shape. We'll be in even better shape if Dan's pipe dream about Al Smith comes off."

But it didn't come off. On election night, on the evening of November 6, in 1928, sitting in the Levy living room, Mark and Sarah and Dan listened to the radio and heard the results pile up as Herbert Hoover won the election in a massive landslide vote. America's repudiation of Al Smith, streetwise Catholic from New York, was overwhelming and complete. There were over twenty-one million votes for Herbert Hoover, as against fifteen million for Al Smith. Hoover garnered four hundred and forty-four electoral votes, as compared to eighty-seven for

Smith — forty out of forty-eight states for Herbert Hoover.

By midnight, the results were beyond dispute, and Dan made his own small political epitaph: " 'You win some and you lose some.' Not very original, but it fits."

"What did it cost us?" Mark asked.

Glancing at where Sarah slept, curled up in a chair, Dan said softly, "Maybe a hundred grand."

"Dumb."

"Yeah, I suppose so. But I like that little sonofabitch. He's got guts. I once said to him that I got my education on fishing boats, and what does he tell me? He got his packing the fish in the Fulton Fish Market in New York. Being a Jew or a Catholic back there in the East, Mark, it's not like out here. Mark, you know what I want to do tomorrow?"

"Sleep?"

"Hell, no. I'm going to rent me a boat down at the docks here, and we'll go fishing."

"Fishing? Are you crazy?"

At seven the following morning, Dan hammered at the door to Mark and Sarah's bedroom. "Fishing!" he shouted. "Get your ass up out of there, Levy!"

Dan found a catboat to his liking. There was a brisk wind on the bay. They sailed for hours, caught nothing, and returned sunburned and relaxed for the first time in months.

"The children will be home for Christmas," Jean said to Dan. "We're not much of a family, but with my father gone, I thought perhaps we might have a civilized family Christmas."

"And how do we go about that?" Dan asked her. "I bet everyone who knows us asks that question. How do the Lavettes go about it? Do we pretend affection? Do I spend days buying gifts for two kids who hate my guts?"

"Dan, they don't hate your guts, as you put it."

"You should have asked me earlier. I have to leave for New York. We're rescheduling, we got labor trouble, we're oversold and just about everything else that can happen has happened."

"Conveniently."

"I suppose so." He took a deep breath and said, "Jean, how long can this go on?"

"As long as I desire. You have no restrictions and no reason to complain. You are free and I am free, and since we are both reasonably discreet in our affairs, I see no reason for either of us to complain."

He let it go at that, not bothering to say that he had no affairs that required discretion. When he wanted a woman, he did what a good many of his business associates did. He telephoned a man by the name of Earnie, and for fifty dollars, a good-looking young woman would arrive at an indicated hotel room, disrobe, and give him what sex he required. He did this infrequently and only to prove to himself that he was still alive. It was without joy and without any aftermath of pleasure.

Actually, he had arranged to flee from Christmas. Anthony Cassala begged him to join his family at San Mateo, and Mark begged him to come with him and Sarah to spend Christmas at Higate with Jake and Clair and with Martha, who would come up from Los Angeles. It would be the first time in months that the entire Levy family would be together — and it would be Dan's first visit to the winery. For years, he had listened to Mark's description of Jake and Clara's struggle to make the place pay, their contract with Rabbi Blum, their subsequent conquest of the Reform and Conservative Jewish synagogues, and, most recently, through the intervention of Anthony Cassala, their first penetration into the sacramental wine purchases of the Catholic Church. But perversely, he had to be alone with his loneliness. There was only one place he desired to be, and May Ling had closed the door there with a firmness he had never believed possible.

Dan took the train to Chicago, and from there he went by air to New York. The ear-deafening roar of the lumbering Ford Trimotors gave him a certain deep sense of satisfaction and relaxation, as if this environment were entirely his own. He ate his Christmas dinner alone in the Plaza Hotel, looking out on snow-covered Central Park, taking a kind of adolescent and perverse pleasure in his condition, buttressed by the fact that he was three thousand miles from those who felt anything toward him, whether it was hatred or love.

At Higate, Martha felt that she was in a dream, and the winery in the upper reaches of the Napa Valley was to her a scene out of another world. Had she forgotten so soon that people lived this way? Jake and Clair had hired a Mexican couple, Juan and Maria Gonzales, to help with the work. They had orders for three thousand gallons of sacramental wine, and with the coming spring they were planning to put fifty acres into grapes of their own growing. They had an enormous fir tree in the living room, piled underneath with presents, and in the big old kitchen, they all sat at a long wooden table of Jake's own making, carving a turkey that he and Clair had raised and slaughtered. Their children sat at the table, Adam, seven, Joshua, five, and Sally, three, sunburned, freckled, healthy. The boys were both redheaded; Sally was like a miniature version of Sarah, with big, pale blue eyes and straight hair the color of cornsilk. Mark looked at them with wonder; did it happen like this, in only three quarters of a century? For Sarah, who had spent her childhood in old Russia, the gap was even greater. She was uneasy among all the accouterments of a Christian Christmas, even though she and Mark had made certain to come with a car piled high with presents. Did they have any religion, she wondered? And what was their life like here in this beautiful and lonely place? Everything on the groaning table was of their own growing or their own making. Even their bodies were different, Jake in blue jeans and blue work shirt, hard-muscled, his face burned dark by the sun, Clair so tall and lean and strong, her red hair tied in back, long and indifferent to the style of the day, without make-up, totally unconcerned with all the variety and elements of life in San Francisco or anywhere else, laughing, apparently as happy as anyone could be. Were these her children and her grandchildren?

Martha was quiet, withdrawn, conscious of her carefully painted nails, her make-up, her precisely bobbed hair. For the rest of them, she was part of that marvelously unreal and fascinating world of Hollywood that lay somewhere far to the south. They asked endless questions that only increased her nervousness and served to make her even more ill at ease. The New York School of Acting had permanently closed its doors. Spizer and Kelly were producing a film at the Great Western Studio. She was to star in it. Uneasily, she told them the plot of the film. The screenplay was being written. But what did she do with herself? How did she pass her day? She was taking voice lessons with a man called Victor Stransky. There was a great deal to do in

Hollywood. She had friends. It wasn't at all as they imagined; it was a serious place where people worked hard, where people were dedicated to their profession.

Desperately, she wanted a drink, but they served no liquor. She breathed a sigh of relief when at dinner Jake brought out a gallon jug of clear white wine, and the talk turned to wine and its making.

"This," Jake said with emphasis, "is not sacramental wine. This is wine," and he underlined the word. "It's a sort of Chablis, but quite dry and good, we think. We made fifty gallons of it, and since we actually made it for ourselves — and for you, of course — it's a sort of bootleg. But if we don't sell it, we don't get into any trouble over it."

"Actually," Clair put in, "we had expert advice. There's a darling little man called Professor Simon Masseo, who teaches chemistry at Berkeley, and he was wonderfully helpful when we made our first batch of wine. I guess he taught us most of what we know, and we made this white wine to repay him. I mean, that's one reason. He was so amazed when he tasted it. Jake and I felt that we had passed some kind of awful college exam. We gave the professor twenty gallons, and when he actually accepted it, it was just the highest praise he could offer."

The glasses were filled and a toast was drunk. Mark and Sarah praised the wine. Martha drained her glass, and Jake refilled it.

"Not that we aren't grateful to Rabbi Blum," Clair said. "And I must say that the Catholics insist on the same dreadful sweet wine that he does. But someday if they ever get rid of this insane Prohibition thing, this is the wine we'll make and sell, I hope. A dry white wine and the wonderful red zinfandel. Poor Fortas. The Feds raided him, and now he's in jail serving six months."

Then Jake had to explain who Fortas was and why he was in jail. Martha filled her glass again. The meal went on. Mark launched into a lecture on air transport. He had finally found the courage to make the flight to Los Angeles and back in the Ford Trimotor, and he gave a vivid description of how it went. Adam pleaded for an airplane ride. Sarah praised Clair's cooking, but then, in Sarah's eyes, Clair could do no wrong. Martha drank wine, unobtrusively, and apparently only Clair noticed that she had filled her glass half a dozen times.

After dinner, in the early twilight, Clair and Martha, both of them wrapped in sweaters against the chill of evening, walked up the hillside behind the big stone house. Clair stopped at a big eucalyptus tree.

"When it gets to be a madhouse down there, you need to have a place to be alone. This is mine. Let's sit here a while and pretend we're still kids back in Sausalito."

"Only I'm not a kid," Martha said forlornly. "I'm not grown up either. God, I don't know what I am."

"Has it been hard, honey?"

"Not hard — just pointless. The days are fifty hours long. Pop gives me all the money I need. Maybe it would be better if he didn't, and then I would have to break my back trying to stay alive, like all the other kids down there, and then when everything else fails, they fall into bed with some louse who gives them five dollars or maybe buys them dinner and then they tell themselves they're not pros, just kids trying to stay alive. I haven't had one damned acting job, Clair. I had a screen test — "

"Well, that's something, isn't it? I mean, from what I've read, to have a screen test."

"Maybe. Who knows? Maybe they'll make the film. But, God, I get so lonely and depressed, and then I buy a quart of bootleg gin and sit in my room and drink, and I guess it helps. I don't think I'm becoming an alcoholic, and then I get terrified that I am, like today. I didn't have a drink yesterday, and today when Jake brought out the wine, I got goose flesh."

"You wouldn't give it up?" Clair asked gently.

"No. I can't."

"Even for a few weeks? Come and stay here. Jake and myself, we won't bug you. Honey, we love you."

"I know, but I can't. I have to see it through. I can't explain either, Clair. I've talked to the other kids about it. No actor can explain what it means. It's like a drug. You begin, and then the whole world revolves around whether you make it or not, and if you don't make it, you might as well be dead."

"No!" Clair exclaimed. "Don't ever say that."

Jean had taken over her father's office in the Seldon Building on Montgomery Street, cleared out the dark oak pieces and the overstuffed leather chairs, and replaced them with pale birch and chintz upholstery. The gloomy Oriental rug on the floor went to an auction house and in its place Jean installed a pale blue, gold, and ivory Aubusson, with drapes to match. Clancy, who had gathered the courage to contest her decision to take over the bank in fairly strong terms, pointing out that the news of a woman bank president might well token disaster, was deeply troubled by these decorative changes, but he bore them in silence. The *Chronicle*, objectively expressing neither approval nor disapproval, did a feature story on the first female bank president in the United States. The bank's business, however, did not suffer; quite to the contrary, riding on the tide of the times, it increased.

One afternoon, sitting in her office, Jean was informed by her secretary that a Mrs. Alan Brocker was outside and would like to see her.

"Did you say Mrs.?"

"Yes."

"A woman?"

"Very much so."

"Well — send her in," Jean said. "By all means, send her in."

The secretary left and then returned, opening the door for a large, handsome, dark-eyed woman who swept into the room, crying, "Darling, you have not forgotten me? It is Manya."

Jean rose, staring at Manya Vladavich whom she had not seen in at least ten years. She came around the desk, and Manya embraced her in a cloud of silk, bosom, and perfume.

"You are more beautiful than ever," Manya declared when Jean had untangled herself. "You are a witch. Or you have sold your soul to the devil."

"More likely the latter. You can't complain, Manya. You look absolutely stunning. What is this Mrs. Alan Brocker thing?"

"What you see, darling. Myself. I have married more money than is in the Bank of England. We have taken fantastic house by the bay, and tomorrow a great party — "

"Manya, stop! Are you telling me that you and Alan Brocker are married?"

"But of course."

"Well, I'll be damned," Jean said, shaking her head and smiling. "You and Brocker. How did you do it?"

"Darling, it would take days to tell you whole story. I am living in Paris where I meet him. He is very lonely, very unhappy. How old you think he is, Jean?"

"Don't you know?"

"He tells me forty-four. He looks older."

"He told you the truth — or close to it."

"Darling, we are five days in Paris. He is so unhappy. I make him go with me to Vienna. You know what is psychoanalysis?"

"Sort of. Dr. Freud's thing?"

"Exactly. We go to Dr. Freud. He is with Dr. Freud for seven weeks, every day. Every day I am like mother to him. Not exactly. After seven weeks, we go to Venice. Three weeks. Then we go to London and we are married. Then we come here. So simple."

"I don't believe it. What on earth did this Dr. Freud do to him?"

"Ah. We shall have to talk about that. Alan's mother, what was she like, darling?"

"A little bit of a thing, as I remember."

"Yes? What does it matter? You are president of bank. Incredible. You are still married? Of course — to the fisherman."

When she left, Jean sat down at her desk, closed her eyes for a few minutes, and then burst out laughing. Alan Brocker and Manya Vladavich. The world was insane, senseless. What had Shakespeare said? "A play written by a madman?" No — she couldn't remember. She conjured up in her mind what it might be like to be married to Alan Brocker, and she wondered why the very notion horrified her so, herself married to a huge, brawling savage who had not taken her to bed in years. And now she sat here, playing this new game of being the head of the Seldon Bank.

She put her head down on her arms and wept.

When Martha returned to her Los Angeles apartment, in the second week of January of 1929, she called Marty Spizer. The telephone company informed her that the phone had been permanently disconnected. She was not unduly alarmed at first, concluding that Spizer had moved. Since she had not been in Hollywood, he might have tried to call her and failed to reach her, and she had not told him about Higate. He might also have tried to reach her at Sausalito and failed there as well. She was certain that he would be in touch with her, and she spent the next few days in her apartment sipping gin and soda and waiting for the telephone to ring.

Finally, she went to his apartment, a tacky, stucco two-story enclosure on La Brea. The landlady there, a stout, slatternly woman, told her in no uncertain terms that "the lousy, four-flushing sonofabitch" had skipped out on the first of the year, owing her five weeks of unpaid rent.

"No forwarding address?" Martha asked uncertainly.

"Cookie, if that little louse left me a forwarding address I'd have him in court right now. No, sweetie pie, he skipped."

Martha was not entirely sober, not entirely certain that she understood the landlady. She managed to drive home, and by then the impact of what she had discovered reached her. Still she tried to reason her way out of it. She had known that since the school had closed, Spizer's funds were minimal. On several occasions she had lent him money, twenty dollars once and fifty another time. The twenty thousand dollars, he had assured her, would have to go entirely toward paying the writer for the screenplay. She kept salving her misery with explanations. He would call; he would turn up; and it would be a fine thing indeed if he came armed with good news and found her drunk.

She poured every ounce of gin in the house into the toilet, and for the next two days she did not touch a drop. When she woke up the morning after getting rid of it, she discovered that she was ravenously hungry. She dressed herself carefully, put on her make-up, walked over to Hollywood Boulevard, and ate an enormous breakfast at Musso and Frank's restaurant. Then she went back, got her car, drove downtown, and spent the rest of the day drifting around and shopping. She returned with a bag of odds and ends of clothing, two sweaters, a blouse, some kerchiefs, and some stockings — none of which she particularly needed. She spent the rest of the evening sitting quietly in her living room, listening to music on the radio. She felt strangely good, like a person in a dream, in a continuing fantasy, a person suspended in time.

The following morning, she awakened very early, strangely enough with no desire at all for liquor. Again she dressed very carefully, brewed a pot of coffee, and satisfied her hunger with that and fig newtons. Then she got into her car and drove over Laurel Canyon Pass down to Ventura Boulevard, turning east. A mile farther on, she drove into the entrance of the Great Western Film Studio. Her progress was halted in front of the swing barrier at the guardhouse, and the uniformed studio guard leaned out of his cubbyhole and asked her who she was there to see.

"Mr. Donaldson. My name is Martha Levy."

The guard consulted his clipboard. "I don't have your name here, miss," he said. "Do you have an appointment?"

"No. But I must see him."

"That may be, miss, but there's nothing I can do about that. I suggest you call from outside and make an appointment." Cars were lining up behind her now, and the guard raised the swing barrier and told her to drive through and turn around and come back out. Instead, Martha drove ahead about thirty feet and then pulled over to one side and parked.

"I told you to make a U-turn and come out!" the guard shouted at her.

She shook her head and sat there.

The guard in the cubbyhole shouted to another uniformed guard, who came over and spoke to him. He pointed to where Martha sat in her car. The second guard walked over to her and said, "Now why do you want to make a scene, miss? You know about studios. No one goes in without an appointment."

"I'm going to see Mr. Donaldson," she said stubbornly.

"Not today, lady. So come on, be a good girl and turn your car around and drive out."

"No, not until I see Mr. Donaldson."

"Lady, this is private property and you are trespassing. You want to make a pain in the ass of yourself, we'll arrest you, and that's going to make a lot of trouble for you. So why not do it the nice way?"

A small crowd had gathered, extras in costume, Indians, cowboys. A tall, heavyset man in a white linen suit pushed through and said to the guard, "What's this all about, Brady?"

"We got a crasher. I'm trying to be polite."

Martha called out to the man in white, "Mr. Donaldson, I must talk to you, please."

He looked at her curiously. "Do I know you?"

"I'm Martha Levy. Marty Spizer introduced me to you. Please. I only want five minutes. Please."

Donaldson stared at her. "All right, Brady. I'll take care of it. Come along with me, Miss Levy," he said to Martha.

She got out of the car and followed him in silence to one of the larger bungalows on the lot. He led her inside, past his secretary into his office.

"Sit down, Miss Levy," he said to her. "You know, I could have had you thrown out. You know why I'm talking to you?"

She shook her head.

"Go on, sit down," he said, nodding at the chair by his desk. "I remember you. I'm talking to you now because your name is Levy. You're the first Jewish kid I've run into on this lot who hasn't changed her name to Adore or Bradford or Simmons or something like that. So it gives you points. Not many, but it's worth five minutes of my time. Now what do you want?"

"I only want to know about my picture," she said forlornly.

"What picture?"

"The picture Marty Spizer is producing."

"That lousy little turd? Sorry. But if Marty Spizer were a magician, I wouldn't let him produce a rabbit out of a hat on this lot."

"He has a deal with you — "

"No."

Tears oozed out of her eyes, blurring her careful make-up. "But he has a deal with you," she insisted. "He's preparing a screenplay. He's going to direct it."

"Spizer?" He stared at her thoughtfully.

"I had a screen test here," she said woefully.

"Anyone who puts down two hundred and twenty dollars can have a screen test here, Miss Levy. It's a service. We're a small studio. It's just a way of augmenting our income. How much did Spizer take you for?"

She shook her head without answering.

"Where are you from, Miss Levy?"

"Sausalito," she whispered.

"Why don't you go back to Sausalito, Miss Levy," he said, not unkindly. "That's the best advice I can give you. That's the best advice I could give a thousand kids in this town. Stay away from lice like Marty Spizer and go home."

She dabbed at her eyes. "I'm sorry. I'm sorry I made a scene outside. I'm sorry I bothered you."

She walked out of Donaldson's office across the lot to her car. Her tears had stopped, and she got into her car.

"Just make a U-turn, miss," the guard said to her.

She drove along Ventura Boulevard and then turned left into Laurel Canyon Boulevard, climbing the hill to Mulholland Drive, a dirt road on the spine of the Santa Monica Mountains. She drove westward, and then parked her car in an open spot, with the whole hazy reach of the San Fernando Valley stretching north beneath her. It was a cool, lovely morning, the valley with its great orange and avocado and lemon and lime groves lying in the early mist like some enormous garden, and eastward, the mighty spur of the San Gabriels. She sat there for perhaps a half-hour, staring at the scene and now and then probing at her own self, forming in her mind a picture of utter emptiness within her, a cloudy, floating emptiness, a feeling that she did not exist, a feeling she had had as a little girl when she would awaken at night in the darkness and be overtaken with terror at the thought that she had disappeared into the consuming dark.

She started the car and began to drive. She increased her speed. Her self had fled, and unless she overtook it, she would live out all her days as an empty shadow. She drove faster and faster, the car careening wildly on the narrow, twisting dirt road.

Polly Anderson, Mark's secretary, came into Dan's office without knocking or being announced, terribly upset, and said to him, "There's a call for Mr. Levy from the Los Angeles Police, and he's somewhere down in the store, and I think it's something awful about Martha — "

Dan looked at her, then picked up the phone and asked for the call. Then he listened, while Polly Anderson watched him. His face turned white, his hand holding the phone trembled, and he whispered, "Oh, my God, no." He listened again. "I'm his partner, his friend. Yes, I'll take care of it." He put down the phone and stared at Miss Anderson.

"Martha's dead," he said. "She died in a car crash."

Polly Anderson began to blubber. Dan rose and eased her into a chair. "Just take it easy, Polly. I'll find Mark and tell him. You just stay here until you feel better."

He left his office and took the elevator down to the store, then walked through floor after floor looking for Mark. How do you do it? he asked himself. How do you tell your best friend that his daughter is dead? How do you tell him that all that's left inside of him is dead and gone and finished?

He found Mark staring thoughtfully at a display of sporting equipment, and Mark said to him, "You know, Danny, I ought to have some sport in my life. Look at all this stuff. I never did any exercise in my whole damn life, and look at this potbelly I'm wearing here. I used to be skinny as a rail. I think I'm going to join one of those golf clubs and take up golf. How about it? Suppose the two of us try it?"

"Come up to my office," Dan said gently. "I want to talk to you."

He saw Dan's face then. "What happened?" he demanded.

"Come up to my office."

Polly Anderson had left and the office was empty. There was no easy way to do it. Dan told him what had happened. "The Los Angeles police called. There was an accident."

"Martha?"

"Yes. Martha's dead."

Mark stared at him. "What are you saying, Danny?"

"Martha's dead. She died in a car crash in Los Angeles."

"I don't believe that. That's crazy. I spoke to her on the phone yesterday. I spoke to her on the phone."

Dan eased him into a chair, and now he began to cry. "Maybe it's not Martha," he said through his tears. "Maybe it's someone else. Danny, what do I do? What do I do? How do I tell Sarah?"

A great belly of gray white fog, shot through here and there with shafts of sunlight, golden, unlikely bars that gave way to thin cold rain, rolled in through the Golden Gate on the morning they buried Martha Levy. Rabbi Blum, bowed with the guilty weight of his years in an irresponsible universe that destroys youth, read the burial service over the grave, and then Sarah cast herself on the fresh soil and lay there sobbing. Dan lifted her up, surprised at how thin, how almost weightless she was in his arms. She clung to him. Mark stood and stared at the grave with unseeing eyes until Jake went over, put his arm around him, and said gently, "Come on, papa. It's over. We'll go home now."

In the background, there was only the poignant sobbing of Maria Cassala and the muted agony of Clair Levy against the lonely foghorns out on the bay.

PART SIX

The Whirlwind

At seven-thirty in the morning, California time — which is ten-thirty New York time — on October 24, 1929, Dan received a long-distance call from his New York manager, Frank Anderson, who said to him, "I hate to get you out of bed, Dan, but this wouldn't wait."

"It's all right. I'm up."

"There's something funny as hell happening with the market. Joe Feld, my broker, called me. I didn't know whether you and Mark were going to the office today. I think you ought to have a look at the ticker."

"I'll be there," Dan said.

It was eight-thirty Pacific Time, eleven-thirty New York time, when Dan walked into his office. The offices opened at nine. He was the first one there, and as he entered his office, the phone was ringing. It was Stephan Cassala.

The first thing he said was, "Dan, have you looked at the tape?"

"I haven't turned the damn thing on. I just stepped into my office. What the devil's going on?"

"There's been a big break in the New York market. The prices are plunging."

"Well, it's happened before."

"Not like this. Twenty, thirty points on a stock. I'm calling because I don't want you and Mark to panic."

"We don't panic," Dan said with some irritation. "We got a few thousand shares on margin, our own money — the hell with it. What goes down comes up."

"That's it exactly. I talked to Crocker and Giannini. There'll be a consortium of banks in the city in the next hour or two, and we'll be buying heavily. The same thing's happening in Chicago and in New York. Pop talked to Clement at the National City Bank in New York, and back there Mitchell and Wiggen and Lamont are putting together a consortium of their own. So don't get nervous."

Dan put down the phone and switched on the ticker tape. But he hardly had a chance to glance at it before the telephone was ringing again. It was Klendheim, his broker: "I need twenty-one-thousand five hundred from you, Dan, and eleven thousand from Mark. To cover your margins."

"When?"

"Now."

"You're out of your mind."

"Do you know what's happening on Wall Street?"

"Give us an hour."

"No more than that. For Christ's sake, Dan, I got thirty customers in the same fix. We've got to have the money."

"Look, my office hasn't opened. No one's here. The moment my secretary comes in, I'll send her over with a check."

Mark entered the office as he was speaking. "Did you hear about it, Danny? Who's that?"

"Klendheim," as he put down the telephone. "He wants margin money."

"How much?"

"About twenty thousand from me, eleven thousand from you."

Mark closed his eyes and calculated. "My God, that doesn't seem possible. That's about one third of our investment."

"You'll cover, won't you?"

"I don't know if we should." Walking over to the stock ticker that was feeding its white ribbon onto the floor, Mark stared at the tape. "I just don't know if we should, Danny. If this is what I think it is, maybe we should just take the loss. It's less than a hundred thousand between us — "

"Less? God damn it, that's a hell of a lot of cabbage!"

"And if it keeps plunging, we could double that. Danny, what did L and L close at yesterday?"

"Fifty-six and a quarter."

"It's on the tape at thirty-four."

Dan walked over and stared at the figures. "Where does that leave us?" he asked.

"That doesn't matter. The fifty-one percent of the company

stock we own has no margin. We own it outright. If it goes down to twenty cents a share, it doesn't make a damn bit of difference to us. Not now." He managed an uneasy smile. "It might give Jean a headache or two. The Seldon Bank has sixteen million dollars pledged against that stock."

"I thought the mortgage was on the property."

"And the stock, Danny. It's all lumped together."

"What about our own stock?"

"What do you think?" Mark asked him.

"Whatever you say."

"All right. I think we ought to take the loss and let go."

Dan was reading the tape. "Here's L and L again — thirty dollars even."

"I'll tell Polly to reach Klendheim and sell us out," Mark said. The phone was ringing again. Dan picked it up as Mark left his office. It was Sarah Levy. "Danny," she said, "I've been listening on the radio and I'm worried about Mark. I don't want him to get too excited over this. I don't care about any money we lose."

"It's all right, Sarah," he said. "It's just a few dollars of our own money, and Mark couldn't seem to care less. It doesn't affect the company in one way or another."

For some months now, Mark had been suggesting to Sarah that they sell the big house at Sausalito and move into one of the new apartment houses in San Francisco. She resisted this. If she had to live with memories, they were here in the old house. She would go to Martha's room and sit there for hours, evoking the image of her daughter. She would handle Martha's clothes, which she had refused to part with. Sometimes she would play Martha's jazz records on the squeaky old Victrola that stood in her room. She had never listened to jazz or understood it or been particularly fond of it, yet she derived a sort of comfort out of listening to the recordings. She found an old diary of Martha's, kept during her thirteenth and fourteenth years. Toward the end of the diary, she found the following entry:

"Today Danny was here and he picked me up in his arms and kissed me. I am absolutely in love with him. He is only sixteen years older than I am. I dream about him a lot. In the best dream, he left that stinky wife of his and asked papa if he could marry me. Papa got very mad but mama said it would be all right. She said it would give her a chance to have a big wedding outside on the lawn. The bad part of the dream came when he never showed up for the wedding at all. His wife came instead."

Sarah found herself laughing and weeping over that. Still a few months short of her fiftieth birthday, she had become old almost overnight. Her blond hair had turned white. She had few resources. She read English with difficulty and she had no taste for novels. The things she had once so enjoyed doing, knitting, sewing, cooking, no longer interested her. She still kept the big old Spanish Colonial house spotlessly clean, but she took no pride and no joy in it. She had never taken too much interest in the garden, leaving it to the gardener, but since Martha's death, she spent more and more hours there. There were some sixty rosebushes in an ornamental circle, and they had been neglected. She began to spray them and clip them and cultivate them. It was there, one afternoon, on her knees loosening dirt with a trowel, that Rabbi Blum found her. He was filled with admiration for the flowers. "A good gardener works with love. You're a good gardener, Sarah." She protested about the trip. "I come slowly," he told her. "Actually, I have nothing to do. I have reached the age where being alive is my only vocation. It gives me an affinity with vegetables and flowers."

They sat in the kitchen, drinking tea. "Do you know," Sarah said to him, "the worst thing I have to endure is that people will not talk to me about Martha. They avoid the subject. Even Mark will not talk about her, and that's what I want to talk about more than anything else. Is that wrong?"

"No, it's not wrong. People are afraid of death. There are people who can't talk about death or think about it. But with Mark, maybe it's too painful. When you get to be my age, Sarah, the separation narrows. It's like an old friend."

"Not a friend."

"Why not? There's a beginning and there's an end. That's not a very profound philosophy, but that's the way it was made. And in between roses grow and bloom and die, and when a bud dies, it's not just and we become angry and hopeless. But the idea of justice is something we put together, not God."

"And what does He put together, a madhouse?"

"That has occurred to me. On the other hand, even a cup of tea has its own good taste."

*

On the twenty-sixth of October, Frank Anderson called Dan and informed him that two thirds of the reservations for the next sailing of the *President Jackson* had been canceled. The following day, Dan left for New York. The train trip to Chicago appeared to him to be endless, crawling, boring, and infuriating; he was locked into his compartment with the world coming apart at the seams. The two days on the train became an eternity in some ridiculous limbo that had nothing to do with reality. He read the papers from cover to cover, first the San Francisco papers, then those picked up at Salt Lake City — his anger increasing because the so-called *news*papers told him nothing he desired to know. In the dining car, he became the object of the kind of inoffensive and meaningless conversation that strangers at a dinner table offer to other strangers; but he had no feeling for chatter, and he found himself being curt and misanthropic. In the lounge car, a woman in her thirties with tired good looks sat down beside him and introduced herself. He fled back to his compartment, wretched and depressed. After this, the plane from Chicago was at least a diversion; and in New York, sitting with the men who ran the North Atlantic division of the shipping line, he tried to quiet the sudden panic and disorientation of otherwise sane and sober businessmen.

It was not a good day, and he slept poorly and fitfully. He had finished the meeting with a decision to cancel the sailing, balancing one loss against another and accepting the lesser of the two, and lying in bed that night, in his hotel room at the Plaza, he tried to grasp what was happening. For years, he had played the fascinating and exciting game of putting together a small empire. He had never been overly concerned with the financial technicalities of the process. Feng Wo and Mark had attended to that. His role had been to devise, to scheme, to invent, to bull and bluff his way through, to dream and imagine and impress people with his excitement and his vitality, and there was always money and more money, once he had learned that a million dollars was easier to come by then a dollar bill if you were broke; and the money generated more money. And now, somehow, it had stopped. A ship that for years had been overbooked was now empty — and so quickly, so incredibly quickly. The empire was coming apart as if it were held together with paste.

He ate breakfast alone in the dining room in the Plaza, a tall, wide-set, handsome man in his middle years, impeccably groomed. Women turned their heads to look at him. His looks were an asset he had carried through the years, granted to him and never evoking much thought on his part. If you looked like Dan Lavette, the doors of the world opened easily.

He sipped his coffee and read the story on the front page of the *New York Times,* realizing that what had happened the previous Thursday was only prelude. Already that day was being called "Black Thursday." What then of today, Tuesday, October 30?

"Stock prices," he read, "virtually collapsed yesterday, swept downward in the most disastrous trading day in the stock market's history. Billions of dollars in open market values were wiped out as prices crumbled under the pressure of liquidation of securities which had to be sold at any price . . . Efforts to estimate yesterday's market losses in dollars are futile because of the vast number of securities quoted over the counter and on out-of-town exchanges on which no calculations are possible. However, it was estimated that 880 issues, on the New York Stock Exchange, lost between $8,000,000,000 and $9,000,000,000 yesterday . . . Banking support, which would have been impressive and successful under ordinary circumstances, was swept violently aside, as block after block of stock, tremendous in proportions, deluged the market . . ."

He finished his breakfast, signed the check, left the hotel, and walked across 59th Street, trying to resolve in his mind the rather extraordinary fact that he didn't give a damn. Where did his personal involvement cease to have meaning? He didn't know. On the one hand, he said to himself, These are your people, the wealthy, the comfortable, the powerful, the doers and the movers; and downtown, just a few miles from here, something is happening that is destroying them. On the other hand, he was thinking, I've had my run. What does it amount to? He had no answers. There had always been questions without any answers.

He crossed the street and walked into Central Park. The sun was shining, the cool October breeze blowing. Women wheeled prams, and the old, horse-drawn carriages lumbered by. He walked to the carousel and stood there for a while, recalling all the times he and May Ling had planned a trip to New York; and then he wondered why the thought of his two legitimate children only now entered his mind. What kind of a bastard are you? he asked himself. It was not by any means an unfamiliar question. Thomas and Barbara were only hours away. Why didn't he want to see them? God Almighty, he thought, what has happened to a man who can't bring himself to face his own children. Yet he could anticipate the situation very clearly. Barbara would look at him, coolly, distantly, her distaste poorly concealed, answering his questions, perhaps dutifully kissing him on his cheek, perhaps not. Thomas would put it into words. "So you finally decided to see me."

"Ah, the hell with it," he said to himself. He looked at his watch. Frank Anderson had begged him to stay a few days more. They wanted to be coddled. They wanted to be told that everything was all right, that Dan Lavette would see to it that their paychecks continued and that the world was not coming to an end. But there was nothing of any importance that he could do here. There were only two things that brought him any real peace: being on a boat and being on an airplane. He walked back to the hotel, packed, and checked out.

Dan moved into a small suite at the Fairmont. His conversation with Jean was brief and to the point. "I suppose I have caused you grief and misery at times, but I have never intentionally caused you embarrassment and discomfort," he said to her.

"That's an odd virtue, Dan."

"Anyway, I can't go on living in this house. I don't know how to explain it any better."

"All right. You've always had freedom of action. Do you want a divorce?"

"Right now, a community property fight would blow everything sky-high. I'd rather wait."

"But you do want a divorce?"

"Don't you?"

"It doesn't matter to me. But that's something you wouldn't understand and I don't intend to explain myself."

A few months later, the situation in Hawaii came to a head. For a month, the hotel had been almost empty, and the Noels, who held a large mortgage on the property, had become increasingly nervous. The whole situation was incredible. Since November, the hotel had dropped from ninety percent occupancy to an uneasy ten percent. When Mark raised the issue with Dan, they were already five days late in their interest payment on the mortgage.

"How much do we owe them?" Dan wanted to know.

"Not a hell of a lot — twenty-five thousand for this payment."

"We've got it. Pay it."

"And then what? The way the hotel stands, we're losing forty thousand dollars a month. We've junked the sailing schedules. The ships are tied up, and we're still meeting a payroll. We've got a tax bill of forty-two thousand on the undeveloped land, and that's three days overdue, and we've got twelve planes on order. There's two million in escrow on the planes, and we're flying to Los Angeles at less than twenty-five percent capacity. Dan, we're not even making the gasoline costs. Without the store and its cash flow, we'd be in over our heads."

"The whole fuckin' empire," Dan said. "What happened?"

"That's what they're all asking. "You've got to have money to ride a ship or a plane — and our customers have had the shit scared out of them. It's falling apart."

"I think we ought to start selling land," Dan said. "We've got at least a thousand acres of the best damn property on the peninsula. We paid more than a million for it, and the price doubled a year after we bought it. So we sell?"

"To whom?" Mark asked sourly. "Would you buy an acre of land today?"

"There's still money. It hasn't disappeared."

"There's still that damn hotel in Hawaii. I think you ought to go there and talk to the Noels."

It was a very different trip without May Ling. He booked passage on Whittier's ship, *Oahu,* and the voyage took forever. Day after day, he paced the deck like a caged animal. He regretted that he had allowed Mark to talk him into this, and when finally he arrived in Honolulu, the Noels proved to be absolutely unyielding.

"Dan," Christopher Noel said to him, "you're asking the impossible." They had been removed from the world, but the world had intruded. They sat on the velvet green lawn in front of Noel's sprawling bungalow, the cool trade wind gently blowing, the sea thundering in across the sand, out of space and time but not unconnected with something called the New York Stock Exchange. "We took one hell of a beating in New York, and now you're asking us to ride the mortgage without interest. We've got half a million dollars tied up in that hotel and the two hundred acres of Waikiki Beach. We can't throw it away."

"Just give the world a chance to breathe. This is panic," Dan insisted, "and panic burns itself out. You know what we've got. We've got the richest and the goddamn strongest country on the face of the earth."

"We're an island, Dan. If we don't survive, we sink into the sea. Who the hell gives a damn about Hawaii? We do. No one else."

"Now look," Dan said, "the hotel's only part of the problem. We own the ships — and without our ships the hotel wouldn't exist. We believed in this and we created it together. We brought you the people. Don't pull the stopper on us now."

"Dan, you've canceled your sailing schedules. Why don't you face this?"

"For a few weeks, yes. I'm leveling with you. We're pinched. We built an airline — one of the pioneers in the industry. That may not mean anything to you now, but someday airlines will connect these islands with the mainland — a few hours, not days. And god damn it to hell, if you can't ride a dream, where are we?"

"You want a free ride, Dan, and we can't afford it."

"Will you give me time to get back and discuss this with Mark?"

"Dan, it's a lousy twenty-five thousand dollars. You're running a multimillion dollar empire, and here we are arguing about a few thousand dollars. What does that say?"

"It says that we're short of cash. That's all it says."

"All right," Noel agreed. "Another two weeks."

Listening dispiritedly to Dan's report of the Hawaiian journey, Mark asked, "Two weeks from now or from when you left him? Ah, it really doesn't matter."

"Why?"

"Because in two weeks or ten weeks, nothing is going to change. Do you know what that ass Hoover is doing? Promoting the sale of apples. You're out of a job, get a crate of apples and sell them on the street. At a nickel an apple, you're elevating the nation's health. In less than a year, we've descended to the level of lunatics."

"What about Hawaii?" Dan persisted.

"You tell me."

"Suppose we send them twenty-five thousand. That gives us another six months."

"For Christ's sake," Mark exploded, "where is your head? In one month of operation, we drop more than twenty-five thousand. That goddamn hotel can bankrupt us. It's over. Can't you understand that? We dropped a hundred thousand dollars in the market because you don't throw good money after bad. People are not going to Hawaii. They're not going to Europe. They're not going to fly on the damned airplanes. It's over."

Dan stared at Mark and watched his face crumble as he covered it with his hands. "I'm sorry," he whispered. "I've been coming apart since Martha died. I'm sorry."

"It's O.K.," Dan said gently.

"Where do I come off talking to you like that?"

"It's O.K., old sport," Dan said. "I've got a skin like a rhinoceros, you know that. If you don't yell, I don't hear."

"We've been together twenty years. We never had a fight before."

"So we needed one. I know how you feel. If I wasn't fat and middle-aged, I'd go out and get drunk and bust up a saloon."

Mark shook his head. "We can't afford that anymore, Danny."

"Right. It costs too much. You know something, I never felt like such a total horse's ass as I did out there in the Islands pleading with Chris Noel. Two words would have been enough."

"Oh?"

" 'Fuck you, Christopher.' No. I should have been explicit. I should have said, 'Take the hotel and shove it up your ass.' You're absolutely right, old sport. We clean house. And don't write off the planes. We'll cut every expense to the bone, reschedule the ships, and concentrate on the airline and the store. We're not licked yet, old buddy. Hell, for two grubby kids from Fisherman's Wharf, we haven't done too badly. We're two interesting citizens, Levy and Lavette. Don't underestimate us."

"We've had our moments," Mark agreed, managing a smile.

*

Stephan Cassala played with his son, Ralph. The little boy, in his woolly Dr. Dentons, with his black curly hair and huge black eyes, was almost too perfect to be true. Stephan always regarded him with amazement, as if he were seeing him for the first time. At six o'clock in the morning, the child would crawl into his bed and awaken him. It was a wonderful way to wake up. "Raphalo," Stephan would growl softly. The little boy would dissolve in laughter. Then the two of them would crawl around the bedroom floor, growling and laughing at each other, while Joanna watched happily. For the past six months, life had been good to her. She was a giving soul and had accepted Stephan's terrible grief at the death of Martha Levy. They had been childhood friends, and he had the right to grieve. Then, when his grief was over, he had been kinder to her than ever before. She had married a good man, she told her mother.

Now, on this day, Stephan played with Ralph, was late for breakfast, and had only a cup of coffee with Maria, who was lamenting the fact that he should leave the house without nourishment, without the strength to take him through the day. His father brooded over the morning paper, oblivious to the world. At half-past seven, they were in the car, driving north to San Francisco. It was a morning like any other morning.

In the car, without looking up from his paper, Anthony said, "Over five hundred banks."

"What?"

"Closed. Destroyed."

"It happens."

"It could happen to us," Anthony said.

"Not likely."

More or less, it was the same conversation they had every morning; the difference this morning lay in the crowd that had gathered in front of the Bank of Sonoma on Montgomery Street. It was only nine o'clock, still a half-hour before opening, yet there were more than a hundred quiet, worried-looking, men and women in front of the bank, and the crowd was increasing. Anthony and Stephan pushed through into the bank, where Frank Massetti, Anthony's son-in-law and the manager, greeted them unhappily.

"It looks like a run," he said.

"Why?" demanded Anthony. "Name of God, why?"

"Didn't you see the paper?"

"So two banks close on the Peninsula? What it has to do with us?"

Stephan said, "Stop arguing. There's a panic, pop, and that's that. Do you want to pay?"

"I die before I stop paying," Anthony said dramatically. "Is the money mine? We are a bank, and I will pay every penny."

"Pop, think about it. We're in no condition to pay every penny. No bank is. We have total deposits that amount to about sixty million. We have close to forty-five million in loans, and we can't call those loans today — or tomorrow — or the next day."

"Why not?"

"My God, pop, don't ask me why not. You know. We got eight hundred thousand with Consuelo Oil. There's no better or more honest man that Sol Consuelo, but he hasn't got twenty cents in cash. And that's only one case. This whole damn country is hanging on a shoestring. You can't call a mortgage today. You just can't."

"How much cash we got on hand?" Anthony asked Massetti.

"Sixty thousand."

"And in the account at Crocker?"

"One hundred and fifty thousand."

"And with Giannini?"

"Seventy-five thousand."

"All right. We got ten thousand with the First National in Chicago and fifteen thousand at the National City in New York. You wire them immediately, now. Stephan," he said to his son, "you go to Crocker and get the hundred fifty thousand and then take the seventy-five thousand from Giannini. We have over three hundred thousand cash. Nine-thirty, Frank, you open the doors and start paying."

"Pop, please," Stephan begged him, "think. There's no way Crocker will give us a hundred and fifty thousand this morning."

"It's our money on deposit there. They got to pay."

"No, they don't!"

"Are you crazy?" Anthony shouted.

"Pop, please, will you think this thing through. It's almost nine-thirty. Crocker's a big bank, but how much cash do you think they have to open with? Maybe a hundred and fifty thousand, maybe two hundred thousand. They don't have to pay it out to me. If they give me fifty thousand, I'll be lucky."

"No, sir. They give you what we got on deposit there."

"Papa, papa, you know better. We don't have to open at nine-thirty. We can post a sign saying we're opening at noon today."

"No! No! Is this how I built a name? A reputation? Is this what I am, Anthony Cassala? I take the sweat and blood of a poor working man, and now I say to him, 'Go to hell! You can't have the money you work for'!"

"For God's sake, give me three or four hours."

"No! Frank," he said to Massetti, "it is half-past nine. Open the doors. We make payment in full."

At the Crocker Bank, the manager told Stephan, "We know what you're up against, Steve, but this damn thing is a disease, a contagion. It's ten o'clock and we've put out fifty thousand dollars. Not a run — yet. But if I give you a hundred and fifty thousand — considering that we still have that, I'll start a run. All we need is one customer told that we're out of cash."

"You've been out of cash before. Every bank has."

"Yes, but not in nineteen thirty. Look, I'll let you have twenty-five thousand."

"Oh, no. No. That's like signing a death warrant."

"For God's sake, why doesn't your father close his doors?"

"Because he's crazy. Because he's a man of honor. How the hell do I know? The point is, he won't close his doors. Now what do I have to do, get down on my knees and plead with you? Take it for granted. I'm on my knees and pleading. Right down the street, something that I gave my life to is being destroyed. I'm begging for help."

"Thirty thousand."

"It's not enough."

"Steve, give me two or three hours and come back. I promise you I'll find some cash."

"Now. It's got to be now."

"All right. I'll give you forty thousand, and sweet God, I hope it doesn't cost me my job."

"O.K., I'll take it. But in three hours, I want a hundred and ten thousand more."

"Steve, don't force me to the wall. In three hours, everyone in San Francisco will know what is happening at your bank, and every bank in this city is going to hang onto its cash like Scrooge himself. I'll get what I can." As an afterthought, he added, "We have fifty thousand on deposit in your bank. We're not going to call it — for whatever that helps."

"Fat lot of good. Well, get the money, small bills. You've never seen my father in a rage."

With a briefcase bulging with money, Stephan raced back to the bank. If anything, the crowd in front was even larger, and now there were four policemen, trying to keep some kind of order among the nervous, pushing depositors. "I work here! Let me through!" Stephan shouted, fighting and shoving to make his way, clinging to his bag of money. Inside the bank, he found his father.

"Forty thousand from Crocker. That's all they'll give me, and I had to get down on my knees and plead for it."

"They must honor our deposit," Anthony cried angrily.

"No law says so. There are a lot of deposits they have to honor. I'm going to Giannini."

He returned with thirty thousand dollars. They were still paying in full, but the cash bins were almost empty.

"Close the doors," he begged his father.

Stony-faced, Anthony stared at him and shook his head.

"You've got to stop it," Stephan pleaded.

"Frank's cashing in our government bonds. We'll pay everyone."

"We can't pay everyone. It's eleven-fifteen, and that crowd outside is growing."

"By two o'clock, we'll have two million dollars."

"And then? What then?"

Anthony Cassala shook his head. "We pay."

"And we destroy ourselves."

"No. They will take confidence. The run will stop."

At noontime, Stephan was in Dan's office, pleading with him and Mark. "Here's a hundred thousand in government bonds. The city's dried up. The run's on us, but every bank in the city has a case of the jitters, and they're hanging onto their cash as if it were blood. We can't even move our treasuries for cash. If you can give me cash for these bonds — "

"The hell with the bonds," Dan said. "We don't carry cash, Steve. You know that."

"But the store does. You got to take in forty, fifty thousand in a day. Mark, if you can let me have it for just twenty-four hours — or take the bonds for collateral. Either way. But I got to have it now — "

"What about that?" Dan asked.

"Whatever we got, Steve. There's about ten thousand in the safe out of yesterday's receipts — we'll clean out the registers. Maybe thirty, forty thousand."

"God bless you both."

Again, Stephan raced back to the bank with a briefcase stuffed with money, but it was like trying to stem the tide with a single outstretched hand. At three o'clock, the Cassala bank closed its doors. At nine-thirty in the morning, it opened them again. At two o'clock, it closed its doors again — its total reserves washed out. It was never to reopen. On the third day after the run began, Anthony Cassala suffered a major coronary infarction while sitting in his office at the Bank of Sonoma. By the time the ambulance reached the hospital, he was dead.

After the funeral, standing with Dan and Mark in the house at San Mateo, Stephan said to them: "It was the morning of the second day of the run, and there must have been four hundred people in front of the bank. We were pushing our way through, pop and me, and this man says, 'Hey, please, Mr. Cassala,' to pop, you understand, not loud but painful, like the voice of a man with a knife cutting him, and he's talking in Italian. I know him slightly, a Sicilian, a laborer, hod carrier in construction or something like that, and pop stops, and he says to pop, not angry, but just soft, 'Mr. Cassala, I don't want to trouble you. You have problems. I have problems. No work for three months. I have a wife and five children. Little ones. Each week I take ten dollars out of the bank. So we live. I got seven hundred and sixty-two dollars in the bank, Mr. Cassala, savings from the day I got married. That's all I have in the world. Without it, we will starve.' Just like that. He wasn't angry. You know, I was never hungry. It's hard for me to understand hunger with my lousy stomach. Pop looked at the man. His name was John Galeno. Then pop took him by the arm and led him into the bank. 'Pay him first, Stephan,' he said to me. Then he said to Galeno, 'You don't take that money home and hide it, you understand? You take it to Giannini's bank, you understand? Put it there. It's safe.' That's not a banker. God Almighty, why did he ever decide to be a banker? The last damn thing in the world he should have been is a banker."

Cold in San Francisco can be as cold as anyplace on earth. It's a wet, damp cold that rides in on eddies of fog and thin rain and eats into the marrow of the bone. It was like that today, and Dan wrapped his coat around him and thrust his hands into its pockets while he stood on the corner of California Street on Nob Hill watching the wreckers take the Seldon mansion apart, stone by stone, brick by brick, beam by beam. The big dining room, where he had sat the first time so long ago, his own Mount Olympus where he had first tasted the food of the gods, stood naked and exposed, the wallpaper peeling away, all the ghosts of the past unsheltered and whimpering in the wind.

There he stood and watched, gripped by the sight, held by some magnet out of a past that was without sense or meaning. Finally he tore himself away and walked down the steep hill toward Montgomery Street, passing the apple vendors and the panhandlers — there but for the grace of God goes Dan Lavette — and emptying his pockets. He was an easy touch. Once, years ago, Jean had said to him with some asperity, "Why must you give money to every bum who approaches you?" But he had always been the other person, a fact which he understood only vaguely. His sense of himself had always been ill defined; only now that things were coming to an end did he begin to feel and sense and touch the person who was Daniel Lavette.

The department store was almost empty. Business had been falling off steadily through 1930, and on a cold, wet morning such as this, the people who still had money to buy stayed at home. He took the elevator up to the offices and heard a bright, cheerful good morning from his secretary. She was a new girl, very young. Her name was Marion something or other. He had always been rotten with names. "Mr. Levy is waiting for you. In his office," she said brightly. "You had a call from New York, from Mr. Anderson. He'll call back. I couldn't say what was keeping you."

Martin Clancy, from the Seldon Bank, rose to his feet as Dan entered Mark's office. "Good to see you, Dan. You're looking fit." Mark, staring out of the window, turned as Dan entered. "A filthy day," he said. Dan apologized for being late. He had stopped to look at the Seldon house.

"A sorry thing to see the old houses go, one by one," Clancy agreed. "But that's progress. You can't stop it."

"Yes, they're selling apples on California Street," Dan agreed. "That's progress too."

"We've been talking about the credit line," Mark put in quickly. "Mr. Clancy's troubled by our delinquency."

"It's only eighteen days," Dan said. "In this best of all possible worlds, Martin, eighteen days are not anything to lose sleep over."

"That's a gratifying thought, Dan. I assure you that the past eighteen days caused me no sleeplessness. What about the next eighteen days?"

"We're talking about a half a million dollars interest. If you're asking me flat out, do we have it? the answer is no. We don't."

"And when will you have it?"

Dan looked at Mark, who sat down at his desk and stared at Clancy. "Mr. Clancy," he began —

"Yes."

Mark cleared his throat. "We've decided to ask you for a moratorium. We didn't come to this decision lightly. You know our condition as well as we do. Even at today's depressed prices, we have a net worth of twenty-five million dollars. I'm not talking about our stock, but about our assets. We have one of the best-run and best-situated airlines in the country. We have twelve magnificent new planes on order. We have a fleet of ships, a department store, and some of the best land around this city. Two years ago, that net worth would have been thirty-five million, so when I say twenty-five million, I'm putting the lowest figure possible on our capital. However, we're a part of what has happened to the country. Dan and I spent our lives building this thing, and we think we can see it through this crisis. That should be in your interest as well as ours. In a sense, the Seldon Bank is our partner."

"Hardly. The Seldon Bank is your lender."

Dan realized that Mark had rehearsed his speech carefully. Clancy was cold and untouched, and Dan felt that he would have given five years of his life to be able to say, "You cold, lousy little bastard. Get out of here before I throw you out." Instead, he heard himself saying, "Martin, Martin — we've known each other a long time. Certainly, you're our lender. And the bank means something to me, a damn sight more than you might imagine.

It goes to my kids. What Mark and I want and propose is best for the bank."

"How do you see that, Dan? You want a moratorium. The bank surrenders a million a year in interest for the dubious pleasure of tying up sixteen million dollars of its capital. Or are you suggesting that the interest become cumulative?"

"That would be unreal," Mark put in. "Unreal and impossible. You know that as well as we do."

"If we can sell our land holdings," Dan said, "we can reduce the debt considerably."

"Why haven't you sold the land?"

"You know why. Martin, we're fighting for our lives. We know what we have. We created it. If you call our loans, what happens to this enterprise?"

"We haven't discussed that. But even if we liquidated, it might be a better situation. The essence of banking is money. I'm sure you know that, and I expect you also know that no bank is exempt from what is happening today. If we declare a moratorium on your loan, the plain fact of the matter is that sixteen million dollars of our money ceases to exist."

"No, no," Mark said. "You can't take that position, Mr. Clancy."

"But I must. You ask for a gift of a million dollars a year. I don't want to appear heartless or cruel, but gifts have no place in banking."

"I'm not appealing to your generosity, Martin. I'm appealing to your common sense. We've lived with this company."

"You've lived too high on the hog, Dan. If you had been content to grow within the bounds of reason, you wouldn't be in this situation today. Well, I'll take it up with the board. It's not my decision in any case."

After he had left, Dan said to Mark, "You know, old sport, if Tony were alive, if there hadn't been that run on his bank — well, Tony's dead. And sure as hell, there's no one else going to give us half a million on our statement."

"What if you went to Jean?"

"That's an interesting notion, isn't it? After I moved out, I served her with notice of intent."

"And?"

"She's not contesting the divorce."

"I never knew Jean too well," Mark said. "I always felt she was as tough as nails. But not vindictive."

"She's the president of a bank."

"A bank your kids own."

"Her kids."

Mark shook his head. "I swear I don't understand that situation, Danny. A child is a child."

"Do you want me to talk to Jean?"

"If you think it will do any good."

"It won't."

"Then what else?"

"I could go to see Gianinni. He was a friend of Tony's."

"Danny," Mark said, smiling ruefully, "you always were lousy on questions of finance. We own fifty percent of the stock in this company, with ten shares to tip the balance to majority, so in a manner of speaking we say we own fifty-one percent. It's the same thing. But when we went public, that fifty-one percent became collateral for the loan. We can't borrow a nickel from any bank. We have no collateral left. Two years ago, I could have walked into Gianinni's bank and said I want to pay off Seldon. He would have jumped at the chance. We were the white-haired wonders then. Today, he'll pour you a glass of wine, pat you on the back, and tell you how he loved Tony Cassala."

They sat in silence for a while. Then Dan said, "I got an idea, old sport."

"Oh?"

"Let's you and me go out and get drunk."

"It's only eleven-thirty."

"Which gives us the whole day."

"Danny, I haven't been drunk in twenty years."

"Then it's high time — right?"

"Right," Mark agreed.

A week after this, Jean telephoned Dan and asked him to lunch with her.

"I'll be happy to," Dan replied. "Where shall we meet?"

"We have our own dining room here at the bank. Just the two of us. We'll have complete privacy, and the food is quite good, Dan."

When he told Mark about the invitation, Mark asked what he thought it might mean.

"Your guess is as good as mine."

"How long is it since you've seen her?"

"About three months."

"I don't know what to say to you," Mark said. "I just don't know what to say, Danny."

"Don't be so fuckin' noble. Tell me to get down on my knees and plead."

"No."

"Do you mean that?"

"You know something, Danny, we got nothing to cry about. When Martha died, I was hit as hard as any human being is hit in this life. After that — hell, there's nothing worse. It's all happened. Sarah and me, we talked about this, more than we ever talked before. I care and I don't care. Yesterday, thirty-five thousand unemployed men demonstrated in New York, and the police beat the shit out of them. Today, a fine-looking old gentleman walked alongside of me, pleading that he'd had nothing to eat for two days. I gave him five dollars, and then I said to myself that what saved his life — five lousy dollars — is nothing to me. We've been in this together for twenty years, and we never took ten minutes to consider the insanity of the whole setup. Maybe a God I don't really believe in works it out in His own way. Anyway, the long and short of it is that we stuck together. Maybe that's the only decent thing we did. I never really questioned any decision of yours and you never really questioned any decision of mine. So I don't want you to get down on your knees and plead with anyone. We never did it before, and this is no time to start."

Dan nodded. "I'll do whatever I can do."

At home that evening, Dan told Sarah about Jean's telephone call and his own response.

"Poor Danny," she said. "There's no way it can be any good. So don't hope for anything, Mark."

Even now, Dan could not look at Jean and remain unmoved. A part of him always responded, a gut feeling that was inexplicable and beyond his control, a cord tying him to her which could never be completely severed; nor had he ever been able to decide whether it was he who had rejected Jean or Jean who had rejected him. May Ling had once remarked rather bitterly, in reference to Jean, that only people who suffer show the ravages of age — a statement which Dan doubted. He had replied that Jean suffered; it was the manner of her suffering that he did not understand. Yet whether or not that was the case, she had reached her fortieth year with her beauty undiminished. There were no bags under her eyes, no wrinkles on her face; perhaps the skin was drawn a shade more tightly over the fine bones of her face, and the veins on the back of her hands were more apparent, but otherwise she was little different from the young woman he had fallen in love with. She wore a blue serge suit with a thin white pinstripe, the jacket open to reveal a blouse of white silk, and her great mass of honey-colored hair had been bobbed, a change which contributed to her youthful look.

It was the first time Dan had ever been to her office in the Seldon Building, and he was taken aback by the style of the room. It was like no office he had ever seen, with its pale Aubusson rug and brightly covered chairs and couch. There were two Picassos on the walls and behind her desk an enormous Monet of water lilies.

"Do you like it?" she asked him, seeing how he stared at it. "I bought it in France. It's the only one of its kind in San Francisco."

"It's damn big."

"Yes, it wants a lot of wall. That's why I have it here. It's a pity. It ought to be where more people could see it. I'm thinking of giving it to the museum."

She had greeted him pleasantly if not warmly, and offered him her hand. She appeared to be amused by his reaction to the office. "Clancy and Sommers are horrified by it," she told him. "It's just not their notion of what a banker's office should be. But then neither am I their notion of what a banker should be. I had Gianinni in here, and he walked all around, looking at things, and then he said to me, 'For you, it's right.' I think that was the highest compliment he ever paid a woman. Anyway, Dan, you seem to be bearing up. A little more gray hair — and you've gained weight, haven't you?"

"Too much lousy beer."

"You haven't smashed up any more speakeasies?"

"I'm getting too old for that."

"Yes, we're both growing up, aren't we? I was very sorry to

hear about Mr. Cassala's death. I know he was a good friend of yours."

Dan nodded. "How are the kids?"

"They'll be home for the holidays. You can see them, you know."

"I know. Are they all right?"

"The last I heard, top shape."

"That's good."

"I've reserved the dining room for us. There'll be no interruptions. I think we have a good deal to talk about, and I think we're both civilized enough at this point to manage it quite pleasantly. Wouldn't you agree?"

"That we're both civilized? If you feel it gives us points, yes, I suppose so."

The bank's dining room, with its long mahogany table where the entire board could dine, was old oak wainscoting and wine-colored velour drapes. "Isn't it dreary?" Jean said. "It's one place I don't dare touch. If I did, old Sommers would have a heart attack. Isn't it strange how we build a city on the edge of the continent and try to copy all the ancient fuddy-duddy habits of the British? We're not respectable and we never were, and yet we spend so much time trying to prove that we are. I ordered a clear soup and lamb steak and some pie and ice cream for dessert. No fish."

"You remembered that?"

"I remember everything, Dan."

"I wish you didn't."

"Does that imply regret?"

"I have regrets. Who hasn't?"

She gave him the head of the table, and she sat on his right, the long empty board stretching out in front of them. Beautiful spode plates rested on lace mats. The silver was heavy, ornate sterling. The glass was Waterford. The white-jacketed waiter served with self-effacing skill, and the food was excellent.

"I rarely eat here," Jean said. "The place oppresses me—particularly this enormous table."

"Your father had one just like it."

"Perhaps that's why it oppresses me. You know, they tore down the house."

"I noticed. Did it make you unhappy, Jean?"

"Yes and no. I'm not too fond of the past. On the other hand, they're tearing down everything on Nob Hill. I thought of forming a committee to buy some of the old houses and preserve them. But I guess this is hardly the time to try to raise money."

"There you have an undeniable truth."

"Yes. Tell me something, Dan, if Mr. Cassala were alive and his bank had not failed, would he have given you the half-million?"

"Yes."

"No if, perhaps, maybe?"

"No. If I had asked him, he would have given it to me."

"Without collateral?"

"My handshake."

"That's interesting. You could establish a relationship like that with another man, but not with a woman, could you, Dan?"

"And what does that mean?"

"I'm not sure. I just wonder sometimes how it all happened with us."

"It happened, Jean. That's all. It happened."

"Do you hate me?"

Dan leaned back and smiled. "That is one hell of a question. No, I don't hate you. I'm not polishing anything — I'm just stating a fact. You see, when you telephoned me, I had no doubts about what this meant."

"You're sure?"

"Pretty damn sure."

"That I'm going to call the loans?"

"Yes." He hesitated, studying her. "Jesus God, you are one damn beautiful woman!"

"Thank you."

"Only — why here? You could have sent a registered letter, or that little shitheel of an errand boy, Clancy? Or did you need this moment, Jean? Was it just too juicy to pass up?"

"That's beneath you, Dan. You've been a bastard, but never small. You never thought small or acted small, and you know damned well that I never did. I didn't ask you here to parade some cheap revenge or to act out some romantic idiocy. I asked you here because I felt that I had to tell you this myself — face to face."

"Without pleasure? Just doing your duty as the president of the Seldon Bank."

"We have no alternative."

"You could give us six months."

"And then it's a million dollars you don't have."

"All right, Jean. You call the loans. What then?"

"We liquidate what we have to and try to manage what's left carefully and prudently."

"Well, you've learned the lingo," Dan agreed. "Carefully and prudently — as opposed to my lunatic operations."

"No, no. I'd like to be open and aboveboard with you. We've been having discussions with Grant Whittier. Your shipping line is worth twelve million. He'll buy it."

"With what?"

"He has a net worth of sixty million, Dan. He has a credit line at Crocker and at Wells Fargo. We would give him the rest. We recoup twelve million there and that puts us out of the danger area."

"You know what you're saying to me?"

"I know, Dan. I know you despise Grant Whittier. But his ships are still moving freight and his company shows a profit. Yours are tied up."

"And the rest?"

"We'll hang on to the airline and the store and the land. I agree with you about air travel, I always have. I don't want to destroy you, Dan. I want to make it possible for you to live."

"And how do you propose to do that?"

"I'm asking you to stay on, to manage the company. We'll pay you well, forty thousand a year to start, and expenses of course. I can be objective about your qualities, and with our board to keep a rein on you, we believe we can turn this around."

"And what about Mark Levy?"

"Mark Levy is nothing. You know that. He's a glorified bookkeeper and he's never been anything else. I'm not denigrating him. I'm simply stating a fact that you know as well as I do — or better."

"You're something. Jean dear, you are something."

She knew the signs of anger. She had seen them often enough in the past, and she said quickly, "I don't want this to degenerate into one of our quarrels, Dan. We're having a business meeting, and I am doing my best to keep it on that level. I have tried with all my heart to be fair and not to offend you."

"I guess you have," he replied slowly. He drew a deep breath and nodded. "All right, Jean, I'll do my best not to be angry, and I'll accept this discussion on your terms. Mark Levy is my friend and my partner. We've been together for twenty years. What am I supposed to tell him?"

"Isn't that a question for you to decide, Dan? If you manage the company, you can employ him or not, just as you see fit."

"At seventy-five dollars a week as a bookkeeper?"

"If you wish. Or at whatever wage you could justify."

"To you?"

"To the board."

"And if I should desire to piss," he said quietly, "do I justify that to the board."

She tightened her lips and sat in silence. The waiter returned and took away the dishes.

"I'm sorry I said that," Dan told her. "I had no call to say that. You're doing the best you can."

"Very well. Now can we continue this in a civilized manner?"

"Yes."

"I made a proposal. You haven't given me your answer."

"You know, Jean," he said thoughtfully, "for weeks now I've been trying to figure out why I played this game. At first, it seems to me, I only wanted you, and I would have burned down the whole goddamn city to have you. Or maybe not. Then I wanted Nob Hill. Or maybe not. Maybe I was empty inside, and I had to fill myself up with something. I never really worked out for myself what it means in this country to be Jewish or Italian or Irish or Chinese or Negro or Mexican, so there's no way I can try to tell you. The only way I can explain it is to say that I did what I had to do because of the way I was. I didn't give a damn about the money. I never cared about money. Right from the beginning, we paid the highest wages in the line, whatever the line was. We're the one big company in this city that never had a strike on our hands. And it wasn't the power either. Oh, I enjoyed the power, but that wasn't it — "

She interrupted. "We're off the subject, Dan."

"Not really," he said. "Not really, Jean — because this is the way I have to answer. Anyway, it's time we had a good talk. We haven't had one in years."

She sighed. "Go on."

"The answer to my question, Jean, was the game itself. It was a kid's game. Either you get a chance to be a kid when you are a kid, or you don't grow up. I was never a kid. My heart bled for my father. God, how I loved him and hated him! He had a rupture. I never told you that. When I was eight years old, I was out in the boat, helping him, my damned hands bloody from the net. Don't let anyone ever tell you that commercial fishing is a sport or a joy. And he'd never take the money and have that goddamn rupture fixed. Every penny had to be saved for a boat of his own, so that his son could amount to something, and my mother be damned. Crap! Why didn't he let me go to school if he wanted me to amount to something? Oh, Christ, I don't want to pile this onto you. I'm only trying to explain. After he died, I said to myself, The hell with his way! It's a game, and you play the game to win, not to sweat your guts out. That's the whole answer. The fun was in the game. I was a kid, I remained a kid. You were part of the game and Nob Hill was part of the game, and the people I played against were the high and mighty, the Whittiers and the Clancys and the Sommers and the Seldons and the Brockers and the Callans. I played in their court and their rules, a wop kid from the wharf and a little Jew who was his partner. O.K. The game's over. Somewhere along the road, I grew up. Maybe not entirely, but sort of. Jean, I swear to God that I appreciate what you tried to do today, but I don't want to manage any goddamn company. You'd just do yourself and this beautiful bank of yours — you'd do them in. I'm a lousy manager. I survived this far because I had Mark Levy and a Chinese by the name of Feng Wo running things and holding them together. No, I don't want it, but thank you."

"And that's your last word?" she asked evenly.

"I think so."

"I won't contest the divorce. You know that."

"I know. Thanks."

"I'll set up a meeting with Thorndyke. Is Sam Goldberg still your lawyer?"

"Yes, but I don't want any meeting with the lawyers."

"Dan, we have to. You know that. There's community property in this state."

"If you mean the house on Russian Hill or anything of yours, I don't want it. I don't want the house or anything that's in it. Just have Thorndyke draw up a release and I'll sign it."

"Why? Do you have so much money that you can afford to throw it away?"

"I have enough."

"Where? You have eight hundred dollars in your personal account at this bank."

"I told you I have enough, Jean."

"You can't do things this way. We have two children. There are problems to be worked out."

"Only if I make the problems, Jean."

"What about visitation rights?"

"If the kids should ever want to see me, I don't think you'd stand in my way. Would you?"

"No, I wouldn't."

"Then let it go at that, Jean." He rose. "It was a good lunch — as you promised. Thank you."

Then she rose and walked with him to the door. There, he paused, looked at her for a long moment, and then bent and kissed her on the lips.

"Not for me, Danny," she said gently, "but you are a hell of a guy."

"Sometimes. Only don't count on it."

"I don't, Danny. Anymore."

Barbara Lavette came down from Boston to Princeton for the football weekend of the Yale-Princeton game. Her brother, Tom, who was a freshman at Princeton, had reserved a room for her at the Princeton Inn and arranged a weekend date with an upperclassman named Robert Toad, who was a member of Ivy, possibly the most prestigious of the eating clubs. Tom had already set his cap for Ivy, and none of this hurt his cause. Dinner that evening at the club had already been arranged, the foursome to consist of Toad, Barbara, Tom, and his own date, Peggy Dutton, a friend of Barbara's and a first-year student at Wellesley. The arrangements had been drawn-out and complex, and at one point had almost fallen through; however, in the end it had all worked out. The two girls would chaperone each other and share a room, and since the Duttons were distantly related to the Asquiths — Tom's grandmother had been an Asquith from Boston — Peggy's family was finally satisfied. Tom had assured Robert Toad that his sister was a stunning girl and that the upperclassman would not by any means be buying a pig-in-a-poke, but even Tom was amazed by the sight of his sister after not seeing her for three months.

Not yet seventeen, Barbara Lavette was almost as tall as her mother. Her bobbed hair was the same honey color, her wide gray eyes cool and knowledgeable, her face firming out in the same strong bone structure. Peggy Dutton, a year older, small, plump, pretty, appeared drab by comparison. Both girls were excited, not only by the fact of their first football weekend but by the whole look and appearance of the town of Princeton. "It's fantastic," Barbara exclaimed. "What a wonderful old place!"

Tom escorted them and their luggage to the inn, explaining that Robert Toad would have been there too, but he was tied up with the glee club. "You'll like 'The Toad,' " Tom told Barbara. "Of course, I don't call him that to his face. But that's what his buddies call him."

"What a hideous name!"

"Not at all. He went to Lawrenceville, and names like that are a mark of distinction there. I wish I had gone there instead of a hole like Groton. He's tall and quite good looking."

"Taller than I am, I should hope."

"Quite. Absolutely."

"Save me from tall men," Peggy Dutton said. "Tom's just the right size."

In their room at the inn, Tom took a flask out of his pocket, with the air of a magician conjuring a rabbit out of a hat. "The good provider. It's bitter cold out and the stands will be even colder."

"I don't want it on my breath," Barbara said.

"Vodka. No smell. Anyway, The Toad won't mind. There are no teetotalers in Ivy."

They all drank a toast to a Princeton victory. "Should we drink to mother's divorce?" Tom asked his sister. "It came through yesterday. Did you know?"

Barbara glanced at Peggy and then at her brother.

"I'm one of the family, almost," Peggy said. "Tom has filled me in. No secrets. You know, I am a sort of fifth cousin of yours — or something of the sort."

"A delicious kissing cousin. Mother called me yesterday, Barby. Very civilized."

"Where did he go?" Barbara asked uncertainly.

"Couldn't care less."

"Don't talk like that!" Barbara snapped at him.

"What's eating you? He's my father, too, and he's been a perfect sonofabitch."

"Children, children," Peggy said. "I will not be party to a family quarrel. These days everyone gets divorced, and if it's done in a proper, civilized manner, all's for the best."

Barbara stood there, looking from her brother to Peggy Dutton, and then suddenly her face wrinkled and the tears began to flow.

"Barby, darling," Peggy cried, embracing her. "What have I said? Please forgive me."

By game time, Barbara was herself again, and she couldn't explain her fit of tears, even to herself. Robert Toad was tall, good-looking, and charming. "Old man," he whispered to Tom, "you've given me my first blind date that wasn't a dud. She's a perfect doll." He had brought with him to the game a sixteen-ounce flask of what he claimed was the "very best, valid imported Scotch," not to be even compared with the rotgut young Tom carried. Barbara disliked the taste of liquor, and she coughed and choked as Toad tipped the flask to her lips. "Girl, you need practice. Don't fight it. Let it go down soft and easy." They were covered by a big steamer rug, and already Toad's hands were tentatively testing Barbara's thighs. He slid his arm around to touch her breast. Oh, my God, she said to herself, what do I do now? I just open my mouth, and there go Tom's chances for Ivy, and from the way he talks, he wants Ivy more than he wants to go to bed with Peggy. It was not that she objected to petting, but she had decided long ago that she would make the choice, and this tall, skinny, glib young idiot was definitely not her choice. She leaned over to him and whispered into his ear, "Please do be careful because I have herpes on my breasts."

"Herpes?" he whispered back. "What the devil is herpes?"

"It's a sort of venereal disease. It's not as bad as syphilis, but it's terribly catching, and I'd never forgive myself."

"You two don't know each other long enough to be whispering," Peggy Dutton said cheerfully. "Come, now, speak up."

Toad's right hand slid away from Barbara's breast and the left hand removed itself from her thigh. Both of Toad's hands appeared above the steamer rug as he edged away from Barbara, and for the rest of the day he was coldly and formally polite. At the dance, after the dinner at Ivy, he did not choose her as a partner even once, watching sullenly as Barbara picked and chose from the cluster of men around her. He spent the evening getting drunk, and said to Tom, when Tom asked him whether he would join him to walk the girls back to the inn, "The pleasure is yours, you little creep. And thanks for nothing."

It was a beautiful, crisp fall evening. In the distance, in the direction of Blair Arch, a cluster of boys were singing, "Going Back to Nassau Hall." The moon was in the sky, and the wind rustled in the dry leaves that still clung to the maples on Prospect Avenue. "It's dreamy, totally dreamy," Peggy sighed.

"Whatever happened with you and The Toad?" Tom asked his sister.

"I can't imagine. But I had a perfectly wonderful time."

"You know, he didn't even dance with you."

"I noticed that."

"Didn't he make a pass at you? I was worried about that, but I figured you can take care of yourself. Not that he's such an animal, but they have a reputation at Ivy."

"Not even a pass."

"Well, there you are," Tom said. "You never know."

At the inn, Barbara told them to go up to the room while she made a telephone call in the booth. "Can you promise us a half-hour of privacy?" Tom asked, grinning foolishly.

"Ignore the little beast," Peggy said unconvincingly.

"Yes, I promise you a half-hour of privacy."

They went upstairs, and Barbara went into the phone booth and called her home in San Francisco, reversing the charges. Jean's voice, thick with sleep and confusion, said yes, of course she would accept a call from Barbara Lavette.

"Darling, what happened? Are you all right? It's eleven o'clock here."

"Oh, I didn't know. Mother, forgive me — I never thought about the time."

"Are you all right? You're not hurt or ill?"

"I'm all right. I guess. I don't know."

"Well, why are you calling?"

"Because you divorced daddy."

"Darling, you knew it was coming."

"Why?"

"Darling, we can't talk about this over the phone. You'll be home for Christmas soon, and we'll discuss it then. Believe me, it's best for all of us. Are you crying?"

"Yes," Barbara replied.

"But why? You were always so angry and provoked at him. You never understood why I remained with him."

"I know."

"Barbara, darling," Jean said, "I'm only half awake. I don't know what to say to you."

"Will we ever see him again?" she asked plaintively.

"Yes, of course you will."

"You're angry at me."

"No, darling. No, I'm not."

"All right."

"Where are you?"

"I'm at the inn at Princeton. Peggy Dutton and I came down for the football weekend. But I'm not going to stay. I don't want to stay. I'll go back to Boston tomorrow."

"Then I'll call you tomorrow night in Boston."

"If you want to."

"Yes, I will. Please, baby, don't cry about this. It's just something that had to be."

"Where's daddy?"

"At the Fairmont, I suppose. Where he's been for most of the past year."

"All right. Good night."

Dan drove down to San Mateo to sell his boat. It had been out of the water for the past eight years and it needed work, and it was a time when people were not rushing to buy boats. Fred Marsha, who ran the marina, offered Dan a hundred and fifty dollars, which he accepted. He then drove to the Cassala's home, where he was expected for dinner. Maria Cassala embraced him and then burst into tears. They left her sitting in the kitchen weeping. In the living room, Dan held Ralph on his lap, while Joanna watched adoringly.

"Life goes on," Stephan said. "Mama cries and goes to

church. She's set a record in candles. She weeps for pop, and she weeps for your divorce and your immortal soul."

"How can you talk like that?" Joanna said. "It's her grief."

"Can you keep the house?" Dan wanted to know.

"There was no mortgage. Pop had insurance. I'm lucky. I got a job at Wells Fargo. We get along, Dan."

"Well, you got the kid and you got a good wife. As for my immortal soul, well, I dropped it on the way up Nob Hill."

"I'm sorry, Danny. I hate to hear you talk like that."

Later that evening, Stephan walked out with Dan to his car. "Danny," he said, "don't let this be the last time. Come back. Please."

"What's that supposed to mean?"

"I don't know. It's just a gut feeling I've got — that we won't see each other again."

"We'll see each other."

"You know what I've been thinking about all day — after the earthquake, when you came into our kitchen and emptied the money from your pockets."

"That was a long, long time ago, Steve."

"I suppose so. Take it easy, Dan."

The next day, Dan sold his car. It was a 1929 Cadillac, but like the market for boats, the market for Cadillacs was thin and tight. The dealer who gave him seven hundred and fifty dollars said to him, "I'm giving you top dollar, Mr. Lavette, believe me. This car will sit in my lot for the next six months."

He checked out of the Fairmont. The bill was six hundred and seventy-two dollars. He paid cash, then loaded his suitcases into a taxicab and took them with him to the office. There he sat at his desk, staring at the bags, his mind strangely blank. He had the feeling of being oddly suspended in time.

Mark came in and looked at the suitcases. "Going somewhere?"

"I checked out of the Fairmont. Can you put me up for a few days?"

Mark nodded.

"Everything shipshape?"

Mark nodded again. "What about the pictures?" he asked, pointing to the walls. "Don't you want them?"

"No."

"They're yours."

"I suppose so. They look good where they are."

"I spent yesterday with Fred Blankfort, the new store manager. He'll be all right. Polly Anderson's staying on, and she knows as much about where things are as I do. Buckley's taken over the airline operation. Sam Goldberg's been working with Thorndyke and his crew all month, and that's all under control."

"Who's paying Goldberg?"

"The company. Thorndyke agreed to that."

"And that about cleans it up?" Dan asked.

"Just about. Whittier's people are taking care of the New York end."

"I suppose they'll fire everyone?"

"There's nothing we can do about that."

"Then we might as well check out."

"Naked we came, naked we go," Mark said, smiling ruefully. "I'll just say goodby to Polly."

Polly Anderson clung to Mark, weeping copiously. "It's unjust," she whimpered, "it's so damn unjust. It's not right."

They walked out of the building, Dan carrying his two big suitcases. "Eleven business suits," he explained to Mark. "Two dozen shirts. Six pairs of shoes. At least thirty ties. God Almighty, I don't know why I'm dragging it with me."

"You'll use it."

"I doubt it."

On the ferry to Sausalito, Mark asked Dan what he had done with his car.

"Sold it. Seven hundred and fifty bucks."

"For that Cadillac? You're out of your mind."

"Nobody wants Cadillacs, old buddy. I didn't do so bad. I paid my hotel bill, and I don't owe a dime anywhere, and I still got a hundred and twenty dollars or so in my pocket."

"Wait a minute. What about the community property?"

"I signed a release. Jean gets it all."

Mark was silent for a while, and then he said slowly, "All right. I don't comment on that."

"That's good, because I don't intend to talk about it."

"How are you fixed? What have you got in the bank, in your personal account, if you don't mind me asking?"

"I don't mind."

"Well?"

"Nothing. I closed out my account."

"Are you telling me you're broke, Danny?"

"Hell, no. Like I told you before, I still got a hundred and twenty dollars in my pocket."

"You crazy bastard."

"You're getting real tough with me, old buddy."

"My God, Dan, it makes no sense, no sense at all. Well, thank God Sarah and I aren't broke. We've got some money put away and the house is free and clear. I've got enough for both of us not to starve."

"Mark," Dan said firmly, "we won't talk about this again. Don't offer me any money. You understand? We're not to talk about money again — not between us and not to Sarah."

"Why?"

"Because I say so."

"O.K., if that's the way you want it."

Sarah had prepared a roast of beef and potatoes and onions and carrots and spinach, sliced tomatoes, home-baked bread, and store cheese with apple pie. Dan sat in the old tiled kitchen, sleeves rolled up, eating hugely and with great relish, washing down the food with Jake's wine, loose and easy and relaxed, the way Sarah had not seen him in years. Mark, too, was less tense, more relaxed than he had been since his daughter's death. "My word," he said, "it was more complicated to wind this thing up than it ever was to put it together. I can't believe that it's over."

"I'll drink to that," Dan said.

"I don't understand," Sarah said. "In a world where men jump out of windows because they've been ruined, you two are celebrating."

"It makes a kind of sense," Mark said. "If only because it's finally over."

"And what about Jean?" Sarah asked.

"What about Jean? We're divorced."

"She did this to you."

"Well, not really," Mark said. "No one did it to us. It was something that happened, and once it started to happen, there was no way to stop it."

Dan slept late the following morning. Fatigue and tension had been building up in him, and he lay in bed until noon, luxuriating in the fact that he had nothing to do, nowhere to go, no obligations, no duties, no plans. Sarah was alone in the kitchen. She fixed bacon, three eggs, and fried potatoes, and Dan ate everything she put in front of him.

"Danny, you haven't eaten like that since you were a kid."

"No? I guess not. Where's Mark?"

"He went down to the marina. There's a bait and tackle shop there that he thought he might buy. It would give him something to do. I wish he'd just take it easy, but I suppose that's something you have to learn when you're young."

"He took it better than I thought he would."

"And you, Danny? No regrets?"

"Sure I have regrets, but not too many. It finished for me before it finished for Mark. Then I was just going through the motions. Funny thing is — I really don't care."

"And now?"

"I don't know. I really don't want to think about it."

"You mean you don't want to think about May Ling."

"Maybe. It's over two years since I spoke to her."

"You're a fool," Sarah said. "It's no use talking to a fool. You and Mark are like children."

"I suppose most men are. Maybe that's why we louse things up the way we do."

After eating, Dan walked down to the village and went into a work-clothes store. He bought a heavy pair of rubber-soled work shoes for four dollars, two pairs of blue denim trousers, and two blue denim work shirts. He paid ten dollars and fifty cents for the lot. He added a small canvas bag to his purchases, and then paid another dollar for four excellent Cuban cigars. It was the first time in twenty years that he had bought anything against the money in his pocket, knowing that what was there was all of it, and while it gave him a strange feeling, it also gave him a curious sense of exhilaration. Smoking a cigar, he walked back to Mark's house slowly and comfortably, a part of the little road he walked on and a part of the bright, sunlit afternoon. He was still short of his forty-first year, ten pounds overweight, but in good health, and he had come out clean. That was something he could not explain to Mark and Sarah. The community property thing — that peculiar California law which divided the personal property of a man and wife equally between them when they divorced

— was the trap. Jean would have gladly given him a hundred thousand dollars, perhaps more, to leave the house on Russian Hill and its contents untouched and in her possession; and then it would begin again; and if he had learned one single thing out of his life, it was to leave the trap untouched. There was no other road to freedom, no other gateway out of the strange, incomprehensible insanity that had been his life for the past twenty years; and he knew that without being able to delineate to himself the fact or the content of the insanity. The ships, the airplanes, the property, the charge accounts, the world where one bought what one desired, food, women, clothes, transportation, and never asked the price or gave a second thought to the price — that world was as insubstantial as a dream. It was over.

When he came down the next morning, he wore the work shoes and the denim pants and shirt. Mark and Sarah looked at him curiously.

"I'll be leaving after breakfast," he told them.

"No!" Sarah cried. "Not now. Not so quick, Danny."

"Where are you going?" Mark asked.

Dan shrugged. "I still have to work that out."

"Will you be back, Danny?"

"Sometime, sure."

When he was ready to leave, carrying the small canvas bag containing the extra pants and shirt, some socks, and underwear, and wearing an old leather jacket, Sarah clung to him, sobbing. Then Mark drove him to the ferry and then to the bus station. "I left the two suitcases in the guest room," he said to Mark. "Put them away, would you, old sport?"

"I can't talk to you. You're a goddamn mule. Never mind about me. But if you don't stay in touch, you'll break Sarah's heart."

"I'll stay in touch."

At the bus station, people turned to watch at the sight of a bald little man with a potbelly hugging a very large man in work clothes. Then the bald little man hurried away, not trusting himself to speak.

At the ticket window, Dan bought a one-way ticket to Los Angeles.

Six months later, Dan Lavette walked out of the Los Angeles city jail, having served ninety days for resisting arrest. He owned a pair of shoes, a pair of worn denim pants, and a denim shirt, all of which he wore, and all of which constituted his total worldly possessions. He weighed nine pounds less than when he had entered the jail. Otherwise, he felt reasonably good, consoling himself with the fact that this was the first time in his forty-one years that he had been sent to prison. The ninety days had been interesting and instructive and now and then deadly boring. There were few books in the jail, but he had gotten hold of a copy of *War and Peace,* which May Ling had often pressed him to read, and he had finished it. He had also read *The Return of The Native* and *An American Tragedy.* He had survived the attempt of a drug-crazed inmate to kill him, escaping with a slight knife cut between two ribs, and he had eaten some two hundred and seventy of the worst meals he had ever tasted, and he had learned the insanity and futility of a system of punishment unchanged since the dawn of what man euphemistically called civilization. He had also spent countless hours lying on a bedbug-ridden bunk, trying to make some sense and reason and validity out of his life, thinking of many things, thinking of his children from the wombs of two women and thinking of the women.

He was only half alive without the women. Within his enormous bulk, there was an almost maudlin gentleness, an aching, pleading need to be loved, to be valued, to be told by word and deed and gesture that he was human, that he was something more than a senseless, ignorant brute; and all of his efforts to prove that to himself by playing the game of the cultured and the mighty were of no avail. When he had purchased the bus ticket to Los Angeles, a part of him was returning to May Ling; and this part of himself he understood better than the part of himself that was afraid to return. Introspection was difficult for him; he compensated for it by doing things; and in prison for the first time in his life he had day after day with nothing to do.

When he came to Los Angeles, he had not gone to May Ling. He argued with himself that he needed a job. He found a room for three dollars a week at the Charlton Hotel in downtown Los Angeles, a wretched little room with a narrow bed, a chest of drawers, a chair, and an overhead, unmasked string light. He lay sleeplessly on the bed and thought about May Ling and told himself that he would find a job first. Main Street was the pit in the sorrowful belly of downtown Los Angeles, a succession of pool halls, speakeasies, vermin-ridden lunch counters, Chinese restaurants, and unabashed whorehouses; and the sorrow was the torment of several thousand men looking for jobs where there were no jobs. At a sign reading WANTED TO CLEAN TOILETS, there were two hundred men waiting. He got two days of work at a lot, scraping the rust from farm machinery that was being reconstituted. He was paid three dollars a day, and no one on the job complained about the pay.

On Signal Hill, oil flowed, as it did from a thousand other derricks spotted around the sprawling, shapeless city, from downtown to Wilshire Boulevard to Venice and Torrance. He found three weeks of work on Signal Hill, where he was chosen out of two hundred men for his bulk and his strength; and for three good weeks he worked in the sun, wrestling with pipe and drill-casing and chains, feeling his muscles harden and his body respond to physical effort. He drew twenty-five dollars a week, and his mind was filled with thoughts of May Ling, with fears and hopes and anticipations — and also with the thought that now she could be married or could hate him, which would certainly have been just and proper — and then he and forty other men were laid off, and there were no more jobs after that. He tried everything. When an advertisement appeared in the Los Angeles *Times,* asking for men over six feet, three inches in height to come to the film studio in Culver City, he made his way there, even though he was an inch short of the requirement. But he was only one among a thousand tall men, and after three hours of waiting, the gates of Metro were closed.

Walking on Third Street one night, he took out the roll of sixteen dollar bills that remained to him and was jumped from behind by two men who were more desperate than he was. He went down, the money flying from his hand, and then when they leaped to grab the money, he flung himself on the two of them, fighting mindlessly and crazily for the small fortune that sixteen dollars represented. A third man joined in, and he fought the three of them; and when the cops came, he was so lost in the violence he had committed himself to that he fought them as well. Beaten, one eye closed, his shirt stained with dry blood, he told his story to the judge and was told in turn that he was fortunate to receive no more than ninety days.

And now it was over, and he walked out of the jail with the clothes on his back and no more.

The distance from downtown Los Angeles to San Pedro is about twenty-seven miles. Dan set out on foot. He had made a simple equation to himself; the fishing boats sailed out of San Pedro, and where boats brought in fish, no one starved. In any case, it was his trade, and if twenty years had gone by since he had stood on the deck of a fishing boat, he had not forgotten. After two hours under the burning Southern California sun, he realized that walking in Los Angeles was quite different from walking in San Francisco. He stopped at a gas station, where he drank from a hose and stood in the shade until the owner told him to move on or he'd call the cops. He started to walk again, and an oil truck slowed and gave him a lift as far as Sepulveda Boulevard. He then walked the remaining seven miles. It was early evening now, and the heat of the sun had exchanged itself for the chill of the night wind off the sea. Attracted by the twinkle of campfires, he wandered onto a weed-grown lot just off Gaffey Street. There at least a hundred jobless, homeless men sat around fires built of driftwood and odds and ends of boards. He joined one of the groups and was made welcome by a nod here and there, no more than that. They were silent men, bent and dispirited. A two-gallon tin of fish and water sat in the coals. When they pulled it out of the fire, they scooped into it with old cans. Dan had not eaten since morning, but he had accepted their warmth uninvited and he had no intention of asking for food. Anyway, he still hated fish. But when an old man sitting next to him lifted a half-cooked piece of mackerel out of the sardine can he was using as a plate and offered it to Dan, he accepted the offer, and realized that he had forgotten that he hated fish — or perhaps to a man half starved, anything would taste good.

One by one, the men around the fire stretched out to sleep. Dan made his own bed on the ground. His thin shirt offered poor protection from the cold, and again and again he awakened shivering. Finally, morning came, and with it the warmth of the sun.

The next four days were like a nightmare; they were the first time Dan Lavette ever lost all control of his life as he lived it. Never before in his adult life did he have the feeling that he was without control. Even in jail, when the man ran at him with a knife, he had remained calm and deflected the blade. Control was the essence of himself as he saw himself, the essence of his masculinity, of his right to have money or not have money, as he saw fit, but always as he saw fit. He might suspend control, but he never had to surrender it before.

Now the old man who had sat next to him at the fire said to him, "It takes twenty-four hours without food to make a bum, or four days without shaving." In four days without shaving, two of them without food, he admitted the fact. He was a bum. They were all bums. San Pedro teemed with bums, because when you had no money and no job and no place to lay your head, you were a bum, and it was just as plain and simple as that. The population of San Pedro was thirty-seven thousand, and for every fifteen of the population, there was a beached seaman, an unemployed steelworker or welder or carpenter out of the dead shipyards, an unemployed stevedore, an unemployed clerk, an unemployed fisherman — dead souls who sat silently on the docks, or shuffled along the streets, or sprawled in empty lots and on the beaches — and who gave a damn that one of them was Dan Lavette? Who gave a damn for human flesh without money?

He sat on a box on Fisherman's Wharf, and stared at the fishing boats, and talked to himself without listening, which was something he had learned to do after two days without eating. Out on the ocean in the distance, with only the top of its masts showing, a ship lay, at least fifteen miles by his calculation, just lying there outside the limit, probably a mother ship for the rumrunners, loaded to the hatches with whiskey; and he tried to remember how long it was since he had tasted whiskey, or a fresh egg, or a piece of decent steak. He remembered May Ling's chiding him for the fat on his waistline. It was gone now. He was fasting, not an ounce of fat on him. Another day or two, and he would begin to stagger. Bums staggered, but not from liquor. It was plain, simple starvation. The trouble was, he told himself, that he had lost his ambition — otherwise he would find that weed-grown lot again, where they cooked fish and fish heads in tin oil cans. Well, he'd sit a while, and then he'd work out that ambition thing. He rubbed the thick stubble of beard on his cheeks, wondering idly how he looked.

And then he heard his name called. A man had come off one of the fishing boats, walked past him, turned, stared, taken a few steps back, and then said tentatively, "Dan Lavette?"

Dan looked blankly at a heavyset man in his middle fifties, burned brown by the sun.

"You're Dan Lavette."

Dan rose to face him and nodded.

"I'll be damned. Don't you remember me? Pete Lomas. I ran your fleet up on the wharf in San Francisco."

"Pete? Yes, sure. Glad to see you."

Lomas was examining him, measuring him with his eyes. "Bad breaks, Dan? Last I heard, you were on top of the world."

"I climbed down."

"Well, a lot of them did. Come on, let me buy you a drink. We'll talk about old times."

Dan shook his head. "No — no, I'd better not."

"Are you hungry? When did you eat last?"

"Hell, no, I'm not hungry."

"Come on. I'm starved. Come on and sit down with me, Dan. Come on."

"No — "

"Ah, cut out the bullshit. Come on. We go back a long way." He took Dan's arm. "Come along, Dan."

"O.K.," Dan said. "I'm lying. I'm broke, I'm hungry. I can't sponge off you, Pete. You find a bum you haven't seen for twenty years, you got no obligations."

"That's a lousy thing to say. Come on."

They walked over to a lunch wagon on Harbor Road, and Lomas ordered ham and eggs and fried potatoes and coffee for both of them. The waitress put down a basket of bread, and Dan couldn't hold back. He began to eat the bread. Lomas watched him. The ham and eggs came. Dan looked up and apologized. "Christ, I'm eating like a pig."

"How long?" Lomas asked softly.

"Two days without anything. They had a soup kitchen going the day before that. Then it closed down."

Lomas nodded. "The sisters from Saint Mary's. They keep it going until they run out of money. They'll start up again soon. They come to me for fish. Go on, eat. You want more?"

"No, this is enough. What do you fish, Pete?"

"Mackerel. I got my own boat. The wife got asthma about ten years ago, and the doctor said she wanted a dry climate. So we came down here and bought a bungalow in Downey. Not that it does her much good, but it's better than up north, I suppose."

"Mackerel? How do you take it?"

"Round haul nets, mostly purse seines. Night fishing, we set out drift nets. A lot depends on the season. We pick up blue mackerel and jack mackerel. There's still a good market, because it's so much cheaper than meat. We bring in two tons a day and sometimes better than that at three to four cents a pound. I got two men in my crew and we work our asses off. I could use a third."

"I'm not looking for charity," Dan said.

"Shit. Your hands will be bleeding and your back broken the first day out, so don't give me no crap about charity. I got respect for you, Dan, so I'm not feeding you any bullshit. I pay eight dollars a day when we fish. That's what I pay my other hands, and that's what I pay you. We go out for ten hours, sometimes more. The pay's the same, ten hours, twelve hours, so I'm not giving you a damn thing I don't sweat out of your ass. Jesus, Dan, you're not the first guy's been on his uppers. If you want a job, I got a job for you. Yes or no?"

"I'll take it," Dan said. "Hell, I'm not a bad fisherman."

"You can say that again."

Mark Levy mentioned the pains in his chest to Sarah, and she was so upset and so insistent that he see a doctor that he refrained from mentioning them again. His stomach had been giving him trouble, and he told himself that it was gas and no more. His plans for buying the bait and tackle shop had washed away. He couldn't see himself standing behind a counter again. For all that he had constantly cautioned Dan through the years, he had played the game with him. It was a wonderful game while it lasted, with the big man storming in and out of the office, an overgrown, easygoing kid building an empire. Well, not precisely an empire; more like an enormous version of the Erector set he once bought for his grandchildren. Yet they had done it, and their ships sailed the seas and their planes flew through the skies when few enough people ever dreamed that ordinary people would travel across the skies as passengers in airplanes.

They had built the biggest store west of the Continental Divide and they had built the biggest hotel in the Hawaiian Islands, and they had done it themselves.

And now Dan had gone, and there had not been a word from him since he had left. There was no one he could talk to about Dan, not even Sarah, nor could he put into words what he felt about him. They had been like brothers, but not even brothers had that easy, noninterfering closeness that had marked their relationship. Through the years he had sat in the office while Dan roamed the country and the world, but vicariously he had reached out and touched and felt everything Dan had touched and felt. Now he did nothing because nothing interested him particularly. He lived with memories. He would sit in the garden with his eyes closed, trying to recall his first meeting with Dan. Probably Dan was no more than six years old the first time his father, big Joe Lavette, had brought him into the chandler shop. Mark's father was still alive then, and Mark remembered how they would talk about the old days when the railroads were being built and there was still gold to be dug out of the earth.

Or else, Mark would wander around the house, room to room, as if he were searching for something he had lost. Sarah watched him in silence, her heart going out to him, unable to help him, unable to bridge the gap that had opened so long ago.

She was not with him when he had the heart attack. She was in the house. He was outside, sitting in the garden, and she found him there, dead from what the doctor described afterward as a massive coronary. Sarah held herself together. She telephoned the doctor, and then she telephoned Jake at Higate. An hour later, Jake and Clair arrived at the house, and it was not until then that Sarah went into the kitchen and sat down and wept.

A few hours later, having pulled herself together, Sarah said to Jake, "I want you to find Danny. I want him to know about this. I don't want Papa buried without Dan here, and I don't want anyone else to talk about him at the funeral."

But there was no trace to Dan, no lead, no direction. As far as the Levys were concerned, he had disappeared from the face of the earth. No one of them had any idea where he had gone or in what direction or how far. Sarah told Jake to try to reach May Ling, who was living somewhere in Los Angeles, but no one of them knew that she had taken the name of Lavette, and there was no Feng Wo listed by the telephone company in Los Angeles.

Six weeks after Dan went to work for Pete Lomas, working six days a week, with the mackerel running heavy and kissing the nets, as they put it, Lomas had to put his boat into dry dock and have the bottom scraped. Dan had three days off. The six weeks had changed him. Lean already after the time in prison, his muscles had hardened and his hands had toughened. He was burned brown by the sun, and he felt better than he had in years.

This day, the day the boat went into dry dock, he shaved carefully, put on a pair of cotton twill trousers that he had bought the same morning and a white shirt and a sweater, and took the interurban to Los Angeles. He divested himself of expectations and tried to will himself to anticipate nothing; but it was not easy. He was unable to control his excitement, yet in all truth he had no notion of what awaited him. It was more than three years since he had seen May Ling. The boy, his son, would be fourteen years old. How do you approach a boy of fourteen and tell him that you are his father? "I am your father who let you down and threw you away." How is it done? What does the boy say? What does he feel?

He located his fear among all the other emotions that beset him. The fear was paramount — fear that May Ling had expunged him from her life. And why not? And then there were other alternatives of fear. May Ling could be dead. As much as he rejected the thought, it kept reoccurring. She could be married to someone else. Her love could have turned into hatred. He had seen love turn into hatred.

No use to think, he told himself. It was almost two years since he had left the house on Russian Hill, and for two years fear and doubt and his own peculiar need for self-flagellation had kept him away.

He left the interurban car at Vermont Avenue and walked to the campus. It was hot now, and he pulled off his sweater and carried it over his arm. At the campus, he experienced a momentary surge of terror, a feeling that his whole world was collapsing around him. The buildings were boarded up. The grounds had been uncared for, the plants dry and yellow and wasted —

as if the University of California in Los Angeles had been flung on the dust heap of the Depression. But then common sense told him that universities do not vanish so easily, and he prowled around until he found a caretaker, who informed him that the entire university had moved to its new campus in the town of Westwood.

A red interurban car, bouncing and jolting, carried him to Westwood, and now a new fear assailed him. Why was he so certain that she remained in the same job? What if this were a dead end? What if nothing but dead ends awaited him?

He walked slowly and uncertainly across the campus, asking directions to the library. The place was bigger than the old campus, new parts of it still in construction, winding pathways and red brick buildings, boys and girls striding past him as if he did not exist. He reached the library and stood in front of it, and now that he was here, his courage failed him, and for perhaps ten minutes he stood without moving. It was almost four o'clock now. There was a pile of lumber about the height of a bench on the edge of the walk, and he went to it and sat there, unable to bring himself to enter the library building.

The minutes passed. He had a dollar Ingersol watch, and, sitting there, he was so high-strung, so desperate, that he could hear it ticking away in his watch pocket. He looked again, and it was four-fifteen. He rose to go to the library and then dropped back onto the pile of lumber. Students drifted by and in and out of the library, and still he waited.

At four-thirty, May Ling came out of the building. She wore a pleated gray skirt that fell to below her knees, a white blouse, and a black sweater. Her long hair had been bobbed. There was a distance of about twenty yards between where he sat and the front of the library, and with the distance, she appeared almost girllike, the same slender, ivory-skinned girl he had met in the apartment in San Francisco in another life and in another time.

She stood there a moment, breathing the fresh air, and he had a sudden sense of panic. She would turn and walk away, never seeing him, and he would remain frozen where he was. But then she looked at him. She remained frozen for a long moment, and finally she walked over to where he was. He stood up, facing her, and she paused about four feet from him, studying him, the heavy work shoes, the twill trousers, the white shirt with the sleeves rolled up, the strong, muscular brown arms and the lean face. She had never seen his face so lean, the skin drawn tight over the ridges of bone. He was not the same man, and yet he was. She came closer and reached out and touched his cheek, in a gesture so typical that he felt tears welling into his eyes. He was unable to speak. He just stood there, staring at her, noticing now that age had not left her untouched, the gray streaks in her hair, the tiny wrinkles around her eyes. The dark eyes met his, directly, searchingly; and suddenly he felt weak and totally drained. He moved back and sat down on the stack of boards, covering his face with his hands, trying to control the dry sobs that wracked his body. He had not been able to weep since he was a child.

May Ling sat down next to him. For almost ten minutes, the two of them sat there in silence, neither speaking. Then May Ling said, "I thought you were dead." Her voice was a whisper. "It was like being dead myself. I read about what had happened to the company, and I waited, and then I telephoned Stephan Cassala at San Mateo, and he told me that Mark had died and you disappeared — "

"Mark died?" he asked woefully. "Oh, my God! When?"

"Four months ago, I guess. He had a heart attack."

"I didn't know."

"Where were you, Danny?"

"In jail."

"Oh, no. No."

"I'm all right now. I was there only three months. But Mark — oh, Christ, this lousy, rotten world!"

"It's a good, beautiful world, Danny."

"We're here and Mark's dead. He wasn't old. He was fifty-one."

"We're here, Danny. I wept enough for you."

He was crying openly at last. Students passing by turned to look at the big, brown-faced man who sat weeping next to a small Chinese woman who clutched his hand so tightly.

"Don't, Danny, please."

He pulled out a handkerchief and wiped his eyes. "Poor Sarah," he said. "Is she all right?"

"I think so. I don't know."

Then he remembered and said to her, "God, you're not married, are you?"

"Who would marry me, Danny?"

He was grinning and weeping at once, rubbing his eyes. "I got a job," he said. "I'm a fisherman again." He shook his head and bent to hide the tears that started again. "I don't know why I'm doing this. God Almighty, I can't sit here crying."

"Come home with me, Danny."

She took his arm, and he rose and walked with her. Even the pain of knowing that Mark was dead could not lessen his sense of being, of existing, the knowledge that this strange, small Chinese woman whose name was May Ling and who was in some way a part of himself was here beside him.

When the University of California in Los Angeles moved to its new campus in Westwood Village, Westwood was still a place of open fields of barley and corn, orange groves, and rolling hills. But hard on the move came the real-estate developers, bloodhounds on the first scent, and soon small tracts of houses began to spring up around the campus. May Ling had bought one of these houses. It was a pretty, two-story frame house, with a living room, dining room, and library on the first floor and four bedrooms on the floor above. The price was sixteen thousand dollars, with an eleven-thousand-dollar mortgage and a cash payment of only five thousand dollars. There was a garden plot in the rear, with a big live oak. Altogether, it was a pleasant, comfortable house, and within easy walking distance of the campus. Dan walked there with May Ling, slowly, hand in hand.

Bit by bit, he told her what had happened, broadly, not in detail. The details would come later. She knew him well enough not to ask why he had waited. She understood his fears — in particular the deep fear of facing his son.

"We'll work it out," she told him. They were in sight of the house now.

"Does he remember me?"

"Of course he remembers you. It's only five years."

"Or a hundred years. What does he feel about me?"

"He's fourteen, Danny. He doesn't know himself what he feels. But he's a good boy. He's earnest and thoughtful."

"What about your father?"

"Danny, Danny, he worships the ground you walk on. Don't you know that?"

"I've never been so scared in my life."

They went into the house. Dan stood awkwardly in the living room, looking at bright chintz, white curtains, and on a table in a corner a picture of himself and May Ling, taken in Hawaii.

"Daddy," May Ling called out, "there's an old friend here I want you to meet. Mama, you too."

Feng Wo came out of the library, balder, thinner, somewhat stooped, his glasses perched on the end of his nose, peering over his glasses at Dan. He stared, then recovered himself, and smiled. "Mr. Lavette," he said, bowing slightly, "what a pleasure! What an unexpected pleasure! I welcome you to our poor home."

So-Toy appeared from the kitchen, wiping her hands on her apron. She stopped short when she saw Dan and just stared. Her husband said something to her in Chinese, and she nodded. Then she began to cry and ran back into the kitchen.

"She will be all right," Feng Wo said.

"Where's Joe?" May Ling asked.

"In his room, I think."

May Ling took Dan's hand and led him upstairs. The door to the boy's room was closed. May Ling knocked.

"Come on in."

May Ling opened the door. The boy was sprawled on his bed, reading. Dan would hardly have recognized him, a big, long-limbed boy who turned to look at them inquiringly. Then he rose and stood facing Dan, tall, almost as tall as Dan, with oversized hands and feet. He just stood there, staring.

Dan shook his head and clenched his fists.

"I don't know what to say," the boy muttered.

"Neither do I," Dan whispered.

"I missed you," the boy said haltingly. "Mama thought you were dead."

"I missed you."

The boy nodded.

"You've grown."

The boy nodded again.

"I don't know what you feel about me," Dan said, speaking with great difficulty. "It's no use saying I'm sorry, but I am. I'm sorry. I should have been with you."

The boy sat down on the bed, staring at the floor. May Ling took Dan's arm and motioned to the door. Dan followed her out of the room, and she closed the door behind her.

"He hates me," Dan said.

"Oh, Danny, he has a scrapbook filled with pictures of you out of magazines and newspapers. He doesn't hate you. Give it time."

May Ling's mother retreated into the kitchen and cooked. When they sat down at the dinner table, the five of them, May Ling refused to participate in the silence. The silence was not for her, and her heart was singing its own song; and if the tall, lean, sunburned man who sat next to her was a stranger to everyone else, he was no stranger to her. There was food enough for a dozen hungry people. She launched into the story of their first encounter, of how she had described each dish explicitly; and the memory set her to giggling. Her son looked at her uncomprehendingly. He had never seen his mother quite like this. Feng Wo watched and listened in silence, a shadow of fear and worry in his eyes. It went through his mind that only a reckless person surrenders to happiness. His daughter was not a reckless person, and no one had yet asked whether Daniel Lavette would go away again. And where had he been?

Dan began to talk. He was a fisherman, he told them. He fished for mackerel out of San Pedro — and then he told how the boats went out and how they rigged the nets and took in the fish, and how they fought the sea when the sea fought them, and how it was to battle through the storm and cold waves. He had never talked about these things before. He had spent his life forgetting. Now he talked with a compulsive necessity, trying somehow to explain that he was content. But it was something he was unable to explain. Feng Wo said to himself that he required no explanations; where a man's life is an obligation to a deed, a word, an action that has not been taken before, the obligation is not conditional. So-Toy, a tiny, wizened Chinese lady, listened without wholly comprehending, and her grandson, Joseph Lavette, let himself be swept into the man's words. He would remember this night all his life, the great sunburned man who was his father, who had ruled the ships that sailed the seas and the planes that sailed the skies, and who was now a fisherman and content to be a fisherman, talking so slowly and intently about how it was to be a fisherman, with all of his past thrown away. The boy did not know how. It puzzled him that an empire could be cast aside, yet vaguely he understood what his father was trying to say. His mother had given him a sense of the fitness of things, a sense of the single lifetime length that spanned this place called California and which had produced him, one-half Chinese, one-quarter Italian, one-quarter French, to be an inheritor not of wealth or power, but of the tangled human forces that motivated these people.

May Ling watched and listen to the single man she had loved and given herself to in the one lifetime she lived. She understood silence and the practice of silence, and that was one of the links with Dan Lavette. He was not an articulate man. When he spoke of what he was and what he did and what he felt inside of himself, the words had to be torn out of his gut. She sensed what this day had been to him and what she had added to the burden by telling him of Mark Levy's death. His life had been smashed and battered, and that was necessary. There was no other way for him to come to an accounting with himself. She understood the illusion of free will, and finally, in his own way and in his own good time, he had arrived at that understanding. It was a great triumph that he was celebrating, but that knowledge would be for the two of them and only for the two of them.

Thus she said almost nothing after he began to speak, only listened. And Dan, glancing sidewise at her, the tiny nose, the perfectly formed small mouth, the delicate image of a woman who might have been formed from porcelain, sensed her calm, her knowledge of the moment, and realized that there was really no need to explain, that what had been had been. Even if he had never returned, they would have been together.

They were married in City Hall, with Feng Wo and his wife as witnesses and with a silent, happy fourteen-year-old boy to complete the wedding party. The clerk was somewhat puzzled that a woman whose name was Mrs. Lavette was marrying a man named Mr. Lavette.

"You're not related?" he asked her.

"Not as blood relations," May Ling replied, smiling.

"Then you were married to another Mr. Lavette?"

"Not legally married, no. We simply lived together," May Ling said brightly. "But he went away a long time ago."

The clerk consulted with another clerk. "You are not at this time married?"

"Oh, no, not at all."

"And you?" he asked Dan.

"I'm not married."

"It's unusual," the clerk muttered. But in the end, the citadels of bureaucracy crumbled, and they were married. The five of them celebrated with a wedding luncheon in a Chinese restaurant near City Hall, where So-Toy complained about the dreadful food and where May Ling remarked that everything tasted like ambrosia, something So-Toy did not understand at all. With a down payment of twenty dollars, Dan had purchased a used 1930 Ford sedan, and after lunch they got into it and drove back to Westwood. May Ling suggested that they devote the rest of the afternoon to a honeymoon of sorts, so after depositing Feng Wo and his wife and young Joseph at the house in Westwood, Dan and May Ling drove out to Santa Monica Beach. Hand in hand, they walked along the beach, and then they sat down together on a rock and watched the waves. Except for the swooping, screaming gulls, the beach was deserted. It was already late in the afternoon. They had been silent for a time, an easy silence that was without awkwardness, the presence of each other being sufficient. And then May Ling asked him, "How do you feel about Jean?"

"I like her. A long time ago, I thought I was in love with her. But I never liked her. I think I do now."

"What changed it, Danny?"

"Leaving her, I suppose."

"And all the rest of it, what they call the good life — you haven't any regrets?"

"I could do it again," he said. "I'm not just talking. I thought about it when I sat there in front of the fire in the lot at San Pedro. There was an old man sitting next to me. He said something about four days without shaving makes a bum. I didn't sleep most of that night, and I thought about it. Start over. Get back to San Francisco. That was no problem. I could ride the rails. I left two suitcases at Mark's house, shirts, ties, suits, shoes. You want the trappings, and then you walk out and make a deal. You don't even need money, only the bluff and the arrogance and knowing how the game is played. There are twenty men in San Francisco who'd make a deal with me. Ships, planes, land. Why even a thing like this bridge over the Golden Gate that they've been talking about for years. I don't know one damn thing about bridges, but I know half a dozen engineering outfits that would be as impressed as hell if I walked into their offices and told them to start drawing up plans for the bridge. Then I'd bull my way into the group that's been talking the bridge all these years, and I'd convince them that I would make it happen, and by God, it would happen."

"But you didn't go back to San Francisco."

"You asked me if I had regrets. It's not a case of regretting anything, May Ling. It's something else. I can't put it into words. When you told me about Mark, the first thing I thought was that Jean killed him when she called our loans and washed us out. But I was wrong. Mark and me, we began to die a long time ago. No. I would have died there in San Pedro or in some flophouse along Main Street before I'd go back. At least it would be a death of my own choosing."

Then, again, they sat in silence, watching a red sun sink to the lip of the ocean. The evening chill rolled in from the sea, and Dan put his arm around May Ling and drew her to him.

On the twenty-eighth of December, in 1933, early in the afternoon, Dan drove up to the house in Westwood, back from San Pedro. He wore his work clothes, stained blue jeans and a blue denim shirt, and he smelled of fish and brine. May Ling met him as he got out of the old Ford, and after he had kissed her and she had made her face at the rank smell of him, she said, "Wait, Danny. There's someone inside."

He stared at her, puzzled.

"Your daughter, Barbara."

"No!"

"Just think about it a moment. She's on her Christmas vacation from college in the East, and she came down here by herself to see you. Drove down. That's her car, across the street there. She's inside, and she's a very nervous, frightened child. Now if you want to, you can go in through the kitchen door and wash up there and I'll bring you some fresh clothes."

He nodded. "Yes, yes, I guess so."

He scrubbed his face and hands at the kitchen sink, washing his body as best he could and then dressing in the clothes May Ling brought him. Her mother and father had retreated upstairs.

"Go in alone," May Ling said. "I'll wait here."

He walked into the living room, and a tall, slender girl of nineteen rose to face him. For a moment, in the shadows of the room, he had the illusion that he was seeing Jean again as he first saw her; and for the same moment, the girl stood and stared at him. He reached out with his hands, and she came into his arms, and he held her there.

"Daddy, I'm so sorry," she whimpered.

"No, baby. There's nothing to be sorry for."

"I missed you. Oh, I missed you so much."

And all he could say was, "Thank you, darling, thank you."

In the book of Lao Tzu and Chuang Tzu, which Feng Wo had translated from the Chinese and which was published by the University of California Press, there were a few lines from the *Natural Way of Lao Tzu:*

> Moved by deep love, a man is courageous.
> And with frugality, a man becomes generous,
> And he who does not desire to be ahead of the
> world becomes the leader of the world.